JOAN JOHNSTON

By Joan Johnston

Mail-Order Brides Series
TEXAS BRIDE
WYOMING BRIDE
MONTANA BRIDE

Bitter Creek Series
THE COWBOY
THE TEXAN
THE LONER

Captive Hearts Series
CAPTIVE
AFTER THE KISS
THE BODYGUARD
THE BRIDEGROOM

Sisters of the Lone Star Series
FRONTIER WOMAN
COMANCHE WOMAN
TEXAS WOMAN

Connected Books
THE BAREFOOT BRIDE
OUTLAW'S BRIDE
THE INHERITANCE
MAVERICK HEART

JOAN JOHNSTON

THE LONER

DELL
NEW YORK

The Loner is a work of fiction. Names, characters, places, and incidents either are the product of the author's imagination or are used fictitiously. Any resemblance to actual persons, living or dead, events, or locales is entirely coincidental.

2015 Dell Mass Market Edition

Copyright © 2002 by Joan Johnston
Excerpt from *Sinful* by Joan Johnston © 2015 by Joan Johnston

Published in the United States by Dell, an imprint of Random House, a division of Random House LLC, a Penguin Random House Company, New York.

DELL and the HOUSE colophon are registered trademarks of Random House LLC.

This book contains an excerpt from the forthcoming book *Sinful* by Joan Johnston. This excerpt has been set for this edition only and may not reflect the final content of the forthcoming edition.

ISBN: 978-0-440-23472-2
eBook ISBN 978-0-307-56969-1

Cover design: Lynn Andreozzi
Cover illustration: Alan Ayers

Printed in the United States of America

www.bantamdell.com

18 20 21 19 17

Dell mass market edition: January 2015

For my daughter Heather
and her husband Peter . . .
May you live happily ever after.

Acknowledgments

I want to thank everyone at Ballantine/Bantam Dell who has helped to make my books the best they can be. The cover art is always spectacular. I want to say a special thank you to all those who do the soldier's work of getting my books into the hands of my readers.

Thanks again to my writing friends who continue to provide the support that makes it possible to survive in this solitary profession—Gloria, Roberta, Rexanne, Pam, Sally, Sherry, Heather, Carla, Pat, and Jasmine.

I'm indebted to my friend Cheryl Hole, assistant district attorney in Edinburg, Texas, for helping me sort out Texas trial procedure. Any mistakes are mine.

Thanks also to the Huntsville, Texas, Chamber of Commerce and the Huntsville Prison Unit for their assistance.

One last thank-you to Lynn Chapman, a reader who was kind enough to look for anomalies between the books in the Bitter Creek series, so all of the characters can be the correct age and have the same color hair and eyes in the first book in the series as in the most recent.

Chapter 1

"WHAT THE HELL ARE YOU DOING BACK HERE IN Bitter Creek?"

Billy Coburn heard the challenge in the low, menacing voice but took his time turning to confront Jackson Blackthorne. He set his cigarette in the corner of his mouth, squinting against the smoke that caught under the brim of his Stetson, and stuck his boot on the brass footrail at the base of the Armadillo Bar. "None of your damn business," he said at last.

Billy saw the anger flare in the older man's eyes and watched his shoulders square as he straightened. Billy almost smiled. Jackson Blackthorne's six-foot-three-inch height wasn't going to intimidate him. He was an inch taller than Blackjack, maybe even broader in the shoulders, and a hell of a lot leaner in the hip. His father—it felt strange to use the word, since he was the man's bastard son—didn't scare him.

"We had a deal," Blackjack said. "I agreed to put that badge on your chest, and you agreed to stay as far from my daughter and this town as you could get."

Billy thumbed a smudge off the silver TSCRA badge that was pinned to a leather folder stuck in his breast pocket. As a result of a deal he'd made with Blackjack, he'd become a field agent for the Texas and Southwestern Cattle Raisers' Association, hunting down modern-day cattle rustlers and horse thieves.

He laid a hand on the Colt .45 holstered high on his hip, met Blackjack's stare, and said, "I've kept my part of the bargain. I've been living in Amarillo for the past two years." Which was about as far as you could go north and west of Bitter Creek and still stay in Texas. "I haven't seen or spoken to your daughter since I left town."

"What I want to know is why you've shown up here now, two weeks before Summer's wedding. If you've got any notion of interfering—"

"I've kept my part of the bargain," Billy repeated, his blood pounding in his temples as he absorbed the stunning news that Summer Blackthorne was about to be married. "I haven't seen Summer in the two years I've been gone. And I made sure before I left that she hated my guts."

That also had been part of the deal.

As far as Billy knew, Summer Blackthorne still hated him. But he felt an ache inside when he thought of her walking down the aisle with some other man. Once upon a time he'd hoped that she'd be marrying him.

But that was a long time—and a couple of significant revelations—ago.

"If you're not here because of the wedding, what are you doing back in Bitter Creek?" Blackjack said.

Billy followed Blackjack's gaze to a booth on the other side of the bar. Summer Blackthorne was sitting there as pretty as you please. And she was every bit as pretty now as she'd been when he'd left her behind two years ago. She was laughing, her head thrown back to expose a long, slender neck. Soft blond curls fell over her shoulders—and onto the male arm that was draped possessively around her. The man must be her fiancé.

Billy hated him on sight. He felt the hairs on his nape stand on end and fought back the jealousy and sense of loss that made his stomach knot and his throat thicken painfully. Summer didn't belong to him. Never had and never would.

"I asked you a question," Blackjack said. "What the hell are you doing here?"

Billy took the cigarette from his mouth, flicked it onto the sawdusted cement floor, and ground it out with his boot. "Like I said, none of your business."

"Look, son, I've had about as much—"

"Don't ever call me son. You haven't earned the right."

Billy saw the irritation flash in Blackjack's eyes. Maybe it was wrong to blame his father for what had happened. After all, it was Blackjack's wife Eve who'd arranged to have Johnny Ray Coburn marry Billy's mother Dora when she turned up at Blackjack's back door unwed and pregnant—and then paid Dora to keep the truth from Blackjack for twenty-five years.

But it was Blackjack who'd come with three hard men and beaten Billy badly enough to put him in the hospital when he wouldn't promise to stay away from Summer. Billy had been lying in the hospital, ribs broken, eyes swollen closed, a dozen stitches in his face, when Blackjack had shown up in his room. Dora had finally told him the truth. And he'd passed it on to Billy.

I'm your father.

None of his physical wounds had equaled the agony he'd felt when Blackjack said those fateful words—which made Summer his half sister...and out of reach forever.

"I won't apologize for what I couldn't help," Blackjack said, meeting Billy's gaze in the mirror over the bar.

"Nobody asked you to."

"I couldn't take a chance on you and Summer getting together," Blackjack said. "You're blood kin."

Billy's eyes narrowed. "No. We're not."

Blackjack's face turned ashen. "Who told you that?"

Billy smirked. "I notice you're not denying it."

"I asked you a question. Answer it."

"I learned the truth from Summer."

"What? How could she possibly know—"

"She heard you and her mother arguing," Billy said. "She knows about her mother's affair with your foreman. She knows she's not your daughter." Which meant he and Summer were not related after all, that there was no reason they couldn't have become man and wife.

"Does she know that you're my son?"

"I didn't tell her." As far as Billy knew, Summer still had no idea he was Blackjack's son.

"When did she— How long has she—"

"She's known the truth the whole two years I've been gone," Billy said. "She came to see me, bawling her eyes out because she'd heard you two arguing and found out about her mother's affair."

Blackjack frowned. "So you knew you two weren't related even before—"

"Even before I made her hate me by telling her you'd paid me off to get out of her life."

"So why did you leave, if you knew the truth?"

"My reasons are my own."

There was no way Billy could explain how much he'd wanted that job Blackjack had offered him. How much he'd yearned for the chance to become someone respectable, to leave behind the labels that had been pinned on him all his life. He'd walked away from this isolated cow town in the middle of the South Texas prairie determined to make something of himself, so that someday he might be the kind of man that Summer would be proud to call her husband. But he hadn't managed to do it fast enough. She was getting married in two weeks.

He was too late.

Blackjack shoved his hat back and rubbed a hand across his eyes. "Why didn't Summer say something to me if she knew I'm not her father?"

"That's the best part," Billy said. "She didn't want you to know she knew the truth, because she was afraid you'd treat her different. I could understand her point."

He saw Blackjack wince. It was an unspoken secret around town that Billy's drunken stepfather had often left bruises with his fists. Billy hadn't understood at the time why nothing he did ever pleased his "father." When he'd found out the truth—that Johnny Ray Coburn's marriage to his mother had been arranged, and that the deed to the ranch where they lived, along with a monthly stipend, had been payments for keeping the truth from Blackjack—he'd understood why Johnny Ray resented all the things about Billy that reminded him of the man who'd sired him.

Billy met Blackjack's gaze, daring his father to bad-mouth his stepfather.

"I didn't know about you being mine when your father—your stepfather—was alive or I would—"

"Would have done what?" Billy interrupted. "Acknowledged me as your son?" He snorted when Blackjack said nothing. "Or played Good Samaritan?" Billy couldn't keep the venom from his voice, but he managed to speak softly enough that only Blackjack could hear what he said next. "Everybody in town knew what was going on in that house. Anybody could have stopped it."

But nobody had. Partly because Billy had been too ashamed to admit that his stepfather was hitting him and made up excuses for the bruises when anyone asked. The beatings hadn't stopped until he was fourteen and started growing—and ended up six inches taller than his "father"—and could defend himself.

A silence fell between them.

Julio Iglesias and Willie Nelson were singing "To All the Girls I've Loved Before" on the jukebox, and the rowdy Friday-night crowd was singing along. The bar was smoky and dark, with the year-round Christmas tree lights that lined the mirror above the bar providing a falsely cheerful glow.

"It doesn't really matter why you're here," Blackjack said at last. "So long as you're gone in the next twenty-four hours. If you're still in Bitter Creek the day after to-morrow, I'll make sure that badge comes off and the job goes away. Is that understood?"

Billy said nothing, simply stared back into his father's

cold gray eyes. What could he say? Jackson Blackthorne would do what he had to. And Billy would do what he had to.

Someone smacked a palm against the glass aquarium at the end of the bar and the dangerous diamondback inside lifted its head and rattled an irritable *chik-chik-chik-chik-chik*.

Billy turned to chase away the man who was bothering the snake—and locked eyes with Summer Blackthorne.

"Billy."

Billy felt his heart leap to his throat, making speech impossible. He searched Summer's face, seeing the wounded look in her hazel eyes, the pouty lower lip, the petal-soft cheeks, the silky golden curls that made him yearn to touch.

At that instant, the bartender showed up and set a baby bottle in front of Billy. "Here's that milk you ordered. I had to warm it up on the stove in back."

Billy saw the startled look in Summer's eyes. He turned toward the bartender and said, "What do I owe you?"

The bartender waved a hand and grinned. "It's on the house. Can't wait to tell folks how Bad Billy Coburn showed up at the Armadillo Bar at two in the mornin' askin' me to fill a baby bottle with warm milk. You gonna suck that up yourself? Or you got a baby somewhere? Didn't hear you got married or nothin'."

The bartender waited expectantly for an answer. Billy felt the hot flush running up his throat as he met Blackjack's speculative gaze in the mirror above the bar. He didn't dare look at Summer. He wasn't about to tell these people why he needed a baby bottle filled with warm milk. It was none of their damn business.

"Thanks," Billy said. He took the bottle and headed for the door, his ferocious look daring any of the drunken cowboys he passed along the way to say a word. He hadn't been called Bad Billy Coburn all his life for nothing. He'd grown up in Bitter Creek fighting everyone and everything. Even if you weren't looking for trouble, Bad Billy Coburn would give it to you.

He shoved his way out the door, then stopped and gulped a breath of cool, fresh air.

I'm not Bad Billy anymore. I'm just Billy.

He'd grown up in the two years he'd been gone. He'd become a respected and respectable man. He was a TSCRA field inspector, a lawman who carried a gun and hunted down bad men. He was no longer looking for trouble.

But goddamn if it didn't always seem to find him.

What were the chances he'd run into Jackson Blackthorne first thing on his return to Bitter Creek? And Summer. She was the last person he'd wanted to see. He'd spent the past two years putting her out of his mind, telling himself he had to focus on making a life for himself before he could ever think about coming back to mend fences with her. He shouldn't be here now. But here he was.

Billy headed for his pickup, his long strides eating up the distance across the potholed asphalt. He'd reached the hood of his battered Dodge when he heard Summer calling him.

"Billy! Wait up. Billy! I want to talk to you."

He could have run. He could have jumped inside the cab and gunned the engine and been gone before Summer caught up to him. But it might be the last chance he had to talk with her before she got married. Before she belonged to another man.

A quick glance showed that the baby strapped securely in the car seat had finally cried himself to sleep. He'd been wailing so loudly and miserably, after being so good during the long drive from Amarillo, that Billy had stopped at the Armadillo Bar to get a bottle of warm milk before driving the last half hour home.

Billy reached through the open window and set the bottle on the seat, then turned and crossed his arms, leaning his hip against the rusted-out fender, waiting for Summer Blackthorne to reach him.

She was breathless when she stopped in front of him, her chest heaving beneath the tailored white Western shirt she'd belted into skintight Levi's. She was wearing her favorite pair of tooled red leather cowboy boots, which cost more than he and his mother and his younger sister Emma used to spend on food in six months.

It reminded him why he'd left the broken-down ranch where he'd grown up to seek a better life. Summer Blackthorne was way out of his class. And nothing much had changed in two years.

"What do you want, Summer?"

She looked anxious and uncertain. He resisted the urge to offer comfort. They'd been good friends—just friends—for a couple of years before she'd gotten curious two years ago and kissed him. There'd been no going back to being friends after that. He'd wanted more. He'd wanted it all, even if she hadn't been sure whether she wanted him as more than a friend. But Blackjack had put a stop to that.

"I hear you're getting married," he said, to make sure he kept his distance—and she kept hers.

"In two weeks," she said.

"I guess congratulations are in order."

"I suppose."

He lifted a brow. "You must like this one, if you agreed to marry him." She'd often told him how much she resented her father shoving young men under her nose for approval. How all Blackjack wanted was for her to marry some scion of a landed family and bear him a grandson who could grow up and run the Bitter Creek Cattle Company, when what she'd always wanted was to run Bitter Creek herself.

She shrugged. "Geoffrey's a good man."

"I suppose he's rich," Billy said.

"His family are old friends of my father. And yes, they're wealthy."

"Do you love him?" Billy didn't know what had possessed him to ask such a question. "Never mind. It doesn't matter."

She looked at him, her heart in her eyes. "Doesn't it?"

"Why did you come out here?" he asked, not bothering to keep the impatience from his voice.

"I . . . wanted to see you."

He spread his arms wide. "If I'm not mistaken, your last words to me before I left Bitter Creek were 'I hate you.' You seemed pretty certain about never wanting to lay eyes on me again."

"You were hateful, if you'll recall. You—"

"What is it you want from me?" he said, staring her down. "You're getting married in two weeks. And I'm heading back to Amarillo."

"My parents were arguing again and . . . I know everything now."

Billy felt a chill run down his spine. He kept his eyes on her, waiting to see what she would say.

"About you being Daddy's son. And that you knew it before you left."

He took a shaky breath and let it out. "Yeah. Well. It's no big deal."

She lowered her eyes to her hands, which were knotted in front of her. "I felt so relieved, because it explained why you went away without a fuss. I mean, if you thought we were related, then of course we couldn't be together. So why shouldn't you accept Daddy's offer?"

Slowly, she raised her eyes to meet his gaze. "And then I remembered that I'd told you that my father's foreman was my biological father. So you knew we weren't related. And you left anyway."

He heard the torment in her voice and felt sick inside. He hadn't wanted to hurt her. He'd wanted to love her, to marry her and live happily ever after with her. But she'd lived her entire life in comfort and ease, and he'd been certain that whatever love she'd felt for him would have died a quick and certain death when she found herself living on a derelict ranch in the dirt-poor surroundings which were all he could offer her. And after what had happened with his stepfather, he'd never take a penny of Blackthorne money, even if it belonged to his wife.

"It wouldn't have worked, Summer," Billy said softly.

"Why not?"

Billy shook his head. "It doesn't matter now. You're getting married and..." He glanced over his shoulder at the child sleeping in the car seat. "I've got responsibilities."

She started toward the pickup and he held up a hand. "Don't wake him. He just went to sleep."

"Are you married, Billy?"

He hesitated, then said, "No."

"Then whose baby is that?"

"Will is my son."

She looked up at him, visibly shocked by his announcement. He realized that he wanted her to see the one good thing he'd accomplished in the two years he'd been gone. He wanted her to see Will.

He stepped aside and she stared, wide-eyed, at the sleeping baby. "Oh, my God, Billy," she said reverently. "He's beautiful."

She reached through the open window and brushed aside a dark, baby-damp curl from Will's forehead.

When she did, Billy's heart clutched. It had been impossible not to wonder what Summer would think, what she would say, when she saw Will. Billy felt proud—and protective—of his son. He'd wanted Will from the moment he'd known of his existence, when the barmaid he'd shared a bed with had come to him for the money to get rid of his baby.

He'd paid her instead to bear the child, and no moment in his life had been more profound than the first time he'd held the soft, fragile weight of his son in his large, workworn hands.

Summer turned to him, her eyes glistening with tears, and said, "I never expected this. You, a father."

She smiled and his heart turned over.

She stepped toward him, her arms widespread to give him a hug. He knew better. She was getting married in two weeks. She would never be his. It could only hurt more if he—

But Summer didn't hesitate. Before he could turn away, she was pressed against him, her breasts soft against his chest, her arms circled around his waist.

His arms just naturally enfolded her. He closed his eyes as he imprinted the feel of her against his body one last time. He stuck his nose in her hair and breathed the flowery scent of her shampoo.

His erection was an unwelcome surprise, and he edged his hips away, not wanting her to know how quickly and undeniably he'd responded to her. He raised his head to look into her eyes, but she kept her face hidden against his chest. He grabbed a handful of her silky curls and tugged her head back so she was forced to look up at him.

Tears had welled in her eyes and one slipped onto her cheek.

"What's this?" he murmured, brushing aside the tear with the pad of his thumb.

"I'm just happy to see you," she said. "I missed you."

Billy hissed in a breath. He bit back the response on the tip of his tongue. *I missed you, too.* Why say the words when they would only cause more heartache?

He saw the shiver run through her before she asked, "Do you love her? The baby's mother, I mean."

Billy snorted softly. "She was warm comfort on a cold night."

"Where is she now?"

"Don't know and don't care."

"I'm so sorry," Summer said.

"For what? There was no love lost between us by the time Will was born. He's better off without her. With me, he'll never know a day when he isn't loved."

He met her gaze defiantly. His son wasn't going to be bruised or beaten or left to wonder what he'd done wrong when all he'd ever wanted was to please his father.

"I gotta go," he said.

But she held on. "Why did you come back?" she asked.

Billy sighed. He might as well tell her the truth. It was going to come out eventually. "My mom's sick. My sister says she's been asking for me."

Billy knew what his mother wanted. Forgiveness for letting herself be bought off by Eve Blackthorne. And for letting his father beat the crap out of him till he was old enough to fight back. Billy wasn't sure he could ever forgive her. But his sister had begged him to come home . . . before it was too late.

"I didn't realize your mother was ill," Summer said, her hand brushing the wrinkles out of the front of his shirt in a gesture that felt like a caress. "What's wrong with her?"

"Cancer."

"Oh, no. Is it bad?" Summer asked.

"She's dying."

"Oh, Billy."

She hugged him again.

It amazed him how much he wanted—needed—that hug. She felt so good in his arms. Like she belonged there.

But she didn't.

"Summer, I gotta go." He put his hands on her shoulders and gently pushed her away. He chucked her softly under the chin in an effort to take the hurt look from her eyes and reminded her why he had to keep his distance by saying, "I guess I shouldn't be surprised that you didn't wait for me to make my fortune and come back for you."

Her brow furrowed. "Was I supposed to?"

His lips curved in a regretful smile as he brushed at a strand of hair that had blown across her cheek. "No, I suppose not."

"You took my father's bribe, Billy. You left and never looked back. You never called me, never wrote me, never did a thing to let me know that you were even still alive."

He heard the anger and resentment he'd been expecting from the first. He was surprised to discover he shared her feelings. "Neither did you."

She huffed out a breath of air. "You were the one who ran away. How could I believe you really wanted me when I realized you knew the truth—and still let my father buy you off?"

Billy resisted the urge to explain. She would never understand the despair he'd felt, the gold ring he'd grasped for—the chance to leave Bitter Creek and make something of himself for her, to be worthy of her.

Well, he'd done it. He had a job he loved and for which it turned out he had a definite knack. The intelligence he'd inherited from Blackjack—which his stepfather had always made him ashamed of showing—had helped him to trap more than one unwary rustler. Now that Summer was marrying some other man, his job was all he had.

And Blackjack had threatened to take it away if he wasn't gone in twenty-four hours.

Billy couldn't afford to lose the work that had given him back his self-respect and, more important, provided the income to support his son. Without that job, he might very well end up back here for good, in a town where he was—and always would be—"Bad" Billy Coburn.

But how could he leave? His mother was dying. He'd come home to Bitter Creek to make arrangements for her care and to find out whether his sister Emma might be willing to sell the ranch where they'd grown up, since he had no intention of ever living on the C-Bar again.

He'd considered explaining the situation to Blackjack and asking for more time to settle his affairs, but he didn't want to end up beholden to a man he hated. Besides, he didn't need help from anybody. He'd figure a way out of this mess on his own.

This sure as hell wasn't the time to stir up trouble by getting involved with Summer Blackthorne again. He had to get away from her before he did something stupid that would make his life harder than it already was.

But he was finding it difficult to let her go, when she was holding him, touching him like she cared.

"What's wrong?" Summer murmured, brushing at the frown between his eyes. Her fingertips haltingly caressed his cheek, then traced the shape of his mouth.

He had lowered his head to kiss her, their mouths only a breath apart, when he realized what he was doing. He caught her head forcibly between his hands. It was hard to breathe with the pain in his chest. He wanted her to go away and take all the hurt he was feeling with her.

"What do you want from me, Summer? A quick lay before you're tied to some man your father handpicked for you? I'm not available."

He saw the shock on her face, followed quickly by anger, as she shoved his hands away.

"How dare you! You know damn well—"

"Keep it down," he said. "We don't want your father or your fiancé to hear us arguing out here and get the wrong idea. Not that a few wrong ideas haven't crossed my mind. And you seem pretty damn willing to indulge in—"

She swung at him with her open palm.

He caught her wrist long before the flat of her hand could reach his jaw. "You always were a spoiled brat. I see you haven't changed."

"You always know exactly which buttons to push," she said furiously, jerking free of his grasp. "I don't know why I let you provoke me."

He kept his arms folded over his chest as the tears brimmed in her eyes.

"I don't want to fight with you," she said, her chin wobbling.

Billy bunched his fists under his armpits and pulled his arms tighter around his chest, resisting the urge to comfort her.

His whole body tensed as she laid her hands on his crossed arms, leaned up on tiptoe, and kissed the cheek she'd almost slapped. "I'm sorry, Billy. I only want us to be friends again. I've missed you. I've missed having a friend to—"

"What about your fiancé? Isn't he your friend?" Billy asked through tight jaws.

She sighed as she took a step back. "Geoffrey is—"

"What the hell is going on out here?"

Billy saw the wariness on Summer's face as she turned and discovered her fiancé striding toward them. She scrubbed at her teary eyes and swiped her hands on her jeans as she said, "You should have stayed inside, Geoffrey."

"I got worried when you were gone so long."

Billy dropped his fists to his sides and widened his stance as Summer's fiancé eyed him suspiciously. He kept his gaze on Summer, wondering how she was going to handle the situation. He didn't want to fight, not on his first day back in town. But he wasn't going to back down if the other man confronted him.

"Let's go back inside," Summer said as she slid her arm through Geoffrey's and turned him back toward the bar.

"In a minute," he said. "I have a few words to say to your friend."

"Geoffrey, please—"

Billy's teeth clamped over a growl as he watched the other man jerk himself free of Summer's grasp.

Geoffrey marched over, jabbed Billy with a stiff finger and said, "I know who you are and what you are. Keep your hands off Summer. She belongs to me."

Billy tamped down the urge to fight for the woman he loved. The only woman he would ever love. He glanced at the baby sleeping in the cab of the pickup. What he wanted had to take second place now. He had to think of Will. He couldn't afford to end up in jail for teaching this asshole the lesson he deserved.

"Geoffrey, please," Summer said, tugging at his sleeve.

"Stay the hell out of this, Summer," Geoffrey said, elbowing her backward.

Summer cried out in alarm as her heel slipped into a large pothole and she began to topple backward. Her arms windmilled in an effort to stay upright, but it was a losing battle. She cried out again—this time in pain—when she hit the ground.

Billy glared at Geoffrey, glanced at Will, and muttered, "To hell with it."

He felt the pain all the way to his elbow when his fist landed satisfyingly on Geoffrey's strong, aristocratic chin. The other man went down in a heap next to Summer.

Billy leaned over, gripped Summer's hands, and pulled her carefully to her feet. "You all right?"

She avoided his eyes by dusting off her fanny and seemed more embarrassed than injured. "I'm fine." She looked down at Geoffrey, who was out cold, and made a face. "You shouldn't have done that."

Billy let go of her hands. "You're right. I know better." He shook his head in disgust. "I couldn't help myself." He gestured toward the fallen man and said, "If he's what you want, Summer, help yourself. I've got to get home."

"Billy..."

He was feeling sick inside, wondering what kind of trouble he'd made for himself, especially when Summer clearly hadn't appreciated the effort he'd made to defend her.

He slid across the hood of his truck without waiting for her to make excuses or explanations and dropped to the ground in front of the driver's side door. He was inside and had the engine revved before she could say anything other than his name.

He leaned across the seat to look at her one last time over Will's head and said, "Good-bye, Summer."

He gunned the engine, anxious to be gone. All he had to do was pop the clutch, give it some gas, and he'd burn rubber out of here. Then he glanced down at his sleeping son.

He couldn't afford to go tearing around town like some teenager. He was twenty-seven years old. He was a TSCRA field inspector—at least for the next twenty-four hours. And he was a father.

Billy let out the clutch and gave the truck enough gas to pull slowly and carefully onto the two-lane road that led home.

Chapter 2

SUMMER WAS BENT OVER GEOFFREY, WHO WAS still out cold, when she heard her father mutter, "I should have known something like this would happen. That Coburn kid is pure-D trouble wherever he goes."

She rose and faced her father in the blue neon light that reflected off the whitewashed adobe walls of the Armadillo Bar. "Then why did you send Geoffrey out here, Daddy?"

"He's going to be your husband. He should be the one to protect you."

"Protect me from what?"

"That no-account—"

"Stop right there," Summer said, taking the two steps to bring her toe-to-toe with her father. "You of all people should know better than to call Billy names."

She could feel the hesitation before he said, "Billy told me that you know about...that I'm not...that you're..."

She'd never known her father to have difficulty speaking his mind. That he couldn't even finish his sentence spoke volumes about how carefully he was treading to spare her feelings. It was exactly why she hadn't wanted him to know she knew the truth about her birth.

Because it would change everything.

She'd struggled for two years with the realization that her dearly beloved father wasn't even related to her. She was neither fish nor fowl. Not a blood relative. Not adopted. She might be legally legitimate, since her parents had been married when she was born, but she hadn't investigated, fearing what she would discover.

The one thing she'd ever wanted out of life was to be mistress of Bitter Creek. But how likely was that once she—and her father—acknowledged that she wasn't even a real Blackthorne? It was far better not to know for sure what her status was. At least this way, she could pretend everything was all right, instead of knowing for certain that it wasn't.

Regrets were useless now. It would be a relief to give up the burden of knowing such an awful secret. She and her father would both have to adjust to their new relationship. Whatever it was.

She looked up and said, "I know everything, Daddy. I have for a long time."

He lifted a brow in question.

"Everything," she repeated, meeting his gaze steadily. "That I'm not your daughter. And that Billy is your son."

Blackjack heaved a gusty sigh, took off his hat, and plowed a rough hand through his silver-tipped black hair, before snugging the expensive Resistol down low on his forehead. "Dear God in heaven. Why didn't you tell me?"

"I didn't want things to change between us."

He started to say something and stopped.

"Say it," she urged. "Whatever it is, Daddy, I can handle it."

"I wanted to protect you from the truth," he said. "So much so that—"

"Daddy, I—"

"Shut up and listen," he said. "The whole reason I've stayed married to your mother for the past two years is that she's been blackmailing me, threatening to tell you the truth if I tried to leave her. If I'd known that both our secrets were out—that Billy's my son, and that you're not my daughter—I'd have divorced her faster than that," he said, snapping his fingers in front of her nose.

"And married Lauren Creed?" Summer blurted.

"As long as this is a night for confessions, yes," her father said. "I love Ren. I've loved her for as long as I can remember. Fate dealt us a bad hand. She ended up marrying Jesse Creed thirty-seven years ago, and I ended up marrying your mother. But Jesse's been dead nearly four years . . . and I'm still not free."

Summer pressed a fisted hand to her heart. She felt an actual physical ache in her chest at the thought of her father in love with someone besides her mother. Despite what he'd told her, she didn't want her parents splitting up. A family in one piece—even if it showed dangerous signs of cracking—was better than a family broken apart.

"I thought you stayed married because Mom would get half—maybe even more than half—of everything in a divorce," Summer said.

Blackjack huffed out a breath. "Two years ago I told her I didn't give a damn, that I'd give her everything. That's when she resorted to blackmail."

Summer gasped, horrified at what she was hearing. It was unthinkable that her father had considered giving up Bitter Creek. His prize possession was a map of the original ranch boundaries drawn in 1864, which hung in a place of honor over the fireplace in the parlor. Each succeeding Blackthorne had purchased, procured, or, in some cases, purloined more land—including her father.

The immense boundaries had been redrawn over the past hundred and thirty-odd years to create an empire that ranged over eight hundred square miles, making Bitter Creek as large as some small northeastern states. She'd always believed her father loved Bitter Creek more than anything or anyone. Obviously, she'd been wrong.

"You love Ren that much?" she asked.

"More than life."

"And you didn't divorce Mom and marry Ren because—"

"Because I didn't want you hurt."

Summer stared at her father, not believing what it seemed he was saying. The ache in her chest was back. She'd never believed he could love her so much when she wasn't even really his daughter. But here was proof that made her throat go tight and her nose sting with tears.

He'd been willing to sacrifice Bitter Creek to have Lauren Creed. *Yet he'd given up Ren because he'd wanted to ensure that Summer remained happily oblivious to the unhappy truth.* She was old enough now, and had made enough choices of her own, to realize the enormity of the gift he'd offered her.

"Daddy..." Her father's face was blurred by tears as

he pulled her into his arms and hugged her tight, rocking her from side to side.

"Everything's going to be all right now, baby. You'll be getting married and—"

"No, Daddy. I won't." Summer pushed at her father's shoulders until he let her go. She tried to look him in the eyes, but the annoyance she saw there caused her to lower her gaze. "I can't do it. I can't marry Geoffrey."

She glanced at her father's face, which was set in angry lines. A tear dropped onto her cheek and slid down. "Please, Daddy—"

"Get rid of those tears," he said, pulling a hanky from the back pocket of his Levi's and offering it to her.

She'd learned very young that tears were effective when she wanted her way. But the days were long past when she wanted her father to see her breaking down in stressful situations. In the two years since she'd turned twenty-one she'd worked hard to have him consider her as someone capable of running Bitter Creek.

She'd hoped that by marrying she could convince Blackjack that she possessed the maturity and steadiness required of someone in control of a ranching empire as vast as the Bitter Creek Cattle Company.

But if her father divorced her mother, there might be no ranch left for her to run. So there was no reason to marry anymore except love. And she didn't love Geoffrey . . . enough.

"You picked Geoffrey," her father argued.

"As the best in a long line of prospective husbands you've thrown at me, Daddy," she said, as she dabbed at her tears with his hanky.

"You told me you loved him."

"I did," she said. *As much as I've been able to love any man.* She'd decided there must be something wrong with her, since she couldn't seem to care deeply for any of the men who'd proposed marriage to her over the years. The man she'd liked best was Billy, and she'd refused his offer of marriage two years ago because she had been too surprised by his proposal to consider her best friend in terms of a husband.

There was something wrong with her, all right. She just had no idea how to fix it.

Blackjack eyed her speculatively. "Are you telling me that two weeks before the wedding you've suddenly changed your mind?"

Her stomach churned and she tasted bile at the back of her throat. Was she really going to end her engagement two weeks before her wedding? Was she really going to hurt Geoffrey like that? What had changed, really? Geoffrey's conduct tonight hadn't been the best, but jealous men weren't known for their rational behavior.

She'd known from the beginning that Geoffrey's feelings for her were considerably stronger than hers for him. But she'd thought she could make the marriage work. Why did the thought of a life with him now seem like a prison sentence?

It made her ashamed to realize how abominably she'd been using Geoffrey. When was she ever going to grow up and act like an adult? When was she going to start exhibiting the responsible, trustworthy behavior she wanted her father to see in her? She wanted his respect. She wanted his approval. And she didn't know what else she could do to earn it, except marry Geoffrey.

She just couldn't do it.

She supposed she was as spoiled as Billy had accused her of being. Sacrifices had never been necessary, because someone else had always been willing to make the sacrifice for her. First Billy, by leaving and taking his secret with him. Then her father, by staying married to her mother to keep Summer ignorant of the truth.

"I'm sorry, Daddy," she said, meeting his gaze and feeling the weight of his disappointment fall on her shoulders.

"I don't know what your mother's going to say about this," he said. "You know how many plans she's made."

Summer nodded dumbly. Her mother had planned everything. Summer's wedding was going to be the social event of the season, with everyone from the Texas governor on down invited to the ceremony at the Bitter Creek First Baptist Church and the reception afterward in the Castle, the thirty-thousand-square-foot wood-frame house which generations of Blackthornes had called home.

Geoffrey moaned.

"We'd better get him back to the Castle," Blackjack said.

Her father pulled Geoffrey upright and slung him over his shoulder like a sack of horse feed, as though he'd never had a life-threatening heart attack four years before.

"Momma would have a heart attack herself if she saw you doing something this strenuous."

"What your mother wants won't be an issue much longer," Blackjack said.

Her father laid Geoffrey in the back seat of the

extended-cab pickup and Summer got in beside him, cradling his head in her lap. As her father drove them home, she used the hanky he'd given her to dab at the blood that oozed from the cut in Geoffrey's chin, where Billy had struck him.

"Oh, Geoffrey," she murmured. "I'm so sorry."

She became aware that he was awake when she felt his hand on her cheek. "Some knight in shining armor I turned out to be," he said. "I'm the one who's sorry."

She pressed his hand to her cheek, then removed it and held it in her own as she stared down into his shadowed face. "Billy and I . . ."

"I'm listening."

That was the problem with Geoffrey, Summer thought. He was a really good man. Someone who listened. Someone who loved her. She'd be a fool to let him go. She'd tried to love him. Really, she had. But the most she'd ever felt for him was . . . affection. She wasn't sure precisely what she ought to feel when she was with him, but the deep respect and liking she felt no longer seemed like enough to plan a lifetime together.

She glanced at her father in the front seat and realized she didn't want to break it off with Geoffrey here, where her father would hear every word they said. The least Geoffrey deserved was the chance to vent his feelings in private. She absently brushed his chestnut hair away from his forehead. "We need to talk," she said softly.

She put her fingertips across his lips and added, "When we get home."

Geoffrey was staying in one of the guest rooms at the Castle, and when they arrived home, Summer stood on tiptoe to kiss her father's cheek and said, "Good night,

Daddy. Geoffrey and I are going to have a nightcap in the library."

Her father lifted a brow but said nothing. She waited at the foot of the stairs until he made it to the top and turned in the direction of her mother's bedroom.

Geoffrey resisted when she led him toward the library. Instead, he pulled her into his arms. When he tried to kiss her, she turned her face away, so his lips only brushed her cheek. He lifted his head and looked down at her, confusion rife in his eyes. He didn't force himself on her, like some other man might. Geoffrey was much too nice to do something like that.

I must be an idiot even to think about letting a good man like this get away.

"What's wrong, Summer?"

"Please, Geoffrey, let's go into the library, where we can talk," Summer pleaded, taking his hand and leading him in the direction she wanted him to go.

"Are you sure this couldn't wait until tomorrow?" he said, gingerly working his chin. "I might be able to talk a little easier by then."

"This isn't going to be easier tomorrow."

"All right, Summer. You know all you have to do is ask."

Summer smiled wanly. Geoffrey was such a *nice* man. She hated doing this to him. He followed her into the library, innocent as a lamb being led to the slaughter.

Once Geoffrey was seated in one of the wing chairs in front of the stone fireplace, Summer began pacing restlessly from one end of a wall of ancient, leather-bound tomes to the other.

"Come here and sit on my lap," Geoffrey encouraged,

patting his knee. "Whatever the problem is, I'll kiss it and make it better."

"Don't patronize me," Summer snapped. "I'm not a child."

He lifted a brow in contradiction.

Summer stopped pacing and marched over to stand in front of him. "Look, Geoffrey," she began, her hands shoved deep in her back pockets. "The truth is..." She couldn't tell him she didn't love him. That seemed cruel. But what other reason could she give him for calling off their wedding?

She pulled her hands out of her pockets and shoved them through her hair. "Oh, God. I don't know how to tell you this."

"Try putting one word after the other."

She glared at him. Anger was good. Anger would get her through this. "All right. Since you want it in plain words, here it is. I can't marry you."

Summer was watching his face, so she saw him flinch, saw the muscle work in his jaw, and the way his Adam's apple bobbed up and down as he clamped his teeth and swallowed back the impulsive retort on the tip of his tongue.

The fire popped and crackled in the silence.

"Say something. Please," she whispered.

He eyed her keenly and said, "What about this Bad Billy character? Your father seemed to think—"

"Billy's a friend. We're just friends," she said quickly, perhaps too quickly. She meant it, but she could see that Geoffrey believed they were way more than friends.

He leaned forward and braced his elbows on his

widespread knees. "I kind of thought something like this might happen."

Summer's eyes went wide as she sank into the wing chair across from him. "What?"

He looked down at his soft lawyer's hands, then back up at her. "I could feel you pulling away, the closer we got to the wedding."

She shook her head. "No, I just—"

"Don't bother denying it," he said, his voice more sad than upset. "I kept hoping. I figured once we were married, you'd let down your guard, and I could make you fall in love with me."

"I never meant to hurt you," Summer said, swallowing over the painful knot of guilt in her throat.

He took a hitching breath and let it out. "I know."

She rose to comfort him, but the instant she did, he lurched from his chair and said, "Don't."

He headed for the door to the library but stopped when he got there, looked back at her, and said, "Will you take care of letting everyone know?"

She nodded. A few moments later, she heard one of the immense double doors to the Castle open and close.

And he was gone.

Summer could hardly believe Geoffrey had left without a fight. Without once raising his voice. With hardly a word of protest. She sank into the wing chair, waiting to feel relief at her narrow escape.

What she felt instead was that awful ache in the center of her chest. If he'd loved her so much, why hadn't he fought harder to keep her? If he'd loved her so much, why hadn't he said something sooner about her apparent defection? If he'd loved her so much, why wasn't he here holding her in his arms, demanding she love him in return? Why had he simply given up? Wasn't she worth fighting for?

Summer hated her conflicting emotions. She had no right to demand Geoffrey release her from her promise and then blame him because he was gentleman enough to do so without making a fuss. But dammit! What kind of man walked away from the woman he loved?

Billy had done it two years ago. Asked her to marry him, and then walked away without a backward look when she'd refused. Now Geoffrey had done the same thing. Was she so unlovable? So little worth fighting for?

Summer could hear her parents shouting at one another. At least they were willing to fight. She wondered if her mother realized the futility of her efforts. Her father loved another woman and apparently always had. Sadly, her mother just as clearly loved her father and apparently always had.

It was a tragedy that had resulted in awful consequences.

Her "real" father, whose name was Russell Handy, had arranged the murder of Lauren Creed at her mother's instigation, in an attempt to get rid of the woman Blackjack had always loved. But the bullet had missed its target, and Lauren's husband Jesse had been killed instead. Handy, who loved her mother, had taken all the blame for the murder and was serving a life sentence in Huntsville.

Since there was no evidence against Summer's mother that would hold up in court, she'd spent eighteen months locked up in a sanitarium. But the "cure" hadn't worked.

She'd come out with her jealousy and hatred of Lauren Creed intact.

Summer could hear her mother's shrill voice getting louder as she descended the stairs, with Blackjack right behind her.

"I will not have her doing anything as stupid as canceling this wedding at the last minute," her mother shouted.

"She's entitled to make up her own mind," her father yelled back. "Besides, she's not the one you're mad at. I am."

At the foot of the stairs her mother whirled, her elegant cream silk peignoir flying around her ankles like a dancer's costume. "And why shouldn't I be mad at you?" she shot back. "It is ridiculous for you to be thinking of divorce at your age. You're too old—"

"I'm still a man," her father raged.

"Who hasn't touched me in two years!"

"I don't want you," he said cruelly. "I want Ren."

"Momma, Daddy, please," Summer begged, crossing into the hall to let them know she was there. She'd overheard them fighting from behind closed doors, but she'd never before seen the naked fury on her mother's face or the loathing that contorted her father's features.

"There's nothing you can do, nothing you can say, to keep me here any longer," her father said.

Her mother stood at the foot of the stairs, Blackjack two or three steps above her. Any second, Summer expected to see her mother spread her arms across the open space, as though she could physically keep Blackjack from leaving.

"Get out of my way, Eve," her father said.

"You'd go to another woman at this hour of the night?" her mother said.

"I'm finally free, Eve. Free. I don't want to spend even one more night under the same roof with you. And now that the truth is out, I don't have to. There's nothing you can do to hurt Summer any more than she's already been hurt."

"I can break this ranch into tiny pieces and sell it to a hundred buyers," her mother threatened.

Summer gasped. "Momma, you wouldn't! She can't do that, can she, Daddy?"

"Watch me!" her mother snarled. "I can and I will."

"You can try," her father snarled back. "Much good it'll do you."

"What is that supposed to mean?" her mother said.

"Just try breaking up Bitter Creek and you'll see," her father threatened. "Now get out of my way."

Instead of stepping back, her mother stayed where she was, forcing her father to take her mother by the shoulders and set her aside. She clung to him as he moved past, her arms wrapped tightly around his neck.

"Please don't do this, Jackson. You're my husband. I love you. I always have. I'll never give you up."

Summer watched, her face pale, her heart skittering, as her father reached up and yanked her mother's arms from around his neck.

"It's over, Eve. You can stop fighting now. I'm leaving. And I'm not coming back."

"We're still married," she said. "If you go to that woman you'll be an adulterer. That won't help your case in court."

Her father glanced significantly at Summer, and then

at her mother. "I think I've got enough evidence of my own to counter whatever charges of adultery you lay against me."

Summer choked back a moan.

Eve glanced at her, then turned to Blackjack and said in a soft, silky voice, "You'd tell the world that your daughter's a bastard?"

"The only person I was ever worried might find out the truth already has," he said. "Summer knows she's my daughter in every way that matters."

That silenced her mother. And filled an empty place inside Summer that she hadn't acknowledged was there.

In the tense quiet, Blackjack walked to the double doors, opened one, and closed it behind him.

Summer glanced at her mother, who seemed to deflate like a balloon. She'd never been close to her mother, hadn't hugged her in recent memory. Yet her mother seemed truly devastated by Blackjack's defection.

She took a step forward and said, "Momma?"

The virulent look in her mother's eyes stopped her in place. "This is all your fault."

"What?"

"Listening at closed doors. Telling secrets you aren't supposed to know, that you wouldn't know if you weren't spying on your parents."

Summer felt the words like a whiplash.

"I hope you're proud of yourself, Missy," her mother said. "Breaking up your parents' marriage."

"That's not fair!" Summer said. "I couldn't help hearing what I did. You were yelling and screaming and—"

"You didn't have to tell him the truth. You didn't have to tell him you know."

"I didn't tell him, Billy did!" The instant the words were out, Summer knew she never should have uttered them.

"That damned bastard son of his! I should have known. Bad seed, both of you."

Summer was appalled at the words coming out of her mother's mouth. "I am not—"

The smirk on her mother's face shut her up. Because the truth was, her real father was a convicted murderer. Oh, God. She couldn't stand this. She understood exactly how her father felt. She wanted to leave this place and never come back.

Except Bitter Creek was all she'd ever wanted. Now it seemed the ranch would be gone, sold away to strangers. And what would happen to her? "Please, Momma, couldn't you let Daddy have the ranch?"

"All that will be left of this empire of his when I'm done is little bitty pieces." She paused, her eyes narrowing, before she added, "Unless you'd be willing to marry Geoffrey after all."

"What?"

"I don't wish to call the governor of Texas and tell him my daughter's wedding has been canceled. Not to mention the other dignitaries I've invited, and the time and trouble I've been through to make this the social event of the season. I know you want Bitter Creek. So tit for tat. You marry Geoffrey, and I might be willing to give Bitter Creek to the two of you as a wedding present."

"How is that possible?" Summer said.

"You heard your father. He doesn't want this place. And I don't intend to let him keep it if he tries to divorce me. The choice is up to you. I can cut Bitter Creek up into pieces and get rid of it, or I can make it a wedding gift to the two of you."

Summer's heart was pounding so hard it hurt. "But I don't love Geoffrey." *And he doesn't love me enough to fight for me.*

"Think about it," she said. "You have until tomorrow morning."

"Momma, please—"

"Don't cry, Summer. Babies cry. I find it irritating in the extreme."

Summer swiped at her eyes with both hands, but when the tears were finally gone, so was her mother. All Summer saw was the hem of her peignoir, floating up the stairs.

"This can't be happening," Summer said as she turned and walked back to the wing chair in front of the fire. She sank into it and stared into the flames. "This just can't be happening."

But it was. And she had until morning to make up her mind what to do.

Chapter 3

"WE'RE ALMOST THERE, WILL," BILLY SAID IN A soothing voice. "One more mile. A couple more minutes. Then I'll get you out of that car seat and get you dry and into bed."

The truck had dropped into a deep pothole in the dirt road that led from the highway to the Coburn ranch house, and the portable crib, stroller, and high chair which Billy had thrown into the back of the pickup when he'd packed so hurriedly had ricocheted noisily around the metal truck bed. At the crash of metal on metal, Will had woken with a cry of alarm and, when he realized he was still strapped into the car seat, began wailing miserably.

Billy had offered his fifteen-month-old son the warm bottle of milk, and Will had sucked it down like a starving calf. But the bottle was empty now, and Will was struggling against the car seat restraints, protesting his confinement with all his might and begging to be let out.

"Out, Daddy."

Billy felt his gut tighten. He hated the sound of his child in distress. But it made no sense to stop when he was so close to home.

"Just a little longer, Will," he said, brushing his hand across Will's baby curls. "You've been such a good boy. We'll be home soon."

"Out, Daddy. Out," Will cried woefully. And then, more angrily, "Out out out!"

Billy couldn't blame his son for being cranky. He felt the same way himself. Especially after his idiotic behavior in the parking lot of the Armadillo Bar.

He had thought he'd grown up since he'd left Bitter Creek. All it had taken was fifteen minutes with the people he'd known all his life, and he'd reverted to being Bad Billy Coburn.

Given a choice, Billy never would have come back to Bitter Creek. But he hadn't been given much choice. His nineteen-year-old sister Emma had called him last night in hysterics.

"Mama's dying, Billy!" she'd cried. "You have to come home."

"You said she has cancer, Emma," he'd replied, the calm voice of reason. "That takes years—"

"She's had it for years, Billy. They just found it. I tell you she's dying! I don't know what to do. I can't take care of her and the ranch and...everything. Come home, Billy. Please, come home."

He'd hung up and called his boss at the TSCRA and told him he needed some time off. He hadn't offered any explanation. His personal life was his own business.

"What about that case you're working on?" his boss had asked.

Billy was investigating what appeared to be a conspiracy among a group of ranchers who were stealing their own cattle, selling them in Mexico, and then collecting insurance for the loss. "The case'll have to wait," he'd said. "I won't be gone more than a week."

His trip was going to be even shorter than that, if he knuckled under to Blackjack's ultimatum.

Twenty-four hours.

It wasn't going to be nearly enough. Not to settle things with his mother and Emma and arrange to put the C-Bar up for sale. Maybe he ought to swallow his pride and explain the situation to Blackjack. Surely the man would back off.

Billy grunted deep in his throat. Jackson Blackthorne wasn't known for showing mercy. The instant he smelled blood, he'd go for the jugular. Better not to say anything just yet. Maybe the picture wasn't as bad as Emma had painted it.

His heart began to pound the way it always had in the past—with fear and anxiety—when he caught sight of the ramshackle wooden ranch house where he'd grown up, silhouetted in the light from the naked bulb that lit the front porch.

Home.

The good memories he had of the place were few and far between. It would have been difficult to return in any event, but he'd brought a little extra baggage . . . a son his mother and sister knew nothing about. He wondered—worried—what they would say. Maybe he should've told them sooner about Will, but he'd been afraid his mother might try and convince him to give Will up, and he didn't want his impressionable—and adoring—teenage sister to know that he'd fathered an illegitimate child.

He drove around to the back door and parked, surprised to see the kitchen light on at this hour of the night.

It was nearly 3:00 a.m. He swore under his breath. He'd given up swearing out loud, so Will wouldn't pick up any bad habits. He'd hoped to get Will in a better mood before he had to introduce him to his family.

"We're home, Will," he said, as he turned to unbuckle the harness that had kept his son secured.

Will clambered toward him as Billy lifted his child into his arms. From the weight of the plastic diaper, it had been soaked several times. "I'm sorry, son," he muttered. "I'll get you dry as quick as I can."

Will stopped crying and snuggled against Billy's shoulder, his nose tucked against Billy's throat, his arms clasped around Billy's neck, his knees dug into Billy's chest. It always amazed him that his child trusted him so completely. He never wanted to lose that trust, never wanted his son to feel betrayed by him the way he'd felt betrayed by his stepfather.

Billy grabbed the diaper bag, which he'd learned never to be without, and headed for the kitchen door. He was careful to avoid the broken step as he hopped onto the covered back porch. To his surprise, the back porch light came on and the screen door screeched open.

"Billy? Is that you?"

"Yeah, Emma. It's me."

He was still blinded by the porch light, so he couldn't see more than her shadow before he stepped inside. He stuck his boot out to keep the screen door from slamming, then turned to greet his sister.

When he got a look at her, his jaw dropped.

Emma was six feet tall in her bare feet and slender as a reed—except where her sleeveless white cotton nightgown visibly bulged over her rounded belly.

"You're pregnant!"

She laid a protective hand over the child in her womb, pointed her chin at Will, and countered, "Whose baby is that?"

"You never mentioned you'd gotten married," he said.

"I'm not," she replied, meeting his gaze defiantly. "Is your wife with you?" She looked over his shoulder toward the door. "Is she coming in?"

"I'm not married, either," Billy said. Will was still clasped against him tighter than a leech, so it was pretty obvious they were together. "Will is my son."

"What happened to his mother?"

"We can talk about that later," Billy said. "I have to get Will dry and into bed."

"Where were you planning for him to sleep?" Emma asked.

"I've got a portable crib in the pickup. He can stay in my old bed until I get it set up." Billy set his Stetson on top of the refrigerator, then pulled the empty bottle from the diaper bag and said, "How about filling this with milk and warming it up, while I change his diaper."

"Sure."

He could feel Emma's eyes following him as he headed down the narrow hallway. He could imagine the questions careening through her mind. It was plain he wasn't the only one who'd been keeping secrets. He could hardly believe it. His teenage sister, unmarried and pregnant! As soon as he got his son in bed, he and Emma were going to have a serious talk.

Billy didn't want to flip on the overhead light in his bedroom, because it was a bare bulb. He felt his way in the dark to the cheap ceramic lamp beside his bed and turned it on. Nothing had changed in the two years he'd been gone, except a thick layer of dust had accumulated.

His old room was the size of a jail cell, and the ancient mattress on the iron-railed double bed sagged in the middle, which was convenient, because it made a safe well in which to lay his son.

Will protested being laid down, but Billy distracted him by saying, "That lady we just met is your aunt Emma." He unsnapped the legs of the cotton sleeper Will was wearing and continued, "She's warming a bottle for you right now. You can drink it while I put your crib together, and then you'll be able to settle down and get some sleep."

Billy had been terrified the first time he'd diapered his son. Will had been so tiny, and he'd felt so clumsy. Those days were long past. He ripped open the diaper tabs, lifted Will by the ankles and removed the diaper, then closed the heavily soaked disposable diaper plastic-side out with one hand and dropped it on the rag rug beside the bed.

He swiped Will's bottom clean with a Wet Wipe, powdered him, and taped on another diaper with masterful efficiency. Then he gave his son a buzzing raspberry on the stomach, listening for Will's chuckle and the feel of his son's hand clutching his hair.

By then, Emma had shown up with the warm bottle of milk. "Here you go," she said, handing it to Billy.

Billy offered the bottle to Will, who eagerly stuck the nipple in his mouth, holding it there with one hand while he twisted his fine black hair in the fingers of the other.

"Will you watch him while I go get the crib?" Billy asked.

"Sure," Emma said, easing onto the corner of the washed-out, knobby-weaved bedspread.

Billy heard Will start to wail the instant he was out of sight and Emma's soft voice reassuring him that Billy would return soon. He hurried out to the truck, grabbed the fold-up crib from the truck bed, and hauled it back inside to his bedroom.

Will pitched toward him the instant he reappeared, straining against Emma's hold, as though Billy had been gone for five months instead of five minutes.

Billy dropped the crib and took his son in his arms long enough to comfort him. "It's okay, Will. I'm not going to leave you."

Billy always felt bad when he had to leave his son in someone else's care, and he'd done it often enough that Will knew what was coming and cried not to be left behind. Billy ended up with a sick feeling in the pit of his stomach that didn't go away until he came back and retrieved his child. It was better now that he'd found Mrs. Caputo, the lady in the apartment down the hall from him in Amarillo, who loved Will like a grandson.

Billy lay Will back on his bed and said, "Hang in there, buddy. I'll have your crib together in no time."

It didn't take long to open the crib and put in the mattress, crib pads, sheet, and blanket. Billy was conscious of Emma watching him and fought the urge to start explaining himself—and confronting her about her pregnancy. When he was done, he picked Will up and settled him in the crib, tucking the blanket carefully around him, down one side, around his toes, and back up the other side.

"Snug as a bug in a rug," he said when he was done.

"Sing, Daddy," the boy said when Billy was done.

Billy glanced at Emma and felt himself flush. He'd read in one of the baby books he'd devoured in the months Debbie Sue had been pregnant, that it was a good idea to establish a bedtime ritual. So he had. He couldn't really blame Will for not understanding that he wanted to forgo it this once. "Not tonight, Will," he said.

"Sing, Daddy," Will insisted.

"It's late, Will."

"Sing sing sing!" Will demanded.

"You'd better sing to him, or he's going to wake up Mom," Emma said, an amused grin on her face.

Billy sat on the edge of the bed facing his son, cleared his throat, and sang in a deep baritone voice.

> *Twinkle, twinkle, little star,*
> *How I wonder what you are.*
> *Up above the world so high,*
> *Like a diamond in the sky.*
> *Twinkle, twinkle, little star,*
> *How I wonder what you are.*

The instant he was done, he popped up and leaned over the crib to tuck the blankets tight one last time. "Now good night," he said, bending over to kiss his son's forehead.

Will yawned and turned over, his hand still in his hair, the song signaling, as it had every day of his brief life, the end of their day together.

When Billy turned to gesture Emma out of the room,

he discovered she'd already gone. Billy darkened the room and headed toward the kitchen for the showdown with his pregnant sister.

He found her sitting at the kitchen table peeling a banana. He lifted a brow and said, "Leg cramps?"

"Yeah. How'd you know?"

"I've been through this," he reminded her.

"They woke me up," Emma explained past a mouthful of banana. "Figured I needed some potassium."

"At least you're taking care of yourself," Billy muttered. He wanted a cup of coffee, but the caffeine would keep him awake. He needed a stiff drink, but he'd been trying to rid himself of all the bad habits that had made his life so wretched before he'd left Bitter Creek. He no longer even smoked in the house, because it wasn't good for Will, and one of these days, he'd finally kick the habit.

But these were extraordinary circumstances.

"To hell with it," he said, opening the cupboard over the ancient Amana refrigerator. Sure enough, he found a half-full bottle of Wild Turkey. He opened the cupboard to the left of the sink and got himself a jelly jar and poured a finger of liquor into it and set it on the table. He pulled out a chrome kitchen chair and turned it around, flattening the sharp edges of torn white vinyl before he straddled it.

He said nothing, just sipped the bourbon, liking the familiar taste of it, the comforting warmth of it as it slid down his throat. He watched Emma consume the entire banana and carefully fold the peel into a heap in front of her on the red Formica table.

"Are you all right?" Billy asked. "I mean, have you had any trouble with your pregnancy?"

She shook her head. "I'm fine. I haven't been sick much. Just a little nausea and leg cramps once in a while." She glanced at him and said, "Will was quite a surprise. Why didn't you tell me?"

Billy and Emma had been close. At least, as close as a brother and sister could be with the seven-year difference in their ages. He'd stayed in Bitter Creek long after he'd yearned to leave, because he'd wanted her to graduate from high school and get a job before he left her alone to make her way in the world.

But two years ago he'd seen his chance and taken it, leaving her unprotected. And look what had happened. He felt guilty and angry and frustrated at the curves life kept throwing him. Her pregnancy was going to complicate everything. Twenty-four hours, hell. He'd be lucky to get out of this godforsaken place in twenty-four months.

"I want to know what sonofabitch took advantage of you," he said, struggling for the rational tone of voice that had been so easy over the phone.

"It wasn't like that, Billy," Emma said. "I love him."

"Obviously the feeling isn't mutual," he shot back.

He heard her swallow several times and felt the knot growing in his own throat. He ought to pull her into his arms and comfort her. It was easy enough to hug Summer. But that was probably because she always made the first move. It was different with Emma.

Hugs were awkward things between Coburns. He'd made sure Johnny Ray didn't beat up on Emma, but that didn't mean she'd gotten any affection.

And she'd been a freak in high school, way taller than most of the boys and skinny as a bed slat, with a head of garish red hair. He'd tried to comfort her, to tell her she'd grow into her body and be pretty someday. But it hadn't happened before he'd left two years ago.

Now, God help him, she was downright beautiful.

It was no wonder some cowboy had come wooing, or that she'd fallen into bed with the first man who'd offered her some attention.

Billy blamed himself for her predicament. If he'd been home where he belonged, no lazy, care-for-nothing cowboy would have been able to take advantage of his sister.

But she'd said she loved the guy.

"Tell me who the baby's father is," he said. "I promise I won't do anything but talk to him."

She eyed him through a sheen of tears and said, "He's gone."

"Dead?"

She shook her head, her bright red hair whipping back and forth across her bare shoulders. "No. He's left Bitter Creek."

"And gone where?" Billy demanded.

"Away."

"That's convenient," he said. "I suppose once you've had the kid and put 'unknown' in the space where the father's name is supposed to be, it'll be safe for him to come back."

He watched the flush of shame and humiliation rise on Emma's fair skin and felt guilty for putting her through the wringer. He was in no position to be lecturing her, when he was unmarried himself and the father of a fifteen-month-old son.

The same thought must have occurred to her, because she said, "You're in no position to talk, Billy."

"Both parents' names are on Will's birth certificate," he pointed out. As though that excused the fact he hadn't married his son's mother.

But Debbie Sue Hudson hadn't wanted to marry him. Or have his baby, for that matter. Billy knew what it felt like to be unwanted, and he'd been determined no kid of his was going to suffer that fate. So he'd taken his son, vowing to see to it that Will always felt loved.

So far, that had meant making sure his son was warm and dry and fed. He'd spent hours talking to Will about all the plans he had for his son's future, which was going to be promising, if Billy had anything to say about it.

Which was a far cry from his own childhood.

Billy hadn't mourned his stepfather when he'd died driving drunk three years ago. Oh, he'd shed a few tears after the funeral. But what he'd really been mourning was the lost dream of growing up with a father who loved him, instead of one who detested and demeaned him.

Which was why he'd been so adamant about protecting his son. And why his current situation was so dire.

He couldn't afford to lose his job with the TSCRA. He needed to be able to prove to a family court judge in Amarillo that he could provide a better home for Will as a single parent than Debbie Sue and her new husband could. The worst of it was, Debbie Sue didn't really want Will. She wanted money.

Sometime after Will's birth, Debbie Sue had overheard two bar patrons discussing how Billy had gotten his job with the TSCRA because he was Jackson Blackthorne's bastard son. She'd decided that with such rich relations, Billy was the goose that laid the golden egg. He'd been paying her a little bit every month to keep her off his back.

Four months ago she'd gotten married, and her new husband had seen the main chance. Debbie Sue had demanded that Billy pay her $50,000 to give up her parental rights. Otherwise, she threatened to haul him into court and seek custody of Will.

Billy was terrified that if push came to shove, she'd do what she said. And she'd win. After all, he'd been "Bad" Billy Coburn all his life. He'd stood before enough judges for doing the wrong thing that he'd seen how they operated. Judges listened to what you had to say, then did what they damn well pleased. He didn't trust a one of them.

He had a high school diploma, and he'd taken a few night college courses in Amarillo, but that was the extent of his education. He had a job, but Blackjack had threatened to take that away from him—and would—if he didn't get out of Bitter Creek. He could get another job. But would it be good enough to convince a judge he was financially stable?

And he was a single male parent. Mothers usually got children who were as young as Will. Not always, of course. But often enough to make Billy's skin get up and crawl every time he thought of facing a judge who had the power to take Will away from him.

If he'd had the money, he'd gladly have paid it to Debbie Sue. He would even have swallowed his pride and gone to Blackjack for cash, if he'd thought there was a snowball's chance in hell he'd get it. But there wasn't.

Billy had no idea how he could come up with that kind of money. His parents' ranch, the C-Bar, was mortgaged to the hilt, and his stepfather had run it into the ground. They had a few head of Angus cattle, but the ranch made ends meet with the stipend Blackjack had promised to pay his mother and sister if Billy went away and left Summer alone. Even that would disappear, he was sure, if he stayed in town more than twenty-four hours.

The day Billy finally told Debbie Sue he didn't have $50,000 and never would, she'd begun court proceedings, telling him to get the money or give up Will.

He would never give up his son.

But what was the judge going to say when he found out that, not only was Billy unmarried and unemployed, but he had the additional costs of caring for a sick mother and a pregnant teenage sister?

He could run. But what kind of life would Will have if Billy kidnapped his son and they ended up looking over their shoulders for the rest of their lives?

"I'll be fine, Billy."

"What?" Billy had been so lost in his thoughts that he'd forgotten Emma was sitting across from him.

"I'll be fine," she repeated. "Now that you're here—"

"I can't stay, Emma."

"Why not?"

"It's complicated."

"Take your time. Explain it to me. I'm not going anywhere."

He wondered how much he should tell her. Not about the custody suit. He wasn't sure he could talk about the possibility of losing Will without her seeing just how close to the edge he was. Maybe he should focus on what arrangements they should make for their mother.

"What's Mom's prognosis?" he asked.

"Not good. The cancer has invaded her organs—lungs, kidneys, liver. She's dying, Billy."

"How long does she have?"

"The doctor doesn't know. A couple of months, maybe."

"Isn't there anything he can do for her? Chemotherapy? Radiation? Surgery?"

Emma shook her head. "It's too late. He can give her something for the pain. She's going to need care. With everything I have to do around the ranch and..." She smoothed her nightgown over her rounded abdomen. "And other things...I realized I couldn't do it all alone. So I called you."

Billy shoved a hand through his hair and blew out a gusty breath. "How would you feel about selling the ranch?"

"What would that accomplish? The shape it's in, no one would pay much for it. Except maybe the Blackthornes. They'd buy it for the land."

Billy grimaced. "Mom paid too high a price to get this place. I'd hate like hell giving it back to Blackjack for nothing."

"That's not the worst of it," Emma said. "Where would Mom and I go? Is your place in Amarillo big enough for the four—" She patted her stomach and revised, "The five of us?"

"There's barely room for me and Will."

"So selling this place is out. Any other ideas?"

Billy swallowed the last of his bourbon and set the jar on the table. "Let me sleep on it. Maybe something will come to me by morning."

"I hope you have better luck than I've had," Emma said. "I've gone round and round with this in my head, and I haven't figured out a solution to the problem."

"I'll think of something," Billy said.

Because if he didn't, he was going to lose his son.

Billy's stomach turned over.

By the time the sun rose again, he had to come up with a plan. He wasn't giving up Will. That simply wasn't going to happen. No matter what he had to do.

Chapter 4

SUMMER WOKE UP FEELING UNHAPPY AND DES-
perate and reckless. If only Billy hadn't shown
up in town last night. If only he'd stayed away
two weeks longer. His sudden reappearance had turned
her life upside down.

She'd tossed and turned all night, unable to decide
what she should do. Her brothers had all made lives for
themselves that took them away from the ranch. Trace
had inherited a cattle station in Australia. Clay was the
attorney general of Texas. And Owen was a Texas
Ranger. All she'd ever wanted was to one day be mistress
of Bitter Creek. Could she marry Geoffrey knowing that
she was doing it simply to realize her dream?

On the other hand, wasn't that why she'd agreed to his
proposal in the first place? Why wasn't she grabbing at
the chance her mother had offered her with both hands?

Her current confusion was all Billy's fault.

His return had reminded her that once upon a time
she'd had a best friend with whom she could share
everything, say anything. And for the briefest moment
before they'd been separated two years ago, she'd felt
things for Billy Coburn that she hadn't known it was

possible for one human being to feel for another. Frightening feelings. Terrifying feelings. Billy had touched someplace deep inside her that she'd kept hidden from everyone, even herself.

What she felt for Geoffrey wasn't nearly so threatening. She could marry him and get the ranch and never have to worry about having those terrifying feelings again.

Unfortunately, she'd already broken off their engagement. She'd have to lie to Geoffrey if she wanted their marriage to go forward now, and she'd never believed herself capable of that sort of deceit.

Summer made a growling sound in her throat. She hated being manipulated even more than she wanted Bitter Creek. First her father throwing Geoffrey at her as a prospective husband, hoping for a grandson to carry on after him. Now her mother offering her Bitter Creek because she was concerned with appearances and didn't want to call off the wedding.

She had half a mind to marry the first man whose path she crossed. That would show her parents she was no puppet on a string!

Summer dressed hurriedly in a plaid Western shirt, crisp new jeans, and her favorite red boots with the Circle B brand hand-tooled into the fine leather, determined to escape the Castle before her mother awoke and demanded her answer. She needed more time to think, and she needed a private, peaceful place to do it.

Summer headed out the kitchen door, undecided whether to ride horseback or take her pickup. She never got past the cherry-red Silverado her father had given her as a twenty-first birthday gift.

It reminded her of Billy.

Summer remembered leaning against the front fender of the big Chevy truck, the warm sun on her face, as Billy Coburn kissed her. Remembered hearing her buttons ping against the cherry-red finish as he tore open her blouse to bare her breasts, his gaze both endearingly reverent and excitingly carnal.

She'd offered him her virginity.

Summer remembered the astonishment she'd seen in Billy's eyes when she'd told him she was untouched. She couldn't blame him for being surprised. She'd spent years running with wild crowds at one university after another, doing whatever outrageous acts it took to get herself thrown out, so she could return to Bitter Creek—until her father made a generous donation to another institution of higher learning and the whole ridiculous scenario began again.

The truth was, between her father and her three older brothers, Trace and the twins, Owen and Clay, no boy in high school would have dared to touch her for fear of his life, and she'd never let a man in college get close enough to seduce her. Owen had done a good job of warning her what happened to an unwary woman when a man started spouting flowery compliments. Forewarned, she'd gotten bored with hearing how her eyes were like topaz jewels and her hair was like spun gold and her lips were like wild, sweet strawberries, and rejected her would-be suitors out-of-hand.

Maybe the reason she'd liked Billy so much from the start was because he hadn't used false flattery to get her attention. Even the lowliest cowhand at Bitter Creek knew who she was, and they'd all tipped their hats in obeisance.

Except Bad Billy Coburn.

Summer grinned ruefully as she remembered the first time she'd come to the stable and found him mucking out stalls. Billy hadn't even acknowledged she was alive. He'd kept right on working as though the barn were empty.

She'd studied him secretly from the safety of the wooden stall while she saddled her horse. Billy was extraordinarily tall and had black hair like her brothers, but his eyes were a brown so dark they were almost black. A day-old beard stubbled his cheeks and chin. His jeans had worn white at the seams and his T-shirt had the arms torn out, allowing her to see the flex and play of corded muscle and sinew as he worked.

Both intrigued and affronted at being ignored—after all, she was an acknowledged beauty and the boss's daughter—she'd contrived a way to force him to speak to her.

She'd led her horse from the stall, stopped near the wheelbarrow into which Billy was forking manure and asked, "Do you think Brandy's hock is swollen?"

Without glancing in her direction, he'd forked another load of manure into the wheelbarrow and said, "Looks fine to me."

"You haven't even looked," she accused. Not at her horse . . . or at her. She might be only sixteen, but she had a grown-up figure which she knew had turned older men's heads. Billy Coburn seemed immune.

"Look," she insisted. Even she hadn't been sure whether she meant at her horse or at her.

He stopped abruptly, leaned his elbow on the pitchfork, and did a slow, sensual inspection of her body that left her pink with mortification.

"Everything looks fine to me," he said in a whiskey-rough voice. "But I think you knew that before you asked."

His eyes were narrowed in contempt, and his mouth had formed a sneer. At least, that's what Summer thought it was. She'd never actually seen anyone sneer before, especially not at her. Without another word, he turned and began forking manure again.

"Just a minute," she said, dropping the reins and taking the two steps to bring her toe-to-toe with him. She thought about reaching out to grab him, but figured that would be like sticking her arm into a lion's cage. It was likely to get torn off.

"I'm speaking to you," she said.

He ignored her.

"Do you know who I am?"

"A little girl playing grown-up," he muttered under his breath.

She was appalled and humiliated. And fascinated.

Didn't he care about his job? Wasn't he worried about losing it? All it would take was one word to her father, and he'd be gone. He must know it. Yet he seemed fearless.

"What's your name?" she demanded.

"Why do you care?"

She frowned. "I'd like to call you something besides—"

"It's not like we're gonna be friends, Mizz Blackthorne," he interrupted. He turned his back on her, leaned the pitchfork against a stall, and moved the wheelbarrow farther down the center aisle. Then he retrieved the pitchfork and went into another empty stall.

"I can be friends with whomever I like," she said, crossing to stand in the stall doorway, blocking his exit.

He glanced at her and lifted a dark brow. "Your father might have something to say about that, little girl."

"My father doesn't run my life."

He snorted. "Right."

"And I'm not a little girl. I'm sixteen."

He leaned on the pitchfork with his crossed hands and grinned, revealing a mouthful of straight white teeth. "You don't say. That old?"

Her breath caught in her throat as she realized how good-looking he was, his shaggy black hair falling over his brow, his dark eyes filled with humor, his smile revealing twin dimples in his cheeks. "How old are you?" she asked.

"Old enough to know better," he said, bending to scoop up another load of manure and crossing toward her. "Move it, kid. I've got work to do. I can't stand here all day jawing with you."

"You're a hired hand. If I want to talk to you, you'll stop and talk," she said, angry at being brushed off.

He dropped the load of manure so close to her boots that she had to resist the urge to jump backward, then threw the pitchfork into the hay and braced his hands on either side of the stall door. He loomed large above her, and she was aware of the dark hair in his armpits and the rivulets of sweat streaming down his throat into his torn T-shirt. He smelled like a hardworking man, musky and . . . different from any other man she'd ever met.

His dark eyes looked dangerous and a muscle flexed in his cheek. "Nobody orders me around, little girl. I'll quit before I let a spoiled brat like you—"

"I'm sorry."

"—order me—"

"I'm sorry," she repeated. She felt breathless, her chest tight, her heart pounding. "You're right. I'm used to getting my own way. And I'm not used to being ignored." Watching his dark eyes, she saw the danger pass, replaced by suspicion.

He looked down at the hand she'd extended to ward him off, as though he were a feral beast. She self-consciously pulled it back and stuck it in the back pocket of her jeans. But that made her breasts jut, and aware of his eyes lowering to look their fill, she yanked her hand out of her back pocket and crossed her arms over her chest.

"What is it you want from me, kid?"

"Nothing." She hesitated, then said, "Just someone to talk with."

He shook his head, took a step back, and dropped his arms to his sides. "I'm not your man."

"Why not?" she said. "You're the first person I've met on this ranch who isn't frightened or intimidated by the fact I'm the boss's daughter. You have no idea how wonderful that is."

He looked skeptical. "Do you know who I am?"

She gave him her most charming smile. "Not yet. You haven't told me your name."

His features hardened. "They call me Bad Billy Coburn."

It was plain he didn't like it. And that he probably deserved it. "You do look pretty ferocious," she teased.

He scowled.

She laughed. "My name is Summer. It's nice to meet you, Billy." She held out her hand for him to shake.

He stared at it for a long time, so long she thought maybe he wasn't going to take it. His eyes looked haunted, like a starving animal that sees the cheese laid on a trap, and knows that if he reaches for it, he's liable to get hurt, but still so hungry that he takes the risk.

He reached for her hand and clasped it in his own. At the touch of his callused hand, a shiver ran through her. She shook off the odd feeling and said, "It's nice to have a friend, Billy."

He released her hand and took a step back. "Have a nice ride ... Summer."

She smiled at him, feeling buoyed by his use of her first name. "Thank you ... Billy."

It was a beginning.

Over the next several years, their friendship had grown. Until she'd spoiled it all two years ago by wanting to know how his kiss would feel. When he'd refused to kiss him, she'd leaned up on tiptoe, right there on his front porch, and kissed him.

And then he'd kissed her back.

Billy's kiss had opened her eyes to what had been missing in every other kiss she'd ever received. His lips had been surprisingly soft and a little damp and had moved against her own seeking pleasure, discovering the wonder of touching her intimately and completely.

She'd felt her skin tingle, felt her blood begin to race, felt a surprisingly heady euphoria that seemed at odds with being touched by a man who'd been her good friend for almost five years without touching her in more than a friendly way. She'd wanted some indefinable something more.

At that fragile moment in time, Billy's mother Dora had arrived home from church. The rest of what happened that day on Billy's front porch was painful to remember.

Dora's face had turned a mottled red and spittle had flown from her mouth as she'd confronted Billy and said, "I won't have you lying with that Blackthorne bitch. Not ever. Do you hear me? Never!"

Summer couldn't remember everything Billy's mother had said, but even now her face went fiery hot when she remembered how that beautiful moment had been turned so ugly.

Of course, now Summer understood why Mrs. Coburn had been so sharp-spoken and upset. Any mother would panic if she thought two children related by blood were about to become lovers. For twenty-five years she'd kept the secret that Billy was Blackjack's son.

And she hadn't known that Summer was not his daughter.

Summer sighed and shifted in the seat of her Silverado as she headed the Chevy toward a towering live oak. She hadn't realized where she was going until she'd arrived. She'd come the back way to the stock pond on Billy's ranch where they'd so often spent private time with one another.

As she pulled her truck to a stop at the base of the ancient live oak, Summer saw a horse ground-tied and eating grass. She should have realized Billy might be here. After all, it was his favorite spot to think, as well.

She found him sitting at the base of the tree, his long

legs extended in front of him, his Stetson pulled low, his hands tearing apart a blade of long-stemmed grass. She knew he must have heard the approach of her truck, but he never acknowledged her. She slid onto the ground beside him and leaned back against the tree.

"Hi," she said.

He glanced at her and said, "What are you doing here?"

"I needed to think. How about you?"

He grunted an assent.

A sudden gust of wind rustled the leaves above them. She squinted and covered her eyes as sunlight stabbed at her through a break in the leafy canopy. She drew her knees up to her chest and laid her cheek on them. "Oh, God, Billy. I'm so confused. I don't know what to do."

She felt his hand briefly on her shoulder before it was gone.

"I know," he said.

She felt a sob building and turned her face away from Billy, not wanting him to see her lose the struggle for control. "I thought I'd grown up so much in the two years you've been gone," she said. A sob broke free, and she made a *grrrrrr* sound of anger and admitted, "And less than twenty-four hours after you get back, I'm reduced to sniveling like some kid whose toy is broken."

"Mind if I join you?"

She heard the humor in Billy's voice and turned to face him. "What have you got to cry about?"

He broke off another stem of grass and chewed on the sweet end of it, staring off into the distance instead of answering her.

"Your mom must be pretty sick," she guessed.

"Yeah. I talked to her this morning. I'd never told her about Will," he admitted.

"Oh, my God. What did she say?"

Billy shrugged. "She was upset. Wanted to know how I could be so irresponsible, getting some girl I didn't even know pregnant, and then trying to raise a kid by myself."

"Oh, Billy." Summer could feel how hurt he was by his mother's criticism, by her utter lack of confidence in him.

"If she wasn't dying..."

"You'd already be gone," Summer finished for him.

Billy tugged his hat down lower, and Summer realized he was hiding tears. She put her arm around his shoulder and leaned her cheek against his arm.

As simply as that, the bond that had been broken when Billy had left two years before was mended. Summer knew what he was feeling, and he knew how much she cared, without a word being spoken.

She waited for Billy to tip his hat up again before she said, "Are you going to stay here and take care of your mom?"

"That's the sixty-four-thousand-dollar question," he replied. "Your father wants me gone in twenty-four hours, or he's going to have me fired from my job."

Summer made a moue of disgust. "My parents are big on ultimatums."

Billy pulled the stem of grass from his mouth and threw it aside. "Problem is, Blackjack doesn't just threaten. He follows through. And I need that job."

The words seemed torn from him, and Summer

looked closely at him, for the first time seeing the strain on his face, the shadows under his eyes, and the gauntness of his cheeks. She laid a hand on his arm and said, "What's wrong, Billy?"

She felt his muscles tighten under her hand, but he didn't pull himself free, so she offered him the comfort of her touch and waited.

"I need to head back to Amarillo," he admitted in a voice that grated with emotion. "But I can't leave my mom here alone."

"Your mom isn't alone. She's got Emma."

"Emma's pregnant. Oh, hell. I didn't mean to let that slip. Nobody knows. She's been keeping it a secret."

"Who's the father?" Summer asked.

"She won't tell me. I don't suppose you know?" he asked, glancing at her.

Summer shook her head. "I haven't seen her with anyone."

"What are you doing out here with me?" he asked. "You and your fiancé get into an argument?"

"Geoffrey and I are no longer engaged. I broke up with him last night after we got home."

He turned to stare at her and she added, "But I might end up marrying him after all."

"Mind explaining that?"

"My father's left my mother for good. When he walked out on her last night, she threatened to cut Bitter Creek up into little bitty pieces before she'd let him have it."

Billy's arm slid around her shoulders and he pulled her close. "That's a bad break for you. So where does Geoffrey fit in?"

She grimaced. "Momma doesn't want the wedding canceled, because she'd lose face with all those important people she's invited. So she's offering Bitter Creek to me and Geoffrey as a wedding present. Of course, that means I'd have to marry him after all."

"Why not marry him?" Billy said, brushing at a leaf that had fallen on the knee of her jeans. "You must love him a little, or you wouldn't have gotten engaged to him in the first place."

"I like him a lot." She shrugged. "I'm just not sure I can ever love him. I think my mother's determined to see this wedding through to the end just so she can thwart my father by giving Bitter Creek to me."

"I don't see anyone holding a gun to your head."

"It's there, whether you see it or not," she said miserably. "I'm sick and tired of my parents manipulating my life. I feel like marrying the first man who crosses my path just to show them I can find my own husband."

He chuckled. "In that case, how about marrying me? I could use a wife."

She stared at him. "You need a wife?"

"No. I just need to be married."

She laughed and said, "Mind explaining that?"

"Will's mother recently got married and is taking me to court to try and get custody of my son. She can provide Will with two parents. I can only give him one."

"I see," Summer said.

"I'm not giving Will up to Debbie Sue," Billy said fiercely.

"How will you fight her?"

"She doesn't really want Will. She wants money. I'll figure out some way to buy her off, even if I have to sell the C-Bar and give her my share of whatever I can get for it."

"What about your mom and Emma? What's going to happen to them if you sell the ranch?"

"I haven't figured that out yet. That's why I'm sitting here thinking."

"I have a suggestion," Summer said, her heart thumping painfully in her chest.

"I'm open to anything."

Summer took a breath and said, "Why not marry me?"

Billy laughed and then sobered. "I'm not in the mood for jokes."

She laid her hand on his cheek and turned his face toward her. "I'm serious. Why not marry me? I won't get my trust fund for two more years, but I get a small settlement—about $25,000—when I marry. Surely that would be enough to hold off Debbie Sue until I get the rest."

"I won't take your money," Billy countered.

"Not even if it's for Will?"

"What do you get out of this?" Billy said.

"I get to make my own choice of husband."

Billy made a snorting sound. "And then what? How long were you planning on staying married to me?"

"I hadn't thought that far ahead. I suppose until I get my trust fund."

"Two years?"

"That would be a fair exchange, wouldn't it? That'll get you through your mother's illness and your sister's pregnancy. Surely by then you'd have another job and be able to prove to a judge that you can make a better home for Will than his mother."

"I'll concede that getting married helps me," Billy said. "I still don't see what you get out of it."

"A chance to help a friend. And to save myself from temptation. I want to manage Bitter Creek so much I'm afraid I'll marry Geoffrey just to get it. I don't want to be as selfish as my mother. Or as ruthless as my father."

Summer tried smiling, but her mouth trembled, so she gave up. "Marrying you gives me a chance to do something good for you...and for myself. What do you think?"

"I think you're crazy."

She got onto her knees facing him. "Think about it, Billy. We're good friends. We like each other. This could work."

"What about the marriage part of it?"

She stared at him in confusion. "What do you mean?"

"I mean the sex part of it. Or had you forgotten that?"

Summer flushed. "I hadn't given it any thought."

"Well, think about it. Am I supposed to spend two years sleeping on the couch?"

"Don't be ridiculous. We could sleep in the same bed and still not—"

He shook his head. "I'm not drawing some imaginary line down the middle of the bed."

"What do you suggest?" she said with asperity.

"I suggest we forget the whole idea."

She shook her head, her ponytail swinging across her shoulders. "No. We're friends. We can manage this, Billy."

"I doubt that," Billy said under his breath.

"I can live without sex if you can. After all, this is simply a marriage of convenience."

"It won't be at all convenient to live without sex," Billy said, lifting a sardonic brow. "But I sure as hell don't want to end up with another child I have to fight to keep."

"I can use birth control if we change our minds later," she said.

"I'm not going to change my mind."

"Fine," Summer said. "So we won't make sex a part of the bargain." She couldn't explain the knot that had formed in her stomach. After all, Billy was making this easy for her. She was going to get independence from her parents at a very small price. Knowing the courts, it would take two years for her parents to untangle their affairs enough to get a divorce. Meanwhile, she would be free of their machinations.

"When are we going to do this?" Billy asked.

"We can go to the courthouse and do it right now, as far as I'm concerned," Summer replied.

"What about that fancy wedding your mother has planned?"

"She'll have to cancel it."

"What's your father going to say when he hears what you've done?"

"I don't really care," Summer said. "Starting right now, I'm making all my own decisions, without regard to what my parents think."

"They're going to be furious," Billy predicted with a grin.

"I really don't give a damn," Summer said. "This is my life. I'm going to live it my way."

"You'll lose Bitter Creek," he said.

Summer laced her fingers together over her knees. "Maybe part of growing up is admitting I'll never be mistress of Bitter Creek and figuring out where to go from there."

Billy stood and reached down to grasp Summer's hands and pull her to her feet. He looked into her eyes, his face as serious as she'd ever seen it.

"I want to be sure you realize what you're getting into," he said. "This has to look like a real marriage—at least for two years. There can be no backing out, no running away. If push comes to shove, I need to be able to show the judge I can make a stable home for Will."

"Of course," she said. "I—"

"I'm not finished," he said, his hands tightening on hers. "I'm going to need to borrow that $25,000 you get when we marry. I'll pay you back—every cent. But that much money in one lump sum—and the promise of more along the way—might be enough to get Debbie Sue to drop the custody suit."

"It's yours," Summer said.

"Thank you, Summer. You don't know what this means to me. I . . ." He dropped her hands. "Just thanks."

She saw the relief in his eyes and something else, a troubled look she couldn't identify. "I'm just glad I can do this for you."

"You have from now until we get to the courthouse for second thoughts," he said. "After that, it'll be too late to change your mind. Between here and there, think long and hard about what you're doing."

"Don't worry, Billy," Summer said. "I know what I'm doing."

"I doubt it," Billy replied. "Just remember. There's no backing out once we're married. A quick marriage and an even quicker divorce would look worse to the courts than no marriage at all. Are you *sure* you want to do this?"

Summer looked into Billy's worried eyes. He flinched as she reached up to brush a lock of dark hair from his forehead. "Don't worry, Billy. You can count on me. I won't let you down."

He unsaddled and unbridled his horse and put the tack in the back of her pickup. "Target can find his way back to the stable. Let's go."

"Maybe I should stop by the Castle first and get some of my things," Summer said.

"You can pack a bag of clothes after we're married," Billy said. "There's no room for anything else at my place."

Summer thought of her canopied bed and her mirrored dresser and the dozens of pairs of shoes in her closet. Then she thought of Billy's tiny jail cell of a room, with its sagging iron-railed bed and narrow chest of drawers.

She swallowed past the knot of apprehension in her throat. She wanted to ask where she and Billy were going to sleep, but she already knew the answer. Her life of luxury was over.

At least for the next two years.

She tried to imagine the shock on her mother's ageless, unlined face, the outrage in her father's cold gray eyes. Better not to confront them. Better to let them find out however they would.

Billy handed her into the passenger seat of her pickup,

then stopped and stared deep into her eyes. "You know what people say about me, Summer. You know who I am and always will be in this town. You sure you want to marry me?"

Summer's voice came out in a rasping whisper. "Yes, Billy. I do."

Chapter 5

LAUREN CREED FELT HER STOMACH LURCH AT the sound of someone knocking on her back door at five in the morning—a bare minute after she'd turned on the kitchen light. She set down the coffeepot and stared into the darkness beyond the screen door trying to discern who was there. She was expecting her elder son Sam, who lived in the foreman's house, to arrive any minute to share breakfast and discuss the division of labor for the day. But Sam wouldn't have knocked.

Something's happened to Luke.

Her heart had been lodged in her throat ever since her restless and rebellious twenty-year-old son had headed to some godforsaken African nation with his National Guard unit five months ago. She lived in daily dread of hearing that Luke had been injured or killed by some machete—or machine-gun—wielding native.

Ren couldn't seem to make her feet move toward the door. She opened her mouth to urge her visitor to come in, but no sound came out. She tensed as someone shoved the screen door open with a groan of springs and stepped inside.

"Oh, it's you." She tried to hold back the sob of relief in her chest, but to her chagrin, it escaped.

"My God, Ren. What's wrong?"

She wasn't sure which of them moved first, but a moment later she was being held tight in Jackson Blackthorne's arms. She let out another sob and wrapped her arms around his waist, amazed that he was here holding her, when she hadn't allowed herself more than a glimpse of his beloved face for the past two years.

"I've been sitting in my truck, waiting for the light to go on," he said in a gruff voice.

"You should have called. I would have let you in."

"I was going to do that, but then I figured it was crazy to wake you up in the middle of the night. I've waited my whole life for you, Ren, but I swear the past two hours have seemed like an eternity."

He rocked her in his arms, his face buried in her shoulder-length hair.

She didn't want to let him go. It felt too good to be held in his arms. But Sam would be arriving any minute, and she didn't dare let him find Jackson here. Sam had warned her what would happen if she ever tried to have a relationship with his father's worst enemy.

Ren leaned back to tell Blackjack he had to leave, that they would have to meet somewhere else later to talk, but frowned as she took a good look at him. His body had felt strong and solid, but his eyes looked haunted and his features looked haggard. He would be fifty-seven next month, with a bad heart that had been corrected with bypass surgery four years ago. Was he ill? Was that why he'd come?

"Are you all right?" she asked, reaching up to touch his cheek with her fingertips.

He grasped her hand and turned it to kiss her palm. "I'm free, Ren. Free of Eve at last."

She felt her heart leap at his words. She searched his face for the joy that ought to be there but was not. He looked anxious and uncertain in a way he hadn't since he'd first come to her thirty-seven years ago to propose ... and she'd refused because she was already pregnant with Jesse Creed's child.

"What happened?" she asked. "Was Eve in an accident? Is she dead?"

He shook his head. "Summer knows everything. There's nothing left for Eve to use as blackmail."

"How did she find out?"

Jackson blew a breath of air out of puffed cheeks. "I met up with Billy Coburn in the Armadillo Bar. He told me Summer's known the truth for the past two years. She overheard her mother and me arguing."

Ren tried to see past the gray stone wall Blackjack had made of his eyes. Why did he still seem so worried? What was he thinking? Now that he was finally free, was he having second thoughts about a life with her? She was afraid to ask, so she said, "Is Summer all right?"

"I should have trusted her more," he admitted. "She said she didn't want things to change between us. That's why she didn't say something to me sooner about her knowing the truth."

Ren pressed her forehead against his chest. "Oh, Jackson. Oh, my dear."

"I plan to start divorce proceedings as soon as the

Houston office of DeWitt & Blackthorne is open for business. Knowing my cousin Harry, I won't have to wait much past daybreak."

Ren lifted her face to his. "What about Bitter Creek?" She couldn't imagine Jackson Blackthorne without the ranch that had been his lifeblood. "Will Eve be able to take it from you?"

He shrugged. "I don't much care. All I want is you."

Ren leaned her cheek against his shoulder. It was hard to believe that the fight between their two families that had begun over a piece of land so many years ago might finally come to an end.

Three Oaks was a small island—a mere hundred square miles of land—in a sea of Blackthorne grass. And Blackthornes had been trying to buy it—or take it forcibly from Creeds—since the Civil War. It would be ironic if the two clans were finally united by marriage now the way they had been when the first Blackthorne married Creighton Creed—against her son's wishes— and started the feud that had survived until the present day.

The conflict had been very much a part of their lives during all the years of her marriage to Jesse. Two years ago, her eldest son had vowed he would murder Jackson Blackthorne—and make it look like an accident—if Ren pursued any relationship with his father's nemesis. She'd believed Sam would do what he'd promised. It had almost been a relief when Jackson wasn't able to divorce his wife.

But her respite had come to an end.

She felt her stomach churn. Sam's feelings hadn't changed. If anything, he hated the Blackthornes more than ever, despite the fact—or maybe because of the fact—that both his sisters had ended up married to Blackthornes.

Four years ago, Callie had married Blackjack's eldest son Trace and taken their two children, Eli and Hannah, and moved with him to a cattle station in Australia, where they'd produced another daughter, Henrietta. Two years ago, Bay had married Owen Blackthorne, and they were now living happily in Fredericksburg with their twin sons, Jake and James. Sam had felt betrayed by his sisters' embrace of the enemy.

But perhaps Sam was entitled to hate Blackthornes. He'd certainly suffered more from the feud than any of his siblings. The Blackthornes had stolen something precious from him. Something he'd never get back.

"You have to leave, Jackson," Ren said. "Sam will be here for breakfast in a few minutes."

"I'm not leaving you, Ren. Not again. Never again."

"Be reasonable," she said, backing away from his embrace. "Sam will need time to adjust—"

"Are you telling me I need your son's approval to marry you?"

Ren heard both arrogance and irritation in his voice. Jackson Blackthorne wasn't used to being told he couldn't have something he wanted. But she'd learned a long time ago that you couldn't always have what you wanted, even if you wanted it very badly.

She crossed to the coffeemaker, using the excuse of making coffee to give her time to think. When she was done, she turned back to Jackson, her hands braced against the counter and said, "Two years ago, you chose your daughter's happiness over your own. Can you blame me for making the same choice now for my son's sake?"

He yanked off his hat and threw it onto the antler rack inside the door, then shoved both hands through his hair. Ren felt her pulse speed up. He looked her in the eyes and said, "I'm here to stay, Ren. Our life together starts here and now... unless you send me away."

"You're not divorced yet. It won't look good in court if you—"

"I don't give a damn anymore. I just want to be with you... before we're both too old and brittle to make love to one another," he added with the hint of a smile.

Ren had rarely seen Jackson smile. She was amazed that he could find levity in the moment. She was still too frightened of what Sam might do. And afraid, now that the moment had come, that the passion which had flared between them so many years ago might have flickered out.

"Jackson, I—"

He must have seen what she was feeling, because his smile broadened until he was grinning. "Do you think it isn't still there? Foolish, foolish woman. All I have to do is look at you to want you.

"It's been that way ever since you were seventeen, and I saw you floating in that pond wearing nothing but a white bra and panties, your eyes closed, that serene smile on your face... and you asked me to come and kiss you, thinking I was Jesse. My feelings haven't changed, Ren. I want you every bit as much now as I did that long-ago day."

She flushed, remembering how husky his voice had sounded that lazy summer afternoon, how she'd heard the rustle of denim and the clink of his belt, before he'd moved silently into the water. How he'd kept her eyes covered with his hand, asking her to live out the fantasy, not wanting her to discover his deception.

Somehow she'd known it wasn't Jesse making love to her in the pond. But she hadn't wanted the dream to end. What had surprised and later shamed her was her behavior after she'd learned the truth. She'd spent the rest of the afternoon talking to, and making love with, Jackson Blackthorne.

It was appalling to realize that she'd found the other half of her soul—and he was not the man who'd fathered the child she carried inside her. She had never made a more difficult decision in her life than whether to marry Jackson Blackthorne or Jesse Creed.

As heir to the Blackthorne name and fortune, Jackson had believed the world was his for the taking. And he'd intended to have her for his wife.

"Marry me, Ren," he'd urged.

"I'm carrying Jesse's child," she'd replied, as though that were answer enough.

"I love you, Ren. I need you."

I need you. The words had seemed to startle him as much as they did her. She'd been so tempted to say yes.

"I'm sorry, Jackson," she'd blurted before she could change her mind. "I can't."

"I promise I'll take care of the baby. He'll never want for anything."

"Except his father's love," she'd said in a whisper. She'd reached up to touch his face, to offer comfort, and he'd grasped her hand and held it against his cheek.

She watched the desperation grow in his eyes as he whispered, "Please, Ren."

She shuddered now when she thought of how much he must have wanted her, to swallow his pride and beg.

"Don't, Jackson," she'd said in a choked voice. "Nothing you say can change the fact that this baby is Jesse's."

"Then get rid of it!"

She'd wrenched free and stared at him, seeing the effort it took for him to control the dark, jealous rage that had prompted his outburst. In that instant, she'd wished the baby had never been conceived. And in the next instant regretted that wish. She'd placed her hand over the tiny life growing inside her, looked into his storm-ridden gray eyes, and said, "You know I can't do that."

"I'm sorry," he'd said. "Just please don't leave me, Ren. I can't live without you. I promise—"

She'd interrupted him in a fierce voice, determined not to let him sway her from the decision she'd struggled so hard to make. "You're a Blackthorne. This child is a Creed. What if your feelings change after the baby is born? I can't marry you, Jackson. I can't take that chance!"

The next day she'd married Jesse Creed. And that same night realized she'd made the wrong choice.

Blackjack watched Ren covertly. Even at fifty-three, she was still gracefully slender, with warm, gray-green eyes and auburn hair that was gray at the temples and smelled like lavender. She wasn't acting as delighted by the turn of events as he'd hoped. She kept throwing Sam up as a roadblock.

He was scared. Was she really worried about her son's reaction to his presence? Or had her feelings toward him changed? Was she wishing he'd stayed with Eve?

He no longer believed in happily ever after. He'd lived too many years in a make-do marriage to be able to imagine any other kind of relationship. It was hard to remember how promising his life with Eve had been in the beginning, even though he'd been urged into marriage by his father, who'd been friends with Eve's father and wanted their two dynasties joined.

He hadn't put up much of a fight. He'd been devastated when Ren married Jesse Creed the day after she'd refused his proposal. He was only twenty, with a whole life ahead of him to be lived without the only woman he was certain he would ever love. Nothing had mattered.

When he'd married Evelyn DeWitt three months later, Ren had still owned his heart. Even so, in the first few weeks of his marriage, he'd begun to admire and appreciate his wife—who'd brought fifty thousand acres of good DeWitt grassland with her as a dowry.

It was hard to remember what Eve had been like all those years ago. So happy. So carefree. Always smiling. Always laughing. When he was with her, he'd been able to ignore the ache in his chest that he felt whenever he thought of Ren. He remembered being surprised that his marriage was turning out so well.

Maybe if Ren hadn't miscarried, everything would have been different. But a horse had stumbled and fallen.

And all their lives had changed forever.

He'd been at the Bitter Creek Regional Hospital with Eve, who was seeing a doctor because she suspected she was pregnant, when he'd overheard two nurses talking and realized Ren had been admitted several hours earlier.

"She was rounding up cattle and her horse stumbled and she was thrown," one nurse said to the other. "The cattle spooked and she got trampled. Her leg got broken pretty bad. And she lost her baby."

"How awful," the other nurse said. "How far along was she?"

Blackjack didn't wait to hear the answer, just headed for the reception desk and said, "Where did you put Mrs. Creed?"

"She isn't receiving visitors," the receptionist said.

"I asked you a question," he said. "Answer it."

"Mr. Blackthorne's family owns the hospital," a nurse told the receptionist, then turned to him and said, "She's on the second floor, Mr. Blackthorne. Room 203."

Blackjack couldn't wait for the elevator. He took the stairs two at a time and ran down the empty hallway, looking from side to side until he found the room he wanted. The door was closed. He debated whether to knock but didn't want to take the chance of anyone telling him he couldn't come in. He pushed the door open and stepped inside.

The shadowy room was lit only by streaks of late afternoon sunlight that escaped through the closed venetian blinds. He could see Ren lying on the farthest of the two railed hospital beds, her eyes closed, her hands folded over her flat stomach. Her toes were all that was visible of her lower right leg, which was covered from the knee down in a thick white cast.

"Ren?" He felt paralyzed, terrified that she was hurt

worse than the nurses had said. Her face was parchment pale, and one cheek had a bandage taped to it.

Without opening her eyes, she turned her head toward the wall and said, "Go away, Jackson."

He crossed and sat on the bed beside her. Tears had dried on her face. He brushed his knuckles across her cheek above the square white bandage. "Are you all right?"

"No." She kept her head turned away.

"I'm sorry," he said.

He heard the gurgle as she swallowed several times.

"Please, Ren. Talk to me." He was frightened by how still she lay. He wanted to pick her up and hold her, but he was terrified of hurting her. "Ren. Sweetheart, I need—"

She wrenched her head around to look at him. "Don't. I'm not your sweetheart. I'm another man's wife. And you have a wife of your own."

He hadn't even realized he'd used the endearment. He met her gaze and saw that what he'd been thinking ever since he'd heard that she'd lost the baby was mirrored in her tortured eyes. *How capriciously the gods play with mortals. How unkind fate is.*

She was free now. But he was not.

He saw something else in her gaze, something greater than regret. And suddenly knew what was causing her so much pain.

Guilt.

Maybe, like him, she'd wished that Jesse's child had never been conceived—and regretted her thoughts as much as he regretted the words he'd uttered aloud. Maybe she believed some prayer she'd spoken in the depths of her despair had been answered in this awful way. What if she'd later realized how much she'd wanted her child? And God had punished her for those earlier, uncharitable thoughts by taking it from her.

He didn't dare ask. He didn't want to know. It was disturbing enough to see her in such anguish.

His heart was thumping in his chest. He wished he could tell her that he'd never stopped loving her, that he still wanted her. But he had a wife. And maybe a child of his own on the way.

Ren's eyes welled with tears, and he watched as she gritted her teeth to still the quiver in her chin. "You should leave," she said. "Jesse will be back soon."

She was right. He had no business being here. She was another man's wife. He'd already let her go once. He had to leave her alone. He had to forget about her and go on with his life.

"I wish . . ." He could have bitten off his tongue when he saw the despair in her eyes as she stared up at him.

The sob seemed to be torn from someplace deep inside her. She tried to turn on her side away from him but cried out in pain and grabbed for her ribs. Blackjack lifted her upright, and her arms groped for his neck and held on tight as she buried her face in the crook of his shoulder.

He felt his heart swell with emotion as he listened to her muffled sobs of grief. He kissed her temple, murmuring what comfort he could, realizing as he held her close—for what might be the very last time—that the loss of this child would force them apart every bit as surely as its birth would have done. Knowing Ren, she would never forgive herself for wanting him when she was pregnant with Jesse's child.

"What the hell are you doing here?"

Ren jerked backward at the sound of Jesse's voice, crying out as her ribs protested.

Blackjack pulled her close again to spare her the pain of holding herself upright. He turned to face the man who'd married the woman he loved. "I heard Ren was hurt. I came to see for myself."

"Get away from my wife," Jesse said, crossing into the room, headed straight for him.

"Jesse, please," Ren cried.

Blackjack saw her face had been robbed of what little color it possessed. She looked frightened and ashamed. It was the shame that angered him.

She was struggling against his hold and whimpering with the pain it was causing her. He let her go and watched as she wrapped her arms around her ribs and held herself tight, as though she might splinter into pieces if she did not. Her eyes were squeezed closed, and her teeth bit hard on her lower lip.

He felt Jesse's hand grab at his shoulder and shrugged it off as he stood and confronted the other man. "We can talk outside," he said.

"We'll talk right here."

Blackjack glanced over his shoulder at Ren. Her eyes were closed, but she could hear just fine. He didn't want her hurt any more than she already was. For her sake, he had to placate her husband.

"There's nothing between me and Ren," he said.

"Right," Jesse said, his lips twisted in scorn. "She told

me what happened between you two—after she cried out your name at the wrong time."

He could see Ren from the corner of his eye. Her eyes were open now and wary, her face suddenly flushed. With mortification? With humiliation? How dare her husband reveal what must have been a very private—and awkward—moment between them?

He could understand Jesse's animosity better. But he wondered just how much of the story the other man knew. Whether she'd told him how they'd made love at the pond, and what a shattering experience it had been for both of them. How they'd spent the rest of the afternoon loving one another, when there had been no question of who he was. That he'd known even then that he wanted to spend his life with her. And that she'd known even then that she was pregnant with Jesse's child.

The child she had lost.

"What happened between Ren and me is in the past," Blackjack said. "I'm married now."

"Then what are you doing here making love to my wife?"

"I came to offer my condolences and—"

"And to see if she'd be your whore again?"

"Watch your tongue," Blackjack said, as adrenaline pumped through his veins. "She's your wife."

"And your lover!" Jesse accused.

Before he could reply, he heard another female cry—this time from beyond Jesse's shoulder. Jesse turned at the sound, and Blackjack saw Eve pressed against the doorjamb, her eyes stricken. He felt his stomach cramp as he realized the disaster his visit here had wrought.

"Eve, I—"

She didn't give him a chance to explain, simply whirled and ran.

He turned his anger on Jesse. "I could kill you for that."

"I only spoke the truth," Jesse said stubbornly. "You're a lowdown, wife-stealing—"

"See to your wife," Blackjack said abruptly. "She needs you." He resisted the urge to vent his anger in violence, as he shoved his way past Jesse and went in search of his wife.

The promising start of his marriage had been spoiled. His wife, it turned out, was pregnant with his eldest son Trace. He hadn't seen Ren again for a long time, and when he had, she'd avoided looking at him. Her husband had remained jealous ever after. And though Eve had professed to love him, even after what she'd heard, her laughter had disappeared.

Over the years, though he'd never so much as spoken to Ren, Eve's resentment of the other woman had grown. He'd felt frustrated, unable to convince his wife that he had nothing to do with Lauren Creed. He'd spent nearly every night of his marriage in his wife's bed, but that one mistake had never been forgotten . . . or forgiven.

Four years ago, Eve had asked her lover his own foreman—to hire someone to murder Ren. The gunman had mistaken his mark, and Jesse Creed had been killed instead.

Leaving Ren a widow and free to marry him.

Well, not quite free. Jesse had passed on his animosity for all things Blackthorne to his children. Surprisingly, their two girls had ended up marrying two of Blackjack's boys. But he was going to have to find a way to make peace with her two sons. Otherwise, there could be no future for him with this woman.

No, he wasn't at all sure that he and Ren would end up together. But he had to try. The rest of his life would be infinitely long and lonely without her.

Blackjack felt his breath catch as the rising sun hit Ren's face through the kitchen window, illuminating her beauty. *Nothing can keep me away from you now,* he thought. *Nothing and nobody.*

"Mom? Are you in there? Are you all right?"

Blackjack saw the terror in Ren's eyes as she glanced toward the screen door. "That's Sam."

He watched as her gaze shifted toward the front door, as though to send him out that way, before she realized his truck, with the Bitter Creek brand painted on the door, was parked out back. Sam already knew he was there.

A moment later Ren's eldest son rolled himself into the kitchen in his wheelchair. Blackjack had to admit there was a startling change in the boy—the man—since the last time he'd seen him, two years ago. Sam must be all of thirty-two or thirty-three now. He'd been in a wheelchair since he was eighteen, when Blackjack's son Owen had tackled him at football practice and broken his neck.

He seemed bigger somehow, broader, stronger. Blackjack realized Sam was no longer using an electric chair. He'd wheeled himself into the room with his own powerful arms and shoulders. Blackjack could almost see Sam's neckhairs bristle when he noted how close his father's mortal enemy was standing to his mother.

"What is he doing here?" Sam said, glancing from his mother to Blackjack and back again.

"I'm here to see Ren," he replied.

"If you've got ranch business, you can call me later. I'm busy right now," Sam said.

It was a dismissal, pure and simple.

Blackjack felt his own neckhairs hackle.

Ren placed a tentative hand on his arm and looked into his eyes, begging for understanding.

He understood, all right. Sam Creed was his stubborn, bullheaded father all over again. Blackjack wasn't about to let some pup's growl spook him, when the big, bad barnyard dog had never scared him away.

"I'm not here for—"

"Sam has taken over the day-to-day business of the ranch," Ren interrupted. "So I have more time to work with the horses."

Blackjack had employed Ren ever since Jesse's death to raise and train his quarter horses for cutting horse competitions. It had given him a reason to visit Three Oaks. He considered making up some business excuse for why he'd come, as Ren obviously hoped he would, to avoid the confrontation with Sam. But that was only postponing the inevitable.

The boy—he had to stop thinking of Ren's grown son that way; there was nothing boyish about him—might as well get used to the way things were going to be. He met Sam's distrustful gaze and said, "I came to see Ren for personal reasons."

"You have nothing to say to my mother that she wants to hear," Sam retorted.

"That's your mother's call."

Sam turned to his mother, apparently expecting her to agree that he should leave. "Mom?"

"I want Jackson to stay, Sam," she said in a quiet voice.

Blackjack breathed an inward sigh of relief but kept his satisfaction to himself. This showdown was between Ren and her son.

Sam turned to his mother and said, "He doesn't belong in this house. Dad would roll over in his grave—"

"What happened in the past is over and done," Ren said.

"Not for me," Sam snapped.

"If you feel you can't stay, Sam, I'll understand," she said.

Blackjack saw the astonishment flicker in Sam's eyes before he said, "You're siding with a Blackthorne over your own family?"

"I hope you won't make that necessary," she said.

"Luke isn't going to be any more pleased about—"

"Luke isn't here right now," Ren countered.

Sam wheeled his chair over to Blackjack, stopping with his knees only inches from Blackjack's, and said, "I want you out of my father's house."

Blackjack resisted the urge to back up. He could see the corded muscle on Sam's forearms where his Western shirt was rolled up, see the veins throbbing in his forehead. He was glad Sam didn't have a gun handy. He looked mad enough—mean enough—to kill.

"I'm here at your mother's invitation," he said. "When she tells me to leave, I'll leave."

"I'm telling you to leave. Now."

Blackjack perused the man—it was no boy who glared back at him—wondering what Sam would do. What kind of physical threat could Sam exert from a wheelchair? On the other hand, you never hit a man when he was down. How was Blackjack supposed to fight someone who wasn't able to stand and face him?

Blackjack glared back, unwilling to fight, unwilling to retreat.

In the end, it was Ren who blinked.

"Jackson," she said. "Please. We can talk later."

He could see how upset she was, how much this was tearing her apart. He could afford to be the bigger man and leave. This business with Sam was just a little wrinkle that needed ironing out. "All right, Ren. I'll go. I'll call you later."

When he saw the smug look on Sam's face, he had to bite the inside of his cheek to keep from saying something he'd regret. That *boy* didn't know it yet, but his reign in this household was coming to an end.

Blackjack turned to Ren, uncurled her balled hands and held them in his own. He wanted to say *I love you,* but somehow he couldn't get the words out with her son watching. He wanted to kiss her, but her eyes said *Don't.*

He squeezed her hands, then let them go. Sam was in his way when he turned to leave.

"Don't come back," Sam said. "We don't want you here."

"Get out of my way."

Sam backed up the wheelchair and made a mocking gesture toward the door. "Be my guest."

Blackjack stopped at the hat rack and settled his Resistol carefully on his head, then pushed open the groaning screen door and let it slam behind him. He resisted the urge to turn and say, *I'll be back.* In the *Terminator* movie, it was the villain who'd uttered those words, and he'd returned to wreak havoc.

Blackjack didn't want to ruin anything. He just wanted to spend the rest of his life with the woman he loved. But as he cranked the engine on his pickup, he stared at the two figures highlighted through the screen door and muttered, "I'll be back."

Chapter 6

SUMMER STARED AT THE RING FINGER OF HER trembling left hand, which was bare of the four-carat square-cut diamond engagement ring which had sat there for the past year. "I didn't think it was possible to get married so quickly and simply," she said to Billy. "No blood test, just a license and a few words said by a magistrate." No wedding band. Not even a kiss at the end of the ceremony. But that would have been a travesty, since the entire marriage was a sham.

She'd been chattering since the moment the ceremony ended and Billy had hustled her into her Silverado and headed for the Castle. Her pickup had air-conditioning, but Billy had said he needed the fresh air and rolled down all the windows. She felt hot and sweaty, and the scorching wind, heated by the unrelenting sun on the asphalt, whipped her hair into her mouth every time she opened it to speak. And she couldn't seem to shut up.

She caught her lower lip in her teeth to stem the tide of nervous words and stared out at the mesquite trees in the pasture, their roots running hundreds of feet beneath the ground, doing battle with the grass for the scarce water that was sufficient to keep only one of them alive.

She bit at a cuticle, then heard her mother's voice in her head telling her what an uncouth habit it was. She dropped her hands into her lap, then loudly cleared her throat, hoping Billy would say something, maybe ask if she was all right.

At which point she would tell him no. She had no idea why she felt so agitated, but Billy was doing nothing to allay her anxiety. Right now, he was busy imitating a stone statue.

"Why don't you say something?" she said. "What are you thinking? What are you feeling? Talk to me, Billy."

"I was wondering how fast we can get that $25,000," Billy replied. "The sooner I pay off Debbie Sue, the better. I want that custody hearing canceled."

Summer felt her heart sink. Of course Billy's first thoughts were about his son. That was the whole reason he'd suggested getting married. But she couldn't help feeling hurt. She'd told Billy she was marrying him to thwart her parents, but she hadn't been able to keep herself from romanticizing the situation.

Sure, they were marrying for convenience, but once upon a time, Billy Coburn's kisses had curled her toes and made her heart gallop. She had to admit that deep down she'd been hoping he'd fall madly in love with her. They'd be short of cash for a couple of years, but eventually she'd have her trust fund and they'd live happily ever after.

The reality was she had two rough, Spartan years ahead of her. And Billy wasn't acting the least bit romantic.

"When and how do you want to tell your parents?" Billy said.

Summer grimaced. "Will you think I'm a coward if I say I'd rather let them find out on their own?"

He glanced sideways at her. "You're my wife now. If you want me there when you tell them, just say the word. Blackjack doesn't scare me."

Summer grinned, but the moment of levity vanished when she thought of what a confrontation between her father and Billy might be like. She shuddered when she imagined the same scene with her mother. "I can't do it right now," she said. "Just let me grab a few things from the house."

"Want me to come in with you?" he said as he stopped her truck at the back door to the Castle.

"No. I'll be quick."

The house seemed empty, but it often did. The servants moved quietly about their duties, and her mother likely was hidden away in her studio at the end of the hall on the second floor, creating another artistic masterpiece. Eve Blackthorne's acclaimed Western oil paintings were featured in galleries all over the country.

Summer had often envied her mother's talent—and resented the time she spent in her studio creating "perfect" paintings from photographic images of Western life, carefully correcting each flaw the camera had captured on film. Her mother painted the world as it might be, not as it was. Sometimes Summer wanted to paint back in a fly-blown sore on a cow, or the rot in a mesquite fence post, or put back in the too-narrow space between a cowgirl's eyes, so her face was distinctively her own.

But she didn't have her mother's talent. She didn't have any talent, for that matter. Oh, she could sit a horse pretty well, and she could dance the two-step and the cotton-eyed Joe with flair. And challenged by her father, she'd mastered the computer programs necessary to manage Bitter Creek.

But she didn't have a college degree. She couldn't sew or cook. She had no idea how to play an instrument or sing on key. And she didn't know squat about babies.

What on earth had she been thinking when she agreed to marry Billy Coburn? She was going to end up being one more responsibility loaded on his already overburdened shoulders. He was going to hate her for taking advantage of the situation when he saw how inept she was with Will.

But she couldn't help being what she was. Maybe she had been spoiled, growing up in a house where everything was done for her. That didn't mean she couldn't learn. And she would.

As Summer tiptoed down the upstairs hall, stepping around the places in the wooden floor that she knew would groan, she vowed that Billy would never have cause to be sorry he'd made her his wife.

She crept into her bedroom, closed the door, and leaned back against the cool wood, staring wistfully around her room. It was everything a young girl could want. A pink canopied bed. A collection of stuffed animals, which she'd used for company when she'd felt alone. An enormous mirror above her dressing table covered with taped-up pictures of her and her family.

She crossed to the mirror and began pulling off pictures. One of her as a three-year-old with flyaway blond curls, holding Trace's hand and staring up at him with a grin on her face. Of her at seven in messy pigtails and ragged jeans, standing between Owen and Clay in their football uniforms. Of her at fifteen in a ponytail, sitting on her horse holding a first-place ribbon for barrel racing, her father smiling up at her.

There were no pictures of her with her mother. Or with friends.

She grimaced and headed for her walk-in closet. She'd just married her best friend in the world. And if she didn't hurry up and pack, he was liable to head for home without her. She grabbed a travel bag from the floor of her closet and opened it on the bed, then began rooting through drawers for underwear, the T-shirts she slept in, and jeans. She was wearing her favorite pair of boots.

Her Western shirts were all ironed and starched on hangers. She found a hanging bag and stuffed in about a dozen. She debated whether to take any dresses, then figured if she hadn't gotten married in a dress, she wasn't going to have much need for one.

Unless they went to church. She knew Billy didn't go to church, but his mother did. She pulled a Von Furstenberg–like print jersey dress from the closet, rolled it in a ball and stuck it in the travel bag with her jeans. She considered the strappy Manolo Blahnik heels she normally wore with the jersey dress, then chose a pair of plain black Cole•Haan pumps and dumped them in on top of the dress.

She looked around the room for anything else she might want or need in the next couple of weeks. She hurried to the small chest beside her bed, opened the top drawer and pulled out her diary—although she called it a journal now—and flipped to her latest entry.

*Broke up with Geoffrey tonight. Feel awful. And
surprisingly free. And frightened, because Momma is
pushing me to make up with him again. Just want to
go to sleep and wake up and have everything be all
right.*

*Billy came home and he has a son! I was never so
shocked in all my life. Billy looks so different. His
hair is just as long as it ever was, but he seems
broader in the shoulders and taller and leaner. I've
always thought he was handsome, but I actually felt
butterflies in my stomach when I looked into his eyes.*

Summer was appalled to see that she'd gone on for
another two paragraphs describing everything she could
remember about Billy Coburn in minute detail. Was she
really so fixated on him? She didn't dare take the chance
of letting Billy see any of this.

She stuck the diary back in the drawer and shut it.
Surely at some point she would be returning to pack
away her things. She'd have to forgo writing in a journal
until then. She turned back into the room, wondering
what else she would need.

And realized she'd forgotten about cosmetics and toiletries—and medications. She got her birth control pills
out of the medicine cabinet, then grabbed toothpaste,
toothbrush, comb, and brush. She considered whether to
take her scented soap and expensive shampoo, then
grabbed both. The day would come when she had to use
unscented soap and cheap shampoo, but there was no
sense denying herself a few luxuries in the meantime.

She grabbed the small bag that held her makeup. She
didn't use much, but she didn't feel dressed in the morn-

ing without some mascara and lipstick. She made herself leave everything else.

She unzipped her travel bag enough to stuff the makeup inside, then looked around to see if there was anything else she couldn't do without. And spotted the stuffed teddy bear that sat in an honored position in the center of her bed.

The bear was small, made of dark brown terry cloth, with a red and green plaid ribbon tied around its neck that had frayed on the ends. One of the two button eyes was missing. She picked up the bear and hugged it to her. She had left Brownie at home when she'd made her forays into university life. And missed him terribly.

But she wasn't a child anymore. Or even a lonely young girl. She was a married woman.

"It's time for me to leave, Brownie," she said to the bear. She laid him back on the bed in his place of honor, then reached for the two bags she'd packed.

An instant later, she dropped the bags and grabbed Brownie. "You can keep Will company," she said to the bear as she unzipped the travel bag and stuffed him inside.

And me if I get lonely . . .

She opened her bedroom door, picked up her bags, and walked out the door.

And ran right into her mother.

"Oh. Excuse me."

"Does this mean you've made a decision?" her mother asked, eyeing the two bags.

"I can't marry Geoffrey," Summer said.

"I always knew you were selfish," her mother replied. "I never thought you were stupid."

Summer gripped her bags tighter, wishing there was some way to stop the humiliating flush burning its way up her throat. She'd always yearned for her mother's approval, strived to earn it, yet somehow never quite measured up. That didn't mean she didn't love her mother, and respect her. She offered the only explanation she could, hoping it would be enough. "I don't love Geoffrey."

"You're being ridiculous. Go unpack those bags while I call Geoffrey and—"

"It's too late for that."

"Geoffrey will forgive and forget. I'm sure you can smooth everything over—"

"I'm married," she blurted. "I married Billy Coburn this morning."

Summer waited for the explosion she was sure was coming. Instead of raging, her mother threw back her head and laughed.

"This is rich. This is perfect. Your father will throw forty fits. His darling daughter married to a saddle tramp without a penny. Even better, your father's very own bastard son. Oh, I love it!" And she sailed off into another fit of laughter.

Summer hadn't thought she could feel any worse. But her mother's laughter made something precious curl up inside her and die. She couldn't even defend herself by saying she loved Billy. And she didn't dare explain the real reason she'd married him. She couldn't take the chance that her mother would do something vindictive to punish Billy for spoiling her plans.

"What does your father say about this?" her mother asked.

"He doesn't know yet."

"I want to be a fly on the wall when you tell him," she said.

"I'm leaving now, Momma. Billy's waiting for me outside."

"I'll just come along and congratulate your new husband."

"Please don't, Momma," Summer said, cringing at the spite she heard in her mother's voice. "There's no need—"

"Let's go, Summer," her mother said.

Summer brushed past her mother and headed down the stairs, walking as fast as she could without running, trying to put distance between them so she could give Billy some warning that her mother was right behind her.

"I can't imagine what you were thinking, Summer," her mother said from behind her. "I thought you had more pride than this. Are you pregnant?"

Summer stopped abruptly in the middle of the kitchen and turned to stare at her mother, her mouth gaping. "Of course not!"

"Then why have you done this?" her mother said, her eyes focused intently on Summer's face.

Summer felt like an ant under a magnifying glass, the kind cruel little boys held, focusing the fierce rays of the sun so that eventually the ant burned to cinders. She didn't want to tell the truth. And she couldn't think of a good enough lie to fool her mother. So she stood there, staring back helplessly. She never felt like this with her father. She could face him toe-to-toe and fight.

But her mother reduced her to this quivering, sniveling

creature without any backbone. Her throat had closed so tight it was threatening to choke her.

"Well?" her mother demanded. "Cat got your tongue?"

Summer couldn't have said a word to save her life.

"What the hell is going on here?" a voice bellowed from the kitchen doorway.

Summer dropped her bags, turned, and ran toward her father, wrapping her arms around him as she careened into him. "Daddy," she sobbed, pressing her cheek against his chest. "Oh, Daddy."

He'd always been her refuge in a storm. Suddenly, she noticed that his body was stiff, and his arms had not closed around her.

She lifted her head and looked up into his face. And saw that he knew what she'd done. And disapproved. His gray eyes were as cold and remote as she'd ever seen them. She looked past his shoulder and saw Billy standing in the doorway behind him, his face pale, his jaw taut.

She took a step back and let her hands drop to her sides.

"Is it true?" her father said.

She focused on Billy's face and tried to divine what he was thinking, but his dark eyes were shuttered. She realized her father was still waiting for an answer—and that she'd been waiting for Billy to provide it. After all, he'd said he would be there to support her.

Well, he was here. But obviously, he expected her to stand up to her father. She didn't want Billy to find her wanting so soon in their marriage. If he expected her to be strong, she'd be strong.

She squared her shoulders and said, "Billy and I are married, if that's what you're asking."

"Goddammit to hell! Have you got maggots in your brain, girl?" her father yelled.

For an instant, Summer thought he might hit her, even though he'd never raised a hand to her in her life. A second later, Billy was standing beside her, his arm around her waist, and the two of them were facing her father together.

She could feel the tension radiating off Billy. His hand was squeezing her waist so tightly it hurt. "Summer and I don't need your permission—or your approval—to marry," he said. "Now get out of our way."

"Billy, I need my bags," Summer reminded him.

He made an irritated sound in his throat but let go of her and turned to pick up her bags. And found himself confronting her mother.

He touched the brim of his hat and said, "Ma'am."

"You're a fool, Billy Coburn," she said. "Like your mother before you."

Summer saw the flush stain Billy's cheeks. She grabbed his arm and tried to pull him toward the door, only to find her father had taken a step closer, blocking their exit.

"Come on, Billy," she begged. "Forget my things. I don't need them."

Billy leaned over and picked up her bags. "We'll be leaving now, ma'am," he said to her mother. He turned and found Blackjack blocking the way. "Step aside," he said.

"Summer's not going anywhere," her father said.

Her mother clapped. "Bravo. Wonderful performance, Jackson. May I ask to what I owe the pleasure of your return so soon, and in such a timely fashion? Did the widow throw you out?"

"This is still my house, Eve. I'll come and go as I please."

"Over my dead body."

"Like I've said before, that can be arranged," her father taunted.

Summer blanched. She and Billy stood between her parents, who stabbed at each other with barbed words.

"Momma, Daddy, please. Not now."

"Why not now?" her mother said. "Your husband might as well know what kind of family he's married into."

"Go upstairs, Summer," her father said. "Where you belong. You can leave, Coburn."

"I'm leaving, all right," Billy said in a steely voice. "And my wife is coming with me."

He took a step forward, his shoulder shoving hard against Blackjack's shoulder and knocking him aside. Summer held her breath, expecting her father to attack Billy as they took the last few steps to the screen door.

"Are you going to let him get away with that, Jackson?" her mother gibed.

Summer realized her father was distracted from confronting Billy by the necessity of making some sort of retort to her mother, like two wolves that attack one another, determined not to share the kill. She heard them snarling at each other as she and Billy shoved their way out the door.

Billy threw her bags into the back of the pickup and said, "Are you all right?"

"Fine," she said, hiding her shaking hands behind her back.

"Then let's get out of here."

She let herself into the passenger side of the cab and buckled her seat belt, which was a good thing, because Billy peeled rubber as he backed out and wheeled the pickup toward the front of the house. He was going dangerously fast as they passed the line of stately magnolias that shaded the asphalt driveway. He accelerated to a pace that became dangerous when ten miles later they left the asphalt and hit the dirt roads that led toward Billy's ranch.

"Slow down," Summer said, both hands pressed against the dash in an effort to brace herself as the truck sailed high after hitting another pothole.

"Have the two of them always been like that?" Billy asked.

"Like what?"

Billy glanced at her but hit another pothole and had to put his eyes back on the road to keep the pickup from careening out of control. "Have they always been so spiteful toward one another?"

Summer felt defensive and said, "All parents argue."

"Your father threatened to kill your mother."

"They always talk like that," Summer said. "It's hyperbole."

Billy lifted an eyebrow.

"Exaggeration," she said, explaining the word.

"I know what hyperbole is."

Summer glanced sideways at Billy. She'd always known he was smart, but she'd assumed his vocabulary was limited because he'd barely made it through high school. She was going to have to be careful not to insult him that way again. Marriage was becoming a minefield, and she'd better tread more carefully.

"Thank you for standing up to my father," she said.

"You're my wife."

She grimaced. "In a fake marriage."

"There's nothing fake about our marriage," Billy said. "It's as real as it gets . . . at least for the next two years."

Except for the sex, Summer wanted to say. But she didn't want to argue. She'd heard enough arguing to last her a lifetime. "I don't want us ever to argue like my parents," Summer said. "Promise me we'll talk things over quietly and reasonably."

"Fine by me," Billy said. "And since you want plain speaking, there are a few things we need to get straight before we get back to the C-Bar."

"I'm listening." Summer realized Billy had slowed the truck to a reasonable speed so he could hold her gaze.

"First, I'm going to need your help nursing my mother and baby-sitting Will."

"I've never done any nursing," she said. And then, since he was going to find out anyway, she admitted, "I don't know much about babies, either."

"You'll learn," Billy said.

Summer bit her lip, then said what she was thinking. "Your mother doesn't like me."

"No, she doesn't," Billy agreed. "The two of you will have to make peace."

"I'm willing. What if she's not?"

"I'll talk to her," Billy said.

Summer wasn't encouraged, but she said, "All right."

"There isn't much to learn when it comes to babies," Billy said. "Just keep them dry and feed them and love them."

"I guess I can do that," Summer said.

"Emma can keep up with the cooking and housekeeping, and I'll manage the chores around the ranch and see what other work I can get. My rent is paid till the end of the month in Amarillo, but I'll need to get up there one weekend to pack up Will's clothes and my stuff and move it all back here, if it turns out I've lost my job. Meanwhile, it'll be roundup time soon, and I expect I can get someone to take me on as hired help."

Summer brightened. "I could do that, too! I'm actually better at ranch work than—"

"I need you at the house," Billy interrupted. "Taking care of Mom and Will."

"But—"

Billy laid a hand on her thigh. The touch felt intimate even though a layer of denim separated his flesh from hers. "I need your help at home, Summer. I'm trusting you to take care of my mom and my son. Think you can handle it?"

"Sure, Billy. No problem."

Sure she could nurse a woman who hated her guts. And take care of a baby when she had no idea how to put on a diaper or what babies ate. And ignore his pregnant sister stalking around, cooking and cleaning and glaring at her, since she had no use for Blackthornes.

Summer inwardly shuddered. She felt like telling

Billy to turn around and take her home. But the memory of her parents at each other's throats kept her mute.

Maybe, somehow, she could make friends with Billy's mother. And get along with his sister. And she would be more than willing to pour out all the love she had to give on Billy's son.

After all, the whole point of marrying Billy was to prove she wasn't as selfish as her mother. Or as ruthless as her father. She might not have any particular talents, but she was willing to work hard. And she never gave up without a fight.

Surely hard work and determination would be enough to see her through the first few difficult weeks of adjustment. And she wouldn't be doing it alone. Billy would be there beside her at night. They'd be able to talk things over, work things out.

As they drove up to the back door of the Coburn ranch house, Summer looked at the one-story frame structure with a critical eye. She'd never paid much attention to its rundown condition when she'd visited Billy before precisely because she'd only been visiting.

Now she noticed that the wood showed through in several places where the white paint had weathered away. The porch roof canted down on one side, and she remembered the middle step leading up to the back porch was broken. The screen was curled up on one corner of the kitchen door, letting in flies.

Billy pulled up to the back door, but didn't shut off the engine. Summer looked at him and smiled tentatively. "Nervous?" she asked.

"I'm not coming in," Billy replied.

Summer felt her heart begin to pound. "Where are you going?"

"I've got to go to the TSCRA headquarters in town to see if there's any chance I can keep my job. I want you to go on in and get settled."

"You can't just drop me off like this," Summer protested. "Does your mother or your sister even know we're married?"

"I called my mother on my cell phone while I was waiting for you to pack and told her I'd be bringing you home."

"What did she say to that?"

Billy's lips thinned.

"What did she say, Billy?" Summer demanded.

"She isn't any more happy about our marriage than your parents," Billy admitted. "But she'll get used to it."

"Please come in with me, Billy."

"You're not afraid of my mother, are you?" he teased.

"Terrified," she said.

Billy laughed. It was plain he thought she was joking. "You're not afraid of anything, Summer."

"We should greet your mother together for the first time as husband and wife," she said. "It's the courteous thing to do."

"It might be," Billy conceded. "But I've got an appointment with the TSCRA that may mean the difference between me being employed in a job with a future or doing menial labor from now on. I've got to go. Do you need me to get your bags out of the truck?" he said.

Summer shook her head in disbelief. Well, the honeymoon was certainly over. "I can get them." She stepped out of the truck and reached into the bed of the truck to retrieve her bags, hefting them over the side with some difficulty. She backed away and stood watching as Billy waved at her and spun his wheels backing up, raising a tail of dust that nearly choked her.

When the dust had settled, she gripped her bags more tightly, then turned and headed for the door. She was going to make Billy proud of her. She was going to make friends with his mother and his sister and love his son more than any mother ever could.

She stood at the screen door and leaned forward in an attempt to see inside. Like Dorothy, she'd been picked up by a tornado and whirled around and set down in a strange and terrifying land. She had a tremendous urge to tap her heels together and chant, "There's no place like home."

Although, in this case, that wouldn't really help. For the next two years, this ramshackle ranch house was her home.

"Who's there?" a voice inside demanded.

"It's Summer Blackthorne. I mean, it's Summer—" She stopped, flustered because her last name was no longer Blackthorne, but Coburn didn't feel right, either.

"Well, girl," the unfriendly voice said. "Come on in."

Chapter 7

 SUMMER SHOVED OPEN THE SCREEN DOOR WITH her hip, stepped inside, and set down her bags. She waited for her eyes to adjust to the gloom after the glare of the afternoon sun. The kitchen was stifling, and Summer remembered that Billy's home didn't have air-conditioning. She felt hot and sticky and realized the only cure was a cool shower, which she wasn't likely to get anytime soon.

When she could see clearly, she greeted the woman who sat at the kitchen table. "Hello, Mrs. Coburn. Billy said he told you we'd gotten—"

"I heard," Dora interrupted.

Summer hadn't seen Dora Coburn for two years. She wouldn't have recognized her if she hadn't known who she was. Billy's mother must have lost thirty or forty pounds. With the loss of flesh, her face had wrinkled in on itself. Her brown hair had turned completely white and she wore it in an untidy bun at her nape, while her dark eyes looked sunken behind black plastic frames. Knobby elbows protruded from the short sleeves of a faded, rose-colored chenille robe that had not only seen better days, but better years.

Summer stood waiting to be invited to sit, or to make herself at home, or to be sent packing. When Dora said nothing, she picked up her bags and said, "I'll put these in Billy's room."

"Don't go in there right now. The baby's napping."

"Oh." Summer waited for further instructions. When they didn't come, she set her bags down again. She decided to take the bull by the horns and said, "I suppose that gives us a chance to talk."

Dora Coburn frowned. "Why did you do it?"

Summer was caught off guard by the blunt question. "For Billy's sake," she replied.

Dora shook her head. "Billy doesn't need a wife. He's doing fine without one."

Summer realized Billy must not have told his mother about the custody suit, and if he hadn't, then she certainly couldn't. "I married Billy because he asked."

Dora snorted. "As I recall, you were set to marry some other fellow in two weeks. What happened to him?"

"I didn't— We didn't— I changed my mind," she said.

"And butted into Billy's life like a she-goat in heat," Dora said, her eyes narrowing. "You've wanted my son ever since you laid eyes on him, and the minute he came back you latched onto him."

"It's not like that," Summer protested. "Billy and I..." They'd been friends, just friends, for so many years. And they still were friends, with one little difference. They were also husband and wife. So what if she was physically attracted to Billy Coburn? That wasn't why she'd married him, no matter what Dora thought. It wasn't even going to be a real marriage, although Summer had no intention of telling Dora that.

"Billy doesn't need the likes of you in his life," Dora said. "Rich, self-centered, selfish, inconsiderate—"

"That's enough," Summer said. She tried not to let the words hurt her. "I would never do anything—"

"Because of you, Billy left home and hasn't been back these two years," Dora said bitterly.

"How can you blame me—"

"If you hadn't come sniffing around Billy, Blackjack never would've sicced his hired dogs on my son. I never would've told Blackjack the truth, and he never would've told Billy. Now you're back to cause more trouble."

"I'm not—"

"You're a pampered brat looking for fun and games. Well, Billy isn't some fancy pair of boots you can wear once and toss away. Best for all concerned if you pick up those bags and leave now, before you hurt my son again."

Summer stood her ground against Dora's verbal assault, but she was reeling. She'd known Dora wasn't going to welcome her. But she hadn't expected this vicious attack.

She took a deep breath and said, "I'm not leaving, Mrs. Coburn."

"You won't like it here," Dora promised. "There'll be no one to cater to your whims, no one to come at your beck and call."

"I never expected there would be."

"If I were healthy—" Dora cut herself off and grabbed at her chest.

"Are you all right?" Summer said, crossing toward her.

"Stay away from me," Dora bit out.

Summer saw the pain on Dora's face. "Would you like something cold to drink? A glass of iced tea?" she suggested, not knowing what else to do.

Dora eyed her suspiciously. "Tea. You know where to find everything?"

No sense pretending she didn't. "Yes, I do," Summer said. She'd spent enough time at Billy's house when Dora and Emma were at church to know her way around the house. "Where's Emma?" she asked as she found two fruit jars in the cupboard and headed for the refrigerator.

"Taking a nap."

That would have sounded odd, except Summer knew Emma was pregnant. She debated whether to say anything, then decided there was no sense pretending about this, either. "Billy told me Emma's pregnant. How far along is she?"

"Twenty weeks."

Summer did the math in her head. Five months. She popped some ice cubes out of the tray in the freezer, then poured herself and Dora each a glass of tea, before returning the half-gallon tea jar to the refrigerator—which she noticed was filled with Tupperware containers that held what she supposed must be leftovers. Her mother gave the leftovers to the servants.

She placed Dora's tea in front of her along with a paper towel, when she couldn't find any napkins, then leaned back against the kitchen counter with her own tea in her hand, rather than joining Dora at the table, since she so obviously wasn't welcome there. She took a sip and asked, "Why aren't you in bed, too?"

It took so long for Dora to speak that Summer thought the older woman wasn't going to answer her. Dora sighed and said, "Got tired of lying around hurting. I can hurt just as easy sitting up."

Summer was surprised at Dora's admission. "Are you in a lot of pain?"

Dora shrugged. And winced. "Some."

"Is there anything I can do?" Summer wasn't sure what Billy's mother might need in the way of nursing care, but she was willing to do anything she could to help.

"You can turn around and go back where you came from."

"You know I can't do that," Summer said. "For Billy's sake."

"My boy can take care of himself," Dora insisted.

"It isn't himself he's worried about," Summer said. "It's Will." She hesitated. "And you."

Dora took a sip of tea and set it back down. "What is it you think you can do for me, Mizz Blackthorne?"

"I'm a Coburn now," Summer said.

"You'll always be a Blackthorne, missy," Dora shot back.

Frustrated by the older woman's animosity, Summer said, "I'm only here to help."

"I'm dying. Nobody can help that."

Summer didn't know what to say. She settled for "I'm sorry."

"Mom? Who are you talking to?"

At the sound of Emma's voice, Summer braced

herself. She'd had little or no contact with Billy's sister, but Emma had been present two years ago when Dora caught Summer kissing Billy on their front porch and called her a Jezebel and a fornicator. If Blackjack's experience with the Creed kids was any guide, Emma would likewise have learned from her parents to hate all Blackthornes.

Summer prepared herself for the animosity she expected by taking a fortifying sip of iced tea.

Emma stopped in the doorway. She was wearing a Western shirt with the tails tucked into a pair of jeans that weren't zipped all the way up, making her pregnancy obvious, because her rounded stomach was at such odds with the rest of her tall, rail-thin body.

Emma's gaze shot from Summer to the two bags by the door and back to Summer again at the same time as she pulled the tails out of her jeans so they overlapped the open zipper. "What's going on?"

"Billy and I got married this morning," Summer said. "I'm here to help out in whatever way I can."

To Summer's surprise, Emma didn't raise her voice or stomp around the room ranting about the mean and ornery Blackthornes. She simply said, "I don't see how you're going to be any help around here."

Summer was stung by Emma's dismissal of her. Of course, she'd realized the same thing herself. But she wanted to help. Surely that counted for something. "I'm willing to learn whatever I need to know."

Emma crossed her arms and said, "Mom, you should be in bed."

"I'm fine, Emma."

"I can see you're in pain," Emma said.

"Lying down isn't going to change that," Dora said. "Why don't you get Summer started on the laundry? Will's about out of the cloth diapers Billy brought with him. The disposables are too expensive for everyday."

Summer opened her mouth to object, saw the challenging look on Dora's face, and shut it again. Billy had said Emma usually took care of the housekeeping, but this was obviously a test to see if Summer had really meant what she'd said. "Sure," she said to Emma. "Let's go."

"Follow me," Emma said.

If Summer had thought about it, she would have realized that she hadn't seen a washer or dryer in the house. They turned out to be hooked up in a little wooden room at one end of the back porch. Emma opened the shed door and Summer was assailed by the strong odor of ammonia.

"We leave the dirty diapers soaking in a pail of water till we're ready to wash them," Emma said. "You'll need to wring them out before you put them in the washer."

Summer stared at the washing machine. To say it was ancient would be paying it a compliment. She wondered whether she should mention to Emma that she'd never done laundry in her life, and that she had no idea how to operate a washer.

Emma had apparently assumed the worst, because she quickly explained how to start the machine, then showed Summer where the Tide and borax could be found and how much to use.

"The dryer doesn't work," Emma said. "When the

machine quits, you'll need to hang the diapers on the line out back. Here's a basket you can use to carry the diapers in. We leave the clothespins on the line."

A moment later Emma was gone and Summer was alone. She took the lid off the diaper pail and reeled backward. "Whoa. That's really rank."

She reminded herself that this was a test—which both women expected her to fail. After all, she was a pampered Blackthorne, who supposedly never dirtied her hands with difficult jobs. Summer grinned. They should have seen her at the last roundup, castrating and branding calves. She'd seen and smelled far worse than what was facing her in that diaper pail.

But she'd done her ranch work wearing gloves. This job required her to reach into the pail with her bare hands, pick up a stinky diaper, and wring it out. Summer grimaced, but reminded herself women had been doing this work for as long as they'd been spinning cloth. She held her breath and reached into the pail.

Once the washer was started, she realized she might as well head back inside until it was done. She didn't knock before she entered the house this time, and she found Emma and Dora sitting at the table in earnest conversation. Emma stopped talking the instant the screen door opened.

"There's nothing for me to do until the washer's done." Summer felt foolish explaining her reappearance, because it should have been obvious why she was back. She resisted the urge to ask for another chore to keep her busy. Instead, she went to the kitchen sink and washed her hands, then refilled her glass of iced tea.

She was aware the whole time that the conversation

behind her had lapsed. She turned and leaned back against the counter. Emma eyed her, then glanced at her mother.

"I'm going to be here awhile," Summer pointed out, setting her tea on the counter. "You might as well finish whatever it was you were saying."

"This is family business," Emma said. "It doesn't concern you."

"Billy and I are married," Summer said. "That makes me family."

"That makes you Billy's wife," Emma corrected. "You can never be part of this family."

Summer felt the flush burning its way up her throat, until she could feel the heat of it in her cheeks. Her stomach had twisted into a knot. Her hands were trembling, and she stuck them in her back pockets.

She didn't know why Emma's statement upset her so badly. The truth was, her marriage to Billy was intended to be a temporary situation. All she had to do was get along with Billy's mother and sister for two years. She didn't have to love them. And they didn't have to like her.

"I have no intention of trying to horn in on your precious family," Summer said irritably.

"Keep your voice down," Emma said. "You'll wake Will."

At that moment, Will let out a howl.

"Now look what you've done," Emma said, shoving her chair back in disgust.

"Don't worry yourself," Summer said, moving past her. "I woke him up. I'll take care of him." She marched from the kitchen in high dudgeon, realizing only as she crossed the threshold into Billy's bedroom that she had no idea how to comfort a crying child.

However, she'd helped deliver her share of calves and colts. How hard could it be?

Will was standing in the crib, and he greeted her appearance with an anguished wail. "It's okay, Will," Summer said in the voice she would have used with a newborn foal. "I'm Summer. I'm going to take care of you."

Will wailed unhappily.

Summer glanced over her shoulder, expecting to see Emma or Dora or both at any second. When no help arrived, she turned back to Will. She reached out a tentative hand to caress his sweat-damp curls, and he screeched as though she'd ripped them out at the roots.

She pulled her hand back and said, "This is silly, Will. I'm not going to hurt you." She tried to think of what Billy had told her—that children only needed to be fed and kept dry and loved. "You're probably hungry," Summer said. "And no doubt you're wet. I think maybe we better start with the loving part, since that seems to be what you need most."

She knew that with horses you had to be firm and show who was boss, or the animal would never obey you. She slid her hands under Will's armpits and lifted him surely and carefully into her arms. "There now," she said, as Will settled onto her left hip. "That wasn't so hard."

Will stared at her from large, wide eyes every bit as dark as Billy's, teardrops suspended from his lower eyelashes. Then he looked past her toward the door, pointed, and said, "Go see Daddy."

"Your daddy's working right now. He'll be back soon." She felt inside the leg of the romper Will was wearing and discovered he was sopping wet. "I think we'd better change this diaper."

Really, she thought. How hard could it be?

She looked around the room for clean diapers and found a couple near his crib, along with powder and some Wet Wipes. That made sense. Remove the diaper, swipe the kid's bottom clean, powder it, then put on another diaper. She'd seen enough movies to know that was the routine.

And enough movies making fun of helpless dads trying to perform this simple procedure to fear that it wasn't as easy as it looked.

She collected the supplies she needed on the bed, then laid Will down, unsnapped the romper and pulled it up to expose the diaper and rubber pants. So far, so good. She tugged off the rubber pants and realized the soaked diaper was leaving a wet mark on Billy's bedspread. She hurried to get the pins unpinned and pulled the diaper off.

Which was when she experienced the first glitch in the process.

Will immediately rolled over and started crawling away from her. She'd stuck the pins in the bedspread as she took each one out, but she was left holding a wet diaper. She looked for the diaper pail, which she realized had been moved outside so the diapers could be washed. She couldn't leave Will alone long enough to take it out there, so she just dropped it on the floor and went scurrying around the bed to intercept the child as he dropped off the other side onto his feet.

"You can walk!" she exclaimed as Will headed for the door lickety-split.

"Daddy daddy daddy!" Will shouted.

Summer scooped him up with a laugh. "Caught you!" she said.

Will struggled to get down. When Summer held on he said, "Down down down!"

"Diaper first, young man," Summer said, carting him back around to the side of the bed where she'd left everything. The instant she lay him on his back he rolled over and tried to escape again. She grabbed him by the ankles and dragged him back. "Come on, Will," she said. "You need a diaper."

Which became obvious as soon as she turned him over and he began peeing onto her shirt. She leaped back, but the damage was done. She grabbed the diaper and covered him until he was done.

Will grinned up at her.

"That wasn't funny!" she said. And then laughed.

She should have known better. She just hadn't realized how dangerous an undiapered little boy could be.

"All right, let's get organized," she said, dropping the second wet diaper beside the other one and picking Will up to keep him from running off. She looked for another dry diaper and realized there was only one left. Good thing she was doing laundry.

"Okay, kiddo, let's see if we can get it right this time."

She had to hold Will down with one hand while she did everything else with the other. Which worked fine until she needed to pin on the diaper. She needed one hand to hold the diaper together and the other to manipulate the pin. "You have to hold still, Will, or I'm going to—"

She stuck him with the pin.

He screamed as though he'd been jabbed with a foot-long hypodermic.

And both Dora and Emma showed up at the door.

Summer knew they were seeing the giant wet spot on the front of her shirt, the wet spot on Billy's bedspread, the diaper soaking into the rag rug beside Billy's bed, and the still undiapered child wriggling and crying on the bed.

"I accidentally stuck him with the safety pin," she explained.

"I told you she couldn't do it," Emma said to her mother.

"I'll just be another minute," Summer said.

"I'll do it," Emma said, shoving Summer aside.

Summer felt like shoving back, but it seemed ridiculous to fight Emma for the right to diaper Will. There would be other opportunities, and she'd learned a great deal in this first encounter.

Emma pinned one side of the diaper and said, "Where's the other pin?"

"I stuck it in the bedspread," Summer said.

They both searched the spread but couldn't find it. "I've got some extras in the kitchen," Emma said.

When Emma picked Will up, Summer immediately saw the missing pin. "I guess Will was lying on it."

No wonder the poor kid had been wriggling and crying, with a safety pin digging into his back.

Emma gave her a look that made her feel like a worm,

laid Will back down, and finished pinning on the diaper. "Those diapers need to go in the pail outside," she said, laying Will over her shoulder and marching from the room.

It sounded like an order, and Summer bristled at the thought of obeying it. But she realized she might as well get used to her position in this household. She was no longer the favored daughter of wealthy parents. She was an unwelcome addition to a struggling household.

She headed outside, wishing she could keep her distance from these two until Billy got home to play peacemaker. She got a bit of a respite because she had to hang the diapers on the line, which she found a surprisingly pleasant chore. The breeze occasionally caught a diaper and slapped it back in her face, but the wet cloth felt cool against her skin and the borax made them smell fresh.

She was sorry when the job was done, because it meant now she had to face the two dragons inside. But whatever flaws there were in her character, cowardice wasn't one of them.

She found Dora sitting at the kitchen table cutting up potatoes to be put in a pot of boiling water on the stove, while Emma was frying pork chops. Will was sitting on the floor at Dora's feet banging a wooden spoon on an upside-down pot.

The scene looked and smelled and sounded surprisingly homey. She felt a wistful desire to be one of them, which died a quick death when Emma turned to her and said, "Took you long enough to hang those diapers. There are green beans in the fridge that need to be snapped."

Summer opened the refrigerator without a word and looked around for the beans. "Give me a hint," she said.

"In the vegetable drawer," Dora said.

Summer opened the drawer and took out the brown bag full of beans and set them on the table. "Where can I find a pot?"

"Left of the sink," Dora said.

Summer found a cooking pot and set it on the table, then dumped the beans out of the bag. She was sitting at the table "snapping beans" when Billy finally arrived.

She was so glad to see him, she had to restrain herself from leaping up and throwing herself into his arms. Of course, that would have been a perfectly appropriate response if they were a real husband and wife. But nothing about their marriage was normal. It was a good thing she didn't do anything so embarrassing.

Because Billy only had eyes for Will.

He opened his arms and said, "How's my boy?"

"Daddy daddy daddy!" Will shoved himself upright, his face a picture of gladness, and tottered on baby feet into his father's arms.

Billy lifted Will up as high as he could, causing the child to shriek with delight, then pulled him down into a ferocious hug, at which point they both laughed with joy.

Summer swallowed over the sudden lump in her throat. She wanted to be loved by someone—anyone—the way Billy loved Will. It must be wonderful to know you were the total focus of someone's life, that his every thought concerned how to make you happy.

She wondered how Billy had learned to be so loving. Not from his mother or sister, she thought, noting that both of them had continued with their chores, although they were both smiling now. She realized she was just like them—watching, but not participating.

Why not? She was Billy's wife. She ought to be greeting him with some sort of affection. She stood and shoved her chair back and crossed to Billy. "Welcome home," she said, putting her arms around his waist on the side opposite from where Will was perched and hugging him.

Billy glanced at his mother and sister before he bent and kissed her on the cheek. "You looked pretty domestic sitting there snapping beans."

"I've been washing and hanging clothes, too," Summer said.

Billy raised a brow and whistled. "You don't say!"

"Don't make fun of me," she said, unaccountably hurt by his dismissal of her efforts. "I'm trying."

Billy gave her a quick kiss in apology. "I think it's great. Really. How have my three girls been getting along?" he said, glancing at his mother and sister.

And that's when the fairy-tale homecoming came to an abrupt and unpleasant end.

"Not well at all," Emma said. "I had to show her how to use a washing machine, for heaven's sake! And she stuck Will with a safety pin."

"It was an accident!" Summer said.

Emma turned with her hands on her hips and said, "A rich bitch like you has no business shoving her way into our family."

"Emma, that's enough," Billy said.

"I don't want her here, Billy. She's upsetting Mom."

"Mom?" Billy questioned. "Is that true?"

Summer stared, stupefied, at Billy. It seemed she was

going to be tried and condemned without a chance to say a word in her own defense.

Dora said, "I don't understand why you brought her here. She's just going to be a burden to everyone."

"I'll never understand why you married her," Emma said. "You haven't seen her in two years, so you can't have been pining away for her. She has no talents to speak of. What were you thinking, Billy?"

"I was thinking we need help around here, and Summer's offered to provide it, plain and simple," Billy said.

"I can handle things without her," Emma said.

"You're the one who called me to come home," Billy reminded her. "Precisely because you couldn't handle everything on your own."

"You and I can manage together."

"Summer is my wife, Emma. Don't make this harder than it has to be."

"Either she goes or I go," Emma threatened.

Summer's heart shot to her throat and stuck there. She turned to Billy, wondering what he would do, what he would say. He couldn't possibly choose her over his own flesh and blood, could he? But she desperately hoped he would.

In the few hours she'd spent in Billy's home she'd realized that there was a feeling of family here she'd never found at the Castle. And she wanted to be a part of it.

She held her breath, waiting for Billy's response.

"You can go anytime you want, Emma," Billy said at last. "Summer stays."

From the stricken look on Emma's face it was clear she hadn't expected Billy to side with his new wife.

Summer realized suddenly that Billy had issued his

ultimatum knowing full well that there were no teeth in Emma's threat. After all, how could his sister possibly leave? Five months pregnant, who was going to hire her to work? And without money for rent, where would she live?

Emma glared at Billy. "If that's the way you want it, fine. I'm out of here." She took off her apron and threw it on the counter.

"Give Summer a chance, Emma," Billy said as she headed to her room to pack. "Please."

Summer thought Emma might relent, but then she met Emma's gaze and realized Emma couldn't relent and keep her pride. Apparently, Coburns possessed every bit as much of that mortal sin as Blackthornes.

"You made your choice, Billy," Emma said. "Now you can live with it."

Billy grabbed Emma's arm as she tried to cross past him. "Emma, wait. Where are you going?"

"Away from here."

"This is ridiculous."

"Not to me," Emma said stubbornly.

Billy let go of her with a sigh. "All right. Go spend the night with one of your friends, if that's what you think you have to do."

"I'm not coming back till she's gone, Billy," Emma said. "I mean it."

Summer had to admire Emma's regal exit. She reminded Summer of herself when she'd had to confront her older brothers. Too bad Emma was leaving. They might have ended up becoming fast friends.

On the other hand, it was nice to know she wouldn't have to face Emma's animosity every morning at breakfast.

"That was badly done," Dora said once Emma was gone.

"There was nothing else I could do," Billy said.

Will began to whine and Billy lifted him up and said, "You're not used to all this fuss and bother, are you, buddy? And I'll bet you're hungry. I sure am. I could eat a bear. How about you?"

Will pointed to his high chair. "Chair, Daddy."

"You bet, kiddo. As soon as we wash our hands." He carried Will over to the sink and washed Will's hands along with his own, then set his son in the high chair.

"Supper won't be ready for a while yet," Dora said.

"He'll be happy with a few Cheerios until the beans and mashed potatoes are done," Billy said.

Dora set her palms on the table and pushed herself up out of her chair. "I'll tend to those pork chops, if you'll put these potatoes in the pot," she said to Billy.

"I'll get the potatoes and put the beans on the stove," Summer volunteered.

Dora shrugged, winced, and said, "If you insist."

Summer was surprised to see Billy pitching in to help with supper. He threw some bacon and diced onions into the beans, and once the potatoes boiled, he got out the mixer, added some milk and butter, and whipped them up. She made herself useful setting the table and pouring everyone a glass of iced tea.

Emma came through the kitchen with a cloth overnight bag just as they put the food on the table.

"Why don't you stop and eat before you go," Billy suggested.

"Not with her here," Emma said.

"I don't want us to be at odds because of Summer,"

Billy said. "Please, Emma. I'm asking you for a truce. We can work this out somehow. I know we can."

"Not when you choose a Blackthorne over family," Emma said.

"Summer is my family now," Billy said.

Emma turned to her mother and said, "I'll call and let you know where I am, Mom." She crossed to Will and kissed him on the forehead. "Good-bye, Will. Be a good boy."

"Good boy," Will parroted.

She stopped in front of Billy and said, "Your new wife won't last a week without all the luxuries she's used to having. Let me know when she takes off, and I'll come home."

With that pronouncement, Emma shoved her way out the screen door and let it slam behind her.

Summer felt sick to her stomach. She glanced at Billy, who refused to meet her gaze. She wanted to promise him he wouldn't regret taking her side. She wanted to tell him he'd made the right decision. She wanted to say that Emma would have to eat her words.

The truth was, she was hot and sticky and had pinpricks on her fingers where she'd stuck herself with Will's safety pins before she'd stuck him. She'd managed to aggravate Billy's sister and had to bite her tongue to cope with the condescension of his mother. She was hungry and she could see that if she wanted to eat around here she was going to have to learn to cook. Now that Emma was gone, it seemed the cleaning was going to fall to her, too.

And she didn't have a clue how she and Billy were

going to be able to sleep in that iron bed of his with the sagging mattress, right beside a baby who was likely to keep them up half the night sniffling and snorting and making strange baby noises.

After supper Dora took Will to give him a bath while Billy and Summer cleaned up the kitchen together. Billy didn't have an automatic dishwasher. It didn't take long before Summer's hands looked like prunes.

"I've got a job," Billy told her as he dumped leftovers in Tupperware containers.

"The TSCRA is keeping you on?" she asked hopefully.

"Nope. Your father had a few words with the local supervisor. There's no TSCRA job for me around here."

"I'm sorry, Billy."

"Doesn't matter," he said. "I got work with one of the local ranchers."

Summer tried to meet his eyes, but he wouldn't look at her. She knew how disappointed he must be, back in Bitter Creek doing menial work for menial wages.

"Maybe you could do something with this place to earn money," Summer suggested.

"Like what?" Billy said.

"I don't know. A guide service for hunters maybe, or a bed and breakfast."

"Where would we put company in this house?"

"Not in the house, in that old bunkhouse out by the barn. It probably needs a new roof, but it has a big cookstove and a serviceable bathroom."

"It would take a fortune to clean it up," Billy said.

"I've got a little money—"

"You're not spending your money on this place."

"What else am I going to do with it?" Summer said.

"Leave it in the bank."

Summer took one look at his stony features and realized she would be wasting her time arguing. But she wasn't giving up on the idea. She'd just have to do it without Billy finding out. Once the place was fixed up, he'd be glad for the extra income. And after all, for the next two years, she was his wife.

Summer had been doing so much thinking, she was surprised to realize she'd finished the last of the dishes.

As she pulled out the plug to let the water drain, Billy whispered in her ear, "Thanks for being here, Summer. I don't know what I'd do without you."

Summer knew in that instant that even if she ended up with pickled fingers from doing dishes and bags under her eyes from sleeplessness and had to eat leftovers out of Tupperware for supper every night, she was going to make it.

Billy needed her. And when friends needed friends, they did whatever they had to do to help.

She turned to Billy and offered him what she'd wanted so desperately herself. Peace. Solace. Love. She put her arms around his neck, leaned her cheek against his chest, and said, "Don't worry, Billy. Everything will be fine."

She heard him swallow noisily several times as his arms tightened around her and he pulled her close. "Thanks, Summer. I need to believe that."

They heard Will laughing in the bathtub.

Billy pulled her hands down and held them in his own for a moment. "I better go spend some time with Will."

"Sure," she said. "See you later."

Summer gulped as she watched Billy saunter down the hall. The next time she saw him, they'd both be getting into the same bed.

Oh, boy.

Chapter 8

"I'M BACK, REN. AND THIS TIME I'M STAYING."

Lauren Creed looked through the screen that separated her from Jackson Blackthorne, then pushed it open and let him in. All the way in. Before the screen door had slammed behind him, muting the afternoon sun, she was in his arms, their mouths meshed. His body was all hard planes against which she fitted her softness, as she stood on tiptoe, her arms reaching up to clasp him around the neck.

She felt him pick her up, his arms tightening like a vise around her ribs as his tongue came searching for the taste of her. She opened wide, wanting the warm, wet intrusion, which mimicked the sexual act. He dragged her arms from around his neck and stood her on her feet, popping the buttons on her shirt as he tore it away, shoving the fabric down her arms, where the buttoned cuffs captured the worn cotton.

They were both breathing hard, and she saw his nostrils flare as he caught the scent of her, saw his eyelids droop as he surveyed the prize he'd finally won.

"You're so beautiful. And mine. At last."

He reached down and took each wrist, one at a time,

and unbuttoned the cuffs, then gently drew the material away. He reached behind her and unclasped her bra and drew it off and let it drop to the floor, then lowered his head and suckled her.

Ren gasped at the feel of his warm, wet mouth on her flesh and grasped at his hair, holding him where he was. She pressed her hand against the hard ridge in his jeans and heard him moan. She traced the shape of him, then cupped him, forcing him to spread his legs so she could caress him.

His eyes were glazed when he raised his head, and she felt the afternoon breeze cool her peaked nipple where his mouth had left it wet. He picked her up, grinned wryly, and said, "Where's the closest flat surface with a little give?"

"That would be a bed," she said, returning his smile, her mouth stretching wide with a responding grin she couldn't repress.

He stopped and looked into her eyes and said, "Not his bed."

"No. Not the bed I shared with Jesse. There's a bedroom downstairs. On the other side of the parlor."

She saw the shadows appear in Jackson's eyes at the sound of Jesse's name and pressed her mouth to his, offering love and peace and forgetfulness.

Comfort wasn't what he wanted. His mouth ravaged hers, demanding more, seeking more, insisting on more.

She gave all she had, every morsel of herself, every bit of her soul.

They made it as far as the buffalo hide on the floor in front of the fireplace. He kicked the coffee table out of the way and lay her down in front of the ash-laden fireplace, reaching for the snap on her jeans and yanking down her zipper. He pulled at her boots and dragged at her socks, baring her to his gaze. His eyes were avid, drinking her in, eating their fill.

She tore at his shirt, wanting him bare, seeking the hard feel of his flesh and the crisp touch of the dark hair on his chest and the feel of a big man, a powerful man, under her hands.

He yanked off his own boots and helped her shove his jeans and boxers down off his hips. And then they were both naked, and he thrust hard and deep, joining them at last.

She looked up into his eyes and felt her throat swell with joy and love and hope . . . so much more feeling than she could contain. "Jackson," she cried. "I can't— It's too much. I can't—"

"You can," he said. "I love you, Ren. I've always loved you. I always will."

His gaze was fierce as his mouth claimed hers, their tongues dueling, their bodies writhing in an ancient dance of love. She felt too much, needed too much, wanted too much. Her heart felt as though it might burst with joy. Then her body did explode with pleasure beyond bearing. She surged against the sweat-slick body that covered her own and held on tight . . . and felt herself sink into oblivion.

Ren wasn't sure how long she remained unaware of her surroundings, but when she woke, she was in bed, covered with a sheet that was tucked up under her arms, the breeze caressing her sweaty flesh. She sat up abruptly and called, "Jackson?"

"I'm here."

She turned and found him lying beside her, the pillow bunched beneath his head, his body covered to the waist with the same sheet that covered her, his eyes focused on her face.

She grabbed at the sheet, which had fallen to her waist, but he reached out and tugged it free.

"Let me look," he said quietly. "I want to see you. I want to make up for all the years I haven't had the right to look."

She thought of how her body had changed in thirty-seven years and turned her face away. She felt his hand on her chin as he gently tugged her face in his direction.

"You're beautiful, Ren. In my eyes you can never be anything else."

She lifted her chin and said, "If you're going to look, then so am I." She pulled the sheet away from his body and let her gaze follow the dark line of hair from his navel downward. And realized her gaze was causing a transformation.

"Thank God everything still works," he said with a chuckle.

She laughed and rolled on top of him, pressing her lips against his throat and straddling his waist. "We're both going to be sore tomorrow," she warned.

"Who the hell cares," he said, as he rolled her back under him and impaled her once again.

She gasped, surprised at how wet and ready she was for him. She closed her eyes and bit her lip and relished the pleasure. Again.

Afterward, they both lay panting, too tired to reach for the sheet. They lay uncovered, the incessant Texas wind cooling their laboring bodies.

Through the open window, Ren heard a truck engine cutting off. It took a moment for the significance of that to register.

"Oh, God. That's Sam."

She bolted out of bed, searching frantically for her clothes. Which was when she realized they were scattered across the floor of the kitchen and lay in messy heaps in front of the fireplace.

Along with Jackson's clothes.

"Get up!" she urged as she tore free the top sheet and wrapped herself in it. "We have to get dressed. We have to—"

He reached the bedroom door before her and pressed it closed, preventing her escape. "Stop it, Ren."

She shoved at him with all her might, her nose burning with tears, her eyes blurring. "Let me out, Jackson. Please. If he comes in and finds—" She leaned her head against his shoulder as she heard the screen door slam.

It was too late now to hide what had happened this afternoon.

She imagined Sam wheeling himself into the kitchen, imagined him following the trail of clothes across the kitchen floor and into the parlor. Imagined him gazing down the hall toward the downstairs bedroom and seeing the closed door against which Jackson now leaned.

She stared up at Blackjack, all hope for the future deadened by fear of what would happen in the next few minutes. Any second her son would knock on the door and . . . she wasn't sure just what Sam would do.

The knock came. And Sam's voice asking, "Mom? Are you in there? Are you all right?"

She glanced up into Jackson's face and said, "I'm fine, Sam."

"Is he in there with you?"

No name, just an emphasis on the *he* and a great deal of contempt in Sam's voice.

"I'm here," Blackjack answered.

Silence on the other side of the door. Ren held her breath, wondering what her eldest son would do. There was no lock on the door. It had broken long ago and no one had bothered to fix it. It must be obvious to Sam what they had come into this room to do. And that neither of them was dressed, since their clothes were strewn across the floors of two rooms.

She knew Sam must be debating the wisdom of demanding that they show themselves. She was hardly decent, wrapped in a sheet, and Jackson, leaning against the door, wore nothing at all.

"I'm not setting foot in this house again until he's gone, Mom. And I mean gone for good," Sam said.

Ren met Jackson's gaze. She was being forced to choose... again. But really, there wasn't any choice this time. The die had been cast.

"I'm sorry to hear you say that, Sam. Because Jackson isn't leaving. He'll be living here with me from now on."

Ren could feel Sam's frustration through the door. Knew he was damning his crippled legs, which kept him from forcing the door and rescuing her from the dangerous ogre who'd stolen her heart from his father. Felt the tension build as she imagined him considering whether to get the shotgun from the parlor, knowing he would eventually realize that the rack over the mantel was out of his reach without help from someone standing on two functioning legs.

There were other guns. Other weapons. She knew Sam wanted Blackjack dead, but he didn't want to spend his life in prison for it, so he'd promised stealth and deception. Her body was wired tight, her heart pounding as she waited to see what her angry son would do.

"Call me tonight," Sam said at last. They could hear his chair being wheeled back down the hall, careening against one wall and then another. Could hear the screen door slam, and then the engine of his truck starting, being gunned viciously, and the shriek of gravel as his wheels spun and he sped away.

She dropped her forehead onto Jackson's shoulder. "We should have been more careful."

"We have nothing to be ashamed of."

She lifted her head and stared soberly into his eyes. "You're still married."

"Not for long," he said flatly. "I called DeWitt & Blackthorne this morning and got hold of my cousin. Harry thinks he can get me into court within a matter of weeks."

"Really?" Ren said. It was hard to believe that all her dreams might finally be coming true. Hard to believe in happily ever after.

"How are you going to deal with Sam?" he asked.

"I'm not sure there's much I can do," Ren confessed, pressing her cheek against Jackson's chest. "Plead with him to be reasonable. Try to convince him that we deserve a chance to be happy together. Tell him it will break my heart if he does anything to harm you."

She reached out to caress Jackson's shoulder blade

with her fingertips, following the length of it to his arm, then letting her hand follow the ridge of muscle along biceps, triceps, forearm, all the way to his large, powerful hand. She intertwined her fingers with his.

"But I'm not giving you up," she said. "Not ever again."

Sam had listened to his mother's latest ultimatum over the phone with tight jaws. No, she hadn't changed her mind over the past week. And she wouldn't. From now on, Jackson Blackthorne would be spending his nights at Three Oaks. She was counting on Sam to act like a sane, sensible adult. And if he didn't think he could behave himself, he could leave Three Oaks for good.

Sam felt a shiver run through him at the thought of leaving the only home he'd ever known. From the moment of his birth he'd been taught to care for the land. And that was what he intended to do. He'd find a way to deal with Blackjack that would get him out of their lives without ruining them in the process.

Sam mentally recited the advertisement he'd posted in the Bitter Creek *Chronicle* the morning after he'd discovered his mother and Jackson Blackthorne in flagrante delicto.

> *WANTED: Woman to do cooking and light*
> *housekeeping. Room and board provided.*
> *Call 555–3792.*

Maybe he should have been more specific about his requirements. So far, he'd had four applicants, any one of whom could have done the job. But he'd found something wrong with each of them. *Too much education. Too little English. Too old. Too young.* He stared at the fifth applicant standing just inside his kitchen door. With her, he could describe the problem in one word. *Pregnant.*

And way, way too pretty. "Don't I know you?" he said as he wheeled his chair a little closer.

She smiled and he felt his heart skip a beat. "I'm Emma Coburn. I was two years behind your brother Luke in school."

"That would make you——"

"Nineteen and pregnant. And unmarried," she added, in case he hadn't noticed the lack of a ring on her finger. "Which is why I need this job. You might have heard my brother recently got married."

Bad Billy Coburn's marriage to Summer Blackthorne was all anyone had talked about the past week. "I heard," Sam said.

"There wasn't room at home for me and her both," Emma said.

Sam both understood and empathized with Emma's plight. But she was still too pretty. And pregnant.

"I need someone to cook and clean for me. Maybe do some bookkeeping on the side." He stared at her bulging abdomen. "You think you could handle that?"

"I'm not sick, just pregnant," she shot back.

"How far along are you?"

"Five months."

"What happens when the baby comes?" he asked.

"Pioneer women had to do chores even when they were nursing their babies. I can do the same," she said, her chin lifted pugnaciously.

He thought of how quiet his simple one-story house

was every morning when he woke up. How empty it felt. He thought of being woken by a crying, hungry baby. Thought of that baby suckling at Emma Coburn's breast. It wasn't at all a carnal vision, but something natural and wholesome and good. A priceless moment of a husband's life he'd been robbed of when Owen Blackthorne had stolen his ability to father children, along with the use of his legs.

Sam had long ago made peace with never having sons or daughters of his own. If Emma came to work for him, he'd have the vicarious enjoyment of seeing her child grow up. It was a tempting prospect.

"You understand you'd be living here in the house with me," he said.

She glanced at his wheelchair. "Uh-huh."

He gritted his teeth. He knew that she, like so many other women, had taken one look and decided that being tied to a wheelchair kept him from being either a physical or a sexual threat. He hated being dismissed as a man simply because he didn't have the use of his legs. He still felt desire. He still needed to be held. He still needed to be loved.

And he could still love a woman. He could still bring her pleasure.

"Do you have any questions for me?" he asked.

"I...uh...heard you're an alcoholic," she said. "I don't want to work for someone who...gets drunk."

Sam controlled his features but couldn't prevent the flush that rose high on his cheekbones. "I'm a recovering alcoholic," he said. "I attend AA meetings, and I haven't had a drink in four years, two months, and sixteen days. Anything else?"

She shook her head, and he watched her hair slide across her bare shoulders like silk.

It would be hell looking at Emma Coburn every day, wanting her to notice him, and being ignored in return. But he needed help. And she had one qualification no other applicant had named. She needed the job because a Blackthorne had come into her life and made trouble for her.

"You're hired," he said. "When can you start?"

"Today. Right now." She took a step backward and pushed open the screen door, then leaned over and picked up a small cloth bag from the back porch. "I've got my things with me."

"Is that all you have?"

She shrugged. "I don't need much."

"There are three bedrooms. Help yourself to either of the ones I'm not using. Then how about fixing supper while I work on the books?"

"Anything particular you'd like to have?" she asked.

"I'm hungry, so something quick. There's hamburger in the fridge. See what you can whip up."

He wheeled himself down the hall and felt her following a short distance behind him. She smiled tentatively at him as he entered his study.

"I'll call you when supper's ready," she said.

"Fine," he said, closing the door in her face. The sexy female sound of her voice had raised gooseflesh on his arms. He felt like a teenager with his first crush. Not that he could feel everything he would have felt as a teenager. He felt nothing from the waist down. Thanks to Owen Blackthorne.

He turned on his computer, determined to work, but

all he could see was Emma Coburn's heart-shaped face, her shiny, fire-engine-red hair, her huge, vulnerable eyes. And her lithe body—with that precious bulge in the middle.

Well, why shouldn't he have a beautiful woman to look at across the breakfast and supper table? There was nothing wrong with looking. He sure as hell didn't have to worry about her looking back. She already had a lover out there somewhere.

Now that he thought about it, he remembered that once upon a time Emma had had a crush on his younger brother Luke. He remembered Luke at sixteen, furious that Emma wouldn't leave him alone, saying that she was always trailing after him like a lovesick puppy.

Well, she certainly hadn't been pining for Luke lately. Some other cowboy had obviously caught her eye. Sam wondered who the fellow was and why he hadn't married her. Sam would have given his eyeteeth to have a kid of his own. The man who'd walked away from Emma Coburn, whoever he was, was a damned fool.

Sam imagined Emma lying on the bed beneath him, then erased that image. He'd be a dead weight on her. He rearranged the two of them in his mind so he was lying on the bed and she was sitting across his hips. Imagined her hair draped across his naked torso. Imagined her stripping off that T-shirt she was wearing and seeing a plain white bra underneath. Imagined reaching up to cup her breast, feeling the warmth and weight of her through the soft cotton. Imagined—

Sam heard a quiet knock at the door and Emma's announcement, "Supper's ready."

"Be right there," he replied. For once Sam was grateful

that his mind hadn't produced the hard-on it would have before his body had been damaged. At least Emma would have no idea of the direction of his thoughts.

As he left his study, he sniffed the air, wondering what she'd done with the hamburger. She'd set the table using paper napkins, because he didn't have any cloth ones, and picked some black-eyed Susans from the flowers growing wild around the back porch and stuck them in a jelly jar that sat in the center of the table.

"I wasn't sure if you wanted coffee," she said. "I found iced tea in the fridge. Which would you prefer?"

"Iced tea," he said as he wheeled himself into place at one side of the square wooden table. She'd set her plate on the opposite side, rather than next to him, which put them a little farther apart, but made it easier for him to enjoy looking at her.

"I decided on sloppy joes, because they're fast," she said, "and because I couldn't find any hamburger buns."

She set a couple of slices of white bread on his plate and spooned a large helping of the saucy hamburger mixture on top.

He took a bite and gasped. "Spicy," he wheezed. He couldn't speak again until he'd taken a drink of tea. Even that didn't ease the burning on his tongue. He pulled off a piece of bread that wasn't covered with sauce and ate that.

"I saw the jar of jalapeños on the refrigerator door and figured it would be okay to add a couple."

"No problem," he said, taking another sip of tea to counter the effect of the hot peppers. "It's good," he added to ease the crease of worry in her brow. "Really good."

She smiled and his stomach did a strange flip-flop.

He couldn't afford to let himself care. Not when he knew he was asking for heartbreak. He made it through the whole meal without a word, but in the end couldn't stop himself from asking, "Who's the father?"

She was taken aback. "I don't see where that's any of your business."

"It might be. If he decided to hunt you up and marry you, I lose my hired help."

"That isn't going to happen," she said, her eyes lowered to her empty plate.

"What makes you so sure?"

She glanced up, then down again. "He doesn't even know about the baby."

"What?" He realized he'd shouted when she jumped in her chair.

She stood abruptly and picked up her plate and dropped it in the sink. "Forget I said anything."

"Fat chance of that," he muttered. "Get yourself another plate. You need to eat more than that little bird portion you took." She opened her mouth to protest and he added, "For the baby's sake."

She grimaced, but opened the cupboard and got out another plate and served herself another portion of sloppy joes. He wheeled his chair around to pull out her chair for her so she could sit down, then pushed it closer to the table.

"Thank you," she murmured.

"Eat."

He kept his thoughts to himself while she ate, afraid that if he upset her again she wouldn't finish the rest of her food, and he'd be responsible for her kid not getting fed. When she'd swallowed the last bite, he said, "Don't you think the father's entitled to know?"

"He wouldn't care," she said.

"How do you know?"

When she looked at him he saw there were tears in her eyes. "Hey. None of that," he said.

She swiped at her eyes and reached for a paper napkin to blow her nose.

"That's better," he said. "Want to tell me about it?"

She set the napkin aside and threaded her fingers together on the table. "I shouldn't," she said. "I mean, you're my boss."

"There's no rule that says we can't also be friends," Sam said. "Especially since we're going to be housemates."

"I suppose," she said.

He wanted her to confide in him. He wanted to know everything about her. He wanted to help her. He wanted her to see him as a whole person. Hell. He wanted her to see him as a man who could protect her and care for her and solve her problems. And love her.

Talk about asking for the moon.

"Tell you what," he said. "I'll make us both a cup of coffee while you talk."

She started to rise. "I can make—"

He put a hand on her arm. "Sit there and relax. I can handle it."

The entire kitchen had been remodeled to make everything accessible to him from his wheelchair. As he measured the coffee into the coffeemaker he said, "I'm listening."

"I'm not sure where to start."

"Would I be likely to know this fellow?" Sam asked. When she didn't speak he turned his head in her direction and raised a brow. "Would I?"

She nodded jerkily.

"Well, well, well. Are you going to tell me who it is?"

She shook her head. "No. Because who he is doesn't matter."

"He fathered your child. It matters."

She shook her head again. "He was drunk. I seduced him."

"Aw, shi— Shucks, girl," he said, cutting out the profanity. "Why did you do a fool thing like that?"

She turned eyes on him that sparked with anger. "I wasn't exactly sober myself." She hesitated, then explained, "We attended the same party. He was more interested in another woman, but when she wouldn't have him . . . I took advantage of the situation."

"I see." He didn't, really. What man wouldn't jump at the chance to have Emma Coburn in his bed? He poured each of them a cup of coffee, then brought hers to the table before returning for his own. "Milk and sugar?" he asked.

"Both," she replied.

When he turned back toward the counter she jumped up and said, "I'll get them."

He fought back the urge to snap at her and said calmly, "You don't need to wait on me, Emma. I'm crippled, but I'm capable of doing most things a man on two legs can do."

"I'm sorry," she said.

He was enchanted by the two roses that grew on her cheeks. "No problem. Assume I can handle it myself unless I ask for your help."

"All right," she said as she set the sugar and milk on the table. "Mind if I ask a question?"

"Go ahead."

"Is it true Jackson Blackthorne is divorcing his wife to marry your mother?"

Sam felt a chill run through him. He met Emma's gaze with narrowed eyes and said, "He may be divorcing his wife. But he won't be wedding my mother. Even if I have to shoot him down in cold blood to stop him."

Chapter 9

EVE BLACKTHORNE HAD PLANNED HER DEATH very carefully, so Jackson Blackthorne would be blamed for it. Tomorrow would be her last day on earth. Tomorrow morning the helicopter she was piloting would crash and she would die.

For a full week after Jackson had moved in with Lauren Creed, Eve had let herself hope that he would realize the folly of his ways and return home to her. After all, if he insisted on divorce, he would have nothing left. Nothing. She'd made it clear she would take everything he'd held near and dear, everything his father and grandfather and great-grandfather had fought to hold onto for generations.

As the days passed and he refused even to speak with her on the phone, it had become increasingly clear that Jackson didn't give a damn anymore about her or their marriage or their life together. He wanted that Creed bitch no matter what he had to give up to have her.

Eve had spent another distressing week going through the stages of grief at the death of her marriage, from denial to anger to bargaining to sorrow. She simply hadn't been able to accept the loss of the man she'd loved body and soul since the moment she'd laid eyes on him. And if she couldn't have him, she was going to make damned sure no other woman would.

She'd been lying in bed alone, staring at the ceiling, feeling the humiliation of losing Jackson to *that woman,* when an idea for the perfect revenge had been born in her head. The plan she'd concocted required her own death, but that was a small price to pay for the anguish she knew Lauren Creed would suffer the rest of her life.

The difficult part had been figuring out how best to kill herself and make certain that Jackson was the most obvious—the only—suspect for her murder. It had taken a great deal of thought, a great deal of research, a great deal of planning. And a little help from someone with something to gain from her death.

Eve had gone through the stages of grief again, this time mourning not the loss of Jackson, but her own ultimate death. Over the past few days, she'd finally reached the plane of acceptance. She was ready and willing to die.

She felt great satisfaction in knowing that Jackson would probably figure out what she'd done but be unable to undo her careful planning. With any luck, he would tell *that woman* of his evil wife's machinations, and the two of them would hold one another tightly in the few days of freedom he had left before they arrested him for murder, knowing that their chance for a life together had been ended by someone they'd both discounted as helpless to thwart them.

Eve was planting enough evidence to show premeditated murder, enough to get Jackson the death sentence. Knowing Jackson, he'd have smart attorneys who'd argue mitigating circumstances, or maybe lessened mental capacity. She'd prepared herself for the possibility he would only end up with a long prison sentence.

But Jackson was old enough that even ten or fifteen years in prison would preclude any chance of happiness with *that woman*. His repaired heart wasn't going to last forever. But it wasn't even his aging body that would do him in. Eve knew that if a man like Jackson Blackthorne was kept in a cell, away from the sun and the wind and the land, he'd shrivel up and die inside.

Less than a week ago she'd finally set her plan in motion. She'd made a point of joining Jackson at the roundup every day. Had insisted on flying with their helicopter pilot so she could relearn the use of the controls, then kicked him out of the cockpit and flown herself for the past two days, even though she had no current FAA license.

The court would want to know why Jackson hadn't stopped her. Unless he'd had a reason for wanting her to continue to fly . . .

She'd stolen his hunting knife with the serrated edge from the locked metal tool kit he kept in the back of his pickup and used it earlier this evening to sever the hydraulic line in the helicopter, then returned it to the locked box. She'd also siphoned off enough gas that the helicopter wasn't going to explode on impact. She didn't want any evidence accidentally burning up. She planned to hide a small homemade explosive device under the pilot's seat that would conveniently "malfunction," leaving all the evidence of Jackson's supposed tampering with the helicopter intact for investigators to find.

She'd taken a few pills from Jackson's stash of heart medication—enough to give herself a heart attack—to dissolve in her thermos of coffee. She'd debated whether to use Jackson's sleeping pills, but she wanted something that was certain to kill her quickly, so she wouldn't be alive when the helicopter crashed. She would arrange to have Jackson personally hand her the thermos tomorrow morning before she got into the helicopter.

She could just hear the prosecutor explaining to the jury how Jackson Blackthorne had threatened his wife the night before her death. How he'd poisoned her in order to keep his fortune and continue sleeping with his mistress. How he'd cut the hydraulic line with his hunting knife so the helicopter would malfunction and appear to accidentally crash, and then arranged for it to explode in a fiery ball on impact to destroy the evidence that would prove he'd murdered his wife.

Oh, it would work, all right.

All that was left was the very public argument she planned to have with Jackson tonight at the barbecue being held to celebrate the last days of the roundup. All of their friends and neighbors would be there. She was sure she could get him to threaten her. It would be nice if she could enrage him enough to strike her. He'd never done it before, but maybe, if she said enough insulting things about *that woman,* she could incite him to it.

Eve looked at herself in the mirror over the dresser in her bedroom. She was still a beautiful woman. Her blond hair was cut short in the current fashion, soft and beguiling around her face. Her blue eyes were striking, her figure trim and spare. She was dressed in a fringed fawn leather skirt and vest with a forest-green silk Western shirt and wore short, high-heeled boots with the Circle B brand tooled into the brown leather.

A woman as beautiful and talented as she was didn't deserve to be abandoned by her husband. Not to mention the mental infidelity she'd suffered during the entire course of their marriage. She'd tried to remove her nemesis once before and failed. Now, even killing Lauren Creed would never bring Jackson back to her. And she couldn't bear to live the rest of her life as a divorced woman.

When Eve was thirteen, her father had divorced her mother and married another woman. Her mother had become invisible to all their friends and neighbors, as though she'd never existed. She'd turned to drugs and alcohol and then showed up at public events, embarrassing Eve and infuriating her father. Following those awful confrontations, her mother had drunk more and indulged in more drugs, along with a series of disgustingly young lovers. Her mortifying decline had ended when she'd killed herself by slitting her wrists three years after the divorce.

Eve's most vivid, most painful memory of that period in her life was overhearing her father say at her mother's funeral, "She should have killed herself three years ago and spared us all the disgrace and indignity of watching her become a lush and a slut."

Eve had no intention of emulating her mother's decline.

Instead of debasing and degrading herself, pining away for a man who'd rejected her, she was going to take firm, positive action. She was going to have the revenge her mother had been denied.

Eve headed down the stairs. She wished it were possible to leave a letter for Jackson, explaining what she'd done. She wanted him to know how and why she'd arranged his ruin. She wanted him to know that she'd ended up hating him as much as she'd loved him once upon a time. And that no man was going to be allowed to spoil her life and get away with it.

She hesitated on the stairs as a thought came to her. She didn't dare leave a letter for Jackson that could be used to exonerate him. But why not leave a note that wouldn't be found for maybe twenty years? Even if Jackson was released from prison when it was found, he'd be seventy-seven. Much too old for a romance with the widow Creed, even if she'd waited all those years for him.

Oh, she liked it. Yes, she'd do that tonight before she went to sleep. Write a note and conceal it where it wouldn't be found for twenty years. But where to put it? How to ensure it wouldn't be found too soon...

The last place Billy Coburn wanted to be was the annual Circle B barbecue. But Summer had told him she'd never missed one, and she didn't want to start now. Besides, she'd argued, what better opportunity for them to greet their neighbors as husband and wife?

Billy was certain the evening would be a disaster. Nobody in Bitter Creek knew him as anything but Bad Billy

Coburn, and he wasn't sure what he'd do or say to the first man who slighted him in front of his new wife. Or worse yet, insulted Summer for getting involved with a no-account, no-good nobody like himself.

"Dance with me, Billy," Summer said as they approached the crowd around a roaring fire, over which a beef carcass was roasting on a spit. A country band wailed over the noise of the gathering, dueling violins daring the two-stepping dancers to keep up with the frenetic pace of the tune.

"We'll be trampled by that herd of buffalo," he said.

"It'll be fun," she said, entreating him with a smile and teasing him with a look from beneath lowered lashes.

He put one hand to her waist and took her hand with the other. "You asked for it."

A moment later they were racing with the crowd, her ponytail bouncing, his boots flying, as they danced in a joyous circle around the spitted meat, like ancient cave dwellers after a successful hunt.

The evening air was warm, and it didn't take long before Billy felt the sweat making his shirt cling to his back. He watched beads of perspiration form above Summer's bowed upper lip and dipped his head to kiss them away as he whirled her in a circle so tight and fast it made her laugh.

Billy grinned at her and felt his heart swell when she grinned back. He was sorry when the music ended. He'd already let her go when the band started playing the "Tennessee Waltz."

He didn't ask her if she wanted to dance again, simply slid his arm firmly around her waist and pulled her close, closer than most of the other couples were dancing. He didn't give a damn. They were supposedly newlyweds. Couples in love were entitled to break a few rules on the dance floor.

Although he'd been married to Summer for close to a month, he'd drawn an imaginary line down the center of the bed that first night, and neither of them had crossed over it. Dancing finally gave him a chance to hold his wife.

He noticed Summer wasn't objecting. In fact, she pressed herself against him, and in the dancing boots she was wearing, she fit him in all the right places. He didn't back off when he felt himself becoming aroused. He noticed she didn't back off either, but her body felt less relaxed in his arms.

He bent and whispered in her ear, "I told you once before, a long time ago, what you do to me."

"I don't want to tease you, Billy," she whispered back. "I mean, since this isn't going anywhere. I mean, we agreed . . . sex wasn't part of the bargain."

That was plain speaking. But that was Summer. Honest to a fault. "I don't mind if you don't mind," he said as he slid his hand down the arch of her back to the rise of her buttocks and urged her against the ridge in his jeans.

She leaned her cheek against his shirt, and he felt her shudder under his hand. He held her close and danced, letting the gentle sway of their bodies against one another feed the need inside him. By the time the dance ended, he was trembling with desire.

He didn't want to let her go.

She looked up at him, her heart in her eyes, and said, "Billy, I think we should—"

Before she could finish, a hand slapped Billy on the back and a familiar voice said, "Never expected to see you here."

Billy turned and recognized one of the kids he'd gone to school with all his life, a one-time partner in crime who was now a respectable rancher with a couple of kids. "Hi, Wade."

Wade offered his hand and Billy shook it. "Going to introduce me to your beautiful wife?" Wade asked.

"You know Summer Blackthorne."

"Know of her," Wade said with a lurid grin as he tipped his hat to Summer. "Never met her. Hello there, pretty lady."

"Hello," Summer said, nodding and smiling back at Wade.

Billy felt himself getting hot under the collar as Wade continued ogling her. "Where's your wife?" he asked.

Wade threw a thumb over his shoulder. "Over there with the other wives. The view is a heap nicer right here."

Billy hadn't expected to feel jealous. Hadn't expected to feel the urge to punch Wade Johnson in the nose. Before he could act, Summer threaded her arm through his and said, "Nice meeting you, Wade. Billy and I need to say hello to my father."

Billy was so surprised, he let himself be led away like a bull with a ring in its nose.

"What a moron," Summer murmured as she glanced back over her shoulder. "I should have let you knock his teeth down his throat."

Billy laughed. "I would have been happy to do it for you."

Summer laughed along with him. "That would have been satisfying. But it's not exactly the impression I was hoping you'd make tonight."

He stopped and stared at her. "Brought your prize hog to market, have you?"

"Don't be an idiot. People are naturally curious about the two of us. They can't figure out why you'd pick someone like me for your wife."

Billy stared at her, then grinned and shook his head. "You never cease to amaze me."

She beamed at him. "I know. Now if I could just convince all these other people how amazing I am, they'd understand the attraction."

"You started to say something at the end of the dance, before we were interrupted. What was it?"

Summer made a face. "It was nothing."

He tipped her chin up. "I was hoping it was something."

"I was going to say I'm tired of trying to stay on my own side of the bed. It's impossible anyway, when the mattress sags in the middle."

"I thought we agreed—"

"You set the terms," she said.

"And now you want to change them?"

"I might."

His body ached, wanting her. It would be so easy to agree with her, to make their marriage a little more real than it was. To add sex.

Only for him, it wouldn't be just sex. It would be making love. And he wasn't sure he could take that chance. He already felt a knot in his stomach every time he thought of what he'd do when their two years together were up. How would he be able to handle the situation if they became lovers? Was the pleasure now worth the pain later?

"You're taking an awful long time to answer," she said. "Which suggests the answer is no."

He reached for her hand to keep her from turning away. "The answer is I have to think about it. We're not kids anymore, Summer. The things we choose to do have consequences."

She placed her palm against his cheek and said, "What happened to the dangerous, risk-taking Billy I used to know?"

"He grew up. He became a father."

"I liked the old Billy better," she said, her lips pouting.

The old Billy wanted to suck one of those pouting lips into his mouth and taste the sweetness of it. The old Billy wanted to palm one of her lush breasts in his hand and work the nipple into a tight bud. The old Billy wanted to lay her flat and thrust the hard, bulging erection behind the fly of his jeans deep inside her.

The new Billy satisfied himself with a quick peck on her lips before he backed off, letting go of her hand. "Your brothers are heading this way."

She turned and watched as her twin brothers Owen and Clay headed straight for them without pausing for the occasional handshake or amenity with anyone.

Billy steeled himself for the verbal—and maybe even physical—attack he figured was coming. Summer backed up against him, putting herself between him and her brothers. He took her by the shoulders and, despite her resistance, moved her to his left, out of the way of harm, in case one of her brothers launched a blow in his direction.

"You lowdown, dirty—"

"Stop right there, Clay," Summer said. "You're talking about my husband."

Even for Billy, it wasn't hard to tell the twins apart. Owen was a Texas Ranger and had spent his life outdoors hunting down badmen. His features were weathered from the sun and his jeans and shirt were worn and soft from a thousand washings. A five-pointed silver star was pinned above his pocket and he had a Colt .45 strapped high on his hip.

Clay had been elected the youngest ever attorney general of the state of Texas and spent his days prosecuting criminals in the courtroom. He looked younger than Owen, but his gray eyes were no less piercing, and his over-six-foot body looked just as hard beneath the blended wool suit pants and white oxford-cloth shirt that had been unbuttoned at the neck, with the conservative striped tie pulled down to make his office uniform look more appropriate for the outdoor occasion.

"Well, well," Clay drawled. "Bad Billy Coburn—"

"That's enough, Clay," Summer warned, stepping back in front of Billy.

He took her by the shoulders again, but she resisted his attempts to move her aside. He gave in and slid his arm around her waist and pulled her back against him, so they presented a united front. "Hello, Clay. Owen," he said, nodding to his brothers-in-law. This was the first time he'd come in contact with them since he'd learned they were also his half brothers.

He saw pieces of himself in them. The chin. The cheekbones. The hair. The nose. But he'd gotten his dark eyes from his mother, while they'd gotten theirs from Blackjack—the ruthless gray eyes of a predator.

"Welcome to the family," Owen said, extending his hand.

Billy was both disconcerted by the friendly gesture and wary of it.

Summer was more direct. "If you have any intention of grabbing Billy and—"

"I just want to shake your husband's hand," Owen said. "I want to wish the two of you well and invite you to visit me and Bay and the kids next time you're in Fredericksburg."

"Where is Bay?" Summer asked.

"She's at home with the twins. They're just getting over the chicken pox."

"Thank you, Owen," Summer said. "We'll try to make it."

She glanced over her shoulder at Billy, and he knew she expected him to shake Owen's hand, which was still extended. Owen, who'd arrested him once for driving drunk. Who'd more than once warned him away from Summer and made it clear he didn't have much use for lowlifes like Bad Billy Coburn.

Billy reminded himself he wasn't "Bad" Billy Coburn anymore. That he'd likely be spending the rest of his life in this sawed-off town. And that it wouldn't hurt to have the goodwill of a respected man like Owen Blackthorne, especially when his son would be growing up and making a place for himself here.

"Thanks," he said gruffly, as he extended his hand.

Owen's grip was firm, but not so tight as to turn the handshake into a contest. When Billy would have let go, Owen held on and said, "I wish I'd known sooner that we're kin. I'd have lent you a helping hand—"

Billy yanked his hand free and said, "Keep your charity to yourself, Blackthorne."

"See what I mean, Owe?" Clay said. "An *ungrateful* yellow-bellied cur. Bad to the bone."

"Say that again when your sister isn't standing between us," Billy taunted, using his hold on Summer's waist to throw her out of the range of the two men's fists.

"Whoa there, boys," Owen said, playing peacemaker. "Shake hands and be friends."

Billy didn't feel like being friendly. He narrowed his eyes at Clay and said, "Takes a yellow-bellied cur to know one."

"Billy, please don't fight," Summer begged.

"If you weren't Summer's husband I'd give you a lesson you wouldn't forget," Clay threatened.

All the unfairness of his situation, all his antagonism toward Blackjack for taking away his livelihood, toward Debbie Sue for blackmailing him, toward his mother for getting sick and his sister for getting pregnant, and the sexual frustration of lying night after night beside a woman he wanted but couldn't have, needed an outlet.

Clay had given it to him.

But he wasn't going to strike first. Billy didn't want Owen-the-lawman to be able to say he'd started it. He needed Clay to make the first move. The smug sonof-abitch was just standing there, certain he was safe so long as he had his brother to protect him and his sister to keep Billy in check.

"Go stand over there, Summer," Billy said, gesturing toward Clay. "Your big brother wants to hide behind your skirt."

It wasn't much as insults go. Billy had said worse. But it was enough. Clay swung without warning.

Clay's fist seemed to move in slow motion, and Billy parried the blow long before it reached his chin, counter-ing with a quick punch to Clay's stomach. Surprisingly solid muscle gave way under the force of his jab, and Clay doubled over. Billy followed with a driving upper-cut that straightened Clay up and threw him backward onto the ground.

Owen stepped in front of him. "That's enough, you bastard."

It was a poor choice of words, and even though Billy could see Owen had realized his mistake, he didn't give him a chance to take it back. "No, not nearly enough," Billy said, his fist driving toward Owen's chin.

Owen's reflexes were better, and he dipped his head aside so Billy's knuckles only grazed his cheek.

"Goddammit. Cut it out," Owen said as Billy's other fist caught him on the ear.

"What the hell's going on here?" a bellowing voice demanded.

Billy was like a wounded animal besieged by preda-tors, knowing only that he had to keep fighting or be lost. Still, he wouldn't have hit an older man, or a weaker one, if it could have been helped. The problem was, Blackjack stepped between Owen and Billy's fist at a point when it was too late to pull his punch.

His bare knuckles smashed into Blackjack's jaw, causing him to grunt with pain and stumble backward into both Owen and Clay, who was rejoining the fray. The two men kept Blackjack upright, but the enormity of what he'd done struck Billy in an instant.

He turned to locate Summer, who stared at him with horror. He looked around and saw a crowd had gathered, all of them with condemnation in their eyes and contempt on their faces.

He didn't need them. He didn't need anyone.

He started to back away, but he wasn't given a chance to escape before attack came from another direction.

"This is all your fault," a shrill female voice cried.

Billy turned toward the accusing voice, but the well-manicured, pointing finger wasn't aimed at him.

It was aimed at Blackjack.

Billy took a halting half-step backward and turned to stare—along with everyone else—at the expensively dressed and elegantly coiffed woman whose gaze pinned Jackson Blackthorne like a hog-tied bull calf she planned to castrate.

"What do you expect when you invite your bastard son to a party where the rest of your family is gathered?" Eve Blackthorne said in a voice loud enough to be heard by everyone there.

"We can talk about this later, Eve," Blackjack said, eyeing the crowd.

"We'll talk about it now," she said, taking another step toward him.

Billy saw Owen and Clay move toward their mother, as though to intercept her, but she either sensed or saw them, because she turned to them and said, "I'm sorry you boys have to witness this, but I've taken all of your father's bad behavior I can stomach. I'm surprised he didn't invite his lover—that Creed woman—here this evening."

Billy heard a gasp from the crowd, but it was Blackjack's face he found riveting. His teeth were clenched and his jaw muscle worked and his eyes had narrowed in fury.

"I excused your fling, even though it bore fruit," Eve continued, sliding a glance in Billy's direction. "But I won't tolerate flagrant adultery. I deserve more respect than that."

He felt Summer's hands grip his arm, her fingernails biting into his skin. He turned to free himself and saw her face was parchment pale, her lips pressed flat. He gathered both her hands in one of his and turned back to the train wreck that was happening before his eyes.

"This is not the time or place—" Blackjack said.

"When is the time?" Eve interrupted. "When you're lying in bed with that woman? When you're fucking her?"

The obscene word was shocking, coming from a mouth as delicate as Eve Blackthorne's. But it had the desired result. Blackjack started toward her with his hands outstretched as though to strangle her, and it was only the intervention of his two sons, each of whom grabbed one of his arms, that kept him from doing it.

"You foul bitch," he spat. "I should have gotten rid of you years ago."

Eve suddenly looked frightened, the way a little girl looks when she realizes she's lost, surrounded by a dark and dangerous forest, with no idea which way to go.

She faltered backward, and several women rushed to surround her, leading her away.

Blackjack shook off his sons like a big buffalo bull shaking off a few irritating rat terriers. "Get the hell away from me," he said. "Show's over, folks," he said to the crowd that lingered, ghoulishly hoping to see more carnage. "I don't know about you, but I need a drink."

The crowd agreed heartily with that suggestion, and Blackjack headed toward the keg of beer and the buckets of champagne and the jars of iced tea that had been set up for his guests.

"What a fiasco," Clay said.

"It's been coming a long time," Owen said. He put his arm around Clay's shoulder, shot Billy a "Stay where you are!" look, and said, "Let's go get a drink."

Clay looked one last time in Billy's direction, but at Owen's urging, followed the rest of the crowd toward the makeshift bar.

Billy let his arm drop from Summer's waist and stood waiting to be condemned for his part in the disaster they'd all just witnessed.

"How could you, Billy?" she said in a soft, agonized voice.

He kept his eyes focused on the retreating crowd as he said, "I didn't have any choice, Summer."

"You baited Clay. You caused that fight."

He turned to her and said, "You knew who I was when you married me. Bad Billy Coburn, the meanest junkyard dog in town. Always was and always will be."

"What does that make me, Billy?"

His throat ached just looking at the hurt in her eyes. "A fool, I guess, for marrying me."

He wanted her to contradict him. He wanted her to fight.

But without a word, she turned her back on him and walked away.

Chapter 10

BILLY LAY IN BED, THE LIGHTS OUT, THINKING about the mess he'd made of his life since he'd come back to Bitter Creek. He felt sick inside, hurting as though he'd been punched hard in the gut and then kicked in the teeth, and finally stomped while he was down. Things were about as bad as they could get.

He'd followed Summer when she walked away from him at the barbecue, terrified that she was leaving him for good. To his surprise, she headed straight for his pickup and got in.

"Take me home," she said.

He gave an inward sigh that she wasn't leaving him. Or maybe she was but just didn't want to make any more of a scene than he and her family already had.

Their trip home was nothing like the drive over. Then she'd been bubbly and excited and smiling and playful. And concerned because he'd been so tense and quiet. She'd asked him whether he was anxious about spending an evening with her family. He'd told her he wasn't used to crowds.

Lying here in bed after the silent drive home, he wished he'd admitted what had really been preying on his mind. That wouldn't have excused his behavior toward her brothers. But maybe it would have explained it.

Billy had found out just before quitting time this afternoon that once the roundup was over, the rancher who'd hired him was going to let him go.

"Blackthorne holds the note to my mortgage," he'd said. "So long as you're working for me, he threatened to foreclose if I'm a day late on the payment. I hate like hell giving in to that kind of threat, but I've got a wife and kids to think about. When the roundup's done, you'll have to go."

He'd be out of a job in three days.

After tonight it was a good bet that no rancher beholden to Jackson Blackthorne—and who wasn't in this tight-knit community where the Blackthornes owned or controlled nearly everything?—was going to hire Bad Billy Coburn. Or sell him feed on credit. Or loan him the money to fix up this place.

Billy felt a spurt of panic. He buried his face in the pillow so Summer wouldn't hear the groan of despair wrenched from somewhere deep inside him and gripped the sheet with both hands to fight off the wave of hopelessness that threatened to overwhelm him.

He would never give up. But it was getting harder to believe he would be able to drag himself out of the bottomless pit into which Jackson Blackthorne had shoved him. His present circumstances were grim. More terrifying was the likelihood that he could expect nothing better in the future.

On his own, he would have spit in Blackjack's eye and dared him to do his worst. But it wasn't only himself he had to consider. There was Will. And his mother. And

Emma, who hadn't even called as she'd promised to assure them she was all right. He'd found out from Joe, who managed the grocery in town, that she was working for Sam Creed. She was as stubborn as he was, and he couldn't really blame her for staying away. Life in this house was . . . tense.

And last, but not at all least, there was Summer, whom he loved with a love as hopeless as everything else in his life.

He had to hand it to her. Over the past month she'd tried hard to be a nurse to his mother and a mother to Will and to help out with chores around the house. But she hadn't counted on her father closing all her bank accounts, which she'd held jointly with him. She hadn't counted on being as poor as . . . he was.

She hadn't quit the marriage. Yet. But every day when he left in the morning, he feared he'd come home and find her gone. After tonight . . . he wasn't counting any chickens.

Blackjack had more than made good on his promise. He'd made Billy's life in Bitter Creek a living hell. Billy viciously punched his pillow, but it was no substitute for the man he really wanted to punish.

It didn't help that Billy had spent the past month sleeping next to Summer without touching her. Sexual frustration led to all sorts of stupid behavior.

Talk about hell.

He'd known he wasn't over her. But living with her and not being able to hold her or kiss her—or even touch her—was taking its toll. He was exhausted and irritable at the end of each day, and all he wanted when he got home was a little peace.

But when he walked in the door, there she was, Will perched on her hip, both of them smiling at him, making him want to gather them up in his arms and hold them.

His eyes would meet hers, and they'd have an entire conversation without speaking a word.

Hi. How was your day?

I learned how to shuck corn. Will said a new word. Your mother isn't feeling well.

Nobody talks to me at work. It's like I'm a leper. But they can't say I don't pull my weight. I do more than my share. Twice my share. I'm determined to prove I'm not Bad Billy Coburn anymore. But someone will say or do something to remind me how it used to be, and I clam up and glare and they back off a little further.

How long can this go on? Let me ask my father—I mean *your* father—to help us out.

Don't mention his name to me. Don't say anything to me. I don't want to argue. I'd much rather hold you. And we both know that isn't a good idea.

She would flush and turn away, because she could see in his eyes what he wanted. That he craved her like a man starved for sustenance, who can see it just beyond his reach. That he longed to put his mouth against hers, to share with her the ebb and flow within him, the ups and downs, the best and worst of his day.

To give solace and to take it.

But he'd kept himself aloof. From her, at least. He'd showered all his pent-up need on his son, who hid his cherubic face in Billy's neck to avoid his kisses and who laughed with delight and pressed his ribs against Billy's chest to avoid his tickling fingers.

And then he'd catch a glimpse of Summer's yearning

face over Will's shoulder and feel an ache that made him want to weep.

Spending the night in the same bed with her was pure torture. Precious, wonderful, delicious torture. She was absolutely right about the mattress sagging in the middle. Although they started out each night clinging to opposite edges of the bed, they awoke each morning entangled with one another in the center.

He'd started waking up when he felt her warmth along the length of him. During those first nights, there were stars aplenty, but no moon in which to discern her features. As the weeks had passed, the moonlight had grown, so he could trace with his eyes the delicate arch of her brow, the bow of her upper lip, the fringe of eyelashes along her petal-smooth cheek. She was so beautiful it made his breath catch.

He'd caressed her hair against the pillow in the dark, marveling at its silkiness. But never her skin, however much he longed to touch. He hadn't wanted to wake her, hadn't wanted her to discover the depth of his need. Hadn't wanted her to tempt him to do what he knew he should not do.

Hold her. Kiss her. Love her.

He didn't dare. His "pretend" wife wasn't going to be around long enough to have a life with him. He'd seen her disillusionment the very first night, when she'd met his eyes in the cracked mirror over the sink in the bathroom, her mouth full of toothpaste. He'd looked around the tiny bathroom and seen what she must be seeing.

The cold water faucet dripped even when it was off. The enamel in the tub was scratched down to the iron. The linoleum was curled where water had flooded once upon a time. And the morning-glory wallpaper was stained brown where rainwater had seeped through a patched hole in the roof.

"It's not the Ritz," he'd said in an attempt at humor.

"It's not that bad," she'd replied. But she'd turned from him after she'd said it and spit toothpaste in the sink.

Which meant it was awful, really, but she was being a good sport about it. He didn't miss the bleak look in her eyes when she lifted her head and met his gaze again in the mirror.

"It's not forever," he'd said.

"Only two years," she'd agreed.

Which was why he couldn't take the chance of giving in to his desire. He didn't want to make love to his wife. He didn't want to give her any more of his heart than she already had. He'd need a little of it to get through the rest of his life once she was gone.

But the truth was, he'd reached the end of his tether, and something had to break. Small wonder he'd taken advantage of the provocation Summer's brothers had given him. Small wonder he'd struck out and proved to everyone he was still "Bad" Billy Coburn.

Billy tensed when he heard the bedroom door open and close. He held his breath as the springs squeaked and Summer slid beneath the sheets. Although the light was out, he'd lifted the window shade and both the moon's white light and a gentle breeze wafted through the open window.

He turned his back on her and rearranged his feather pillow, using that as an excuse to put more space between them. Not that he wasn't aware of her every time she stepped into a room. Hell. He'd recognize her distinctive female scent anywhere.

"Billy."

He could tell from the sound of her voice that she was facing in his direction, so he didn't turn to answer her. "What?" he replied in an equally low voice.

"You need to speak to your mother."

She'd caught him off guard, because he'd been expecting her to bring up what had happened that evening. He wondered if this was her way of easing into a discussion of what he'd done. He knew he ought to apologize. Knew he'd been in the wrong. But it wasn't easy.

Or maybe this really was about his mother. Even that thought boded no good. The possibility that now he was going to have to play peacemaker between Summer and his mother was damned close to the straw that would break the camel's back. "Why do I need to talk to my mother?" he said irritably.

"She's dying."

Billy sat bolt upright and glared at Summer. "I know that. Why the hell do you think I came back here to Bitter Creek?"

She pushed herself up on one arm. A smarter woman, a more experienced wife—or someone who hadn't been raised as a Blackthorne—would have kowtowed. He recognized—and welcomed—the martial tilt of Summer's chin as she sat up straighter.

The moon reflected off her eyes like red-hot coals in the darkness. The oversize white T-shirt with the neck torn out that she was using for a nightgown slid off one shoulder, exposing more skin than he wanted to see.

"Your mother needs your forgiveness," she said.

"She sure as hell doesn't deserve it!" he shot back. "Any more than your mother does. When people are wrong they're wrong."

"Keep your voice down. She'll hear you."

"I don't give a damn if she does."

"You'll wake Will," she warned, glancing in the direction of the crib that sat in the corner of the room. Will made a snuffling sound, then was quiet.

The last thing he wanted was to wake his son. Will was teething and had been fussy and tearful before he fell asleep.

"Let's get out of here," he said, thrusting his feet over the side of the bed and reaching for his jeans, which he'd thrown over a ladder-back chair beside the bed.

He'd been sleeping in a pair of pajama bottoms to avoid being naked in the same bed with her—the clothing as much for his sanity as her modesty. The layer of cloth had more than once saved him from doing what he shouldn't.

He dragged his jeans on over the pajamas, stalked to the door barefoot, and stood there holding it open, waiting for Summer to join him. She grimaced and stood, giving him a glimpse of lacy pink panties before she straightened the shoulder of her T-shirt so the scrap of cotton covered both shoulders. He sucked in a breath when he realized it barely covered the tops of her thighs.

He opened his mouth to tell her to put something else on, but she put her finger to her lips and whispered, "Shh," then marched ahead of him through the door and down the hall toward the kitchen.

She didn't stop there. She inched open the screen door slowly enough to mute the groan of springs, then held the door open for his exit, before easing it closed behind them.

It was blessedly cool outside on the back porch. He thought she was going to sit in one of the rockers, but to his surprise, she headed for the back steps, making sure to miss the one that was broken—he kept meaning to fix it—before heading for the barn.

Which was when he realized they were not going to have a civilized discussion. Summer would need the privacy of the barn only if she intended to raise her voice. He already felt defensive. He was sorry he'd let her marry him. Sorry he'd gotten her into this mess. Sorry she had to live like this when she was used to so much better. And damned sorry he'd taken a swing at her sorry-assed brother.

But he couldn't apologize. Wouldn't apologize. She was a grown-up. She'd known what she was getting into. If she wanted to call it quits, that was fine by him. He'd pay back the $25,000 from Summer's trust that he'd borrowed to pay off Debbie Sue and her money-grubbing husband if he had to work till he was a hundred. There was no real harm done.

Except he'd married the woman he loved . . . but never made love to her. And now she was leaving him. And once she was gone, there wasn't much chance she was ever coming back.

He reached over her shoulder to lift the latch on the barn door and pulled it open, gesturing her inside. She hit the light switch and the bare overhead bulb blinded them. He closed the door behind them, locking them inside, then turned.

The T-shirt had slid off her shoulder again, and he caught a glimpse of her pink undies when she reached up to shove her hair away from her face.

Suddenly, he knew there was no way he could live through the speech that was coming. He wanted her, needed her. She was here, and he might not ever have another chance.

He didn't give her any choice, just closed the distance between them and captured her against the length of him.

"Billy—"

"Don't fight me," he said as he claimed her mouth. "Don't fight me. Don't—"

He took her deep, fast, plundering what he'd been denied for years and years and years. He'd wanted her so long. Since the first time he'd laid eyes on her. He'd made himself her friend, because he knew she'd never want a troublemaker like him. But by some miracle, some freak of fortune, she'd become his wife.

He wanted her. And he wanted her to want him.

"Love me, Summer. Love me, please."

He tore her T-shirt in half, baring her to his gaze, staring at her breasts, so lush, the pink nipples peaked. "You're so beautiful. So perfect."

He didn't lift his gaze to her eyes, afraid of what he'd find. He couldn't bear to see shock or disgust or dismay. He could feel the stiffness in her body, her reluctance, her resistance.

He set out to woo her, kissing her throat, letting his

breath warm her ear, his work-rough hands plumping her breasts. His hips pressed urgently into the cradle of her thighs, letting her feel his arousal.

She moaned, and he felt the warmth and wetness of her mouth against his throat.

Oh, God. She was kissing him, making shivers tear across his flesh. He wanted inside her now, this instant. But if he took her now, it would all be over too fast. He didn't want this moment to end. He made himself slow down. Made himself savor the moment, because it might be all he had to remember in the years to come.

Her hands shoved their way into his hair and she leaned into him, her hips pressing back against his own. He'd thought he was hard. She made him harder.

She was loving him back. He hadn't imagined it. Could hardly believe it.

He lifted his head and looked into her eyes. And shuddered at what he found. Acceptance. And a desire as fierce as his own.

He picked her up and carried her to one of the stalls, grabbing a saddle blanket along the way. He threw it down onto the straw and kicked it open, then laid her down. He shucked his jeans and pajama bottoms, then pulled off her panties. Though her breathing was labored, she lay quiescent as he braced his hands on either side of her and lowered his body onto hers. He felt her shiver as their flesh met.

The stall smelled of hay and horses and leather and was shaded from the harsh light above them by a wall of knotholed wooden planks. Billy looked into her eyes, and saw they were shadowed, fearful, worried. His body was taut with the need to thrust inside her.

"I want you," he rasped. "I need you."

"I want you, too," she said breathlessly.

His heart lurched. It seemed he'd been waiting an eternity to hear those words. They'd only been married a month, but he'd loved her—how many years? He couldn't stop to count now. His mouth was needed elsewhere.

He kissed her throat, and her guttural moan made his groin tighten. He touched her with his hands everywhere, seeking the places that made her undulate against him, the places that made her moan and writhe with need, the places that made her gasp with surprise and delight.

She was already wet when he finally slid a finger inside her, but tight, very tight. He added another finger, and she stiffened.

He made a grunting sound and she said, "What's wrong?"

"Nothing," he said.

She stiffened and said, "Something's wrong. Tell me."

He met her gaze and said, "You're small."

She looked frightened. "Am I? Is that bad?"

He hadn't expected her fear, wasn't ready for it. "Have you had problems before?"

"Before?" she echoed.

"When you've made love," he said.

"I haven't ever done this before."

He withdrew his hand. "Are you telling me you're a virgin?"

She blushed fiery red, crossed her arms over her breasts, and turned her face aside.

He grasped her chin and made her look at him. "Are you untouched?"

"Yes," she whispered.

He lowered himself beside her and pulled her into his arms, holding her tight and rocking her. "Oh, God," he said. "I never dreamed...I never hoped. Thank you. Thank you."

"You don't have to thank me," she muttered against his shoulder.

An enormous swell of joy made his chest feel like it might burst. The joy came out as laughter. "I wasn't thanking you," he said. "I was thanking God."

"He had nothing to do with it," she said. "I just never found anybody who made me feel...like you do when you kiss me."

"What about Geoffrey?" he asked.

"He agreed to wait until we got married."

"Thank God."

She hid her face against his shoulder and asked, "Why did you stop?"

"I was surprised." He lifted her chin again, so he could see her eyes and added, "And pleased."

"I don't know how to do this. I won't be able to please you."

"You already please me," he said. "And we'll teach each other what we like."

He frowned as he realized he was probably going to hurt her, because she was a virgin. And that he might not have another chance to show her how good it could be between them.

"What's wrong now?" she asked.

"You see too much," he said.

"Just tell me."

"I'm afraid I'll hurt you."

"Isn't it supposed to hurt the first time?"

He shook his head. "Not always. Anyway, I don't want to hurt you ever, at all."

"What you were doing before didn't hurt," she said. "It just felt... strange. I felt... full."

He felt his erection pulsing. He kissed her and rolled over so he was under her, settling her on his lap with her legs on either side of his hips. "I think this will work better if you're the one controlling things."

"I like the sound of that," she said with a mischievous grin. She laid her hands flat on his chest and leaned forward to kiss him deeply, languidly. "I'd be happy just kissing all night."

"Then that's where we'll start," he said.

He started over from the beginning, kissing her, caressing her, letting her discover what made her feel good, arousing her passion. He was glad he knew enough to bring her pleasure. Selfishly glad she had never given herself to another man. Dying from the need to be joined with her.

At long last she moaned and said, "I want you inside me. How should I— What should I—"

He lifted her hips and positioned her so that he was poised to broach her. "Your call," he said, his breath caught in his throat. "Take all the time you need."

She pushed downward a little with her hips and made a grunting sound, then slid back up.

He moaned.

"Did I hurt you?" she asked.

He gripped her hips to keep her from bolting, as it

seemed she might. "I'm fine," he said. "It felt good. Really, really good," he said, explaining the noise he'd made.

"Oh." He heard the surprise in her voice. And the satisfaction. "How's this?" she asked, sliding back down.

"Good. Great," he corrected. "Keep it up."

She grinned and sank lower, pulled back up, then inched farther down. "Oh," she said. "It does feel good. I'm so full. You're so hard."

He gripped her hips but resisted the urge to push her down, determined to let her join their bodies at her own speed. "Are you all right?" he asked.

She flinched as she finally settled on top of him. "You're big," she said, wriggling around.

He moaned again. "Good God, woman. You're killing me."

She started to rise, and he gripped her hips and held her down. "Now it's my turn."

He turned her beneath him and watched the concern on her face turn to surprise, and then delight, and finally ecstasy, as they moved together in the ageless dance of lovers.

He touched her with his hands, finding the bud that had unfurled just for him. "Stay with me," he urged as he felt her body begin to convulse, even as he felt his own racing toward orgasm. "Stay with me."

And she did, her hips arching upward, her head thrown back, an unnatural sound that was part groan, part savage snarl issuing from her throat. He felt his seed erupting into her, and held her tight as his growl of satisfaction joined her own.

They clung together, sweat-slick bodies still joined,

lungs bellowing, unwilling to let the real world back in, denying for a few more precious moments the troubles that had brought them here in the first place.

Billy would have fallen asleep if he hadn't been so aware of the woman in his arms. He wanted to be sure she was all right. He wanted to know he'd brought her pleasure.

He wanted to be sure she had no regrets.

He waited until his breathing and hers had slowed and separated their bodies. At long last, he opened his eyes and found her staring back at him. With wonder. And fulfillment.

"We should be getting back to the house," he said.

She lowered her gaze and bit her lip, then looked into his eyes and said, "Billy, we need to talk."

He felt like jumping up and running. He didn't want to hear what she had to say. Before he could move, she leaned forward and kissed his lips, gently and sweetly, and said, "Please, Billy."

He sighed in resignation. If she was going to leave him, there was nothing he could do to stop her. "All right, talk," he said brusquely. "What is it you want to say?"

"You need to talk with your mother."

When he tried to object, she put her fingertips against his lips.

"Please listen to me. She wants to apologize. She wants to—"

He grabbed her wrist and moved her hand away from his mouth. "What difference can it possibly make?" he said. "It's all over and done with. She can't change the past any more than I can."

"She can say she's sorry."

"Then what?"

"You forgive her, so she can die in peace."

Billy snorted. "Why should I?"

"Because she's your mother, and you love her," Summer said.

"Have you forgiven your mother for what she did to you?"

Summer looked startled. "What do you mean?"

"For having an affair with another man and conceiving you with him. For letting Blackjack believe you're his daughter. For letting you believe it. And for admitting the truth when she knew it would hurt you."

"I . . ."

"I'll forgive my mother when you forgive yours." Billy rose and reached for his pajama bottoms and dragged them on, then threw his jeans over his shoulder. She dragged on her pink undies.

He picked up her torn T-shirt and handed it to her. "Sorry about that. Maybe it can be mended."

"I'll throw it away and get—" Summer stopped and stared at him, stricken. She could no longer afford to throw things away and buy new.

"I'll mend it," she mumbled.

He grabbed her hands and pulled her onto her feet, then took the T-shirt and stuck her arms in the holes, dressing her as though she were Will's age, then pulling the two sides together in front. "I'm sorry," he said. "I'm sorry I got you into this."

She leaned up on her tiptoes and kissed him on the mouth, her lips a little damp and incredibly soft. "I knew exactly what I was doing, Billy," she said. "And I'm not sorry. So there."

"I'm glad," he said. "Thank God you're taking birth control pills. At least we don't have to worry about you getting pregnant."

She blanched. "Uh-oh."

"That doesn't sound good."

"I only started taking pills because I was going to marry Geoffrey. I brought them with me because I thought I'd finish the month, but when you said it wasn't going to be a real marriage, I stopped taking them."

"So where does that leave us?"

She shrugged. "I have no idea."

Billy shook his head. "I never should have come out here with you."

"It's not that bad."

"Not that bad? I've seen how unhappy you are, Summer. I know you want out of this marriage. The last thing I want to do is get you pregnant!"

"I'm not sorry we did this," she said, her temper flaring. "And if you are—"

He pulled her close and pressed her cheek against his chest. "You were wonderful. Tonight was a memory I won't forget. But we can't do this again, Summer. We can't be taking chances. I already have one kid I can barely afford to support. And your father's cut you off, so—"

"I can get a job—"

"Who'll take care of Will and my mom? We have to be realistic—"

"It's too hard—"

He pushed her an arm's distance away, grasping her shoulders so tightly he saw her wince. "Life is hard. The sooner you understand that the better."

Summer jerked herself free and snarled, "Fine. We won't do this again. I wouldn't want to add to your burdens by getting pregnant."

She turned and headed for the door.

"Summer," he called after her.

She stopped but didn't turn around.

"Being with you was wonderful. Tonight was a memory I won't forget."

She angled her head to look at him over her shoulder and said, "Unfortunately, neither will I."

Chapter 11

SUMMER PRETENDED TO BE ASLEEP WHEN BILLY woke the next morning. Will's painful gums had kept him from sleeping soundly, and she'd gotten up with him in the middle of the night and stayed up till nearly dawn. Billy had offered to help, but she'd reminded him that he had to spend the next day on horseback, while she could sleep in. She was counting on Billy to feel too guilty to wake her up to have coffee with him, a wifely duty she'd performed every morning over the past month.

She couldn't face him after last night.

She'd been more than a little frightened at the prospect of having sex for the first time with Billy, because he had a reputation with women that was as wild as his reputation for making trouble. She was afraid he wouldn't want to bother with someone who had no experience.

She'd thought all that stuff about men desiring their wives to be virgins was propaganda to keep women from experimenting. She'd been surprised—and moved—to see how much it meant to Billy that he would be the first man to make love to her. It had warmed her heart to see how gentle and tender—and passionate—a lover he had been.

She'd been basking in the glow of their lovemaking, her heart full with everything she'd just experienced, when he'd proceeded to rip and tear and stomp out what remained of their precious interlude together.

He thought she wanted out of the marriage. He expected her to cut and run now that the going had gotten tough. It hurt to know he had so little faith in her.

And, oh, by the way, making love to her once was plenty. He didn't want any child of theirs coming into the world by mistake, so he was willing to forgo any further activity of that sort. It was humiliating to think something that had meant so much to her had meant so little to him.

Summer rolled over and stared at the crack in the ceiling plaster. It seemed she'd been trying to prove herself all her life—first to her father and now to Billy—and always came up wanting. She felt like running far, far away. Tahiti sounded perfect, strange and exotic, an ideal escape from all her troubles.

Who was she kidding? Since her father had cut her off, she didn't have the cash for a bus ticket to Mexico.

She punched the pillow and rearranged it under her head. As tempting as the thought of flight was, she couldn't leave Billy in the lurch. He needed her. Will needed her. And, though Billy's mother was often difficult—actually, a real pain in the ass—Dora needed her.

For the first time in her life, Summer was an indispensable part of a family. She felt strings of responsibility—and love—tugging at her, holding her to this ramshackle homestead.

She stared at the chipped nail polish and ragged cuticles of the hand lying not far from her nose. She'd never thought too much about how easy her life was at the Castle. She'd always worked hard, but whenever she'd needed a break, there'd been some hired hand to take up the slack.

The past month had been a wake-up call. The day-to-day effort necessary to take care of Billy's son and his mother and do chores around the house and barn was exhausting and tedious. The worst part was knowing there was no relief to be had.

Summer realized how few real challenges she'd faced in her life. How seldom she'd been forced to dig deep for reserves of energy or spirit in the face of adversity. The temptation rose again to do what Billy feared she would do—to cut and run.

She kept imagining the look of disappointment and disillusionment in Billy's eyes when he came home and found her gone. She couldn't bear to hurt him like that. She'd have to find the fortitude—somewhere—to keep going.

Summer shivered. What if she dug down deep for the strength to carry on and discovered it wasn't there? She tried to imagine herself living Billy's life, being knocked down over and over and getting up every single time to fight again. In the same situation, would she have kept on slugging?

Summer understood Billy's defiance far better now that she'd walked a mile in his shoes. She'd never realized just how hard it was to stare disaster in the face and thumb your nose at it. She just wished he hadn't felt he had to fight her whole family to prove himself.

She took a deep breath and let it out. Her moment of truth had come. In her mind's eye, she dusted off her fanny. She'd been knocked down, but she was up again. And by God, she was determined to fight. It was her turn to confront her father and make it plain she was Billy's wife and nothing he said or did was going to make her turn her back on him.

When the phone rang, Summer waited to see if Billy or his mother would get it. After four rings, when neither of them had picked up the phone, she lunged out of bed and scampered barefoot into the kitchen, where a phone hung on the wall.

"Hello," she said breathlessly.

"Oh, I didn't expect to get you," a male voice said. "I was hoping to catch Billy before he left."

"He's already gone," Summer said.

"Damn. Oh. 'Scuse me, ma'am."

Summer waited for the caller to say more, but the silence dragged on. Finally she said, "Is there a message I can give him?"

A nervous cough, and then a gruff voice that said, "This is Harvey Kemper. Billy's been working for me. I wanted to let him know I won't be needing him anymore. I told him there'd be work for a few more days, but last night at the barbecue Mr. Blackthorne made it clear—" He stopped, apparently realizing who he was speaking to, and finished lamely, "I won't be needing him anymore."

He sighed and there was another pause, and Summer imagined Harvey Kemper rubbing the back of his leathery, sun-browned neck. "I suppose I can tell him that when he gets here," Kemper said.

"Thank you for calling." Summer held the phone for another moment, then hung it gently back in the cradle and sank into one of the kitchen chairs. She reached down to straighten the curled vinyl that was scratching the underside of her thigh, but that irritation reminded her how hopeless Billy's situation had become. She jumped up and began pacing the kitchen, from one end of the worn linoleum squares to the other.

Had her father been making threats all along? Summer stopped at the sink and stared out the kitchen window past a faded gingham curtain toward a field of dry brown grass that stretched as far as the eye could see. She pressed her palm against her stomach, which spewed acid.

It was time Billy got a break, and she was going to convince her father to give it to him. All he really needed was his TSCRA job back. She wasn't sure what argument she would use on Blackjack, but she'd come up with something.

Having decided to act, Summer immediately felt better. She smiled wryly. Her stomach was still flipping and flopping around at the thought of facing down her father, but that couldn't be helped. Time to get moving.

With any luck, Dora would be having one of her "good days" and she'd be able to watch Will while Summer "ran an errand."

She poured a cup of coffee for Dora from the pot Billy had left and made a slice of dry toast, which was all Dora could keep down these days, then put coffee and toast on a tray and headed down the hall.

Dora's bedroom was lit by narrow beams of early morning sunlight that shot through holes in the ancient roll-up shades that covered the windows. Summer set the tray on the table beside the brass-railed double bed and said quietly, "Mrs. Coburn?"

Dora whimpered as she rolled over.

Summer's groin twisted as she imagined the other woman's pain. She leaned down and straightened the pillows behind Dora as she struggled to sit up, then straightened the covers around her legs, which looked like sticks beneath the sheets. "How are you this morning?" she said, knowing the answer before she asked.

"How do you think I am?" Dora replied peevishly, reaching for her black plastic glasses and shoving them onto her face. Her dark eyes looked even more sunken through the thick lenses. She was wearing an old-fashioned flannel nightgown that was too warm for the weather, but even so, she often complained of a chill in her bones.

Summer dug deep for the patience to deal calmly with Billy's mother. "I've brought coffee and toast."

"I'd rather have slept in," Dora said, at the same time reaching for the lap tray.

Summer started to help and was told, "I can do it myself!"

The tray tilted dangerously, and Summer reached to straighten it without a word.

"I have to go out this morning," she said. "I'll take Will with me."

"He was up half the night crying," Dora said.

"I'm sorry if he kept you up," Summer replied.

She waited for Dora's sharp retort, but when it didn't come, she met the older woman's gaze. Dora's brow was furrowed, and her dark brown eyes looked troubled. "I don't understand you," she said.

"I don't know what you mean," Summer said, flustered by Dora's probing stare.

"Why are you doing this? It isn't what you're used to. Don't try telling me you don't mind living here. I've seen your face when you don't think Billy's looking."

Summer flushed. "I want to help Billy."

"You think it helped to marry him?" Dora shook her head. "All you did was raise that boy's hopes. And bring disaster on him. The sooner he faces the life he's destined to lead—"

"Billy doesn't dream impossible dreams, Mrs. Coburn," Summer interrupted, angry for Billy's sake. "All he wants is a decent life for himself and his son. And he wants to take care of you and Emma. Is that asking so much?"

"It is when you have an enemy like Jackson Blackthorne."

"My father—Billy's father—won't keep Billy down for long. You'll see—"

"He clipped your wings pretty good."

Summer made a growling sound in her throat. "He took away my money. He can't keep me from living my life the way I want to live it. I still have choices."

Dora made a snorting sound. "Yeah. Like what? Starving in a hovel with your father's bastard son."

"Why are you so bitter? Why can't you be happy for Billy?"

"Because it's my fault he ended up coming back here," Dora said in an anguished voice. "If I weren't sick, he would've stayed where he was, and you damned Blackthornes couldn't have made his life a living hell again!"

Summer flinched at being included in the group Dora had vilified. "Billy will never let Blackjack get the better of him," Summer said. "You watch and see—"

"I won't be here to see what happens. Goddammit, girl, use your eyes and see what's staring you in the face. I'm dying. And there isn't a damned thing I can do about it. It's killing me to lie here and do nothing to help my son. To know he can't forgive me for what happened, for not defending him when he was helpless to defend himself. And to know he'll be fighting another battle alone—"

"He won't be alone," Summer said. "I'll be here."

"You can't count on a Blackthorne for anything but more trouble," Dora shot back.

Summer sat down next to Dora and took her hand, hanging on when Dora tried to pull free. Summer covered the wrinkled, age-spotted flesh with her hand, feeling the bony knuckles under her palm. She looked into Dora's eyes and said, "I promise you that Billy—and his son—will always be loved."

Summer had loved Will from the first moment he'd smiled up at her. Promising to love Will was easy. She wasn't as comfortable making such a promise where Billy was concerned. To be honest, she needed more time to sort out her feelings about Billy, especially after what had happened in the barn last night.

But it was time Dora didn't have.

Dora needed reassurance that someone would be looking out for Billy when she was gone. Summer had no qualms about making such a pledge. She would always be Billy's friend. And friends took care of friends.

Dora pulled her hand free and said, "You can leave Will here if you've got errands. I'm feeling downright spry this morning." She winced as she spoke, so Summer knew she wasn't as well as she pretended to be. But it would be a lot easier facing down her father without Will on her hip.

"Fine," Summer said. "I won't be gone long. I'll bring Will in once he's dressed and fed and set up the playpen so you can keep an eye on him."

"I can dress and feed him," Dora said.

"I know," Summer replied. "But I like doing it, and that'll give you a little more rest before you have to be up and about."

The truth was, Summer didn't simply *like* taking care of Will, she *loved* it. Of all the chores she had to manage, taking care of Billy's son was far and away the most fun. She'd never felt anything like what she felt when Will reached out to her, asking to be picked up.

Her insides turned to mush when he curled his tiny body against her and put his arms around her neck and made a baby sigh of satisfaction. She felt pure delight when he grinned, exposing his tiny front teeth. And her heart turned over with love and joy at the sound of his laughter.

Summer stared down at Will, who was still sleeping soundly. She brushed aside a dark curl on his forehead, and he made a snuffling sound. It would be a shame to wake him up just so she could have the pleasure of dressing and feeding him. He hadn't slept any more last night than she had. She swallowed her disappointment and turned to dress herself. If she hurried, Will might sleep until she returned.

On her way out the door, she stopped by Dora's room and said, "I decided to let Will sleep. If you're feeling bad when he wakes up, give me a call on my cell phone, and I'll come back and get him." Her cell phone was paid up for the month. She might as well use it while she could.

"Take as long as you need," Dora called after her, as Summer headed for the kitchen door.

"I will," Summer said. Since the C-Bar had once been part of the Bitter Creek Cattle Company, it was only twenty-five miles from Billy's house to the back door of the Castle. Summer spent the drive over calculating what she would say to her father.

She half expected to find one or both of her brothers having a cup of coffee in the kitchen, since they'd come home for the annual barbecue, but was relieved when the only person she found was the housekeeper Maria. She said good morning but didn't bother to ask where she might find her parents. She already knew.

Her father would be in the library, which also served as his office, organizing the day's work. Her mother would be upstairs in her studio painting.

But she found the library dark, the blinds closed, the desk surprisingly bare of papers, the room vacant. "That's strange," she muttered.

It had never occurred to her that Blackjack wouldn't be home. He'd stomped out of the house the night she'd broken up with Geoffrey, but he had come back the very next morning. And even though her parents had argued in public last night, something they'd never done before,

Summer had been certain her father would be at his desk this morning because it was from there he managed his vast ranching empire.

Her mother would certainly know where he was.

Summer left the library and bounded up the stairs, taking them two at a time, hurrying down the hall to her mother's studio. She knocked, but didn't wait for an answer, because her mother ignored the rest of the world when she was working.

To her astonishment, her mother's studio was also vacant, though bright sun streamed in through the skylight and bare windows and reflected off the white walls. The room smelled strongly of turpentine, and Summer crossed and screwed the lid on an open can. She wiped her hands on a rag she found on the counter, which was cluttered with squeezed tubes of oil paint, some of them also open. She wondered how her mother kept from suffocating while she worked.

The trip across the room brought her close enough to see what her mother was painting. Summer stood stunned, gazing at the canvas in awe.

Eve Blackthorne didn't merely paint beautifully, she only painted beautiful things. Her work had always been a source of quiet splendor and grace in a turbulent world. Which made the canvas on her mother's easel all the more horrifying.

Summer had never seen anything so vicious. So violent. So terrifyingly merciless.

Threatening purple storm clouds roiled across a lavender sky. A longhorn cow was backed up against a wood-railed fence, knee-deep in snow, her head lowered, one horn impaling the writhing body of a slavering wolf.

Another wolf gripped her by the throat, while a third razed her flank with razor-sharp white teeth. Her calf lay dead at her feet, its throat ripped out, blood staining the wind-drifted snow.

It was obvious the besieged animal could not survive, that it was only a matter of time before she succumbed to the ferocious attack and was devoured, along with her calf.

As Summer stared at the painting, her stomach convulsed in fear and revulsion and pity. Yet she couldn't take her eyes off it. What had happened to her mother in the month Summer had been gone that had caused her to paint a scene like this? What did it mean?

Summer left the room on the run, nearly stumbling and falling down the stairs in her haste to get back to the kitchen. "Maria," she called out. "Where are my parents?"

Maria backed up against the sink as Summer came barreling into the kitchen. "At the roundup, Señora Coburn."

"Where's my mother?" Summer demanded impatiently.

"At the roundup," Maria repeated.

"*Both* of them are there?" Summer asked, astonished.

"*Sí,* both," Maria replied. "Your mother, she went to be with your father. To fly the helicopter." Maria made a circling motion with her finger.

Summer couldn't believe her ears. "What? Mom hasn't been on a roundup since we were kids. Are you sure?"

"*Sí,* Señora. Your father, he does not come here anymore, so your mother, she goes there to be with him."

Summer had stopped breathing as she listened to

Maria's recital. When her lungs started to burn, she gasped a breath and exhaled a prayer. "Dear God."

It seemed her father had actually left her mother, and apparently long before last night. And that her mother had joined him at the roundup to force him to spend more time with her.

"Where are they? I mean, where on Bitter Creek?" she asked.

"In the north pasture, Señora."

"Thank you, Maria," Summer said as she ran out the door. She couldn't explain her sense of urgency. She only knew she had to get to the site of the roundup without delay.

Even so, it took her nearly an hour to drive the forty-five miles of dirt roads to the holding pens in the north pasture where the calves would be branded, castrated, and vaccinated. She could see the dust and hear the anxious cows bawling for their lost calves long before she reached the first of the corrals.

She glanced up as she heard the *whup whup whup* of a helicopter driving cattle toward the pens. Several cowboys worked on horseback to keep the animals calm and moving in the right direction. She tried to see who was flying, but the sun reflected off the glass bubble, keeping the pilot a mystery.

Her mother's family, the DeWitts, had been among the first cattlemen in Texas to use helicopters to drive a herd during the roundup, and her mother had talked her father into the practice. She'd been his first pilot. He never let her fly when she was pregnant, but in the old days, in between children, her mother had always helped with the roundup.

Summer watched the helicopter veer dangerously toward a stand of squat mesquite trees, then rise over them at the last instant. The risky maneuver had her heart pounding. Her mother had always taken that sort of death-defying risk. But she wasn't as young as she used to be, and it had to be fifteen years since she'd flown a helicopter.

Summer gunned the truck engine, bouncing through potholes as she raced to reach the chuck wagon and branding fire, where she was most likely to find her father and the answer to who was flying that helicopter.

She braked her Silverado to a skidding stop when she spotted her father, whose head loomed above the men working around him. "Daddy!" she called, as she headed toward him, walking briskly, but not running, so she wouldn't spook either horses or cattle.

He broke from the circle of cowboys and headed toward her. "What are you doing here, Summer? Is something wrong?"

"Who's flying that helicopter?" she asked.

Her father glanced up as the helicopter zoomed past a lone, towering live oak, then back at her and said, "Goddamn that woman, taking chances like that."

"Is it Mom?" she asked anxiously.

He took off his hat and swatted it against his Levi's, raising a cloud of dust, then settled the Resistol back low on his forehead. "Yep."

"What's she doing up there? Are you crazy? Is she?"

"Couldn't stop her," Blackjack said. "Believe me, I tried."

"Why is she doing this?" Summer asked, watching as her mother pointed the nose of the helicopter at another bunch of cattle and started them moving toward the pens. "I didn't even know she had a current pilot's license."

"She doesn't," her father replied.

"Then why are you letting her fly?"

Her father gave a disgruntled snort. "You try keeping her on the ground."

"You're bigger than she is. You can—"

Blackjack laughed bitterly. "And have her accuse me of physically abusing her? When we're headed for divorce court? Not on your life."

"Daddy, you have to—"

Her father interrupted her with a dismissive wave of his hand. "Why did you come here, Summer? What do you want?"

Summer glanced one last time at the helicopter, then turned her attention to her father. "I want you to give Billy back his job with the TSCRA."

"I told Billy not a half hour ago that there's no work for him anywhere in this part of Texas, and he might as well sell out and move on. Did he send you here to beg for him?"

Summer blanched. "Billy was here?"

"Sure as hell was. Got to hand it to the kid. Didn't argue with me, just listened, then turned and left."

"Billy left without fighting? Without an argument? I don't believe you."

Blackjack shrugged. "Believe what you want. That boy—"

Summer was enraged at her father's dismissal of Billy, enraged at the thought of Billy giving up. Billy would never give up. Her father had to be lying. "That *boy* has more integrity and courage in his little finger than—"

"Whoa, there, Missy," her father interrupted.

Summer bit her lip. Attacking her father wasn't going to get Billy back his job. She made herself speak slowly and carefully. "It isn't fair, Daddy. Billy hasn't done you any harm. It isn't his fault I wouldn't marry Geoffrey. The choice was mine."

Her father made a disgusted sound, and she hurried to speak so he wouldn't interrupt again.

"Billy has a son to support. His mother's sick, and his sister's pregnant. He has responsibilities. He needs his job to take care of them. Please, if you ever loved me, will you do this for me?"

"You know I love you," her father said gruffly. "But—"

"Billy's more your blood than I am. He deserves a helping hand."

"It's because he's my blood that I don't want him married to you," Blackjack said. "I want him gone from here. Gone from your life."

"That isn't going to happen, Daddy."

"Then he's got zero chance of getting a job around here."

Blackjack started to turn, but Summer laid a desperate hand on his arm. "Are you saying that if I left Billy you'd help him? That you'd give him back his job with the TSCRA?"

"Are you saying you'll leave Billy if I do?" Blackjack countered.

Summer felt her throat tightening and swallowed painfully. "I can't—I won't—divorce Billy," she said. He needed to be married to protect his rights in court. "But if you give him back his job, I'd be willing to move back home. At least for a while until...until we can get all this sorted out."

Blackjack's eyes narrowed. "I'm not living at home."

"All the more reason for someone to be staying at the Castle with Mom," Summer said. "Is it a deal?"

"You promise to keep your distance from Billy?"

"If you give him back his job with the TSCRA, I'll move back home." Summer thought about her mother's promise to sell Bitter Creek when she divorced Blackjack. "So long as there is a home."

"Done." Blackjack held out his hand and Summer shook it, then turned to leave.

"Where are you going?" Blackjack said.

She stopped and glanced at him over her shoulder. "To tell Billy he's got his job back." And to find someone to keep an eye on Dora once she was gone.

"Be sure you don't stay long. We can use some help here."

Summer glanced at the helicopter, once again flying dangerously low. The first thing she intended to do was talk her mother out of the air. She had no business—

Summer gasped. The helicopter was headed for that lone live oak again. And it didn't seem to have enough altitude to get over it. "Pull it up, Mom. Up. Up. Up!"

Summer was running toward the tree, shouting as she went, but the helicopter had a mind and will of its own. "Mom!" she shouted. "Mom!"

She was a hundred yards away when the helicopter seemed to bounce off the tree, then tipped sideways, so the blades chopped into the ground, breaking off and flying in all directions. Summer ducked as a piece of metal tore past her head like shrapnel. Then she was moving again, running, breathless, desperate to reach her mother.

Chapter 12

Summer heard someone screaming and realized the horrible sounds were coming from her. She fought against the iron grasp that kept her from reaching the crumpled wreckage, clawing at the sinewy arm wrapped around her waist from behind. "Let go of me, damn you. I said let go!"

"Settle down," an angry voice said, and the arm clamped around her chest so tightly she struggled to breathe.

Summer saw the cowboy who'd reached the wreckage stick a hand inside the cockpit, then look a little past her and shake his head. She turned to see who he'd been signaling and realized her father was holding her captive. "I have to get to Momma. She's hurt, Daddy. Please let me go," she begged. "Momma's hurt."

"She's dead, Summer," her father said.

"No," she said. "No." She didn't want to believe him, but the distress in his eyes, the tremor in his voice, were too real. "She can't be dead. She can't!"

"I'm sorry, baby. She's gone."

Summer sagged against her father as a low moan tore from her throat. She felt him pick her up in his arms and pull her close as he turned and strode away from the crash.

She shoved her face hard against his chest and grabbed him around the neck, holding on tight. She and her mother had never been close. They hadn't even been friends. So why was her throat so tight it hurt to swallow? Why couldn't she stop sobbing?

"I want to go home," she said.

"We're heading for the Castle now," her father said as he set her in the passenger seat of his pickup.

"I want to go *home*," she said through the open window as he closed her inside the pickup. "I want Billy."

"You can call him from the Castle," he said. "I need to be there to meet with the authorities and make arrangements for your mother's body to be brought home."

Summer stared at the wreckage, then at her father, who was sliding behind the steering wheel of his pickup. "How can you walk away from her?" she said. "How can you just leave her there?"

"We left each other a long time ago," her father said.

"You're glad she's dead!" Summer accused. "Now you can marry that Creed woman and still keep everything!"

"I'm not sorry she's dead," Blackjack corrected as he met her gaze. "That's a whole other thing. And I would've married Lauren Creed even if we had to live on bread and water the rest of our lives."

That was a hard truth for her to hear. Especially right now.

She couldn't believe her father could be so callous about her mother's death. Then she saw his hands were trembling. And that his jaw was clamped so tight the muscles jerked. "Daddy..."

She reached out to touch his arm and he turned his head away and she heard the gurgle as he swallowed several times.

"Daddy..."

He started the engine, his movements jerky. "You coming or staying?" he said, his voice like a rusty gate, his gaze focused straight ahead, his eyes narrowed.

Summer was torn in two. She wanted to stay and offer comfort. But she couldn't leave her mother alone. She shoved open the door and got out, slamming it behind her. She faced her father and said, "I'm staying here with Momma. She shouldn't be alone."

He hesitated, then said, "Do what you need to do. I'll be back when the authorities show up."

"You never should have let her fly."

"You're right," he admitted. "I should have stopped her. Hindsight is always twenty-twenty."

"Why didn't you stop her?" she asked, tears clogging her throat. "Why didn't you make her go home?"

He rubbed a hand over his eyes. "Goddamn that woman. I don't know. Maybe I was hoping that exactly what happened would happen."

Summer gasped, and Blackjack made a pained, grunting sound.

"Hell, I didn't mean that. Summer, I didn't mean it! Don't go off half-cocked and—"

She didn't hear the rest of what he said. She'd already turned her back on him and walked away. Her knees kept threatening to buckle as she headed toward the downed helicopter.

A cowboy stepped in front of her and said, "Don't think you want to get any closer, Missy. There's a bit of gas on the ground. Could be everything'll go up in flames."

Summer shuddered. "I have to see her. I have to be with her."

"Your father'd have my hide if I let anything happen to you," the cowboy said.

"Then get a fire extinguisher from one of the trucks and keep an eye out for smoke!" Summer retorted.

"Yes, ma'am."

The cowboy stepped aside and Summer walked the rest of the way to the crushed helicopter on unsteady legs. She expected a lot of blood. She braced herself for some sort of mutilation. But her mother sat upright, belted into the seat without a visible wound. She might have been sleeping, except her mouth was contorted in a grimace of pain, and her eyes were wide open.

Summer reached out a trembling hand and closed her mother's eyes. Then her knees buckled, and she sank onto the grass near the crumpled mass of metal. She heard her cell phone ring and dug it out of her breast pocket.

"Summer? Are you all right?"

She sobbed at the sound of the one voice she'd wanted to hear. "Billy? How did you know to call me?"

"One of your dad's men called and told me what happened. I'm on my way. I'll be there as quick as I can."

"Hurry, Billy. I need you. Please hurry."

"I'm coming, Summer." He hesitated, then said, "I'm sorry about your mother."

"I never forgave her, Billy. For Russell Handy. I didn't get the chance."

It wasn't until she blurted that admission to Billy that Summer realized her unfinished business with her mother was responsible for so much of the anguish she felt. Now she would never have the chance to confront her mother about the affair with Russell Handy that had resulted in her birth. Or forgive her and find some sort of peace.

Summer's bitter grief was also fueled by the way her mother had died. It seemed so senseless.

What had made her mother so desperate to spend time at this roundup with her father? How had she ended up so jealous of Lauren Creed?

Summer would never understand why her father hadn't been able to love her mother the way he loved that other woman. It seemed awful that her mother should end up dying this way—flying a helicopter she wasn't qualified to pilot—so she could spend time with the husband who'd abandoned her.

That also meant her mother had to take a great deal of the blame for her own death. She should have been more careful, Summer thought angrily. She should have found some other way to be with Blackjack. She should have let herself be persuaded not to fly!

The forty-five minutes Summer waited for Billy seemed endless. She spent the time with her knees pulled up to her chest, her head down. No one spoke to her. No one bothered her. She was aware of the hot sun on her shoulders, the breeze feathering her hair, the cattle lowing in the pens where work had ceased.

"Summer."

Summer looked up to find Billy bending toward her and launched herself into his welcoming embrace. He held her against him, crooning solace in her ear, rocking her back and forth.

"Come on," he said. "Let's get out of here."

When she resisted, he stopped and held her at arm's length. "There's nothing more you can do for her, Summer."

"I don't want her to be alone. I can't just leave her here. I have to stay until . . . I have to stay."

She prepared herself for an argument, for a physical fight, if need be.

Billy kicked aside a shard of metal and sat down on the grass, pulling her into his lap. "All right. We'll wait here till someone comes to get her."

"Thank you, Billy," she murmured against his throat.

Her tears had dried. The sobs seemed stuck in her chest. "I wish . . ."

"I know," he said.

She let the warmth of his body and the strength of his arms comfort her. She heard the siren long before the paramedics arrived. She wondered why they bothered announcing their presence. There was no traffic out here. No suffering victim listening for the wailing siren that promised surcease from pain.

To her surprise, her brother Owen led a cavalcade of vehicles that included the sheriff, the paramedics, and her father. She struggled upright and helped pull Billy to his feet, then faced the oncoming horde.

Owen had his arms open when he reached her, and she walked into them and held him tight around the waist. She saw his eyes were red-rimmed, though there were no tears visible now.

"Are you all right?" he asked, glancing at Billy, who stood to the side with his hands in his back pockets, one hip cocked.

"Are you?" she replied, looking up into her brother's face.

His eyes were tormented. "She wasn't a good mother," he bit out. "Why the hell does this hurt so much?"

"I don't know," Summer admitted. "Did you reach Clay? Has someone called Trace in Australia?"

"I called Clay. Dad contacted Trace. He and Callie will be here for the funeral."

A fresh spurt of tears blurred Summer's vision. What a sad reason for her eldest brother to be coming home. She blinked the tears away in time to see the sheriff and her father examining the cockpit, while the paramedics freed her mother from the seat belt and lifted her onto a wheeled gurney.

"Accident, you say?" the sheriff said to her father.

"She was flying erratically," her father said. "Taking dangerous chances."

"Didn't know your wife did any flying these days," the sheriff said.

"Eve had a mind and a will of her own. There wasn't much I could do to stop her."

The sheriff lifted an eyebrow but didn't contradict Jackson Blackthorne. "You call anybody from the NTSB or the FAA to come look at the wreckage?" the sheriff asked.

"No. I didn't think of that."

"I'll take care of it," the sheriff said. One of his

deputies was stringing crime-scene tape around the helicopter. "Don't let anyone touch anything before they get here," the sheriff said.

The crime-scene tape caused Summer to stare. "Why are they doing that?" she said to Owen. "There hasn't been any crime. This was an accident."

"All accidents like this have to be investigated," Owen said. "It's the law."

It dawned on Summer what that meant. Her mother's body would have to be cut up by a medical examiner. The thought made her feel nauseated. She tried to swallow the bile that rose in her throat, but lost the battle, and leaned over and vomited onto the grass.

A moment later Billy was beside her, a handkerchief in his hand. She grabbed it and wiped her mouth.

"Come on, Summer. You need to lie down," he said. "Let's go home."

Which was when Summer realized that her mother's death hadn't done a thing to change Billy's circumstances. He still didn't have a job. And the only way her father would give it back to him was if she left Billy and moved home to the Castle.

She had the perfect excuse to make the break without Billy even knowing that it was going to be permanent. It made sense for her to stay at the Castle for a few days to help her father with arrangements for her mother's funeral, and to be there to mourn with her family and accept the condolences of their friends and neighbors.

Once Billy had his job back with the TSCRA, he'd be able to support his son and himself. And once she was gone from the house, Emma would surely come home to take care of Dora.

"I need to go back to the Castle," she said. "You understand, don't you, Billy? Daddy will need someone in the house until the funeral, and maybe for a little while afterward."

She watched the struggle on Billy's face. And realized he'd been expecting her to break and run for so long that even a good excuse couldn't camouflage her desertion. He obviously believed this was the beginning of the end for them. And he was thinking about whether to fight to keep her.

"All right," he said at last. "I suppose the whole family will want to be together to mourn."

She opened her mouth to say *You're my family now,* but the words wouldn't come. Billy would never be welcome at the Castle. He was a reminder of how her father had betrayed her mother, a reminder of all the things that had gone wrong with her parents' marriage, all the things that had led to her parents' estrangement, and finally to her mother's death.

The sound of her father's angry voice tore her attention from Billy.

"How the hell would I know how it got there!" Blackjack said.

"You can see it's an explosive device," the sheriff said. "Who'd want to kill your wife?"

Summer started toward the helicopter at a brisk walk, but she was running by the time the sheriff finished his sentence. Her brother and Billy were right behind her.

"What's going on?" Owen asked.

The sheriff pointed under the seat where her mother had been sitting. "Take a look at that."

Owen bent down for a closer look, then rose and

turned on Blackjack. "Do you know anything about this, Dad?"

"Why the hell would I?" her father said angrily.

Summer looked from her father to her brother and asked, "What is it, Owen?"

"Some sort of explosive device."

"What is it doing there?"

"At a guess, somebody wanted to make sure this helicopter didn't come down in one piece," Owen said, staring at their father. "But it must have malfunctioned. Which makes me wonder if there's any other evidence of foul play that device was supposed to destroy."

"Why are you looking at Daddy like that?" Summer asked her brother.

"Who else has a reason to want Mom dead?"

"Maybe that device wasn't intended for Mom. She isn't the only one who's been flying this helicopter. Who knows how long it's been there?" Summer argued.

Owen looked speculatively at the device, then at his father. "Who else has been flying this thing?"

"Randy Tucker," her father answered. He turned and called for the pilot, who was standing among the cowboys who were waiting for further orders.

"What is it you need?" the pilot said when he reached Blackjack.

"You got any enemies you know of?" Owen asked.

"No, sir," the pilot said.

Owen pointed out the explosives and said, "You know anything about that?"

"Shit, no!" the pilot said. "It wasn't there when I checked the helicopter before Mrs. Blackthorne's flight this morning."

"You have some reason to check the floor around the seats?" Owen asked.

"I wouldn't normally, but this morning I spilled my coffee and had to wipe it up."

Owen turned to Blackjack and said, "Seems Mom was the target after all."

"Are you accusing Daddy?" Summer asked.

"You know anybody else who wanted Mom dead?"

"The device didn't even explode, but the helicopter crashed anyway," Summer said heatedly. "Doesn't that prove it was an accident?"

One of the paramedics said, "I'd say she died before the copter crashed. Heart attack, maybe."

"There was nothing wrong with my mother's heart," Owen said.

The paramedic shrugged. "Then stroke maybe. An autopsy will tell the tale."

"Daddy didn't want Momma dead," Summer said. "He's innocent."

"But a heap of people heard him say last night that he wanted to be rid of her," the sheriff said quietly.

Summer stared at the sheriff, then at her father. Everyone might have heard her parents argue last night, but everyone wouldn't know that they'd had the same argument a thousand times over the past ten or fifteen years. That they'd said the same things—and worse—to each other time and again. That didn't mean either really wanted the other dead. Even though theirs hadn't been a love match, her parents had been committed to one another.

At least, until recently they had.

"Stay close to home till we get this straightened out," the sheriff told her father.

"I'm not going anywhere," Blackjack replied.

"Come on, Summer," Billy said as he gripped her elbow. "It's time to take you home."

"There must be some explanation for this, Billy," she said as he led her toward his pickup. "That device must have been intended for someone else."

"Take off those rose-colored glasses, Summer, and take a good look around you. Blackjack has always done what was necessary to get what he wanted. This time he just got caught at it."

Summer jerked her arm free and turned to confront Billy. "You're wrong. I know my father. He isn't capable of murder."

"That's where we differ. I think he's a ruthless sonofabitch, capable of anything."

Summer's neckhairs bristled. "Why would he need to kill her? He'd already left her. He'd already given her everything."

"Exactly," Billy said. "Can you see a man like Blackjack, who's spent his life building a place like Bitter Creek—a ranch that's been in his family for generations—just giving it all away?"

"He said he didn't care about the ranch. He said it wasn't important."

"Yeah. Sure."

"Besides, Lauren Creed has a ranch where they could live."

"Three Oaks isn't Bitter Creek," Billy said. "Not by a long shot."

"Blackjack is innocent," Summer said. "You'll see."

They'd arrived at the back door to the Castle. When Billy shut off the engine it ran for another thirty seconds before it quit. "Need to tune this damned thing," he muttered.

They sat in silence for another thirty seconds before Summer said, "Will you come for the funeral?"

"What is your family going to think if I show up?"

"You're my husband, Billy. It would cause gossip if you didn't come."

"All right," he said.

"You can meet me at the church, and we can go together from there to the cemetery," she said. Which would avoid the awkwardness of having Billy show up at the Castle with her whole family there.

Summer leaned over and kissed Billy on the cheek. She was surprised when he caught her shoulders and pulled her close and kissed her hard on the mouth.

"I'm coming to get you when this is over, Summer."

She didn't say anything. It would be easier to turn him away once she was behind the solid walls of the Castle. But she was aware for the first time of what she was giving up to help him. There hadn't been many men like Billy in her life. When she'd needed him, he'd put her first, just dropped everything and come running. And provided a rock-solid shoulder to lean on.

And, glory of glories, he was willing to fight to keep her. It had been sweet to hear him swear he was coming back to get her.

She wanted him to pick her up and carry her back home with him right this minute. But for his sake, she couldn't allow that to happen. For once, she was the one making the sacrifice. She had to stay at Bitter Creek, so Billy could have back the job he needed to take care of Will and Dora and Emma.

"Good-bye, Billy," she said. "Take care of yourself. And give Will a hug for me."

"You can give him one yourself in a couple of days."

Summer stepped out of the pickup and quietly closed the door behind her. She took a step back and waved at Billy.

He had trouble starting the engine, but once he did, he gunned it several times, then popped the clutch and spun the wheels as he backed the truck and headed away from her.

Summer hurried through the kitchen, responding to Maria's offers of condolence with a brief nod, then turning away before the look of sympathy in the woman's eyes brought her to tears again.

She hurried upstairs to her bedroom and shut the door behind her. She looked around her and realized she'd left all of this far behind her when she'd married Billy.

The scents of expensive perfume on her dressing table, which permeated the room, made her feel nauseous. She raked them all into a drawer and closed it. The stuffed animals on her bed seemed childish, and she brushed them all to the floor, then threw herself onto the bed and stuffed a pillow against her mouth and howled in pain.

The day had been a disaster.

Her mother was dead. Her marriage was over. She hadn't realized until she'd said good-bye to Billy just how much she wanted a life with him. She hadn't realized until she'd said good-bye to him just how much she loved him.

Summer sat bolt upright in bed.

I don't just like Billy Coburn as a friend. I love him. I'm deeply, hopelessly in love with him.

She grabbed the pillow again and stuffed it against her mouth to stifle the wail of misery that erupted. She loved Billy, and because she did, she had to stay away from him. Billy needed his job with the TSCRA. If she insisted on being his wife, her father would punish him by taking away his livelihood again.

There seemed to be no solution to her dilemma.

And no time to think about it over the next few days. Summer lay down the pillow and scrubbed at the tears on her face. There was work to be done. The house needed to be prepared for the arrival of her brothers, and for her mother's family, the DeWitts, who would be coming as well.

There would be time once her mother had been grieved and buried to think about her own problems.

And it was going to take quite a bit of thinking—and ingenuity—to figure out a way to convince her father that she belonged with Bad Billy Coburn.

Chapter 13

EVE BLACKTHORNE'S FUNERAL WAS DELAYED IN order to complete the autopsy required by the accidental nature of her death. The coroner's examination revealed that Eve had died of a heart attack. The attack had been precipitated by an excess of a heart medication in her system which no doctor she was currently seeing had prescribed for her. However, Jackson Blackthorne did have a prescription for the medication, and in fact, a half-empty bottle of it was found in the medicine cabinet in his bedroom.

Preliminary tests of the coffee remaining in the thermos on board the helicopter, which several cowboys told the sheriff they'd seen Blackjack hand to his wife as she strapped herself in, showed it possessed lethal amounts of Blackjack's heart medication.

The sheriff himself had been a witness to the scene the night before Eve Blackthorne's death during which Jackson Blackthorne said he should have gotten rid of his wife a long time ago.

The investigator for the National Transportation Safety Board had discovered that the main hydraulic line had been severed, and that the loss of hydraulic fluid had brought the helicopter down.

The sheriff had searched Blackjack's tool kit—with his willing permission—and found a serrated hunting knife with traces of hydraulic fluid still on the blade.

The homemade bomb under the seat possessed a simple timing mechanism—a watch that Owen remembered his father giving to his mother for their anniversary several years before. It had stopped working and she'd given it to Blackjack to send back to the manufacturer for repair.

Obviously, it still wasn't working right. It had failed to detonate the homemade bomb that had been put there allegedly to destroy all evidence of Eve Blackthorne's murder.

"Everyone thinks I did it," Blackjack said, as he paced the length of Ren's bedroom from one wall to the other. "Do they really think that if I wanted my wife dead I'd be stupid enough to leave so many clues pointing right back at me?"

"Are you going to be arrested?" Ren asked.

Blackjack couldn't look her in the face. Her eyes were too frightened. "If I had to guess, the sheriff will serve his warrant at the funeral."

"Will they keep you in jail until the trial?"

"I'm a solid, law-abiding citizen with roots in the community—and the judge is a friend of mine. I'm sure I can make bail. That isn't going to help much if I can't figure out who hates me enough to kill my wife and frame me for it."

"She did it."

"What?"

"Eve did it," Ren said, her eyes huge and liquid with sorrow. "To keep us apart."

He crossed and sat beside her on the bed and lifted her into his lap. "No, sweetheart. She didn't want us together, but she was too selfish to kill herself."

Ren shook her head. "You underestimate her. She was full of hate and envy. Think about it. Who else had access to all those things? She was the only one in a position to make it look like you murdered her."

Blackjack frowned. "It doesn't make sense. What does she gain?"

"I told you. She keeps us apart. You might have forgotten, but I haven't. She arranged a death once before to separate us, but it didn't work. This time she's planned more carefully."

"Damn her to hell," Blackjack said.

"I'm sure she's there now, laughing at the two of us," Ren said.

"If she did do it, she didn't do it alone," Blackjack said thoughtfully.

"What makes you say that?"

"She'd need help with the bomb, for one thing. And figuring out where to cut the hydraulic line and maybe even how much medication to dose herself with."

"Who would she know with that sort of knowledge, who'd also be willing to help her?" Ren asked.

"Damned if I know," Blackjack said. "But I sure as hell intend to find out."

"When's the funeral? I mean, will you have time to find out before you're arrested?"

"Hell, the funeral's tomorrow."

"Can't you explain all this to the sheriff?" Ren said.

Blackjack sighed. "He'd probably point out that I could just as easily have aimed all the evidence at myself with the intention of arguing that nobody as smart as I am would make so many dumb mistakes. No, I've got to find the bastard who helped Eve make all this happen."

Ren shivered and said, "Hold me."

"I am holding you."

"Lie down with me," she amended. "Make love to me."

She didn't have to ask him twice. Blackjack laid her down, but refused to let her undress him. "I want to take my time, love."

He'd missed all the hours of necking when they were teenagers, the eager anticipation of the sexual act with the woman he loved. Missed the teenage anxiety of not knowing when or if he'd ever feel the silky texture of her skin. Of wondering whether her nipples would be pink or dusky brown.

In one insane moment on a sunny afternoon, he'd become her fantasy lover. The experience had been something he'd never forgotten, and the spiritual bond they'd forged that long-ago afternoon had been strong enough to tie them together for a lifetime. But he'd never had the opportunity to sip at the fount. He'd swallowed everything whole without fully tasting.

Now he feared he would never have the chance to love her at his leisure.

He kissed her sweetly, as though they were newly met, as though kissing was all they could do. He deepened his kisses and reached for her breast tentatively, as though he'd never touched her before, as though he expected her to be innocently shy. And in fact, she tensed for a moment at the first hesitant brush of his knuckles against her clothing.

He reached beneath her shirt to unhook her bra, not nearly so clumsy as he'd been as a youth. Petting brought heated bodies and panting breaths. He kept his hands above her waist, as though that was all he was allowed.

Blackjack backed off to let the wanting grow. He kissed Ren's mouth, letting his tongue taste her, plumping her lips with his, nibbling gently on her lower lip. He tongued the frenulum behind her upper lip, then tested the sharpness of her teeth. Suddenly, he thrust deep, in an imitation of the sex act.

Ren moaned and her body arched toward his.

He held tight to her waist, keeping them separated, imagining them as young and innocent lovers, without any knowledge of what it meant to go all the way. Except it was impossible not to know, when they were both experienced adults.

He hadn't been nearly so patient as a young man. He hadn't appreciated the finer points of necking and petting. His aim had been to achieve the ultimate pleasure as quickly as possible and repeat it as often as he could. Now he knew how to savor a fine wine...and a fine woman.

"I love you, Jackson," Ren said, her kisses increasing in fervor.

"I love you, too," he said, keeping his kisses slow and easy, refusing to be rushed. "I want you to leave Three

Oaks and come live with me at the Castle," he murmured.

She leaned back and stared at him, her eyes troubled.

He pulled her close again and kissed away the wrinkles in her brow. "Not right away," he said. "But soon. As soon as you can."

"What am I supposed to do about Three Oaks?"

"I thought you told me Sam could manage it on his own."

"He can."

"So give it to him," Blackjack said.

She broke away from their embrace and sat up. "I don't want to do that."

"Why not?"

"Because then this damned feud will go on for another generation."

"I don't want your land, Ren," he said, caressing her cheek with his thumb. "I want you."

"I know that," she said, brushing aside his hand. "But you can't have me without the land."

He smiled ruefully. "What is Sam going to say about that?"

"The land isn't his, it's mine, to do with as I please. It seems to me the best thing to do is merge Three Oaks and Bitter Creek. Once the two spreads are united, there won't be an excuse for our families to fight anymore."

"Some folks don't need an excuse," Blackjack said. "I figure Sam is one of those. How's he going to take all this change?"

"He won't like it, but he'll get used to it. He can handle the cutting horse end of the business. Sam's got a good eye for a fast horse with a quick stop."

"You think he'd be willing to work for me?" Blackjack asked, lying back and crossing his arms behind his head.

"What choice will he have?"

Blackjack grimaced. "He could leave. Have you considered that possibility?"

"It's a risk I'm willing to take for the chance to end this feud."

"All right, then," he said. "Once I get myself cleared of murder charges, we'll work it out so that when we get married, Three Oaks will become a part of Bitter Creek, and all our kids will inherit equally."

She snuggled back down against him, waiting until his arms enfolded her again before she spoke. "I like the sound of that," she said. "Our kids. What about Summer . . . and Billy? Shouldn't they both be included, especially now that they're married?"

"I'm not convinced their marriage is going to last," Blackjack said.

"Why not?" Ren asked. "I believe they genuinely care for each other."

Blackjack thought of the deal he'd made with Summer to come home in exchange for giving Billy back his job. "I don't want to encourage it," he said.

"It seems to me you owe that boy more than you've given him. Considering everything, he's turned out to be a pretty decent man."

"He's not good enough for Summer," he said.

"Not good enough? Or not rich enough?"

"Is it wrong to want more for her?"

"A good man is worth a great deal," she said, leaning over to kiss his mouth.

"I think you may be right about her loving him," Blackjack admitted reluctantly. "She agreed to come home if I'd get him his job back."

"Think of all the trials that boy has suffered and still managed to triumph. That's your blood in him."

"He did have quite a reputation with the TSCRA. His boss had twenty fits when I said I wanted him fired. Told me I was a jackass for depriving the Association of someone as talented and whip smart and steadfast as Billy Coburn. Not a 'bad' word about him," Blackjack admitted.

"He's a fighter, Jackson. You'll never put that boy down for long."

"I don't want to put him down. I just want him to leave Summer alone."

"Why not help the two of them, instead of standing in their way?" Ren said.

"That boy would as soon spit in my eye as take any help from me," Blackjack said.

"Surely a clever man like you can figure out a way to get him to accept it."

"I'll think about it," Blackjack said. "Come here, Ren, and kiss me."

He slid a hand around her nape and she willingly bent over him, their mouths meeting in a kiss as tender as any they'd ever shared.

The sound of a horn outside the window made her jerk away. She jumped off the bed ahead of him and raced to the window to look out. "It's the sheriff's car," she said. "What do you suppose he wants here?"

"Best way to find out is to go down and ask," Blackjack said.

Ren grabbed for her bra and struggled to get it back on, while Blackjack headed down the stairs ahead of her. He shoved open the screen door and invited the sheriff inside, surprised when his deputy stepped in behind him.

"What's going on, Sheriff?" he asked.

"Jackson Blackthorne, you're under arrest for the murder of your wife Evelyn DeWitt Blackthorne."

"Aw, come on, Grady. Can't this wait till after the funeral?" Blackjack said in disgust.

"I have to cuff you, Mr. Blackthorne. Turn around," the deputy said.

Blackjack felt the hot flush start on the back of his neck. "It's Sunday, Grady. It's going to be damned hard to find a judge to come to a bail hearing before Monday morning."

"Put your hands behind your back, Mr. Blackthorne," the sheriff said, "so my deputy can cuff you."

Blackjack wanted to resist, but he could hear Ren coming down the stairs, and he didn't want her involved in some ridiculous fracas. He turned around and felt the cold metal cuffs being ratcheted down tight on his wrists.

It wouldn't be the first night he'd ever spent in jail. He'd gotten in trouble once in his misspent youth and his father had left him in the Bitter Creek County Jail overnight to think things over. It wasn't an experience he wanted to repeat. The place was lit up too brightly, and it smelled of vomit from the Saturday-night drunks who were its usual tenants. But he wasn't being given a choice.

"I want to call my lawyer," Blackjack said as he turned to face the sheriff.

"You can call him from jail," the sheriff replied.

By then, Ren had reached the kitchen. She stared in alarm at his cuffed wrists. "What's going on?"

"I've been arrested a day early," Blackjack said.

"Why?" she asked, her eyes wide with fright.

"To keep the two of you from fleeing, ma'am," the deputy blurted.

The sheriff glared at him, but the cat was already out of the bag.

"What are you talking about?" Blackjack said.

The sheriff straightened his gunbelt nervously, then said, "We know about the trip you planned with Mrs. Creed, Mr. Blackthorne. Once the NTSB confirmed that your helicopter had been tampered with, we had the FAA check to see if you'd booked a flight anywhere. You hadn't booked a commercial flight, but your corporate pilot had filed a flight plan based on an e-mail you sent him last week."

Blackjack stared at the sheriff blankly, then exchanged a look with Ren, whose lower lip was clasped in her teeth. It took him a moment to figure out what Ren had apparently already divined. "Goddamn that woman," he muttered.

"A trip going where?" Ren asked, when Blackjack didn't.

"Costa Rica, ma'am," the deputy supplied. "They don't have an extradition treaty with the U.S."

"Bad move, Mr. Blackthorne," the sheriff said. "You're going to have to stick around to stand trial for murder. And since it's doubtful bail will be allowed when you've proven yourself a flight risk, you're going to have to wait for trial in jail."

Blackjack was sorry now that he'd allowed himself to be handcuffed, because he thought he might have been able to take the two men and escape with Ren. Costa Rica didn't sound like a half-bad idea, especially when Eve had arranged to leave a hanging noose so tightly knotted around his neck.

"Let's go, gentlemen," he said.

"What can I do?" Ren asked frantically.

"Call my lawyer Harry Blackthorne, at DeWitt & Blackthorne in Houston," Blackjack said. "Tell him what's happened. Then get some sleep. And don't worry about me. I'll be fine."

He left her standing in the kitchen, her eyes forlorn. She knew how high the odds were stacked against him. And fate seemed determined to keep them apart.

He had to hand it to Eve. Her trap had been cleverly baited, artfully sprung. And he was well and truly caught.

Sam felt relieved at his mother's narrow escape. Jackson Blackthorne was in jail. With the wealth of evidence mounting against him, it didn't look like he'd be getting out in this lifetime. Sam had been shocked, however, when he learned his mother had planned to run away with the blackguard. He hadn't foreseen that. He just thanked his lucky stars it hadn't happened.

Eve Blackthorne's funeral had been held that afternoon, and the town was full of mourners from all over the country who'd come to pay homage to the famous artist. Sam had seen her art up close, and while it was technically amazing, it left him emotionally cold.

When the knock came on his kitchen door, Sam hurried to answer it, grinning broadly when he saw his older sister Callie standing there with his nephew Eli, his niece Hannah, and his littlest niece Henrietta. He saw them every Christmas, but it wasn't often enough.

"Come in, come in," he said, waving them inside.

"Hi, Uncle Sam," Eli said.

"Good Lord, boy, you must've grown six inches since I saw you last!" At fifteen, Eli looked more every day like the Blackthorne he was.

At eight, Hannah was too old to climb into his lap the way she used to do. But she helped three-year-old Henrietta scramble into his arms. "Hey there, Henry. How ya doin'?" he said.

"Take me for a ride," Henrietta said. "Go fast!"

Sam laughed and said, "Let me greet your mother first."

He looked up at Callie and realized, now that she was no longer standing behind her children, that she was pregnant. "Looks like you've been busy," he said with a smile.

She patted her round belly and smiled at him. "Should be here before Christmas."

"Boy or girl?" Sam asked.

"We don't know yet. I'd love another girl. Trace would like a boy."

"Where is he?" Sam asked. Normally Trace Blackthorne came visiting with Callie and the kids. Sam didn't like the man, but he was cordial for Callie's sake. To his chagrin, he was indebted to Trace, who'd forced him to sober up and learn to drive, and renovated this house so Sam could live in it, all because he'd loved

Callie and wanted her family to be independent enough that she could marry him and leave Three Oaks.

"He's spending some time with Owen and Clay. They're going over the facts and the timeline of events that led up to their mother's death, looking for anything that might clear Blackjack or lead to another suspect. They haven't found zip. The evidence against Blackjack is overwhelming, and of course, they know their parents' marriage has been especially rocky lately. I'm afraid Summer is the only one clinging to hope that her father will be cleared."

"He ought to be convicted," Sam said. "He's guilty as sin."

"It doesn't look good for him," Callie conceded.

"Can I go horseback riding, Mom?" Eli said.

"Can I go horseback riding, Mom?" Hannah parroted.

Callie made a face at Sam. "Please excuse their manners, but would you mind if they go for a ride?"

"Francie and Homer are in the corral. I brought them in from the pasture when I heard you guys were coming," Sam said. "You know where the tack is."

"Thanks, Uncle Sam," Eli said as he raced back out the door for the stable.

"Thanks, Uncle Sam," Hannah echoed, following after him.

"I want to go riding, too," Henrietta said, tugging at Sam's shirt.

"Sure, sprite. Just give me another minute to talk with your mom."

"Don't take off for that ride around the house with Henry right away," Callie said.

"Why not?" Sam asked.

"Because Bay and her twins left the Castle a few minutes after me. They should be here any minute."

Even as she finished speaking they could hear car doors slamming.

"Slow down," Sam heard Bay shout.

A moment later two tiny boys trotted into the house on stubby legs and ran over to stand in front of Sam's knees.

"Hi, Sam," his sister Bay said. "Once Jake and James heard Callie's kids were headed this way, they insisted on coming for a visit, too."

"I'm glad they did," he said. "Hello, Jake. Hello, James."

"We had chicken spots!" Jake said.

"We had to scratch!" James said.

"I'm glad to see you're all better," Sam said. "What can I do for you today?"

"Ride, Unca Sam," they said together.

Sam turned to greet Bay and laughed. She was also pregnant. Which reminded him of Emma. "There's someone the two of you have to meet."

"Hang on to my shirt, Henry," Sam said to the little girl, as he caught up one eighteen-month-old boy in each arm. "Give us a push, will you, Callie? Come on along, Bay."

"Where are we going, Sam?" Bay asked as she trailed Callie and the wheelchair.

"You'll see." He directed Callie through the house and out the front door onto the porch, where Emma sat in one of the two white wooden rockers knitting.

She stood up immediately and set her knitting aside.

The instant she did, Sam's two sisters exchanged wide-eyed glances with him.

"Sam! You didn't say anything about getting married," Callie chastised. She turned to Bay and said, "Why didn't you tell me?"

"I didn't have a clue," Bay said.

Sam realized he'd embarrassed Emma and set the twins on their feet so he would be able to take one of her hands and explain. "I'm sorry, Callie, Bay. I didn't mean to give you the wrong idea. I'm not married. This is my housekeeper. You remember Emma Coburn, don't you, Callie?"

Callie's jaw dropped. "You're so beautiful! Oh, I'm so sorry. That came out wrong. It's just, the last time I saw you—"

"I was fourteen and looked like a bed slat," Emma said with a grin.

"Exactly," Callie said with a laugh.

"How did you end up working for my scapegrace brother?" Bay asked.

"He needed help and I needed a job," Emma said.

"Ride, Unca Sam," the twins said, dragging on his arms.

"I've got to go," Sam said. "I'll leave you three girls here to get acquainted."

Sam ignored the desperate look Emma shot him. She didn't have any female friends that Sam knew of, and with pregnancy in common, the three women should have an easy time finding things to talk about.

He spent the rest of the afternoon wrestling with his niece and nephews, feeding them cookies, and enjoying a glass of iced tea on the porch with his sisters and Emma. It was one of the most enjoyable days he'd spent in a long time.

There was a silver lining in every dark cloud, he thought. If Jackson Blackthorne hadn't murdered his wife, Sam wouldn't have had this chance to get together with his sisters and introduce them to Emma.

He wanted Callie and Bay to like Emma, because he was pretty sure he was going to make her one of the family. That is, if he could convince her to marry him.

He had reason to hope.

Just yesterday, after he'd done some carpentry work in the heat of the sun, he'd taken off his T-shirt on the back porch to wipe down the sweat behind his neck and under his arms.

And caught her watching him.

She'd made a startled sound and hurried away from the screen door, but he'd been encouraged. A woman didn't spend time looking at a man who didn't interest her.

She'd glanced at him more than once this afternoon, as he'd played with the children on the back porch. He wanted her to consider him as a potential father. He loved kids, and he wanted her to see that being in a wheelchair didn't keep him from being both a source of authority and a good deal of fun.

As his sisters made their farewells, each of them hugging Emma, he sat in his wheelchair on the back porch beside her, his arm draped possessively around her waist.

The tail of dust from their Jeeps was just settling

when Emma pulled away and said, "I wish you hadn't done that."

"Done what?"

"Introduced me to your sisters as though I were something more than your housekeeper."

Sam realized he could explain away what he'd done or use it as an opportunity to let Emma know how he felt about her. "I wish you were more than my housekeeper," he said. "I think you're a very special person, Emma. I'd like to get to know you better."

He heard her swallow noisily. "I'm pregnant," she said.

He smiled. "I've noticed."

"That doesn't bother you?"

He looked her in the eye and said, "I can't have kids of my own. I think of you being pregnant as a gift from God."

She smiled and said, "You're a very special man, Sam Creed."

He reached out a hand to her and waited. It was a long wait, but at last she put her hand in his. He tugged her toward him, and when he could reach her waist, he lifted her into his lap.

"I'm always surprised at how strong you are," she said, bracing herself on his muscular shoulders as she settled into his lap. "And since you caught me looking, I'll admit you have some pretty spectacular abs. But I'm too heavy to be sitting on you."

He smiled again. "You're light as a feather."

"You couldn't feel a feather," she said tartly, "and I assure you I'm no feather."

"Please don't go," he said, looking up into her eyes.

She stayed where she was, but she kept both hands in front of her, folded together in her lap.

He rubbed a lock of her bright red hair between his fingers, then lifted it to his nose and inhaled the scent of her shampoo. "Women always smell so good."

She laughed softly and leaned over to smell his hair. "I'm glad you think so, but we're using the same shampoo."

He laughed, too. And raised his face just as she lowered hers. He felt her hesitation and waited, letting her come to him.

The touch of her lips was electric. There was nothing wrong with the feeling in his lips, nothing wrong with his taste buds. He was overwhelmed with sensation as her soft lips pressed against his, pliant and giving.

"Relax," she said as her arms slid around his neck. "I can feel your shoulder muscles are all bunched up."

"I haven't done this in a while," he said. "I'm a little nervous."

"That's all right," she said, lowering her mouth to his. "I haven't done much of this lately, either."

But she was damned good at it, Sam thought, as she pressed butterfly kisses on his neck and throat, then let her tongue trace the shell of his ear. "Let me," he said, returning the favor.

She moaned in pleasure and tightened her hold around his neck.

"Emma," he murmured. "I want to see you."

She froze in his arms. "I'm ugly. My breasts are enormous and—"

Sam laughed. "I'm sorry, Emma, but men pay a fortune to see pictures of enormous breasts. I promise you I'll enjoy them."

She crossed her arms over her stomach and said, "I stick out a foot."

He put his hand on her pregnant belly for the first time, his touch reverent. "Believe me, I find this belly of yours a bonus."

"You're just saying that to get me naked."

"Is it going to work?"

She laughed and stood up. "Not on the first date. What kind of girl do you think I am?" She sobered as she realized what she'd said. Pregnant and unwed, she was exactly "that kind of girl." She stared at him from stricken eyes, then hurried from the porch.

"Emma, don't go. Emma, it doesn't matter."

But of course it did. She was pregnant with some other man's child. Some man she'd seduced...as she'd just now been seducing him. And the bastard had left her high and dry. Why should Emma think he would treat her any differently?

To make matters worse, he was her boss. What if things went wrong between them and he decided he wanted her gone. What would happen to her if she lost this job?

He was going to have to take his time and tread carefully. He was going to have to find a way to convince her that he wasn't like the man who'd taken her favors and abandoned her. He had to convince her that he was willing and able to take care of her and her baby. That he wanted to be a husband and father.

And her lover.

Sam realized he was trembling. He wasn't sure what kind of lover he was going to be. He hadn't had sex with a woman since he'd lost the use of his legs. He'd tried once with a prostitute in Houston, but the whole thing had seemed so sordid he hadn't wanted to repeat it. The fact was, he never knew when or whether he could get it up. It happened when it happened.

He would have to love her in other ways.

She'd revealed her insecurities about being seen naked. He hadn't been able to share his own. He'd made himself as strong as he could from the waist up, where he still had functioning muscles and feeling and spent enough time in the sun to toast his skin a rich brown.

But from the waist down, he was as white as a dead fish, and his muscles were atrophied from disuse. He was afraid she wouldn't think he was much of a bargain. He was glad she'd put off the moment of truth, so he could hang on a little longer to his dream of what it would be like the first time they made love.

In his mind it was always perfect, wonderful. She was understanding and forgiving of his shortcomings. He was a considerate and tender and satisfying lover.

But he didn't dare wait too long. There was always the chance her lover would find out she was pregnant and come to claim her and the baby. He wanted her legally tied to him long before that happened.

"Sam?"

Sam turned to find Emma standing in the kitchen doorway. "What is it, Emma?"

"I was going to take a bath and cool off. I wondered if you might like to join me."

Sam thought of all the reasons he should say no thanks. And how often he'd fantasized about exactly what Emma was suggesting.

"Go start the water," he said at last. "I'll be right there."

Chapter 14

SUMMER HAD FORGOTTEN HOW MANY DEWITT cousins she had, but she was reminded when they all showed up for the funeral and she had to find places to put them in the Castle.

Her grandfather DeWitt had been married twice, so Eve and her sister Ellen had a stepsister Elizabeth. Her aunt Ellen had two sons about Summer's age, while her aunt Liz had three sons and a tomboy daughter. Crazy as it sounded, all the kids were DeWitts, since both sisters had married distant DeWitt cousins.

It was easy to tell which males went with which aunts, because Aunt Ellen's sons were both blonds, while Aunt Liz's boys had hair as dark as any Blackthorne. The tomboy had short spiked hair dyed blue.

The DeWitts owned a ranch nearly as large as Bitter Creek, and each of the three DeWitt girls, Eve and Ellen and Elizabeth, had been named as one another's heirs to ensure that the land stayed in one piece. Aunt Liz had died five years ago. Now that Summer's mom was dead, Aunt Ellen was the sole owner of the DeWitt ranch.

Because the DeWitts had always had more sons than their ranch could keep busy, they'd embarked on many and varied businesses. In the early twentieth century one enterprising DeWitt and an equally ambitious Blackthorne had started a law firm in Houston called DeWitt & Blackthorne. Now the firm had offices in every major metropolitan area in the United States and the capitals of several foreign nations.

Ellen's sons were both already attorneys and Summer learned that two of Liz's three sons were headed to law school. No word yet what the tomboy daughter planned.

Her cousins seemed to have a friendly rivalry going over who would be the richest by the time they were thirty. Considering the high jinks they'd pulled and the tricks they'd played on one another over the years, she was betting they'd all end up in jail long before then.

It had been a relief when Trace and Owen and Clay came home, even though the addition of Trace and Owen's wives and all their kids made the Castle crowded and chaotic. Her father had been around when her brothers and their families first arrived, but when Owen-the-lawman began asking questions for which her father had no answers, he'd disappeared.

Summer had a feeling she knew where he'd gone, but whenever anyone asked, she said he'd asked to be alone to grieve. Her suspicions were confirmed when the sheriff came by to inform the family that he'd arrested Blackjack at Three Oaks for murder, reiterating the overwhelming evidence, and explaining why Blackjack was unlikely to be allowed to post bail.

"I don't care how much evidence there is," Summer had told the sheriff. "My father didn't murder my mother."

When she'd looked around the library, she realized

that every one of her brothers believed he was guilty. But they were only looking at the facts. And the facts didn't tell the whole story.

Maybe because she'd been a girl, Blackjack had revealed more of himself to her than to her brothers. She knew Jackson Blackthorne better than any of them, and their father—and yes, he was *her father* in every way that counted—wasn't capable of doing what he'd been accused of doing.

"You'll be sorry you didn't stand behind Daddy," she said. "Because you're wrong about him."

But she had no idea how to prove her father innocent. And it was troubling—frightening, actually—to know that both Owen and Clay, who'd spent their lives catching criminals and prosecuting them, sided with the sheriff.

When she was finally alone in the library, Summer had another troubling thought. If her father was in jail, how was he going to help Billy get his job back with the TSCRA? And if Billy didn't get his job back, how was he going to survive?

Then it dawned on her that if her father was in jail, someone would have to run Bitter Creek. Since her brothers all had lives that took them away from the ranch, the job would fall to her. And since she would need help, she could make Billy her foreman and pay him to provide it.

Summer sat at her father's desk and ran her fingers over the scars left in the wood by spurs and bootheels over the years. Bitter Creek had been run from behind this desk for generations. And now she was sitting here.

She picked up the phone and punched in Billy's number, telling herself to stay calm and choose her words carefully. Billy was a proud man, and she wanted him to accept the job.

"Hi," she said.

"Hi," he replied.

"I wanted to make sure you're going to be at the memorial service at the First Baptist Church. It starts at two."

"I'll be there."

"I'd like us to go from there in the same car to the cemetery," she said.

"Fine."

"There are limousines for the family."

"Fine."

"Are you all right?" she asked. Billy wasn't normally talkative, but he sounded downright taciturn.

"I'm fine."

She wished she could see his face. Then she would know what was wrong. Because something was. She thought about confronting him over the phone, but realized she didn't want to start an argument that he could end by hanging up.

"I'll save a seat for you at church," she said.

"Fine," he said, and hung up.

Summer laid the phone very carefully in the cradle. Probably he was just nervous about having to meet all her relatives. It was a sure bet he wasn't looking forward to being in the same room with her brothers. A lot of eyes were going to be on him, comparing him to the other Blackthornes, noting all the similarities—and all the differences.

Summer wondered if Billy had a decent suit to wear. When he'd buried his father, he'd worn a shirt and tie, but no jacket. He'd said it was because of the heat, but Summer remembered doubting that he had one.

She picked up the phone to call and offer Billy one of her brothers' suits, then put it down again. Somehow she knew he wouldn't take it. And he'd be insulted by the offer. He'd know she was worried about appearances, something he disdained. And really, what difference did it make what he wore?

She'd made him her friend when he dressed in ripped T-shirts and jeans and defied anyone to judge him by appearances. Once he was here at Bitter Creek helping her run things, everyone would have to acknowledge what she'd known for a long time. There was a great deal more to Billy Coburn than the clothes on his back. He was as good a man as any Blackthorne.

When Summer reached the church just before 2:00 p.m., Billy wasn't there. She made excuses for his absence as she greeted her parents' friends and neighbors at the church. "He's coming. His mother hasn't been well."

She waited until the very last second before she agreed to be seated in the front pew and then wouldn't let anyone else sit beside her, leaving a looming space between her and Trace and his family. Owen and Bay and their twins sat in the pew behind her, along with Clay. She managed a smile over her shoulder when Owen laid a comforting hand on her shoulder.

"He'll be here," she whispered. He'd said he was coming.

But the organist, who'd also arrived late, started playing and the minister was making his way to the pulpit and Billy still wasn't there. Summer couldn't imagine what had happened to him. What if he'd had an accident? What if he was lying dead beside the road?

The minister said a prayer, but Summer kept her eyes open during the whole of it, glancing back down the aisle furtively in search of her missing husband. It was all she could do to keep herself from leaping up and running from the church to hunt for him. Where was Billy? Why wasn't he there?

Summer couldn't listen to the service. She was too aware that Billy had left her alone in this most public of moments. Too aware of the pitying glances her brother Trace shot in her direction. Too aware that she wanted her brothers' approval of her choice of husband, and that Billy had let her—and himself—down by failing to show up for her mother's funeral.

Summer closed her eyes to cut off the tears sliding down her cheeks and suddenly felt herself being nudged sideways on the wooden bench by a male hip, at the same time as a handkerchief was thrust in her hand. Summer opened her eyes, and the instant she saw Billy, smothered a sob of relief in the handkerchief. "Where have you been?" she whispered when she could speak. "I thought something terrible had happened to you."

"We'll talk about it later," he said. "Hold Will, while I set down some of this stuff."

Summer realized Billy had brought a diaper bag with him, along with a handful of Will's toys. Will clambered into her lap, Brownie clutched tight under his arm, and pointed over her shoulder at the twins behind her, giggling at the sight of the two identical boys.

Summer felt herself smile inside. This was how it was

supposed to be. Her and Billy and their little boy, a normal, happy family, just like her brothers' families.

Summer didn't hear any more of the end of the service for her mother than she had of the beginning, because Will provided a constant distraction. Summer wondered why Billy hadn't left him at home and realized that might explain why he was so late. Maybe Dora had taken a turn for the worse. She waited until they were alone in a limousine together, headed for the cemetery, to ask, "Is your mother all right?"

"She's having a bad day," Billy said. He set Will on the floor with a pegged wooden PlaySkool toy and handed him a tiny wooden hammer.

"I didn't want her to have to take care of Will," Billy explained, talking a little more loudly so he could be heard over Will's pounding. "So I brought him along, figuring I'd drop him off and let Emma take care of him this afternoon. When I got there, I changed my mind."

Summer saw the morose look on Billy's face and said, "Is Emma all right? Is there some problem with her pregnancy?"

"Emma's just fine." He turned to her, his eyes alight with anger, and said, "I caught her sitting on the back porch in Sam Creed's lap, the two of them coiled around one another like snakes. I could hardly tell where one began and the other let off."

Summer laughed. "Good for Emma!"

"She's a pregnant woman. She's—"

"Still a woman," Summer interrupted. "Being pregnant doesn't turn you into a mushroom, Billy. I say again, good for her. Sam Creed is a hardworking rancher, and any woman would be lucky to have him."

Billy harrumphed. "Once their lips were unlocked, he had the nerve to tell me he's proposed to Emma."

"Why are you so upset?" Summer asked. "Don't you think Emma wants to marry him?"

"If I hadn't left Bitter Creek to seek my damned fortune, if I'd been home to take care of her, Emma would never have gotten pregnant, and she wouldn't be forced into marrying the first man who asks, just to get a father for her baby."

"Sam wouldn't have proposed to Emma unless he loved her. And from what you say you saw, it appears she's just as much in love with him. If he loves her, they're bound to be happy together. There's nothing to blame yourself for. Just be happy that Emma's found someone who'll love her and her baby. When are they getting married?"

"Sam wants to make it soon. He wants the baby to have his name."

"See, I was right. He does love her. And he'll love Emma's child like it was his own. Just you wait and see."

Billy glanced at her and said, "She hasn't said yes... yet."

Summer smiled. "She will."

When they arrived at the cemetery, Summer talked the chauffeur into watching Will while he played on the floor of the back seat, so she and Billy could spend some time at her mother's graveside.

Summer made sure Billy said hello to each of her brothers and their wives before they moved off to stand alone at the head of her mother's casket.

"I wish my mother could be here to see this," Billy said.

Summer turned to him, startled by the comment.

"Eve Blackthorne caused my mother a lot of heartache," he said. "She arranged for her to marry my father. She gave them a piece of land so my mother would have a home she wouldn't want to leave, tying her even tighter to that mean bastard. She paid my mother to keep my existence a secret from my real father. And she made my stepfather ashamed of himself for taking money to marry a woman he didn't love and raise a son he didn't want."

"I'm sorry you've lost your mother," Billy said. "But I can't say I'm sorry she's gone."

Summer didn't know what to say. It was impossible to defend her mother against Billy's charges. They were true. And she had no station of her mother's goodness with which to counter them.

Summer didn't know how she was supposed to feel. She only knew what she felt, a horrible, breathtaking ache inside because her mother—humanly flawed and unhappy—was dead.

When the limousine delivered them back at the church, where Billy had left his pickup, he asked, "When are you coming home? Will misses you."

"I miss him, too," Summer said. "Surely you can see I have to stay at the Castle, at least until my father's been cleared. Somebody has to run things."

Billy finished strapping Will in his car seat and turned to stare at her. "I do see. At last, you get to be mistress of Bitter Creek."

"The work is there. Someone has to do it. I could use your help."

He shook his head. "That's your dream, Summer. Not mine."

"Why can't it be yours, Billy? What's wrong with us making a life together at Bitter Creek? No more worry about money. Ever."

She watched Billy's eyes narrow. Saw his lips flatten.

Will cried and strained against the car seat. "Go, Daddy."

"We're leaving soon, Will," he said, all signs of anger at her gone from the voice he used with Will. He closed the door and headed around the front of the pickup, Summer on his heels.

"What's wrong with my suggestion? You're entitled to a piece of Bitter Creek," she said to his back. "You're a Blackthorne, too."

He whirled on her and said, "All being a Blackthorne has ever meant to me is a bloodied nose or a punch in the kidney. I don't want any part of it. And neither should you. There's not one drop of Blackthorne blood in your veins!"

Summer stared at Billy, her face bleaching white.

"I'm what Blackjack has made me," Billy said. "And so are you. The way I figure it, that makes us pretty much the same. Nothing and nobody."

Fury rose in Summer at Billy's indictment of her and of himself. Her cheeks flamed and her hands balled into knots of anger. Her voice vibrated with rage. "You can't deny who you are, Billy, any more than I can. You're a Blackthorne through and through. And so am I!"

"I don't want a thing from him. And I won't take charity from you."

"You already have!" she snapped.

She saw the shame flare in his eyes before he turned

and started moving again. She could have bitten off her tongue, but it was too late. The words had been spoken.

He reached the driver's door before she managed to grab his arm and force him to face her again.

Before she could speak, he said, "I'll pay you back every penny of your goddamned $25,000. And when I have, I never want to lay eyes on you again."

She stumbled backward as he got into the truck and gunned the engine, then glanced at Will, and gently let out the clutch and slowly rolled out of the parking lot.

Summer had to stop herself from running after him. This time she was definitely right, and he was wrong. He would come to his senses. He would take her back.

She loved him and she wanted to spend her life with him. Why was he insisting it could only be on his terms?

Summer scraped her hands over her eyes. She wasn't going to shed one more tear over Billy Coburn. He'd made his choice. And she'd made hers.

She crossed the church parking lot, got into her truck, and drove home to the Castle. Where she belonged.

A week went by and Billy didn't hear a word from Summer. He'd expected her to back down, but so far it hadn't happened. He hadn't realized how much he'd let himself hope. Hadn't realized how much of his heart he'd given to her. There was nothing left for him if she didn't come back. The thought of a future without her wasn't just bleak, it was goddamned black.

He was repairing the broken step on the back porch when he spied a dust cloud in the distance, which cleared to reveal Summer's cherry-red Silverado coming down the road.

He debated whether to stop working and put his shirt back on and wash the dirt off his face and hands, but he didn't want her to think he'd been expecting her—in case she hadn't come to apologize. He braced the replacement step between the porch rail and a sawhorse while he used a hand saw to cut it down to size. The excess wood fell to the porch as Summer arrived at the bottom of the steps. He braced his shoulders as though for a blow, waiting to hear what she'd come to say.

"Hello, Billy," she said, her hand over her eyes to shade them from the sun.

He took the cigarette from his lips and ground it out on the porch, then brought the board with him as he hopped down, and laid it in place on the risers. He jerked when Summer grabbed a couple of nails from the bag he'd set on the ground, thinking she was going to touch him. But she just leaned down to pick up the hammer from where he'd left it and handed it to him, along with the nails.

"Thanks," he said, sticking the extra nails in his mouth, so they'd be handy, and pounding the first one in, securing the step in the corner.

"I figured you were going to be stubborn about this," she said over his pounding. "So I decided that I'd be the one to give in."

Billy felt a swell of satisfaction. *She's coming back. Thank God.* He pounded the nail flat, then pulled the extra nails from his mouth and turned to face her. "I've missed you," he admitted. He owed her that much at least. "I'm glad you're back."

The pained look on her face should have warned him, but he chose to ignore it and asked, "Do you have a bag in the truck? I'll bring it in for you."

"I'm not moving back in with you, Billy."

He stared at her another minute, then stuck the nails back in his mouth and turned once more to the porch step, taking out his frustration and despair on the nail he pounded into the wood.

"I need your help, Billy," she said. "Please, stop that and listen to me."

He pulled the nails from his mouth and threw them onto the ground, then dropped the hammer and turned to her, his arms crossed over his chest. "I'm listening. What is it you want?"

"I want you to find out who murdered my mother."

"Hasn't the evidence already established that?"

She put a hand on his crossed arms and looked up at him with beseeching eyes. "I was listening when you told me about your work as a TSCRA field agent, Billy. How good you were at finding rustled cattle, when no one had a clue where they were. How you found missing horses when they'd disappeared into thin air. If anyone can save Blackjack, you can."

"I'm not interested."

"If you won't do it for him, do it for me. And for yourself. He's your father, too, Billy, whether you like it or not."

"What's in it for me?"

She flushed and he knew she thought he meant money. He didn't want money. He wanted her as his wife. In his bed. Loving him. He just had no idea how he could make that happen.

255

Apparently, she'd learned from their last encounter because she didn't offer him money. "You get my gratitude," she said at last. "And the satisfaction of knowing the wrong person won't be punished for my mother's death."

"I don't have the time," he said. "Or the freedom." She knew full well he had to take of his mom and his son.

"I've already spoken with Emma," Summer said. "She agreed to baby-sit Will and check in on your mother while you help me."

"She did?" he asked skeptically.

"It wasn't easy convincing her," Summer conceded. "But she came around."

"What did you promise her?" Billy asked.

"That I'd pay for a hired nurse when the time comes that your mother needs one," Summer admitted reluctantly.

"Dammit, Summer—"

"My agreement with Emma doesn't concern you, Billy. All I want to know is whether you'll help me out or not."

"Are you going to come back here and live with me while I'm investigating?"

"You know I can't," she said. "I've already told you there's too much to be done at Bitter Creek. Please, Billy. My brothers are only looking at the evidence found at the scene. They don't think Momma would have killed herself. They believe Daddy's guilty. You're my only hope."

"I need to get this step back together," he said, turning

away from her and searching out the nails he'd discarded, making sure he found them all so there wouldn't be one for Will to find when he was playing outside. He picked up the hammer and began pounding in another nail.

"I'll wait to hear from you," Summer said as she backed away. "I'm counting on you, Billy. Don't let me down. Please."

Once her Silverado was on its way, he sank down onto the bottom step and stared after her. He heard the screen door screech open and leaped up to help his mother into one of the rockers on the back porch. "You shouldn't be up," he said.

"I couldn't help overhearing," she said as she set the rocker in motion.

Billy slumped down with his back against the porch rail, his arm on one raised knee, his other leg extended so his boot was grazed by the tip of his mother's rocker. "She wants me to help prove Blackjack is innocent, when it's a good bet he's guilty as sin."

"He didn't do it," Dora said.

"How do you know that?" Billy said belligerently.

"If he'd wanted her dead, there were a thousand less incriminating ways to do it."

"In other words, because all the evidence points to him, he didn't do it?"

"Exactly," Dora said. "Jackson Blackthorne is no fool. To be honest, this looks more like Eve's work."

Billy stared at his mother in confusion.

"She loved manipulating people, using them without regard to the pain she was inflicting. She was as vicious and heartless and cunning as a wolverine."

"That doesn't sound like the kind of person who'd kill herself to make her point," Billy said.

"That's probably what she counted on people thinking." Dora stopped the rocker and sighed. "Or maybe I'm completely off the mark. Maybe it was someone else who wanted to be rid of Eve and needed a scapegoat."

"Like who?" Billy said, brushing at the flies that were attracted by the sweat on his brow.

"You once told me that the way you'd become such a successful TSCRA agent was that you always followed the money," Dora said. "Where does it take you in this case?"

"Summer ended up with Bitter Creek," he said. "That was the biggest prize."

"Go on," his mother said. "Who else stood to benefit from Eve Blackthorne's death?"

"Ellen DeWitt," Billy said. "She ended up the sole heir to the DeWitt ranch, and probably a lot more besides."

"How much are we talking about?" Dora asked.

"The estimate I got from one source put the value of the incorporated ranch and its subsidiaries at about sixty million."

Dora whistled.

"I don't know whether the family was in financial trouble and needed quick access to cash assets. But Ellen's got two sons who could've helped her plan the murder and pull it off," Billy said, feeling his adrenaline begin to flow.

"Good," Dora said. "Now think of who might have helped Eve if she planned her own death."

Billy rubbed away a spot of perspiration that was

worming its way down the center of his chest. "She used Russell Handy last time, but he's behind bars now."

"That doesn't mean he didn't help her. He was foreman at Bitter Creek for a lot of years. He'd know all about the hydraulic line on a helicopter and how to rig an explosive. He supervised anything and everything that had to be done on that ranch."

"But why would he help Eve Blackthorne now?" Billy asked. "She's the reason he ended up in prison."

"Why don't you go and ask him?" Dora said. "The sooner you find out who killed Eve and get Blackjack out of jail and back home at Bitter Creek, the sooner you'll get your wife back."

Billy stared at his mother in amazement, then laughed out loud. "Why, you wily old coyote."

"There's always more than one way to skin a cat," she said with a smile.

"I thought you didn't approve of Summer," Billy said, eyeing his mother.

"The girl's got gumption," Dora said gruffly. "Now how about helping me back to bed?"

Dora started to walk on her own, but she was so frail, Billy picked her up once they were inside and carried her into the bedroom. He tucked her into bed and then sat down beside her. "I don't want Summer back if she's only coming because there's no place for her at Bitter Creek."

"There will always be a place for her at Bitter Creek," Dora pointed out. "Even if Blackjack comes back. But maybe when he does come home, she'll realize that she belongs here with you."

"Thank you, Mom," Billy said.

"You're welcome. I only wish I'd spoken my mind sooner in the past. I wish . . ."

Billy pulled his mom into his arms and hugged her tight. "It's all right, Mom." He hesitated, then said, "I forgive you."

She sobbed once, but made no other sound, just clung tightly to him as they comforted one another.

Chapter 15

WHEN SUMMER CAME TO SEE HER FATHER IN the Bitter Creek County Jail, she found he had company. Lauren Creed sat across the table from him in the visitors' room. It was difficult for Summer to face the woman who'd caused so much heartache for her mother and still be cordial. "I didn't know my father had a visitor. I'll come back later."

"I'll leave," Ren said, rising.

"No," Blackjack said, grabbing for her hand. His hands were cuffed together in front of him, and also cuffed to the table, so he was brought up short. "Stay, Ren. We haven't finished."

"Your daughter—"

"There's nothing Summer has to say that you can't hear," Blackjack said.

It was plain to Summer that whatever time her father had left before he was convicted by the weight of evidence against him and either executed or sentenced to life in prison, he was determined to spend with Lauren Creed. What was it about this woman that had so captured his heart? She wasn't nearly as beautiful as Summer's mother.

At that moment Ren looked up at her, and Summer saw empathy and sympathy and compassion. And a kindness that she'd never found in her mother's striking blue eyes.

Summer didn't want to like this woman. Didn't want to understand her father's choice. She turned to Blackjack and said, "I only came to tell you I haven't made any progress yet in finding out who helped Momma commit suicide."

"So you believe it *was* suicide?" her father said, arching a dark brow.

"I don't have any other suspects besides you, Daddy, and I don't believe you're responsible. Which only leaves Momma."

"Your mother had some help," her father said. "You need to keep hunting until you find whoever worked with her to frame me."

"I'm glad to hear you say that, Daddy, because I've asked Billy to do exactly that."

Her father was silent a moment. "He agreed to help?"

"Not yet. But he will."

"I wouldn't bet on it," Blackjack said. "That boy hates my guts."

"True. But I believe in justice," Billy said as he entered the room.

"Billy! You came," Summer said, rising to greet him. She gave him a quick hug and a peck on the cheek, as though he were some friendly acquaintance rather than her husband.

Billy slid an arm around her waist and lowered his head and kissed her like he had the right to do it. And didn't care whether her father liked it or not.

Summer was breathless when he let her go. She could have kicked Billy when he turned to Blackjack, his eyes hooded, his mouth curled in a sneer, as though defying him to say anything. And she wanted to kiss her father when he failed to rise to the bait.

"Pull up a chair," Blackjack said.

"I can't stay," Billy said, cocking a hip and setting his hands to his waist. "I came by to let Summer know that I'll be out of town for a couple of days hunting down the truth about whether or not you're a murderer."

Summer saw the dull flush rise on her father's cheekbones. "I'll go with you," she said, to forestall the eruption she feared was coming.

"What about Bitter Creek?" Billy said. "You told me you needed to be there to run things."

"I do. But I—"

Blackjack interrupted with, "Ren can relay any problems to me here in jail, and I'll give orders to the men what to do."

Summer stared at the petite woman her father seemed so determined to make a part of his life. Ren's eyes were lowered, but her hand clasped Blackjack's tightly.

"I suppose that will work," Summer said.

"There's no need for you to leave Bitter Creek," Billy insisted. "I can handle this on my own."

"I want to go," Summer said. "Don't bother arguing. My mind is made up."

"Suit yourself," Billy said with a shrug. "But I'm leaving now."

"I need to pack a few things," Summer said.

"You can buy a toothbrush, and I've got a clean T-shirt you can borrow to sleep in."

Summer stared at him, wondering why he was making this more difficult than it had to be. How much trouble was it to stop by the Castle and let her throw some things into a bag?

Then, like a light bulb going on, she got Billy's message. If she insisted on coming along, he intended to spend the night with her. She met his hooded gaze. And they weren't just going to sleep.

Summer realized she might not have another chance to make Billy fall in love with her. If things didn't go well for her father, she might end up having to stay at Bitter Creek. And the way things stood right now, Billy might very well refuse to join her there. She wanted the chance to convince him they belonged together, to make love to him one more time, in case they ended up apart.

"Make a decision," he said. "It's all the same to me. But today's Thursday, and if the courtroom stuff cranks up on Monday, we haven't got a helluva lot of time."

Summer felt her stomach roll at this reminder of how drastic her father's situation had become. The grand jury was being convened on Monday, and unless she and Billy could come up with some new evidence, it wasn't going to take long for them to indict her father. They only had three days to find out the truth.

"Let's go," she said.

It wasn't until she'd walked out of the jail into the sunlight that Summer realized she'd turned her back on Bitter Creek without a second thought. She could tell herself she'd done it for her father's sake. But the truth was, she'd done it to spend three more days with Billy.

She got into his pickup, and as he started the engine asked, "Where are we headed?"

"I thought I'd start by visiting your aunt Ellen. She's the one who inherits the DeWitt fortune now that your mother's dead. Then I thought I'd head up north of Houston to Huntsville to talk to Russell Handy."

"Do you really think he could have anything to do with this?" Summer asked, her eyes wide.

"The only way to find out is to ask," Billy replied. "On the way back, I want to stop off in Houston and see your great-uncle Harry at DeWitt & Blackthorne."

"Why do you need to see Daddy's lawyer?" Summer asked.

"Because your great-uncle Harry is also the executor of your mother's estate," Billy said. "He may not tell us anything—like a priest, a lawyer has to keep his secrets—but you never know what he might let slip."

"It sounds like you've done a lot of thinking about this," Summer said. She turned her face into the breeze from the open window. The air smelled of the earth, the blooming mesquite, and the cattle that roamed the grassland. The hot wind tore the hair around her face from her ponytail, and she pulled out the band and let it fly free.

"Your nose is going to get sunburned if you stick it out that window the whole trip," Billy said.

Summer grinned at him. "Do you realize this is the first time we've been away from Bitter Creek together?"

"We didn't exactly spend our youths traveling in the same circles," Billy pointed out.

"None of that matters now," she insisted. "The point is, we could travel the world together. We could—"

"You're forgetting something, Summer. You didn't marry a rich man. You married me."

"You're forgetting something, Billy. You didn't marry a poor woman. You married me."

She resisted the urge to fill the silence that grew as he absorbed what she'd said.

"I don't want your money."

"Not even if it means Will would have a more comfortable life?" She put up a hand to cut him off. "I didn't say a better life. I don't believe money can buy happiness. It never made my mother happy, anyway. And it's been nothing but a burden to me. But the fact is, in two years I'll inherit a great deal of money from my trust. Think of what we could do with it, Billy. We could travel. We could buy more land."

"Your father's the first one in line whenever a rancher goes belly-up in Bitter Creek. I don't see us outbidding him. Assuming there is an us," he said. "I thought we agreed this marriage wasn't going to last more than two years. Has something changed that I don't know about?"

"Nothing's been changed but the subject," Summer said. "We're pretending, Billy. Playing 'What if?' So what if my father outbid us? We don't have to build an empire with land," she said, frustrated by Billy's unwillingness to join in the game. "Maybe we focus on breeding a better bull, or we start a stable of blue-ribbon quarter horses. What I'm saying is, my money can make it possible for us to realize our dreams."

"Your dreams," Billy corrected.

"Only because I've been the first to say them out

loud," Summer countered. "Surely you've dreamed of what you'd want to achieve if money wasn't a problem. Fess up, Billy. What would you be doing with your life, if you'd grown up with all the advantages of a Blackthorne?"

He eyed her sideways and was silent for so long that she thought he was going to put her off again. But at last he said, "I think all my dreams were about how I could earn enough money to achieve my dreams. I never got much beyond making the money. Because I never figured I would."

Summer's throat constricted at Billy's admission. She'd never realized how little he'd hoped for in life. "The money's there, Billy. What would you like to do with it?"

"I'd want to be sure Will has funds set aside for college," he said.

"Done."

"I'd make sure my mother has the best medical care she can get."

"Done."

"I'd want to make sure Emma and the baby have everything they need."

"Done."

"And I'd want to fix up the house for you, put in some air-conditioning and a dishwasher and a decent washer and dryer. Maybe redo the bathroom and add another one. Paint the house white with green shutters and have a green front door. I'd put in some red flowers around the porch, and I'd plant a tree out back, so there'd be shade in the evening."

"Thank you, Billy," Summer said. "I'd like that. Now, what about you? What do you want for yourself?"

Summer had a feeling Billy had never allowed himself to want anything—so he wouldn't be disappointed when he didn't get it. She watched him struggle to voice the dreams he'd never allowed himself to dream.

"I'd want . . . I'd like . . . I want respect," he said.

"Oh, Billy," Summer said, her heart clutching. "You already have that."

He shook his head. "I want to be a respected member of the community. The kind of man other men tip their hats to. The kind of man women don't cross to the other side of the street to avoid. Money can't buy me that. I'm not sure I can ever have that if I stay here in Bitter Creek."

Small towns were unforgiving, Summer knew. Billy's past would always follow him. "It won't be as easy to earn respect here in Bitter Creek," Summer said. "But it seems to me it would be a lot more satisfying to prove yourself to the people who've known you all your life, who know where you came from and how you started out, than to a lot of strangers."

"Easy for you to say."

Summer felt frustrated by his unwillingness to accept the goodness in himself that she saw in him. "Look at yourself, Billy. You were always a hard worker. You always took care of your mother and your sister. You just carried a chip around on your shoulder and dared anyone to try and knock it off. And because of who you were, a lot of men tried. And nobody beat you, Billy. *Nobody*. Not even Blackjack."

"I sold out," Billy said. "I took the job he offered me and ran as far and as fast as I could."

"No. You grabbed at a once-in-a-lifetime opportunity. And you made it work. When life threw you another curve—when Debbie Sue Hudson got pregnant—you stepped up and took charge and have a wonderful son to show for it. How can anyone not respect you, Billy? You're a strong, generous, loving man."

Summer hadn't intended to get so carried away, but it was high time Billy realized he was a lot better than most of the men she'd met out in the world, who'd had every advantage and possessed wealth and good looks and never become as worthy of respect as Bad Billy Coburn.

When Billy's lips curved into a smile, Summer let out the breath she'd been holding.

"Remind me to hire you to walk two feet ahead of me and let people know before I arrive what a wonderful person I am."

"I'd be proud to do it, Billy. Because you *are* a wonderful person."

"I appreciate the vote of confidence. But I haven't forgotten that you liked me when I really was Bad Billy Coburn."

Summer made a face. She could see she wasn't going to change Billy's mind. "I suppose only time will tell," she said. "But you haven't been paying attention if you think people in Bitter Creek haven't noticed the difference in you."

"If you say so," he grudgingly conceded.

"Well?" she said, arching a brow. "What do you want to be when you grow up, Billy?"

He glanced at her, then said, "Working for other men all my life has made me realize there is something I want."

Summer waited with bated breath.

"I want to be my own boss. I want my own place, with enough of a nest egg to be able to support my family and still have time to play catch with my sons and go riding with my daughters and make love to my wife. Maybe that doesn't sound ambitious enough to you, but—"

"That sounds wonderful," Summer said. "Wonderful."

Billy eyed her sideways. "Well, you asked. So that's what I want."

They'd been headed north on U.S. 77 nearly two hours and were approaching the turnoff to the DeWitt ranch, located southwest of Victoria, before Billy spoke again.

"Your aunt's expecting us," he said. "When we get there, let me ask the questions."

"What if I think of something you've forgotten?"

"That won't happen." Before she could protest, Billy added, "But if it does, feel free to speak up."

The DeWitts' ancestral home had been built in the early 1840s, when Texas was still a Republic and the DeWitts had raised cotton. The white frame structure emulated the magnificent Southern mansions built before the Civil War in Georgia and Alabama and Mississippi. Its towering Doric columns held up a second-story gallery porch, and the pitched roof revealed windows on the third floor, where house slaves had once slept.

"I thought Bitter Creek was impressive," Billy said. "This place puts it to shame."

"They might have a bigger house," Summer said pertly. "But we own more land."

Billy grinned. "I should have known."

When Billy knocked on the kitchen screen door, he expected to be greeted by a servant, who would lead him through a maze of rooms to some elegant parlor, where he'd be greeted coldly by a carbon copy of Eve Blackthorne. After all, blood was blood.

He was taken aback when he and Summer were greeted by Ellen DeWitt herself, who was in the kitchen baking, wearing an apron that covered a simple cotton print dress, her feet stuck in furry pink house slippers. Her hand, when she reached out to greet Billy, was dusted with flour.

"Oh, so sorry," she said with a laugh, as she wiped it off on the food-spattered apron.

When she extended it again, Billy realized she was looking at him over reading glasses that were perched on the end of her nose.

This woman did not remotely fit his image of a cold-blooded murderer. But as TV detectives were quick to point out, evil sometimes came in benign packages.

"Hello, Aunt Ellen," Summer said as she followed Billy inside. She gave her aunt a hearty hug and said, "The kitchen smells wonderful. What's in the oven?"

Ellen DeWitt pulled off her glasses and threw them onto a cookbook that lay on the cobalt-blue ceramic-tiled counter. "Sourdough bread, which I love, and bake for company just so I can brag I made it myself. Then I got the insane idea to whip up this Christmas

Bohemian Braid recipe, and yes, I know it's the middle of July."

Billy looked at the pile of dough on the central island, which Summer's aunt Ellen had divided into three long rolls.

"How can you forget something like how to braid?" the older woman lamented. "I mean, that's impossible, right?"

Summer was already at the sink washing her hands and laughing at her aunt. "I think you made that up because you know how much I like to play with dough."

Her aunt smiled...benignly. "I'm glad to see you, Summer. And your husband." She focused her attention on Billy, who stood still for her scrutiny. "We didn't have much chance to talk at the funeral. I'm glad you came to visit."

"We aren't here for a social call," Billy felt compelled to point out. He was liking the woman too damned much. He needed to keep his objectivity.

"Oh?" she said, as she crossed and put her hands on Summer's shoulders, watching as Summer efficiently braided the dough. "Why have you come?"

"To ask if your sister Eve gave you any indication that she feared for her life, or that she intended to take her own life."

Ellen DeWitt's brow furrowed. She turned away from him to retrieve a baking sheet for the bread and instructed Summer how to get the braided bread from the counter to the aluminum sheet, and then into a second preheated oven.

Billy waited patiently. He'd learned that if he didn't

ask questions, witnesses often filled in the uncomfortable silences.

At last, Ellen turned back to him and said, "I had a phone call from Eve a week before her death which, in retrospect, is somewhat distressing."

"Uh-huh," Billy said.

"She asked me about Max's heart condition. She wanted to know what medication he was using. She asked rather... intimate questions about what effects it had on Max."

"Max?" Billy said.

"Uncle Max was Aunt Ellen's husband. He died two years ago of a heart attack," Summer volunteered.

Billy frowned Summer into silence, then turned back to Ellen and said, "I don't want to make you uncomfortable, but can you tell me exactly what Eve asked?"

Ellen lowered her eyes and rubbed her hands on her apron. "She wanted to know if Max's heart medication made him... unable to perform in bed," she said in a rush. "She seemed to think Jackson might be having trouble... Anyway, she wanted to know if I'd had any problem like that with Max, since Jackson was taking the same medication Max took."

Ellen looked up at Billy and said, "We discussed how important it is to get the dosage right, because too little medication might result in a heart attack—but too high a dosage could actually cause an arrhythmia and lead to death."

Billy marveled at Eve Blackthorne's devious mind. She'd acquired the information she'd wanted about the correct lethal dosage of heart medication from

Ellen without Ellen ever being the wiser. Until it was too late.

Or maybe Ellen was making up the story to make it look like Eve had killed herself. Although, if that were the case, why make up any story at all?

"I took her questions at face value," Ellen continued. "But now I have to wonder whether she might have been asking for some other reason."

"What reason is that?" Billy asked.

Ellen met his gaze and said, "My sister was not a happy woman."

Billy thought that was perhaps the understatement of the year. He said nothing.

"When I heard about the heart medication in her system, I thought she might have taken it on purpose," Ellen said. "But . . ."

"But?" Billy prodded.

"Eve told me in the same phone conversation that she and Blackjack hadn't been getting along well. And the circumstances of her death aren't remotely typical of a suicide. It looks a great deal more like she was murdered. And the most logical suspect seems to be—I'm sorry, Summer—her husband."

Summer gasped at this indictment of her father.

"I suppose that means your sister didn't ask you about helicopter hydraulic lines or explosives during that conversation," Billy said.

Ellen managed a smile. "No. Just heart medication. Can the two of you stay for dinner?"

"Sorry, ma'am. We—"

"Please, call me Aunt Ellen," she said. "After all, we're family."

Billy saw the imploring look Summer shot him and said, "Thanks for your help, Aunt Ellen. But we've got more traveling to do today. I have just one more question."

This time Ellen waited for him to speak.

"You're the sole beneficiary of your sister, is that correct?"

"Yes."

"What's your financial situation like?"

Aunt Ellen made a face. "I had no reason to want Eve dead," she said. "The DeWitt family is disgustingly rich. I don't need Eve's share of the corporate profits, if that's what you're getting at."

This had turned out to be a dead end.

"I guess we'll be taking off," Billy said.

"Heading up to Huntsville?" Ellen asked.

Billy snorted softly. So much for clandestine investigation. "Yes, ma'am, we are."

"Russell Handy won't tell you anything that would hurt Eve," Ellen warned. "If you want him to help you, make sure he thinks you're on her side."

"Thank you, Aunt Ellen," Billy said. "I appreciate the advice."

Summer crossed to kiss her aunt on the cheek, and Billy found himself doing the same thing when Ellen crossed to say good-bye to him.

"Don't be strangers," she said as she let the screen door slide closed behind them.

Billy headed the pickup toward Victoria, where they'd pick up U.S. 59 to Houston. "I like your aunt," Billy said. "How did she end up so different from your mother?"

"Momma was older than Ellen, and I think it hit her a lot harder when Grandpa DeWitt divorced their mother."

"Divorces can do a lot of damage," Billy agreed. "Almost as much damage as two people staying together who ought to get the hell away from one another."

Billy felt Summer's hand on his arm, an offer of comfort. He felt like shrugging it off, but that would be admitting the pain that he so seldom let anyone see. So he let it be.

Billy got on the Sam Houston tollway, which kept him out of Houston, and shortly after lunchtime he took the exit heading north on I-45. "You hungry?"

Summer rubbed her stomach. "Starved."

"There's a barbecue joint just off the interstate in Spring. How does that sound?"

"Do we have time to stop and eat? When do we have to be at the prison?"

"There are some advantages to having a Texas Ranger for a brother-in-law," Billy said. "Owen made arrangements for us to see Handy whenever we get there this afternoon."

"When did you call Owen?" Summer asked.

"When I realized that the sooner I got Blackjack cleared and out of jail the sooner you'd be free to come back home to me."

Summer stared at him. "And you thought that's all it would take to get me to leave Bitter Creek? My father back at the helm?"

"A fellow can always hope." Billy was glad they'd arrived at the barbecue joint, because the conversation was stepping toward dangerous ground.

The barbecue consisted of stripped pork and links of pork sausage served right onto sheets of waxed butcher paper placed in front of them—one sheet up, one sheet down—to prevent the grease from seeping through to the red and white checked plastic tablecloth. The only eating utensil offered was a tinny-looking soup spoon that came with the cup of pink-tinged pork fat and pinto beans.

Ketchup dispensers had been filled with barbecue sauces that ranged from sweet to red-hot. Billy grabbed for the sweet and noticed Summer reached for the red-hot.

"I like it spicy," she said when she saw him staring.

He grinned. "I can see that."

The meal was a primitive delight, from the use of fingers, to the necessity of gnawing on bones for the last morsel of tasty gristle.

"How did you find this place?" Summer asked.

"I had engine trouble the last time I traveled to Huntsville and ended up spending the afternoon here. You might have noticed there aren't a lot of dining choices."

Summer's head came up, and she dropped her bone on the butcher paper. "When was this? Why were you traveling to Huntsville?"

"Two years ago, before I headed to Amarillo. I wanted to see your biological father."

"What for?" Summer asked.

"I wondered how a man could know he had a child and not acknowledge it."

"What did you find out?"

"That your mother wasn't any more honest with him than she was with Blackjack."

"What do you mean?"

"Russell Handy didn't know he was your father until I told him two years ago."

Chapter 16

THE HUNTSVILLE PRISON UNIT, FORMERLY called "The Walls" for its infamous redbrick walls, was among the oldest Texas prisons. In 1848, it had been built on farmland, so inmates could work the fields. It could now be found smack in the middle of downtown Huntsville, its redbrick walls more daunting for the modern razor wire that topped them. No inmates were likely to escape, if the numerous and meticulous procedures involved in getting inside were any measure of prison security.

A half hour after Billy and Summer arrived, they were sitting on the opposite side of a glass partition from Russell Handy. The odor of ammonia through the fine mesh screen at the bottom of the glass partition was strong enough to make Billy's eyes water, and he wondered what the hell they were using to mop the floors in here.

He kept a close eye on Summer, wondering how she felt seeing Handy for the first time since she'd discovered he was her biological father. When she rubbed at her eyes, he wasn't sure if it was the ammonia or her emotions getting the better of her.

Because of things Handy had told him two years

before, Billy knew that Summer and her father's fore-man had spent a great deal of time together doing ranch work while she was growing up. Billy imagined Eve Blackthorne must have gotten quite a charge out of see-ing them together, especially since Blackjack was proba-bly around most of the time, too.

"Hello, Russ," Summer said.

"Hello, Missy," he replied.

Handy still had the wiry frame and weathered fea-tures of a man who'd spent his life working outdoors on horseback, but he'd developed a nervous twitch in his right eye and his hands were never still.

Summer scrubbed at her eyes again and said, "We came to ask some questions."

"It's good to see you," Handy said, his dark eyes eat-ing up the sight of her. "I heard you got married." He shot a quick glance at Billy and said, "Congratulations."

"We have some questions," Summer repeated.

Billy could see she didn't want the visit to become personal, but he couldn't help empathizing with Handy. It was a shock to find out someone that you'd known for years was actually related to you. He ought to know. But they didn't have a lot of time. And there were questions that needed to be asked and answered.

"We've come to see if you can give us any informa-tion about Eve Blackthorne's death," Billy said.

"What is it you think I know?" Handy said, an edge in his voice. "I haven't been down to Bitter Creek lately."

"But you had a phone call from someone in Bitter Creek two weeks ago," Billy countered.

Summer opened her mouth to speak, and he put a hand on her thigh to silence her.

"How do you know that?" Handy asked.

"I'm a good investigator," Billy said. "What about it, Mr. Handy? Who called you?"

Handy ran a nervous hand through his hair. "All right, it was Eve. But it had nothing to do with her accident. It was private."

"Please, Russ, if you know anything about Momma's death, you have to tell us," Summer said.

It was obvious to Billy that they'd had a good relationship long before the Bitter Creek *segundo* discovered they were related. He watched as Summer reached out to Handy, then realized the glass was there, and awkwardly pulled back her hand.

Handy must have been more than a little partial to her. Because when her eyes locked on his, the foreman started talking.

"It wasn't anything," he said. "Eve just needed some information. She said your dad had moved in with that Creed woman and the men needed to blow out some tree stumps and she didn't know how to get to the dynamite."

"Are you telling me there isn't another cowboy at Bitter Creek who'd know where to find those explosives?" Billy asked.

"They all knew where they were stored, but nobody knew the combination to the munitions safe except me and the boss."

Billy frowned. "He didn't share that with the man who took over for you?"

"Evidently not," Handy said. "Or Eve wouldn't have called me."

Billy exchanged a look with Summer. Now they knew

where her mother had gotten the dynamite. The next question was who had helped her fashion the bomb.

"Did you discuss anything else?" Summer asked, her fingertips reaching out again, this time matching up to Handy's against the glass. "Anything at all?"

Handy hesitated, then said, "She was pretty broken up about your dad leaving her."

Summer's hand came down and knotted with the other in her lap. Handy's stayed there for a moment before it also disappeared. "Anything else?" Summer asked.

Handy shook his head, his dark eyes intent on her, his jaw taut.

"She didn't ask you how to make a bomb?" Billy said bluntly.

"Hell, no!" Handy looked from Billy to Summer and back again. "Is that what happened? Did a bomb bring down her helicopter? I saw pictures on TV, but there weren't any details."

"There was a bomb under her seat, but it never exploded," Summer said.

Handy looked like he was in pain, and Summer's hand once more found its way to the glass.

"I'm so sorry you're in here," she whispered.

Handy's eyes were dark pools of anguish. "God, how I loved her."

"And I love my father," Summer said.

This time Handy's fingertips left the glass first. "I'm sorry how all this turned out. Your father was my friend."

Billy watched the tear roll down Summer's cheek, saw her swallow hard and rasp, "Then won't you please help us?"

Handy sniffed and backswiped his eyes. He shook his head once in indecision, then turned to Billy and said, "What do you want to know?"

"If you were Eve Blackthorne, and you wanted to make a bomb, how would you go about finding out how to do it?"

"I'd talk to somebody who handles a lot of explosives," Handy said.

"Who would that be?" Billy persisted.

"Any of the men in the Bitter Creek National Guard unit, the combat engineers. They all work with mines. One of them would know how to rig a bomb."

Billy had been in Bravo Company himself before he'd moved away to Amarillo. He suddenly knew who Eve Blackthorne might have asked to instruct her.

"I guess we better be going," Billy said, as he rose abruptly.

Summer looked surprised, but rose along with him. "Good-bye, Russ," she said. "I ... It was nice to see you."

"It was good to see you, too, Missy."

There was no way for them to physically touch through the glass. Neither mentioned seeing the other again. Neither mentioned writing. Billy waited to see if either had anything more to say, but when neither of them spoke, he put a hand to the small of Summer's back and ushered her from the room.

Once they were free of the prison walls Summer said, "He really loved my mom."

"Yeah. Too bad for him."

"He was always good to me."

"I suppose that's something," Billy said.

"It's everything," Summer said. She turned to him and

asked, "Why did we leave in such a hurry? What did I miss?"

"I think I might have figured out who taught your mom how to rig that bomb."

"I'm listening," Summer said as she stepped into Billy's pickup.

Billy hurried around the hood and slid in beside her before he spoke. "Luke Creed."

"But he's somewhere in Africa with the National Guard, engaged in 'a humanitarian effort to locate and disarm mines,'" Summer recited, recollecting as best she could what the article in the Bitter Creek *Chronicle* had said.

"Exactly," Billy said. "Who better to teach someone how to make a bomb than someone who knows how to dismantle one? I figure she got a kick out of using Ren's son to help frame Blackjack."

"Okay, Luke has the expertise," Summer said. "But he's been gone for nearly six months. My parents only separated a month ago. When would he have given my mother her lesson in bombmaking?"

"He could have done it over the Internet. If your mother followed the pattern we've seen, she arranged it so Luke never knew who he was giving his lesson to. Maybe she went to an Internet café somewhere and pretended to be some guard buddy of his, or impersonated a professor at some university. She could find him easy enough through the local guard, and guys his age always know where they can find a computer to log on."

"Or maybe she just typed in 'How to Make a Bomb'

and the details came up on the screen," Summer suggested. "How would we ever prove it one way or the other in court?"

"Circumstantial evidence can add up," Billy said. "It's convicted more than one felon."

"Why would Luke tell us the truth, if it's going to help Blackjack?"

"He'll tell the truth because he's been subpoenaed and is under oath. It's too bad what we've got so far isn't enough to clear Blackjack."

"Why isn't it?" Summer asked.

"You'd be asking a jury to make a pretty big leap to get from two seemingly innocent conversations and an exchange of intellectual information on the Internet to a woman planning her own death. A good prosecutor could take it apart in no time."

"So this trip was a waste," Summer said, slumping down in her seat.

Billy started the engine. "Yeah, maybe. But we have one more stop to make."

"Right. The offices of DeWitt & Blackthorne, where Uncle Harry rides to the rescue," Summer said sarcastically. "I should point out that Uncle Harry's way over eighty and hasn't thrown his leg over a saddle since he was seventy-five."

Billy laughed. "Some of those old codgers are pretty smart. Maybe he'll have some ideas to help us out."

"He is smart," Summer conceded. "I just don't see any way out for Daddy. I'm scared, Billy."

Billy reached for her hand and squeezed it. "Don't give up yet. We'll spend the night somewhere in Houston and hit your great-uncle Harry's office first thing in the morning."

"My family has a penthouse apartment on Woodway. We can stay there," Summer suggested. "That way I won't have to buy a toothbrush or borrow your T-shirt to sleep in."

Billy didn't relish the idea of spending the night in Blackthorne territory. But it was bound to be more comfortable than the Motel 6 he could afford. "I was looking forward to seeing you in my T-shirt," he said.

"You prefer cotton T-shirts to sexy lingerie?" Summer asked.

"I don't think I've ever seen anything sexier than you in a T-shirt," Billy said. "But then, I've never seen you in sexy lingerie."

"Get us to Houston," Summer said, "and I'll see what I can do."

Summer spent the drive back to Houston hunkered down in her seat thinking. It was hard being the child of three such notorious persons. She'd read enough to know that heredity was at least partly responsible for who a person turned out to be, with environment shaping the rest, and that scientists differed on which of the two was more important.

Summer felt her heart beating frantically, like a butterfly slapping its fragile wings against an unforgiving jar. What if she was doomed to be like them? Surely she could choose the course she took. Surely there was some hope she could be a better person than her parents.

"You've been awful quiet," Billy said.

"I shouldn't have married you, Billy."

"Why not?"

"I took advantage of you."

"Do you see me complaining?"

"The thing is, I wish I'd been more honest with you in the beginning."

He raised a brow but said nothing.

Summer couldn't bear the silence, so she said, "I didn't only marry you because I wanted to get away from my parents. I had this crazy idea that you'd fall in love with me and we'd live happily ever after."

"Not so crazy, when you think about it."

Summer's breath caught in her throat. "Really?"

"I've always liked you, Summer. You know that. I really thought . . . I mean, I hoped . . . We might have done okay together."

"Might have?"

"We'd have had to work at it. I'm too proud. You're too stubborn. But I figured we had as good a chance as most of being happy together, or I wouldn't have married you in the first place."

"But you needed money—"

"It wasn't the money, Summer. I was desperate, but I could have left town and kept my job and figured out some other way to take care of my mom and Emma. I wanted to marry you. I've wanted it for a long time."

Summer stared at Billy, her jaw agape. "Why didn't you say something sooner?"

His lips twisted wryly. "If you'll recall, I did."

Summer thought back to the time two years ago when Billy had proposed to her, and she'd refused. And the moment a few weeks later, when she'd been running from who she'd discovered she was, and she'd proposed to him and he'd turned her down. "I suppose timing is everything."

She opened her mouth to tell him that she was glad this time the timing had been right, because she'd discovered that she loved him, but he spoke first.

"We didn't marry for love, Summer. But some of the best marriages happen when people like and respect one another."

Summer felt her heart sink. What about love? She loved Billy and she wanted his love. Was that asking so much? "What are you saying?"

"That I'd like to treat this marriage as something that will last beyond the time we set for it to end."

Summer didn't know what to say. Didn't know how to feel. She shot a surreptitious look in Billy's direction. "I'm not sure I know what you're getting at."

"I'm saying we make a good team. That I like being with you. That I want to keep on spending time in your company. That we ought to plan on staying married for the long haul."

Nothing about love in any of those statements, Summer noticed. Commitment. But not love.

Summer wondered what would happen if she just admitted her feelings to Billy. But what if he didn't— couldn't—love her back the way she loved him? Friendship just wasn't enough anymore. She threaded her fingers together in her lap and focused on them as she said, "I don't think that's a good idea, Billy. I mean, I think it's important to be in love with the person you plan to spend your life with."

The ball was in his court. If he had feelings for her, surely he would declare them now. She'd given him the perfect opening.

But all he said was, "Yeah. I suppose you're right."

Summer gave Billy directions to get to the penthouse on Woodway and exchanged an amused glance with him when the concierge at the desk gave them the key, then glanced at the small gym bag that was all Billy had brought along and asked, "Do you need help with your luggage, sir?"

"I think I can handle it," Billy said, slinging the bag over his shoulder.

A fast ride up the elevator, and they were inside the penthouse, which was filled with memories for Summer.

"Nice place," Billy commented as he dropped his bag on a silk-upholstered chair.

"I'm surprised you didn't put up more of an argument when I suggested it."

Billy shrugged. "It's a lot closer to the offices of De-Witt & Blackthorne than a motel somewhere along the freeway."

Summer headed straight for the pictures on the baby grand piano. "There are so many good times captured here. I want to go back and live them all over again."

"But then you'd have to live the bad times all over again, too," Billy said as he joined her. "Owen and Clay looked a lot more alike in high school." He pointed to a picture of Summer dressed in pink tights, standing between her brothers and said, "I never knew you took ballet lessons."

"Just for the blink of an eye. Which was how long I

lasted with the piano and the flute. It seems I had no affinity for instruments either large or small," she said with a grin.

"I guess you needed to find one just the right size," Billy said as he took her hand and placed it over the fly in his jeans.

Summer laughed and slid her palm down to cup him, feeling the length of him grow hard beneath her hand. "Amazing how much fun it can be to play, once you've had a little practice."

When she looked into Billy's eyes, it suddenly wasn't a game anymore. This was serious. She loved him. And though he liked her and admired her and obviously desired her, he didn't love her back. Summer felt a growing sense of desperation.

"Love me, Billy," she whispered. She purposely hadn't said "Make love to me." There was a difference. She wanted Billy to see it. She wanted Billy to feel it.

He kept his gaze focused on her as he lowered his head and touched her lips with his in a gesture of infinite tenderness. Oh. It felt like love.

But his eyes were dark and dangerous. A second later he scooped her up in his arms and said, "Which way?"

She pointed him down the hall toward her penthouse bedroom. He shoved a handful of stuffed animals off the bed, then tore off the bedspread and lay her on the cool sheets, following her down.

He popped the buttons on her shirt, and she smiled inwardly as one pinged off the headboard. He shoved her bra straps off her shoulders and dragged the bra out of the way as his mouth latched onto her naked breast. This was the lover she'd wanted, a little rough because he was impatient to touch, impatient to taste.

He stopped long enough to yank off her boots and pull down her jeans and underwear and finally unsnapped her bra when she couldn't get it undone, before throwing it across the room.

Summer laughed as he gave his own clothes the same crude treatment, tearing at cloth and buttons until he was as naked as she was. But there was no more foreplay. She gasped as he gripped her hips and drove into her in one swift thrust.

He stopped and stared into her eyes. She thought he was going to speak, but instead, he leaned over and kissed her hard on the mouth, a kiss of claiming, of absolute possession.

His hands moved over her, touching, testing, until she was alive with sensation. She arched her back as his mouth once more claimed a breast, her hands clutching his silky hair as he suckled her.

His lips continued their delicious torment at her throat, and she tasted the salt on his shoulder and nipped at his flesh as she sought to give back the pleasure she took. His love bites became harder, more savage, as his body pumped into hers, but she felt only an exquisite pleasure that pulsed and grew.

He buried his face in her neck, binding her hands on either side of the pillow, giving her no chance of escape. She drove her hips up to meet his, writhing beneath him as they both sought the pinnacle of pleasure. She cried aloud and heard a wrenching groan tear from his throat as they found what they'd sought.

They both lay heaving, their bodies sweat-slick, and for the first time Summer was aware of the ice-cold air-conditioning. She shivered when a blast of air hit her heated flesh. "It's cold in here."

Billy released her hands and started to rise off of her, but Summer slid her arms around his waist and held on, wanting to feel the weight of him, not wanting the closeness to end.

The words *I love you* were on the tip of her tongue. All she had to do was say them. She didn't think Billy would mind. It was a good thing to love someone.

But not if he didn't love her back.

Summer didn't speak, and when Billy lifted himself and slid to her side, she didn't stop him. He reached down and pulled the sheet up to cover them, then put an arm around her and nestled her close.

"This is nice," she said, as she slid her fanny into the niche created by his thighs.

"Yeah," he agreed. "Nice."

"Are you hungry?" she asked. "We can order something from the concierge downstairs."

He nuzzled her neck. "Not for food," he said.

She opened her eyes and turned to stare at him over her shoulder. "You can't possibly—"

"That was just an appetizer," he said. "Now I'm ready for the main course."

Summer grinned. It seemed there were some things she hadn't known about Billy Coburn. "Have you always been this insatiable?" she asked as she turned in his arms and kissed his throat.

He took her head between his hands and forced her to

look at him. "I was never like this with anyone else. Only with you. I'm always hungry for you."

It wasn't love. But it was still a precious feeling. Summer turned her face up for his kiss, felt the gentleness of it, felt his need. She moaned as Billy once more filled her full.

Chapter 17

EMMA COBURN HADN'T EXPECTED TO FALL IN love with Sam Creed, or she never would've gone to work for him. She hadn't known what to say when he asked her to marry him. She liked Sam well enough, but she didn't trust men. And with good reason. The men in her life hadn't exactly proved trust-worthy.

Johnny Ray Coburn hadn't been any girl's dream of a father. He'd only hit her once, but there were other ways of hurting a person without using your fists. Billy had been there to protect her physically, but neither of them had known how to give comfort to one another. And even though she knew Billy had to leave when he did, she'd felt betrayed when he took the TSCRA job and moved to Amarillo.

Then there was the father of her baby. It wasn't his fault he'd used her body and given her nothing in re-turn—except a baby, of course. She hadn't asked for more.

Sam had come into her life at a vulnerable time. Her mother was too wrapped up in her own pain to notice Emma's. And when Billy answered her call and came home, her foolish brother thought that what she needed was help running the C-Bar, when what she'd really hoped for was a strong, sympathetic shoulder to cry on. She'd felt cheated when she saw how easily he shared a hug with his new wife, when he'd never offered her one.

Emma had needed someone to hold her close, to tell her everything would be all right, to remind her she was a good person and would be a good mother. Sam had offered her a job, and in the short time she'd worked for him, proceeded to do all that and more.

How could she not have fallen in love with him?

Although, to be honest, when she'd first interviewed with Sam, what she'd seen was the wheelchair, not the man. He'd seemed so . . . safe. She'd had no qualms about living in the same house with him, certain that she could simply pull free and outrun him if she ever felt threatened.

Emma smiled. How naïve she'd been. Sam Creed was a great deal stronger than he looked sitting in that wheelchair. She'd figured that out when she accidentally caught him with his shirt off, late one night in the kitchen.

Cotton pajamas covered his legs, but his upper body reminded her of sculpted stone, muscle and sinew and bone chiseled out precisely by some master artisan. She'd wanted to touch. She'd leaned across him into the refrigerator to get some cream for her coffee, bracing a hand on one of his shoulders, and felt the warm flesh ripple powerfully beneath her fingertips.

She'd lain in bed that night and wondered about the rest of him, about the part that had been paralyzed since he was eighteen. Wondered how a man in a wheelchair made love.

Tonight she would find out.

"Emma, is it all right if I come in?"

"Yes, Sam."

The door opened and he wheeled himself into the room. Emma sat up straighter in bed. When she'd first come into the house, she leaped to help Sam at every turn. He'd soon made it clear that he could take care of himself and that if he wanted her help, he'd ask for it. She made no move to help him now, simply waited in bed for her lover to come to her.

She'd seen his lower body before, when he'd taken a bath with her, and it was as weak and frail as his upper torso was healthy and strong. When she'd invited him into the bath, it hadn't occurred to her to wonder how he would get in and out. But he'd laid a board across the tub and levered himself out of his wheelchair and onto it, and then levered himself off the board and into the tub, inviting her with a smile to join him.

Emma quivered when she remembered how it had felt to sit before him, enfolded in his arms, to have him caress her breasts and to have his lips tease her neck and throat. She hadn't done any necking before. She'd just had sex. Once. In the front seat of a Chevy pickup.

She'd been nervous and shy in the tub with Sam, but he'd been infinitely patient. He'd made her feel beautiful, even with a belly sticking five inches out in front of her. His hands had marveled at the shape of her, marveled at the child growing inside her, made her realize what a miracle it was . . . what a miracle she was.

That had scared her right out of the tub. She'd jumped up dripping water and grabbed for a towel to cover herself. She was poor white trash. Always had been. And she was nothing more in this house than Sam Creed's cook and housekeeper. She had no business listening to such nonsense.

But Sam had repeated his compliments. Often. And made her believe them. She was beautiful. The child growing inside her was a precious gift. She was funny and smart. She was a good cook. She was a kind and loving woman.

She was afraid to believe it would last. She was sure Sam would change his mind about her once he got to know her better. But the more she tried to hide herself from him, the more he'd sought out her innermost fears . . . and eased them.

He made her believe she was as capable of being loved as she was of loving. Although she wasn't quite sure yet what making love to Sam would be like. She didn't think he could have an erection, but they hadn't talked about it . . . yet.

She knew he used a Foley catheter to collect urine during the day, and that he wore the bag on the inside of his jeans when he was dressed. He'd tried removing it out of her sight when he'd come into the bathroom to bathe with her, but she'd wanted him to think she wasn't embarrassed by the way he managed his bodily functions.

Of course, she'd been terribly embarrassed, and he'd realized it when her pale skin had blushed a fiery red at his matter-of-fact explanation of what he was doing. But he'd looked at her and grinned and said, "At least you'll never have to worry about me leaving the toilet seat up."

That had made her laugh and eased the tension. She'd noticed he often made jokes when he could see others were uncomfortable with his disability. But the more she'd gotten to know him, the more she'd realized it was a defense mechanism to hide the hurt. It had been hard not to step between him and the rest of the world, but she'd seen that he didn't want or need her protection.

He only needed her to hold him and love him.

And because her need for love and affection was the equal of his, they'd come to a more than satisfactory meeting of the minds. Holding and touching and kissing had become a commonplace part of their daily life. It was time to move on to the next step. To lovemaking.

"I see you're already naked," Sam said.

Emma pulled the sheet a little tighter under her arms. "I thought that would be easier. I see you had the same idea."

Sam was sitting in the wheelchair wearing nothing but a towel wrapped around his waist. "Are you nervous?" he asked.

"No."

He tilted his head and looked into her eyes and she felt the telltale flush rising up her throat and admitted, "Yes, a little. All right, a lot."

He smiled crookedly and admitted, "Me, too."

"Have you . . . done this before?"

"I had a steady girlfriend in high school. We experimented quite a bit. Since then . . . I tried it once after my accident, but it wasn't too good for either of us."

"I see."

"So we'll both be finding our way," he said as he stripped away the towel and levered his naked body onto the bed beside her. "I think maybe this will work better if I'm in the middle. It'll give us more room to play."

She got out of bed, still holding on to the sheet to keep herself covered. He grinned and tugged it out of her hands and said, "You know I like to look at you."

She stood before him feeling beautiful because his warm brown eyes told her she was.

When he'd shifted himself into the center of the bed, with the pillows she'd been using stacked behind him, she asked, "Where would you like me?"

"How about sitting on my lap facing me?"

It was impossible not to notice the absence of an erection. "Will I be too heavy for you?" she asked, glancing at his legs.

"I'll be fine." When she hesitated, he said in a low, husky voice, "Come here, Emma. I want to kiss you."

That invitation got the desired response. She was on his lap lickety-split, her arms around his neck, her naked breasts pressed against his powerful chest, her lips pressed to his for the promised kiss. There was a little more of her between them than there had been a month ago. She was six months pregnant.

She loved kissing Sam. He put a lot into his kisses, languorous kisses, ravishing kisses, tender kisses, savage kisses. She hadn't known there were so many ways that mouths could meet and emotions be shared.

His hands traversed every part of her, face, throat, shoulders, breasts. So far all their loving had been done above the waist—with the exception of the adoring attention her growing belly had received.

They leaned their foreheads together so they could both watch as Sam shaped her rounded belly with his large, callused hands. His hands revered her, honored her, enjoyed her.

He leaned back and looked into her eyes and said, "Emma, have you ever had oral sex?"

Emma tried not to look shocked. She'd heard about it. Giggled about it in high school. But she didn't know anyone who'd actually done it. She cleared her throat and said, "No."

"Does the idea of oral sex upset you or disgust you?"

"I'm . . . not exactly sure what all is involved," she admitted.

"It would involve me kissing you here." Sam slid a hand across her belly and down between her thighs.

Emma jumped a little when Sam's hand closed over her, because he'd never touched her there before. "Why would you want to do that?" she asked, aware of a rising tension between her legs where he was touching her.

"Because it would bring you pleasure," he said. "And I would enjoy it."

Emma wasn't sure she believed him. That part of her body had always been taboo, and she couldn't imagine what Sam would find enjoyable about kissing her down there.

"Would you like to try it and see if you like it?" Sam asked.

Emma suddenly realized, without Sam saying it, that plain old ordinary sex, the "Wham, bam, thank you, ma'am!" kind of sex she'd experienced, was apparently not possible. Sam was offering her the only kind of sex he was able to share with her. If she refused, their intimacy would be confined to kisses and touches. Sam was saying there was more they could have together, more they could do, an act that would bring her pleasure and him enjoyment.

She'd be a fool to say no.

But Emma couldn't help being a little daunted. "You'll stop if I don't like it?"

Sam nodded. "Just say the word."

"All right," Emma said. "What do you want me to do?"

"Right now, let's just lie down together and hold each other."

Emma was grateful for the offer of something so easy to do, something she'd wanted to do for a long time. They both pulled the pillows from behind Sam, leaving one for each of them to lay their heads on as they turned to embrace one another on the bed.

Holding led to caressing. Emma's hands roamed Sam's body, wanting to bring him pleasure. "What can you feel?" she asked. "Where can you feel?"

Sam took her hand and lowered her fingertips to a spot just at his waist. "Here," he said, "I have feeling. Below this point, there's nothing."

"So you can feel this," Emma said as she kissed his shoulder.

"Uh-huh."

"And this," she said as she lowered her mouth to his nipple.

"Uh-huh."

"And this," she said, as she laved his nipple with her tongue and then bit gently.

Sam moaned.

"I guess you can," Emma said, a grin widening on her face. She made Sam lie still while she kissed the front of him, then made him turn over, so she could press angel kisses down his spine from the soft down at his nape to the dimples above his buttocks, where he couldn't feel them anymore.

"My turn," he said.

Emma took one look at her belly and laughed. "I haven't been lying on my stomach much lately."

"Then lie on your back," Sam said. He braced his arms on either side of her and kissed his way down to her belly, sliding slowly down the bed, stopping at all the interesting places he found along the way.

Emma couldn't help tensing as his head moved downward. He lifted her legs and slid them over his shoulders and she felt his silky hair against her thighs. She froze as his mouth touched her, and gasped as his lips and tongue sucked and darted and lapped, until the pleasure was almost unbearable. Emma arched upward, her body bowed by the strength of her response, no longer embarrassed by what he was doing, or the groans and moans he elicited from her, because he made it feel right and good.

"Sam!" she cried, grabbing at his hair.

He met her gaze and said, "Do you want me to stop?"

She shook her head vigorously. "God, no. It feels so good, I can't...I want..."

But by then he was kissing her again, making her pulse race and her thighs clench and her body ache. Her hands tightened on his hair and she held on, her body bucking upward as he held her hips in his hands and made love to her, giving her pleasure beyond anything she had imagined possible.

"Don't!" she cried suddenly. "Stop! I can't— I—"
She was in the grip of something larger than herself, her body trembling and aching and finally erupting with

sensations so powerful she cried out with pleasure and with pain.

She lay against the pillow, her chest heaving, her mind dazed, her body drained. She felt the mattress sink as Sam pulled his body up the bed until he lay with his head beside her.

"Are you all right?" he asked.

"No," she said, tears blurring her eyes.

"I'm sorry," he said, pulling her into his arms. "I'm so sorry, Emma. I didn't mean— I would never want—"

"Shut up, you stupid idiot," she said as she pressed her nose against his throat. "That was the most beautiful, most wonderful, most amazing thing that's ever happened to me. I had sex for the first time and made a baby and it was awful. Painful and awkward and humiliating. With you ... Sam, with you it was so different. I felt treasured and loved and there was so much ... pleasure."

Sam brushed her hair away from her face and kissed her nose and then her lips. "I'm sorry your first time wasn't good for you, Emma. But honestly, it's often painful the first time. I want you to marry me, Emma. I want you to be my wife. But you should know that sex is a big part of marriage. I can't give you more than what we just had."

Emma kissed his lips again, tasting herself there, and looked into Sam's eyes. "I love you, Sam. Even if we didn't have this, I'd love you. But this is ... so wonderful," she said with a laugh. "I don't know what you were so worried about."

Sam grinned. "I can't imagine."

"When are you going to make an honest woman out of me?" Emma asked.

"What?"

Emma arched a brow. "Or maybe now you're thinking 'Why buy the cow when the milk's free?'"

Sam laughed and said, "Emma Coburn, will you marry me?"

She looked into his warm brown eyes and said, "Yes, Sam. I would love to be your wife."

"Good. As soon as—"

The knock on the door surprised them. They didn't get many visitors and none in the middle of the afternoon. Emma scrambled out of bed and grabbed for the clothes she'd left folded on a nearby willow rocker. Sam made it back into his wheelchair just fine, but he hadn't brought any clothes with him into Emma's bedroom.

"Hellfire and damnation," he muttered.

"Hello! Anybody home?"

Sam grinned. "That's my brother Luke! He's home from Africa!" He grabbed the sheet from the bed to hide his shriveled legs and said, "Take your time getting dressed, then come and meet us in the kitchen."

Emma stood with her bra in her hand and stared at the closed door. Dear God. She'd hoped she'd be married to Sam before Luke got back. Because he was going to take one look at her and realize there had been repercussions to their brief interlude six months ago.

She'd loved Luke since she was twelve, but he'd never looked twice at her. Until that fateful night, when they'd both been a little drunk.

Luke had realized too late she was a virgin, but her hymen had been intact and there'd been some blood and there'd been no denying it when he'd confronted her. He'd been angry at her for not telling him. Angry that she'd let him make love to her for the first time in the front seat of a pickup. Angry that he'd let himself make love to her when what he'd really wanted was another woman, the girl he'd dated all through high school. The girl whose engagement party they were both attending.

Her first sexual experience had been exactly the way she'd described it to Sam. Painful and awkward and humiliating. But what they'd done had started a child in her. And however much she wished it wasn't true, Sam's brother was the father of her baby.

"I'm not dressed," Sam called to Luke. "Come on in and make yourself at home."

Sam should have realized Luke wouldn't wait in the kitchen. A moment later his younger brother sauntered into Sam's bedroom, looking fit and tanned. He was taller than Sam had been at the same age, and a lot more lanky, with dark brown hair and gray-green eyes that were old beyond his twenty years.

"What are you doing in your skivvies in the middle of the afternoon?" Luke asked. "If I didn't know better, I'd say you'd been enjoying a little—"

Sam couldn't help the flush. He kept right on dressing as Luke walked up and stood in front of him.

"Talk about a wolf in sheep's clothing," Luke said with a grin. "You've got a girl here somewhere, haven't you?"

With his jeans on, Sam didn't feel quite so exposed. He pulled a T-shirt over his head and said, "Not just a girl. The girl I'm going to marry."

Luke whistled and clapped. "Hallelujah and hosanna!

My big brother is in love. Who's the lucky girl? Anyone I know?"

"I'm the one who's lucky," Sam said. "And it's definitely someone you know."

"Don't tell me. Let me guess." Luke named four girls in quick succession who'd all had crushes on Sam when he'd played football in high school.

"Nope. I'll give you a hint," Sam said. "Once upon a time she was skinny as a bed slat."

Luke frowned. "Hell if I can remember anyone who—"

"Bright red hair."

Luke slapped his forehead. "Emma Coburn!" He stared hard at Sam and said, "Emma Coburn? How did you two meet?"

"She's been cooking and cleaning for me for the past month or so since Blackjack moved in with Mom."

Luke scowled. "I couldn't believe it when you wrote me what was going on with the two of them. That sonofabitch is right where he deserves to be now that he's in jail. How's Mom taking it?"

"She's pretty broken up. She doesn't believe he's guilty."

"She wouldn't," Luke said disgustedly. "When are you and Emma getting married?"

"As soon as we can get the church reserved." He hesitated, then said, "She's pregnant."

Luke's jaw dropped. "Wonders never cease." He crossed and picked up Sam's hand and gripped it hard. "I thought ... I mean, I figured you couldn't ... I mean, the doctors said you couldn't ..."

Sam pulled his hand free. "I wish—"

At that instant Emma knocked on the door and said, "Are you two coming out of there anytime soon?"

Before Sam could stop him, Luke hurried to the door and pulled it open. He stopped dead in his tracks when he saw Emma's belly.

Sam watched Emma's face bleach white as she met Luke's gaze.

Luke's head swung around to Sam. "I thought you said she'd only been working for you a month. She's got to be—"

"She's six months pregnant," Sam confirmed. "I was trying to tell you. The baby isn't mine. It's—"

"Mine," Luke said in a harsh voice. He turned back to Emma and said, "Isn't that right, Emma? That baby is *mine!*"

Sam's heart skipped a beat. Maybe more than one. He was staring at Emma, expecting her to deny it. Needing her to deny it. But she wouldn't look at him. Her eyes were lowered to her hands, which protectively surrounded her belly.

Sam wheeled his chair over to the door, forcing himself between Luke and Emma. "Is that true, Emma? Is Luke the father?"

"Yes."

Her voice was so soft he barely heard the word, but it shattered his world. "Why didn't you tell me?" He saw the desolation in her eyes, but the pain he felt in his own chest was excruciating. How could he marry her now? The answer was he couldn't. She was pregnant with his brother's child, for God's sake!

A tear dripped off her chin and fell onto her blouse.

"What am I supposed to do with you?" Sam said, rubbing angrily at his stinging eyes.

"Couldn't we go on the way we were?" Emma said.

"No."

"Why not?"

"Because I couldn't stand to look at you."

He saw Emma cringe and knew she'd misunderstood him. She thought he hated her, when the exact opposite was true. He couldn't bear to look at her because it would tear his guts out. And he sure as hell couldn't marry her. Not now.

"You and Luke should marry," he said. "I'll make the arrangements as soon as possible."

Luke looked at him, startled. "I'm not in love with Emma," he said. "And if she was going to marry you—"

"You're the father of her child. You'll do the right thing and give that child your name, or you're no brother of mine!"

"What about Emma?" Luke countered. "What if she doesn't want to marry me?"

"Emma's child needs a father, and you're it," Sam said implacably.

"Emma, say something!" Luke shouted.

Sam's fist connected with Luke's solar plexus with a satisfying *thwack*. "Don't shout at her. She's in a delicate condition."

Luke massaged his belly with his hand and glared at Sam. "You're plumb crazy."

"Crazy or not," Sam said, "as soon as the church is available, you're marrying Emma Coburn."

Chapter 18

Summer could feel the noose tightening around her father's throat as though it were choking her. Her mother had done her work well, and it was beginning to look like there was no way to prove his innocence. Uncle Harry was the last hope they had of discovering information that might clear her father.

As she and Billy drove into the high-rise parking garage that adjoined the steel and glass DeWitt & Blackthorne office building, she voiced her fear aloud. "What if Uncle Harry can't help us?"

"Let's not borrow trouble," Billy said. "Let's wait and see what he has to say."

The computer directory on the main floor of the towering building told them Harry Blackthorne had his office on the 40th floor, but they had to go through rigorous security before they could get on the elevator.

"Probably noticed how many Texans out there with guns don't like lawyers," Billy said.

"At least Uncle Harry is harmless. Why are you so nervous?"

"Don't like courtrooms. Don't like judges. Really don't like lawyers," Billy muttered.

The receptionist on the 40th floor was immaculately groomed and could have modeled for a New York agency. "Mr. Blackthorne is expecting you," she said. "Follow the hallway to the left. It's the corner office."

Summer noticed that the anxiety Billy had let her see downstairs was absent when they entered Harry Blackthorne's office.

The older man, who was as tall as all the Blackthornes and had ice-blue eyes and a full head of silver-gray hair, rose and stretched out his hand to Billy. "Good morning," he said.

"Good morning, Mr. Blackthorne," Billy replied.

"Call me Uncle Harry," the older man said with a genial smile as he released Billy's hand.

Summer took a step closer and rose on tiptoe to kiss the old man on the cheek. "Hi, Uncle Harry."

"It's good to see you, Missy. I'm sorry it's under such sad circumstances. Why don't you two sit down?" Harry said, gesturing toward two brass-studded burgundy leather armchairs on the opposite side of his desk. "And let's get down to business."

"I noticed you were expecting us," Billy said. "How did you know we were coming?"

"Mrs. Creed called on your father's behalf and told me you were on your way. I would have been in contact with you anyway, Summer. As you know, I handle both your parents' estates. A few weeks ago your mother sent me an envelope to be passed on to you in the event of her death. Since you're here, I can deliver it to you in person."

Summer exchanged a look with Billy. Was it going to

be this easy? Had her mother left a note explaining everything and exonerating Blackjack?

"I got it out of the safe this morning," Harry said, shuffling through the papers on his desk. "Here it is."

Summer recognized the vellum envelope with the Circle B brand in the corner. She took it and stared down at her name in her mother's handwriting. She turned to Billy and said, "Should I open it now?"

"It's up to you."

"It might be something legal," Summer said, glancing up at her great-uncle Harry.

Harry Blackthorne shrugged. "I'm afraid I don't know. The envelope was sealed, and I put it away never imagining I'd be handing it over so soon."

Summer ripped open one end and pulled out a piece of Bitter Creek stationery. She let the envelope slip to her lap as she read the letter.

Dear Summer,

If you're reading this, I'm no longer in this world. I've always feared what your father might do to have that Creed woman. If the circumstances of my death are suspicious, be sure you tell the authorities how your father threatened me. Remember, if he's prosecuted for my death, Bitter Creek will be yours at last.

Your father says he loves that woman above all else. She'll realize someday that it's the land he loves more than anything or anyone. That will be his downfall, of course. Like those who came before him, he never could give up a single acre of it, and he always wanted more.

Well, my darling daughter, I've given you the only clue I intend to offer to the puzzle I'm certain you're trying to solve. I've left the answer for you to find. Someday you may see it under your nose, but with any luck at all, it will be long after Jackson Blackthorne has been sent to hell and is rotting there.

> *Love and kisses,*
> *Eve*

Summer's heart was pounding as she finished reading and she felt nauseous. How could her mother believe she would betray her father to have Bitter Creek? Had her mother really believed her life was in danger? Summer couldn't believe she'd really been afraid. But what had provoked her to write this letter so close to her death? And what "answer" had her mother left for her to find?

This letter suggested there was another letter somewhere that would answer the question of what had really happened to her mother and which might provide the key to free her father. All she had to do was figure out where that "answer" was hidden.

Summer read the letter again. And again.

"What does it say?" Billy asked.

"It says there's a clue in this letter to what really happened. But I don't see it!"

"Let me take a look," Billy said.

Summer passed the letter to him and studied his face while he read it. He looked at her, his brow furrowed. "This doesn't say anything helpful that I can see. But it sounds like she's left another letter somewhere that explains more."

"That's exactly what I thought," Summer said.

"May I take a look?" Harry asked.

Billy glanced at Summer, who nodded, and he handed the letter over to the lawyer.

"What is she talking about, Uncle Harry?" Summer asked.

"Damned if I know," Harry said. "But what's here doesn't help your father in the least. If anything, it implicates him by suggesting that your mother knew he loved another woman and had threatened her."

Summer choked back a sob. "Do you recognize the clue she's said is there?"

"It's as much a mystery to me as it is to you," he said, handing the letter back to her.

"Did she leave anything else with you?" Summer asked. "What about her will? Is there anything written there that might be useful or be the 'answer' she mentioned?"

Harry shook his head. "I'm sorry, Missy. Just who gets what and when. Maybe that letter you're holding will mean something to your father."

"Of course!" Summer said, jumping up. "You can fax it to the jail and—"

"That's not a good idea," Billy interrupted.

"Why not?" Summer asked.

Billy looked at the lawyer, who deferred to Billy with a nod. "Because the law enforcement officer who receives the fax would see that it implicates Blackjack. And it could become evidence against him."

"Then we'd better get going," Summer said. "We have to get this to Daddy right away." Her uncle was already on his feet, and Summer kissed him on the cheek again and said, "Thank you, Uncle Harry. If you think of anything, please leave a message for me at the Castle."

Uncle Harry patted her on the shoulder and said, "I hope you can figure it all out. I don't think your father had anything to do with what happened to your mother."

"Thank you, Uncle Harry."

Summer was already gone from the room when Billy turned back and said, "Just out of curiosity, why do you think Blackjack is innocent?"

"Because if he'd murdered Eve, you'd have found his fingerprints on her throat."

"Gotcha," Billy said.

Billy caught up with Summer in the hall, where she'd stopped to talk to some guy in a thousand-dollar suit. It took Billy a moment to recognize him. It was Summer's former fiancé.

"Billy, you remember Geoffrey, don't you?" Summer said, putting herself between the two men as she introduced them.

Geoffrey offered his hand and said, "Congratulations on your marriage. You're a lucky man."

Billy didn't want to shake the other man's hand, but there was no way out of it. "I know I am."

In his head Billy was making the comparison Summer had to be making, between the handsome, well-dressed, well-educated—and rich—lawyer she'd turned down, and the man in blue jeans and a weather-worn Western shirt she'd married. He forced himself to control the belligerence that always rose when he felt defensive.

"I've never seen you in your milieu, Geoffrey," Summer said as she looked him up and down. "You look like you can knock them dead in court."

"Well, I'm a little more effective there than I seem to be in your average parking lot," Geoffrey said as he eyed Billy and rubbed his chin. The lawyer was smiling to make a joke of it, but Billy felt his neckhairs hackle at the reminder of how badly he'd wanted to shove good-old-Geoffrey's teeth down his throat.

Billy put a possessive arm around Summer's waist and said, "It was nice seeing you, but we have to go." He was glad she moved with him, because he wasn't sure what he would have done if she hadn't.

When they got past the receptionist Summer turned on him and said, "What in the world got into you? I was afraid that if he said one more word you were going to punch him in the nose."

"If he had, I would have," Billy said.

"What is your problem?" Summer said. "I didn't choose him, I chose you."

"Yeah, but why, Summer? What I don't understand is why? He's got everything a woman could want. I've got nothing."

"I want a *man,* Billy. Geoffrey is a boy dressed in grown-up clothes. You're so much more than he could ever be. You're determined and courageous and you never, *ever* give up."

Billy stared at her. He hadn't known how much he'd needed to hear her say what she was saying. He turned his back on her and swallowed noisily. He felt her at his shoulder and turned his face away.

"I know I should have said this a long time ago, because I've felt it for a very long time. I love you, Billy."

It was everything he'd ever dreamed of hearing her say. Everything he'd ever hoped. He'd turned to tell her he loved her, too, when the elevator doors opened with a loud *ding*.

The elevator was full of people, and Billy bit his tongue to keep from spilling his feelings in front of them. She was fidgeting, and he grabbed her hand and held it tight.

"Take it easy," he murmured. "We'll figure it out."

"When did you start caring about Blackjack?" Summer whispered.

"I don't care about him. I care about you." He wanted to say more, but he needed privacy to do it. "I don't want you unhappy. If that means saving Blackjack, then that's what we'll do."

"Thanks, Billy," Summer said as she squeezed his hand.

Summer practically ran from the elevator to Billy's old Dodge and was inside waiting for Billy when he got there. They would be on their way in a moment, with plenty of time and privacy ahead of them for him to tell her that he loved her.

Except his pickup wouldn't start.

"Perfect!" Summer said, pounding the dash. "This is just perfect."

Billy got out and put the hood up to look at the engine. "Damn," he said.

"What is it?" Summer said, joining him.

"Alternator."

"How long will it take to fix that?"

"Couple of hours, if I can find the part."

"What do you mean, 'if' you can find the part?"

"It's an old truck, Summer. Parts aren't always easy to find."

"Then leave it. We'll find another way to get back."

"I'm going to need my truck, Summer. I can't just leave it here."

"Why not? It's a piece of junk. We'll buy another one."

"With what money?"

Summer stared at him without blinking, and Billy realized she must be expecting some sort of inheritance from her mother.

"How much?" he said flatly.

"Not more than a couple of million," she said. "Most of her estate was land, and that went to Aunt Ellen."

"Sonofabitch," he said. "Why did you marry me, Summer? You sure as hell weren't hoping I'd be able to take care of you, because you can take damned fine care of yourself!"

"I told you why," she said, standing toe-to-toe with him. "I love you."

He wanted to believe her. What other reason could she have for staying with him? He wanted to tell her that he loved her, too. Had always loved her. Would always love her. The words were on the tip of his tongue.

But what kind of man lived off money provided by the woman he loved? He wouldn't be able to face himself in the mirror. It had ruined his father, turned him into a mean, slothful drunk. Billy couldn't bear to end up that way. But he knew in his heart that sooner or later he'd resent Summer's money. He couldn't help it.

It might be old-fashioned. But he wanted to be the one to take care of her. And that was never going to happen.

"What do you want to do, Billy?"

He wanted to call around town and find an alternator and fix his pickup. But they were running out of time to save Blackjack. Summer needed him now more than she ever had. He would just have to swallow his pride and let her spend her money to get them both home.

He slammed down the hood and said, "Let's go buy a new truck."

Sam's house was empty. Again. For a short time it had been a home full of love and laughter. And he'd given it all away. To his brother. But how could he have fought for Emma, when it meant stealing away his brother's child?

After his ultimatum to Luke, Emma had finally spoken. She'd turned to his brother and said, "I need to pack a bag. Then I'd appreciate a ride back to the C-Bar."

She hadn't spoken a word to him.

Luke had glared at him, sullen and defiant. "I don't have to marry Emma to be a father to my kid."

"Emma deserves a husband," Sam had said. "Your child deserves his father."

They hadn't spoken another word while they waited for Emma. It hadn't taken her long. It was a small bag, and not heavy, but Sam moved forward to take it from her. She pulled it out of his reach and said, "I'm not a cripple."

She bit her lip, but he'd already backed away. She didn't protest when Luke took the bag for her and said, "You ready?"

She nodded. She didn't look at him when she said, "Good-bye, Sam."

"I'll see you at the wedding," he'd said.

She hadn't replied, just turned and walked out the screen door. Luke had let it slam behind them.

Sam had left the house in his truck and returned with a bottle wrapped in a brown paper bag. He'd poured himself a glass of Jack Daniel's and set it on the kitchen table and stared at it. He wanted a drink. He needed a drink. He figured if there was ever an excuse to take one, this was it.

He fingered the glass, knowing how dangerous one sip of liquor could be for an alcoholic. Only, he already knew he wanted more than one drink. He wanted the oblivion to be found in the whole bottle. Because he didn't think he could bear seeing Emma become his brother's wife.

Sam dropped his head into his hands. He didn't see what else he could have done. Luke might think he didn't care now, but what would happen when he was a little older and realized what he'd given up?

God, why hadn't Emma told him? Why had she let him make love to her—fall in love with her—if she'd known how impossible their situation was?

He took the glass in his hand, gripping it hard, but before he got it to his mouth, he was interrupted by a knock.

"Sam? Are you in there?"

He set the glass down and crossed to the door but didn't open it. "I guess Luke told you what happened," he said to his mother through the screen.

"He did," she said. "May I come in?"

"I don't want to talk about it," Sam said.

But like mothers everywhere, she couldn't let well enough alone. "I think we have to talk about it," she said.

Sam backed up as his mother opened the screen door and came inside. "I'm having a drink," he said. "You want to join me?"

"Nothing for me right now," she said, eyeing the bottle of Jack Daniel's and the glass of liquor on the table. "I just want to talk."

Sam crossed back to the table and said, "I'm listening."

She sighed and sat across from him at the table. "I should have told all you kids the truth a long time ago. Four years ago, I had a golden chance to tell your sister Callie what I'm about to tell you, but I choked and told her a lie instead."

"What are you talking about, Mom? You've completely lost me."

"I know something about what you're going through right now, how confused you're feeling, and—"

"How could you possibly know what I'm feeling?" Sam said in a harsh voice.

Her eyes met his, and he almost couldn't bear the look of sorrow he saw.

"There's a reason why your father and I never celebrated our wedding anniversary," she said. "The math wouldn't have added up. I wasn't pregnant with Callie when I married your father." She paused, swallowed hard, and said, "I was pregnant with another child."

Sam stared at his mother, his jaw agape. Before he could say a word, she raised a hand and cut him off. "I'll tell you what all this has to do with you. Just let me say it in my own way."

He saw her hand was trembling as she shoved the hair back from her face. To give her credit, she looked him in the eye as she continued her confession.

"I was already pregnant with Jesse's child—although we weren't married—when I met and fell in love with Jackson Blackthorne. Neither of us expected it to happen. It just happened."

"Then Dad was right to be jealous of Blackjack," Sam said, his stomach churning.

"Please, Sam," his mother said. "Just listen."

Sam sat back in his wheelchair and crossed his arms. "I'm listening."

"Jackson asked me to marry him," she continued. "But I refused. Not because I didn't love him, but because I was pregnant with Jesse Creed's baby and Jackson was a Blackthorne and I couldn't imagine how that could ever work out."

"How did you— What happened to the baby?" Sam blurted.

The tears welled in her eyes and he knew the answer before she spoke.

"I lost it. I had an accident and miscarried in the fourth month. But Jackson had already married Eve, and she was pregnant with Trace. It would have been impossible for us to divorce our spouses and marry each other without causing everyone pain.

"Unfortunately, I'd made the mistake of saying the wrong name at the wrong time, so your father knew I loved another man."

"I can't believe what I'm hearing," Sam said.

"Believe it. I wouldn't be telling you any of this, except I see history repeating itself. You can't let your brother marry Emma when you love her yourself. It will make you miserable. And I promise you it will make Emma unhappy. And Luke will only resent the fact his wife loves another man."

"Emma will learn to love Luke."

Ren shook her head. "She'll be Luke's wife, but she'll always yearn for you."

"Like you did for him?" Sam snarled.

His mother lowered her chin to her chest, and a tear dripped onto her cheek. "Yes. As I did for Jackson." She looked up at him, eyes glistening with pain, and said, "Don't you see, Sam? You can't make Emma and Luke care for one another any more than you can stop yourself from loving Emma."

"What about Luke's child? What happens to the baby?"

"With God's grace it'll be born healthy and strong, and you'll love it and raise it as your own."

"What happens when Luke gets a little older and realizes what he's given up?" Sam argued.

"Luke wants to go back to school. He wants to be a lawyer. I don't think marriage to Emma, especially with a child on the way, will fit into those plans very well."

Sam shook his head. "That's crazy. Luke, a lawyer? He's spent a helluva lot more time on the other side of the law."

"He told me he wants to be in a position to make the law work for us Creeds for a change. I'll tell you something else, though perhaps I shouldn't."

Sam waited, watching his mother press her fingertips to her lips as she made up her mind whether to speak.

"Luke is in love with another woman."

Sam nearly choked. "I don't believe you! He'd have said something to me."

"It's true. He's in love with her. But she's in love with another man. In fact, she's engaged to him. So you won't be doing Emma any favors forcing her into marriage with Luke."

"She'd be marrying the father of her child," Sam said stubbornly.

"Have you heard a word I've said? You've got Luke believing that he owes it to Emma to marry her. And I'd be willing to bet Emma's hurt enough and angry enough to go through with it to spite you.

"Don't let them do it, Sam. Don't make the same mistake I did. You can spare everyone so much pain, if you'll only let your heart rule your head."

They sat in silence while Sam considered his mother's advice. He ran a finger slowly around the rim of the glass, craving a taste of the whiskey inside. His gut hurt. His throat hurt. His heart hurt.

At last he said, "I'll think about what you've said."

Ren rose and crossed to Sam and took his head in her hands and kissed his forehead. "I love you, Sam. You deserve a life filled with happiness. Don't be too afraid or too bullheaded—to reach out and grab for it."

Sam let the door slam behind his mother without moving from where he sat. His chest physically ached, he missed Emma so much. It was hard to imagine Blackjack, who'd been an ogre all Sam's life, aching like this. Hard to imagine his mother pining, as he was pining, for someone who was beyond her reach forever.

Sam didn't want to understand. He didn't want to forgive. He didn't want to hurt like he was hurting. He grabbed the glass of whiskey and threw it against the wall, shattering it and leaving a trail of Jack Daniel's on the flowered wallpaper. Before he could change his mind, he picked up the bottle and wheeled himself over to the sink and poured it down the drain.

His mother had given him a great deal of food for thought. He needed a clear, sober head to digest it.

Chapter 19

SUMMER WASN'T SORRY SHE'D TOLD BILLY SHE loved him. But it had definitely made things awkward between them. The subject hadn't come up again the entire time they were hunting down a truck dealership, or during the long drive back to Bitter Creek from Houston in their shiny black Dodge Ram 4X4. She kept waiting for Billy to say the words back to her. But he never did.

Summer bit nervously at her cuticle, then forced her hand back into her lap. She just wished she knew one way or the other. Did he love her? Or didn't he? She opened her mouth to ask and shut it again. She didn't think she could keep on working with him if she knew for sure that he didn't. Better not to push for an answer right now. Better to be in limbo than in hell.

"I think we should go straight to the county jail and show Blackjack the letter," Summer said.

"I'll drop you off," Billy said. "You left your truck in town Thursday, so you can get back to the Castle on your own. I need to go home and check on Will and my mom. She said she'd call Emma if she needed help, but Mom tends to push herself harder than she should."

Summer was stung that Billy didn't want to follow through with her on her mother's letter. It was as though he were cutting himself off from her, making it clear they were headed for different destinations.

"I'll call you after I talk to Blackjack," she said.

"Yeah. Sure," he said as he stopped in front of the jail.

There was no kiss good-bye, no endearing farewell. She might have been a hitchhiker he'd picked up on the road.

Summer got out and stood at the curb as Billy drove away. She had the awful feeling that he was driving out of her life forever. Of course, that was ridiculous. But she shivered as she turned and walked into the jailhouse.

Summer wasn't surprised to see Ren Creed sitting with her father, but she was a little annoyed. She wasn't sure whether she ought to bring out her mother's letter now, or wait until Ren had left.

"What did you and Billy find out?" Blackjack asked.

"Nothing that would clear you," Summer replied. She glanced at Ren, remembered how her father had insisted on including Ren the last time they'd spoken, and said, "When we went to see Uncle Harry, he gave me a letter Momma left with him."

"That sounds promising," Blackjack said, reaching out and squeezing Ren's hand.

Summer focused on her father and ignored their clutched hands. "There are clues in this letter that there's another note somewhere. But I can't figure them out. I was hoping they'd mean something to you."

Summer handed the letter to her father and watched as he laid it open on the table and leaned over to share it with Ren.

"This statement about the land being my downfall seems important. But there's not much here to tell us what she really means," Blackjack said, shaking his head. "You're right that she's left something to find. Whatever it is, she's hidden it in plain sight."

"What do you mean?" Summer asked.

He pointed to the letter. "See here, where she says 'Someday you may see it under your nose'? Bet you everything I've got her hiding place is something you see every day on the ranch, something so common-place you'd never suspect it of being the key to the puzzle."

"That's no help!" Summer protested.

"Sure it is," her father said. "You just have to go through everything in the Castle piece by piece and look for a scrap of paper in a drawer or some film negative in a photograph album or a key to a safe-deposit box hidden in an old shoe."

"That could take forever! The grand jury is being convened Monday."

"Then you'd better get hopping," Blackjack said.

"I'll come and help," Ren offered. She must have seen Summer draw back because she added, "If you don't mind."

"Summer will be glad for the help," Blackjack said.

"Yes, I will," Summer agreed. After all, her father's life was at stake. "I'll call Billy and see if he can come over, too."

Summer offered Ren a ride because she expected the other woman to say she had her own pickup, but to her surprise, Ren accepted. Summer wasn't sure what the two of them would talk about during the drive home.

Summer couldn't help thinking of Ren the way her mother had, as the *other woman*.

"I wanted a chance to speak privately with you," Ren said, once Summer had her Silverado on the road.

Summer tensed and gripped the wheel tighter. "Oh?"

"I want us to be friends."

Summer made a sound that was half snort and half guffaw. "You've got to be kidding."

"Not in the least."

Summer stared at Lauren Creed, appalled at the woman's gall. It took the blare of an oncoming car horn to get her eyes back on the road.

"I can see I've taken you off guard," Ren said.

"I'll say," Summer retorted. "You're the enemy. Why would I want to be your friend?"

"Because I love your father. And we got married this afternoon."

Summer swerved the pickup onto the shoulder and braked to a skidding stop, killing the engine before it died on its own. She searched for Ren's ring finger, looking for a diamond at least the size of her mother's. But there was no ring at all there, only a bare white space where a ring used to be.

Ren's hands were settled calmly in her lap. "Jackson was afraid to tell you. He knows how you feel, and he doesn't want to lose you from his life. But you see, we've loved each other for a very long time, and he wanted to be certain that whatever happens to him, the feud between our families will end with us."

Summer turned the key and gunned the engine, burning rubber as she accelerated. "I'm turning around—"

She felt Ren's hand on her arm and jerked free, nearly running the pickup off the road before she stopped again. Her chest was heaving, her stomach rolling.

"We've had papers drawn up to merge Three Oaks and Bitter Creek," Ren said into the silence.

Summer dropped her forehead with painful force onto the steering wheel. She would have made some exclamation of shock or dismay, except her throat had closed so tight she couldn't speak. She lifted her head and stared at the other woman, the blood pounding in her temples, her whole body shaking.

"You might wonder why I'm telling you all this now, instead of waiting to give you this news when I'm with your father. The truth is, his heart isn't as strong as he wants you to believe. I couldn't take the chance that you'd upset him."

"Upset *him*?" Summer croaked. "How could he? How could you both?"

"We love each other. We wanted the feud to end."

"You think this is going to stop it?" Summer asked incredulously.

"There's nothing left to fight over," Ren said. "The land now belongs to all our children equally, the profits to be paid in even shares."

Summer asked the question that was of primary interest to her. "Who's going to run Bitter Creek?"

"Sam will continue running the cutting horse operation at Three Oaks. Your father will manage things at Bitter Creek, presuming he's cleared of the murder charges against him."

"And if he isn't?"

"We haven't considered that alternative."

Summer was still dazed. Still unable to absorb Ren's revelations.

"Maybe I should drive," Ren suggested.

"I can manage." Summer reached up with a shaking hand to turn the key in the ignition. She checked the sideview mirror, glanced over her shoulder as she'd been taught, then merged slowly and carefully onto the two-lane road.

"I'm sorry this has come as such a shock to you," Ren said.

"Just not sorry enough to leave my father alone," Summer said bitterly.

"As I said, we've loved each other for a long time. I know it's difficult for you—"

"You bet it is!"

"I thought since you've fallen in love yourself, you might understand. You don't choose who you love. And you can hide your feelings, but they never really go away."

"I don't need a lecture from you," Summer said. But she understood exactly what Ren was saying. Summer hadn't been able to love anyone but Billy Coburn. And she would love him till the day she died, whether he loved her back or not.

Understanding helped, but it wasn't the same thing as acceptance. Acceptance was going to take a little longer. In the meantime, Summer couldn't bring herself to be openly rude to Ren, not now that she was Blackjack's wife.

When they arrived at the Castle, Ren followed her inside without a word. Summer turned to her and said,

"Why don't we go upstairs to start? You can work in Trace's bedroom. I need to call Billy."

Summer used the phone in her own bedroom, closing the door so Ren wouldn't hear if she broke into tears on the phone. "My father married Lauren Creed this afternoon," she wailed as soon as Billy answered.

"I guess we should have seen it coming," he said. "I have to admit I never thought they'd go through with it."

"Ren said they've drawn up papers merging Three Oaks and Bitter Creek."

There was silence on the other end of the line.

"Did you hear what I said?"

"I heard. Where does that leave you?"

Without anything, Summer thought. What she said was, "I don't know. I wondered if you have time to come over and . . . and help with the search."

She didn't ask him to come and comfort her. She was afraid she might fall to pieces if all he offered her was friendly comfort, when what she wanted—needed—was his love.

"Emma and Sam broke up," Billy said. "She's pretty distraught, and I don't want to leave her alone. If it's all right, we'll both come over. We'll have to bring Will along. Will that be a problem?"

"No," Summer said. "I've missed him." And she had. Her life with Billy seemed all the more priceless now that she'd lost it. "Tell Emma I'm grateful for the extra help."

While she waited for Billy to arrive, Summer searched her mother's studio. It was the place where Eve Blackthorne had spent most of her time and seemed the most likely place where she'd bury her secret. Summer started by checking the back of her mother's final paint-ing—the longhorn attacked by wolves—looking for some paper concealed in the frame. When she found nothing, she covered the disturbing canvas with a cloth.

The rest of her thorough search was equally fruitless and frustrating, so Summer welcomed the sound of Will's laugh and Billy's heavy bootsteps coming down the upstairs hall. She stepped beyond the door, crouched down on one knee, and opened her arms.

And Will came bounding into them. "Hi, Mer," he said, which was the best he could do with her name.

"Hi, scamp," she said, rising as she gave him a big hug and a raspberry on his neck.

Will giggled and wriggled in her arms, and she was struggling to keep from dropping him when Billy came to the rescue, enfolding both of them in his arms.

"I told Emma to start in the kitchen," Billy said. "Not that I think your mother ever set foot in the place, but maybe because of that she figured we'd never look there."

"So of course that's where she's hidden the note," Summer finished for him. "How are we ever going to get through this house in two days?"

"One room at a time," Billy said.

"I've been all through Momma's studio and didn't find a thing. All the time I was looking, I kept wondering if she'd left a message in invisible gesso that requires a secret decoder, like lemon juice, to make it appear on the canvas."

Billy chuckled. "I wouldn't put it past her. She was pretty devious."

"Then I remind myself that she said I'd find what I'm looking for 'right under my nose.' That seems to eliminate invisible gesso."

"And suggests it's something you might smell. Which means something in the kitchen," Billy said.

"Or a flower vase."

"Or bathroom toiletries."

"Or perfume!" Summer headed for her mother's bedroom with Will in her arms and Billy on her heels. "Mother loved Chanel No. 5. She said it was a classic scent that would never go out of style."

She set Will on the carpeted floor and searched her mother's dressing table for the perfume she knew her mother used exclusively. "There's something here!" she said excitedly, tearing away a piece of paper that was taped to the bottom of the perfume bottle.

Billy stood at her shoulder as she opened the tiny piece of paper and read, *"Too obvious. Keep Hunting. E."*

"Damn her!" Summer said, tearing the paper into tiny pieces. "She's treating this like a game. A man's life is at stake!"

They heard Emma yelling from the kitchen, "Billy, I've found something!"

Billy grabbed Will and they headed down the stairs on the run, joined by Ren, who'd heard Emma's shout. They all arrived breathless in the kitchen to find Emma holding a note similar to the one Summer had found.

"I found it on the bottom of a pickle jar in the refrigerator." Emma held it out to Summer. "It says, *'Don't be so literal. E.'* "

"In other words," Billy said, "what we're looking for is something in plain sight, but not something that has a smell."

"Unless this is all part of the game," Summer said.

Billy cocked a questioning brow.

"These notes are easy to find and suggest we're searching in the wrong place. What if she planned it so we give up when we find these useless notes and miss the real note, which turns out to be attached to a flower vase or . . . or . . ."

"Or in the barn, which is full of interesting smells," Emma said.

"Oh, God. I haven't even let myself think she might have hidden a note out there. It's enormous. And there are just too many hiding places."

"Let's stick with the house for now," Billy said.

"I've about finished with Trace's room," Ren said. "Where would you like me to look next?"

Summer rubbed a hand across her eyes. "The twins' room, if you don't mind. It's next door to Trace's."

Ren left and headed back up the stairs.

"I still have more work to do here," Emma said, turning away and opening the cupboard under the sink.

"Where do you want me?" Billy said.

"Bring Will, and you and I can search the library. Maybe Momma put her note in with some of Daddy's papers."

"Or in one of the thousand or so books in there," Billy said.

Summer crossed the threshold of the library that also served as her father's office, took one look at the immense wall of leather-bound tomes, and glanced back at Billy, unable to keep the hopelessness from her eyes.

Billy set Will on the Turkish carpet, handed him a small silver globe from the desk, and said, "Have a ball, kid." Then he turned and took Summer in his arms.

"Oh, Billy." Her arms closed around his waist and she pressed her cheek against his chest, so she could hear his heartbeat. "I'm so afraid we're not going to find any letter. And if we don't—"

He tipped her chin up and kissed her gently on the mouth. "What happened to the indomitable spirit of the girl I fell in love with?"

Summer drew in a breath. She looked into Billy's eyes, hoping he was at last returning the offer of love she'd made to him. But his dark eyes remained shuttered, and the word *love* didn't come up again.

"It's hard to be brave when there's so much at risk," she said.

"I know," he said. "But that's when you have to forge ahead, despite all the odds."

Summer realized that was what Billy had done all his life. That was what had allowed him to survive under the harshest of circumstances. That was what made him a good father and a good friend and the man she loved.

"Thank you, Billy," Summer said as she released him and stepped back.

"Ready to go to work?"

"Ready. Let's start with the books."

By Monday morning, when the grand jury convened, Summer and Billy and Emma and Ren had still found nothing. Summer spent the endless days that followed desperately searching for her mother's mysterious letter with anyone she could find to help. And the very long nights alone, wondering how long it would take the grand jury to hear the evidence against her father. And how quickly they'd move to indict him for murder.

Early on, she'd asked Billy to stay with her, but he'd said it would be too disruptive for Will to stay in a strange place, and he didn't want to leave his son alone. And besides, his sister was often weepy and sad and he needed to be home with her. He also needed to spend time with his mother, whose health was failing, since she saw only the nurse Summer had provided—as promised—during the day.

Summer knew they were all excuses. If Billy had wanted to be with her, he could have managed it. But she didn't argue. Maybe it was better this way.

Late Thursday, when there was still no word from the grand jury, Summer let herself hope they might not indict after all. When everyone who was helping with the search had gone, and the servants had left for the day, she sat down at the kitchen table, exhausted, and sipped at a cup of coffee, hoping the caffeine would help.

She tensed when the phone rang, afraid to answer it. After six rings, she leaped up and ran for it. "Hello?"

"Summer? It's Uncle Harry. The grand jury indicted."

"Oh, no!" she moaned. "No."

"Your father will be going to court tomorrow morning to hear the indictment read and to make his plea."

"I won't be there," Summer said. She had to stay home and search for the letter that might clear him. As she gripped the phone, she had the terrifying thought that her mother had lied about the letter to give her hope, when there was none.

"I know he'd like to see you there," Uncle Harry said.

Summer didn't say anything. She didn't want to sob into the phone. So she hung up.

She had one day left to find that goddamned note. Because tomorrow, her father would plead "Not guilty," when his only defense was, "Of course we argued, Your Honor. All married couples do. But I didn't murder my wife."

She punched Billy's number into the phone. She could hear Will crying in the background when Billy answered. "You have to come back. Please. I don't want to be alone."

He must have heard the panic in her voice, because he said, "The grand jury indicted?"

"Yes. I have to find that letter, Billy. I need you here."

"I'll be right over," he said. "Does Ren know?"

At that moment, Ren appeared at the screen door.

"She's here now," Summer said.

"See you soon," Billy said and disconnected.

"Come in," Summer called to Ren as she hung up the phone.

Ren stepped inside and let the screen door ease closed behind her. "I'm so sorry," she said.

A week ago, this woman had been a stranger. But when Ren opened her arms offering comfort, Summer flew into them. She gripped Ren hard, sobbing against her shoulder. "What are we going to do?"

She felt Ren's hands on her hair, comforting her in a way her mother never had. "We're going to keep looking."

Summer took a step back and swiped at her eyes. "Sorry about the tears."

Ren took a step forward and gently brushed Summer's hair back from her shoulder. "None of this is your fault, Summer."

"Sure. Right."

"I mean it. All of this was set in motion long before you were born."

Summer hadn't realized until Ren said something how guilty she'd felt. She wanted to believe her.

Ren smiled and said, "I know your father doesn't blame you."

"Really?"

Ren nodded.

"Billy's coming over," Summer said.

"We can use all the help we can get. Shall we start again upstairs?"

"I'll search Momma's studio again."

"Guess I'll head for Trace's bedroom."

Sometime later, Summer heard Billy hailing her and hurried downstairs to find him and Will—and Emma— in the kitchen. "What are you doing here?" she asked Emma.

"Billy said you needed help. I thought maybe I could make us all some supper."

Summer saw the kitchen table was already set. "How long have you been here?"

"I brought the chili and cornbread muffins I'd made for our dinner," Emma said. She turned the muffins out of the warm tin into a basket and set them on the table.

"Bless you," Summer said. "I'm starving."

"So's Billy," Emma said. "Even Will's starting to complain."

Will was sitting on the floor banging on a couple of pots with a wooden spoon.

"Mer!" Will cried when he spied her.

Summer reached out her arms and Will dropped the spoon and clambered into them. He hugged her tight and she hugged him back. She met Billy's eyes, fighting tears. "I'm so glad you're here."

He took Will from her and settled the little boy in the high chair Summer had found earlier in the week in the attic.

"Eat, Daddy," Will said plaintively.

Billy reached for a muffin, broke it open, and blew on it to cool it before handing half to Will, who stuck it in his mouth and began munching happily.

Ren came into the kitchen with dust and cobwebs clinging to her hair.

"What happened to you?" Summer asked.

"I found an entrance to the attic in the closet of your brother's bedroom and decided to go up for a look," Ren said.

"No luck?" Billy asked.

Ren shook her head as she sank into a chair at the table. "I think Eve's sent us on a wild-goose chase."

Summer exchanged a look with Ren and thought of indomitable spirits and intrepid hearts. She fought back her own despair and said, "The note is here somewhere. And come hail or high water, we're going to find it!"

They were almost done with supper when they were surprised by a knock on the screen door.

"Who could that be?" Summer said, leaning around Billy to see.

Emma crossed to the screen door and stood there without opening it.

"Who is it?" Ren asked.

Emma stepped back as Sam rolled his wheelchair into the kitchen. "Mom called and told me you could use some more help with the search," he said.

Summer was astonished by the appearance of Sam Creed. There was no one who had more reason to hate the Blackthornes. She didn't understand what he was doing here.

Until she saw the byplay between Sam and his mother and Emma.

"If you've come here to cause Emma any trouble, you can leave now," Billy said.

"I'm not here to cause trouble for anyone," Sam said. "I came to help."

"Why would you want to help my father?" Summer said.

"Because whether I like it or not, what hurts Blackjack hurts my mother. And I don't want to see her in pain."

That made sense. "We can use the help," Summer admitted.

"You're still in time for supper," Ren said. "Find yourself a place at the table. Emma's made us some corn muffins and chili."

Summer could hardly believe what she was seeing as she looked around the table. Enemies sitting together, sharing food and conversation.

"Why don't you show Sam the letter?" Emma suggested to Summer. "He's smart about things like that."

"All right," Summer said. Will was lying in her arms, drinking a bottle and playing with his hair, almost asleep. "It's in my back pocket. Billy, can you get it?"

She angled her hip and Billy pulled out the letter she'd been carrying around with her. Summer watched it pass from hand to hand down the length of the kitchen table until it reached Sam.

"This part about the land is important," Sam said, tapping the letter with his finger.

Summer looked at Ren, who said, "Jackson said the same thing."

"She mentions the Blackthornes never having enough of it. Didn't your mother bring a portion of DeWitt land with her when she married your father?" Sam asked.

"Yes, she did," Summer said.

"So the Blackthornes would have needed to redraw their property lines to show—"

"Oh, my God." Summer jumped up abruptly, jostling Will so his bottle fell onto the floor. Will cried out, and Summer cooed to him in apology, retrieved the bottle, then dropped Will and the bottle both into Billy's hands and said, "I know where it is!"

Everyone at the table jumped up to follow her, Sam bringing up the rear, as Summer headed into the parlor.

"There," Summer said, pointing to an aging yellow map hanging over the fireplace that showed the original boundaries of Bitter Creek. "It's in plain sight, right under our noses, and it's something Daddy has forbidden any of us ever to touch, because the paper behind that glass is so old it would disintegrate if it were handled. It's Bitter Creek as it was when the first Blackthorne built his home here."

Billy handed Will to Emma and stepped up onto the low stone wall that surrounded the fireplace so he could reach the map framed above it. The map wasn't large, but the wooden frame, apparently as old as the map itself, was heavy.

Billy stepped down with the framed map and set it on the arm of one of the wing chairs that faced the fireplace, turning it so all of them could see the back of it.

Summer's heart sank as she looked carefully over the wooden backing and found nothing that seemed remotely like it might be a note from her mother.

Billy leaned closer to the map itself and said, "I think I see something sticking out from under the map, a piece of paper that isn't aged like the rest."

"Can you get to it?" Summer asked.

"I'd have to separate the map from the backing to see whether it's something . . . or nothing."

"I don't give a damn about the map," Summer said. "You can tear it to shreds for all I care. Just find out what's under it."

Billy grinned. "I don't think that's the attitude your mother expected you to have. I think she counted on you wanting to preserve this piece of your heritage badly enough that you'd handle it with velvet gloves and wouldn't look too closely at it."

Eve had apparently glued the black mat upon which the map was mounted both to the glass in front and to the quarter-inch plywood that backed the frame, so there was no way to remove the map without breaking the glass, which would necessarily damage the wafer-thin paper.

"I can't believe Momma glued all this together," Summer said. "Or that she left that scrap of paper so visible."

"She promised her clue would be under our noses," Billy said. "And she's made sure the map has to be destroyed to get to it."

Summer gulped. "What if it's one of those fake notes, like the others we found? And we ruin Daddy's map for nothing."

"I guess that's a chance you'll have to take."

Summer glanced at Ren, then turned to Billy and said, "Go for it."

"You sure?" Billy asked, as he prepared to break the glass with the horn handle of the jackknife he carried in his jeans pocket.

Summer nodded, then took a deep breath and held it while Billy broke the glass. She was still holding her breath as he picked out the shards of glass and set them carefully in the ash-laden fireplace.

Summer exhaled noisily and said, "I can't stand the suspense. Is it the letter we've been hunting for, or not?"

The map began disintegrating as Billy tugged at the tiny scrap of white paper behind it. But it turned out to be more than a scrap. As ragged pieces of the priceless map fluttered to the floor, a sheet of Bitter Creek stationery emerged.

"Oh, God," Summer said, tears welling in her eyes. "We found it."

"Read it," Ren said, her voice hoarse.

Billy held the vellum in front of him and began reading.

My darling daughter,

If you're reading this, I have the satisfaction of knowing that your father has lost at least one thing he holds dear. That map of Bitter Creek was his pride and joy.

I hope he's lost a great deal more. I've learned to hate him as much as I once loved him. I couldn't have lived knowing he'd left me for that woman. So I planned my own death to make it look as though your father murdered me.

I've been very clever about it, getting everyone who had something to gain from my death to tell me what I needed to know without ever letting them know how I intended to use the information. I especially enjoyed arranging the flight to Costa Rica.

But it's no fun being the only one who knows just how clever I've been. So I've left this letter as a legacy for you to find—if you can.

> *Love and kisses,*
> *Eve*

Summer sobbed with relief and heard Ren weeping beside her. "Will this be enough?" she asked Billy.

"Seems to me your uncle Harry can use it to free your father."

"Thank God," Ren whispered.

"Then I take it we're done here," Sam said.

"Looks that way," Billy said.

"Can I give you a ride home, Emma?" Sam said.

"I'll go with my brother," Emma replied.

"I could use a ride," Ren said. "One of the hands dropped me off here."

"Sure, Mom," Sam said as he turned to wheel himself out of the parlor.

"Sam," Summer called after him.

He stopped and glanced at her over his shoulder.

"I don't know how to thank you," Summer said.

"No need. Creeds take care of each other. And we're all one family now."

Chapter 20

SUMMER STOOD IN THE VESTIBULE OF THE FIRST Baptist Church with Emma Coburn, who was dressed in a full-length white silk wedding gown with a heart-shaped neckline and capped sleeves that did nothing to hide her advanced pregnancy. They were waiting for the church organist to arrive.

Flossie Hart was always late. Summer wondered why people didn't just tell her church events began a half hour earlier. But she supposed Flossie saw them posted in the bulletin—as this wedding had been—and came when she felt like showing up.

There was no one in the church other than the bride's and groom's families, because the bulletin had also stated that the couple preferred to have a private ceremony and would entertain guests at a reception following the wedding at the home of the groom's newly married mother.

Because of Flossie's tardiness, there was no music to temper the utter silence that had descended once both families were seated. And with so few people in the high-ceilinged country church, every sound echoed, so no one was inclined to talk, even in whispers. The church radiated with red and gold light from the stained glass windows that lined both walls, making it feel even warmer than it was.

Dr. Robert Truman, whom everyone called Pastor Rob, stood in his robes at the pulpit, and Luke waited nearby, while Sam, his best man, sat in his wheelchair next to his brother. Dora, the mother of the bride, sat on the aisle in the first pew on the left and kept dabbing her nose with a lace-edged hanky. Billy sat beside her, Will perched on his lap, impatiently shooting glances over his shoulder toward the church door.

Summer smiled at Billy and waved, then mouthed, "I have no idea why she's so late."

She knew why Billy was anxious for the ceremony to start. He wanted it over with so he could get away from Blackjack, who was sitting on the aisle opposite him with his new wife, the mother of the groom.

Billy kept shooting furtive glances at his sniffling mother and then glaring at Blackjack. It was an explosive situation, to say the least. If Flossie Hart didn't arrive soon, Summer wasn't sure there wouldn't be fireworks.

Her father turned and glanced back at her, and she smiled and waved at him, too. Summer couldn't believe how quickly and efficiently Harry Blackthorne had gotten Blackjack exonerated once he had her mother's letter in hand.

Her father had been sent home the same night they'd found the letter. And since he'd already married Lauren Creed, they'd moved right into the Castle together. Her father's new wife had done nothing overt to make Summer feel uncomfortable in her own home, but with Ren there and Blackjack back at the helm, Summer felt like a fifth wheel.

And she had nowhere else she belonged. Emma had stayed at the C-Bar for the two weeks until her wedding. When Summer had told Billy about Blackjack and Ren moving in together, and that her father had taken back the reins to Bitter Creek, Billy hadn't said a word about her moving back in with him. So she hadn't, either.

Summer wasn't sure what she was supposed to do now. It had seemed best to let things ride until after Emma's wedding. Once she and Luke were married, they would move into the main house at Three Oaks. That would be the logical time for Summer to move back in with Billy. That is, if Billy wanted her to move back in. Summer still wasn't at all sure about his feelings.

"Summer."

She turned to Emma, who'd clutched Summer's wrists and dragged her back out of sight in the vestibule. "What's the matter, Emma?"

"I'm not sure I can go through with this."

Summer felt like saying, "Of course you can!" Her own situation would worsen if Emma ended up leaving the church unmarried and moved back in at the C-Bar. But she bit her tongue and asked, "What's wrong, Emma?"

"I don't know if Luke can ever love me," Emma said.

"Then why are you marrying him?"

"Because this is his child I'm carrying. And because from the first time I saw Luke, I always dreamed of marrying him."

"Then I don't understand the problem," Summer said.

Emma took a deep breath and said, "I think I might be

in love with Sam." She put a hand to her trembling lips and said, "I know I am."

"How does Sam feel about you?" Summer asked.

"He said he loves me. But he thinks this baby—" she slid her hands lovingly around her belly—"should have his father's name."

"He'd still be a Creed if you married Sam," Summer pointed out.

Emma laughed through her tears. "I suppose that's true."

Summer took both of Emma's hands in hers. "I can't know what's right for you, Emma. All I can tell you is that my father married my mother when he loved someone else and ended up pining for that lost love forever after. You should marry for love. Everything else will sort itself out."

Emma gripped her hands and might have said something else, except at that moment, a tremendous swell of organ music filled the church.

Summer let go of Emma's hands and backed up hurriedly to look down the aisle. Flossie Hart must have come in through a back door, because she was sitting at the organ, a flowered hat on her head, performing some Bach piece at a tempo that suggested she was in a hurry to get the music played to make up for being late.

Billy was waving at Summer to start down the aisle. She turned back to Emma and whispered, "Time to go," and began moving at a hurried step-together, step-together, step-together that matched the accelerated music. She was halfway down the aisle when she realized Emma hadn't said whether she was going to go through with the wedding. Or not.

When she reached the front of the church, Summer turned and waited to see whether Emma would appear. The first measures of the "Wedding March" filled the church with joyous sound, and everyone except Dora stood up and turned to face the bride, who was coming down the aisle alone. Billy had offered to walk with Emma, but she'd told him she'd rather do it by herself.

Emma was the least radiant bride Summer had ever seen. Her mouth never curved in a smile. Her gaze was somber, her tread measured. Flossie had slowed the tempo to accommodate Emma's ungainly size. But finally, Emma reached the front of the church and the music stopped.

Summer looked at the groom and his best man and wasn't sure which of the two looked more miserable. Someone should stop this fiasco. Someone should say something.

But it wasn't her place to speak. It wasn't her life. She wasn't the one marrying the wrong man.

I've already married the right one, Summer realized as she looked in Billy's direction. He was the man she wanted to spend her life with, and she was as bad as Emma, not getting what she wanted because she was too fainthearted to speak up. She knew Billy must care for her. She just had to get him to admit it. Surely that shouldn't be too difficult. Especially if she was willing to take the risk of being honest with him.

"Dearly beloved," the preacher intoned.

Summer missed a lot of what Pastor Rob said next, because she was too busy making eye contact with Billy. Who was looking right back at her. Most of the time.

That is, whenever he wasn't pulling his suit buttons out of Will's mouth or tugging Will's hands out of his hair, or rescuing his mother's hanky from Will's clutching baby fingers.

"If there is anyone here who knows any reason why these two people should not be joined in holy matrimony, let him speak now, or forever hold his peace."

Summer wasn't sure who spoke first. It might have been Emma. Or Luke. Or Sam. Or Ren. Or Billy. Or herself.

Billy had dropped Will in his mother's lap as everyone came out of their seats and congregated at the front of the church shoving aside the standing vases of gerbera daisies Blackjack had provided on either side of the pulpit. All talking at once. All stating reasons why the marriage they'd come to witness—or participate in—should be called to a dead halt.

"Hold it! Hold it!" the preacher said. "One at a time. Young lady, since you're the bride, I believe you should speak first."

Emma turned to Luke and said, "I'm sorry, Luke. I can't marry you. I'm not in love with you."

"Good," Luke said. "Because I'm not in love with you, either."

"Why, you—"

Emma plopped into Sam's lap, effectively ending any chance he had of attacking his brother. "It isn't Luke's fault that I'm in love with you, Sam. It isn't his fault that there's no other man I'd rather spend my life with or raise my child with than you."

Sam looked up at Luke, who said, "You ought to

marry the girl, Sam. She loves you. I know you'll be a good father. And your kid will have a great life with the two of you as parents."

The tears Summer saw in Sam's eyes before Emma bent to kiss him on the mouth made her nose sting. She swallowed over the knot growing in her throat as she turned to share the moment with Billy. Who had tears in his own eyes.

Summer didn't stop to think, she just walked into Billy's arms.

"I love you, Summer," he said as he closed his arms around her. "I want to spend my life with you. I don't care that you're rich and I'm not. I'll figure out some way—"

"You're rich too, young man," a voice said over Summer's shoulder. "There's a couple of million in an account with your name on it at my bank."

Summer felt Billy grab her arms and push her away from him as he stared over her shoulder at Blackjack. Billy's gaze shifted back to her, his dark eyes narrowed, as angry as she'd ever seen him.

"What the hell is going on here, Summer?"

"I don't know," Summer protested. "Believe me, Billy. I have no earthly idea what Daddy is talking about."

"It's simple," Blackjack said, staring into Billy's wrathful eyes. "I've acknowledged you legally as my son."

Billy hadn't wanted to come to Emma's wedding because all the crying she'd done the past week had convinced him she was making a big mistake. But he'd never told her what to do in the past, and he didn't think he should start now.

The other reason he hadn't wanted to attend her wedding was because he hadn't wanted to see Summer in such a suggestive setting. When the preacher started talking about loving and honoring and cherishing, he'd been looking right at Summer and thinking how he wanted to do all those things for her and with her the rest of his life. And that he was an idiot for worrying about something as unimportant as which one of them had more money.

When Will looked up at him and grinned, and then put his shoe in his mouth to chew on it, Billy realized he wanted a lot more children, and he wanted to make them with Summer.

When his mother caught his hand and held it tight and looked at him with tears in her eyes, he was reminded that he didn't have all the time in the world to fool around. Folks never knew how long they had on this earth and a wise man made the most of it—by spending his life with someone he loved.

Billy suddenly knew that even if it made him an interfering brother, he couldn't let Emma marry Luke. So when the preacher asked who objected, he'd jumped up and yelled.

But he hadn't been the only one. It seemed no one in the church wanted the bride and groom to go through with the ceremony, including the bride and groom. Billy had been proud of Emma for speaking up, and moved when he saw how tenderly Sam Creed held her in his arms. He'd felt such joy for his sister welling up inside him that he'd searched out the one he loved to share it with.

Billy had convinced himself that he could handle being a poor man married to a rich woman. He wouldn't ever be completely comfortable with the notion, but he figured it was a small price to pay to spend his life with the woman he loved.

But he hadn't wanted or needed Blackjack's charity. The offer of it had been an ugly slap in the face.

And then Blackjack had said the words that Billy had never been able to admit he wanted to hear. The words that any child who grows up knowing he doesn't belong, who knows he's connected somewhere else than where he's landed, longs to hear.

"I've acknowledged you legally as my son."

Billy clamped his teeth together to keep his chin from wobbling.

"I've arranged for you to have the same trust fund your brothers each received when they turned twenty-five," Blackjack continued. "It's only a couple of million, but it'll give you the freedom to do whatever you want with your life. You can tell me and the rest of the world to go to hell. Give it away, throw it away, leave it there to rot. What you do with it is up to you."

Billy opened his mouth to speak and closed it again, because his throat was swollen closed.

"You got anything to say?" Blackjack said with a wry smile.

"I never wanted money from you," Billy managed at last.

Blackjack put a hand on his shoulder and said, "Don't you think I know that, son? That's why I gave it to you.

Because you never asked. You're a good man, Billy Coburn. You deserve a share of what's mine. There's good Blackthorne blood running through your veins."

Blackjack turned to Summer and said, "And it seems I owe you a wedding present, young lady."

"Daddy, there's no need—"

"So I'm giving you Bitter Creek to care for and nurture and pass on to the next generation of Blackthornes." He glanced at Ren and added, "And Creeds." And finally at Billy and said, "And Coburns."

Billy saw the stunned joy in Summer's eyes as she absorbed the enormity of her father's gift.

"Daddy, I—"

"You deserve it, honey," Blackjack said. "I know you can handle the job, because you've been doing it the past two years. I plan to stay busy running the rest of the businesses I've invested in. I'll be at my desk if you need any advice. But I have confidence you can run the ranch on your own."

Summer turned to look at Billy. She seemed a little dazed and disbelieving. She turned back to her father and said, "Daddy, I don't know what to say. I don't know how to thank you."

"Give me a hug," he said. "And we'll call it even."

Summer laughed and threw herself into her father's open arms. In a matter of moments she pulled free and turned back to Billy. "Bitter Creek is ours to run, Billy."

Billy grinned, glad that what he felt inside was simply joy for her. "Yours to run. But I'll be glad to help."

She put her palms on his chest and looked up into his eyes and said, "Do you mind, Billy? Is it all right?"

Was it all right for her to realize her dream? Was she

so afraid he'd ask her to give it up? Billy knew suddenly what he wanted from life. What he'd always wanted.

"I just want to make a home at the C-Bar with you and Will and whatever kids we have. And I want to spend my life loving you."

Summer lifted up on tiptoe and kissed him on the mouth. "I'm glad, Billy," she said, tears brimming in her eyes. "So very glad."

Blackjack slid his arm around Ren's waist and said, "Are we going to have a wedding here today or not?"

Sam spoke up and said, "I've got a license I picked up when . . . Earlier," he finished hastily. "All I need is someone to say the words for me and Emma."

They all gathered around Sam and Emma as the preacher started again with, "Dearly beloved—"

"You can skip all that," Blackjack said. "Get on to the important parts."

Billy crossed to Summer and stood behind her. As Sam repeated his vows, Billy repeated softly to her, "I promise to love you and honor you, cherish you and respect you. I want to have children with you. And I want to grow old with you, knowing that we're two parts of one eternal, infinite, and undying whole."

Summer reached for Billy's hand, and as Emma said her vows, she whispered, "I promise to love you and honor you, cherish you and respect you. I want to have children with you. And I want to grow very, *very* old with you, knowing that we're two parts of one eternal, infinite, and undying whole."

"I now pronounce you husband and wife," the preacher said. "You may kiss the bride."

Billy turned Summer into his arms and felt her hands

slide around his nape and into his hair. "I love you," he said.

"I love you, too, Billy."

Billy kissed his wife. And felt someone tugging on his trousers.

"Kiss me, too, Daddy, Mer," Will said.

Billy leaned down and scooped him up. "You got it, son."

Will smiled happily as Summer and Billy each pressed a smacking kiss to his cheeks.

Letter to Readers

Dear Readers,

I hope you had a good time with the Blackthornes, Creeds, and Coburns in *The Loner.* Luke Creed is back in my next book in the Bitter Creek series, *The Price,* but the series moves to the law offices of DeWitt & Blackthorne in Houston. Hope you'll come along for the ride!

If you missed Trace and Callie's story, *The Cowboy,* or Owen and Bay's story, *The Texan,* you should be able to order them on the Internet or find them in your local bookstore.

If you'd like to read more about the Blackthorne family, look for my Captive Hearts series set in Regency England, including *Captive, After the Kiss, The Bodyguard,* and *The Bridegroom.* For those of you intrigued by the Creeds and the Coburns, check out the Sisters of the Lone Star trilogy, *Frontier Woman, Comanche Woman,* and *Texas Woman.*

You can find more than forty of my novels in digital form wherever eBooks are sold. If you have comments or suggestions you can reach me through my website, www.joanjohnston.com, find me on Facebook at www.facebook.com/joanjohnstonauthor, or tweet me at www.twitter.com@joanjohnston.

Happy trails,
Joan Johnston

Read on for an exclusive sneak peek
at the next sizzling contemporary Western
romance by *New York Times* bestselling author
Joan Johnston

SINFUL

Where power, money, and rivalries rule—
and love is the best revenge.

Coming soon from Dell

Chapter 1

Her name was Eve. Not Evelyn or Eveline or Evette. Just Eve. The day she was born, her father, King Grayhawk, took one look at her large blue eyes, soft blond curls, and bowed upper lip and whispered, "Eve." Apparently, she reminded him of some woman he'd fallen in love with as a younger man. That Eve, he'd declared, was the only woman he had ever loved.

Those words, spoken as her mother lay recovering from labor, must have been the final insult, because Eve was still a babe in arms when her mom ran off with one of King's cowhands. Eve had grown up with the knowledge that her birth had caused a terrible rift between her parents. That marital fracture had left her and her fraternal twin sisters, Taylor and Victoria, and their older stepsister, Leah, as motherless children.

Eve felt burdened by her name. It didn't help that she shared it with the woman who'd tempted Adam to sin in the Garden of Eden. In high school she was teased and taunted as she began to acquire seductive curves. She was sure one of those pain-in-the-butt Flynn brothers had started it, but the other boys had quickly followed his lead.

"Show me an apple, and I'll eat it," a boy would say, "so long as you come along with it, Eve." Or, "Too bad you ate that apple, Eve, or we'd all still be running around naked," followed by a lurid grin.

She'd gotten pretty good at sending back zingers like, "If God had seen you naked, Buck, He might have decided He made a real mistake only taking out a rib." But the constant innuendo made Eve's teenage life miserable.

That was the least of the trouble those four awful Flynn brothers—Aiden, Brian, Connor, and Devon—had caused her and her sisters over the years.

From her father's rants at supper, Eve had known he was feuding with Angus Flynn. It wasn't until she was eight years old that she understood why. Angus's older sister, Jane, had been King's first wife, and Angus blamed King for his unhappy sister's death from an overdose of barbiturates. Eve had no idea whether her father was innocent or not, but he was sorely tried by Angus's efforts to blight his life.

The animosity should have remained between their fathers, but it had bled onto their children. Angus Flynn's four sons were infamous around Jackson Hole for wreaking havoc and causing mischief. After their aunt Jane died, as though a switch had been flipped, the Flynn brothers began aiming all that tomfoolery toward Eve and her sisters. It didn't take long before King's Brats, who'd done their own share of troublemaking around Jackson Hole, were giving as good as they got from those wild Flynn boys.

Eve could remember vividly the year fourteen-year-old Leah's blueberry pie had been mysteriously doused with salt at the Four-H competition. Her stepsister had retaliated by shaving the flank of fourteen-year-old Aiden's Four-H calf so it looked like it had the mange.

Some of the mischief she and her sisters perpetrated was merely a nuisance. Like putting an ad in the paper for a cattle auction at the Flynn ranch, the Lucky 7, beginning at 6:00 a.m. on a Saturday morning, offering their prize bull for sale, when no such auction existed.

Eve had helped Taylor and Victoria punch a tiny hole in

the gas tank of Brian's truck, so that when he and Devon headed off to hunt deer in the mountains, where there was no cell phone reception, they'd ended up making a long, bitterly cold walk back to civilization.

The Flynns had retaliated by placing slices of bologna in a vulgar design on the hood of Taylor and Victoria's cherry-red Jeep Laredo. The next morning, when her sisters pulled the deli meat off the hood, the preservatives in the bologna caused the top layer of paint to come off as well, leaving the distinct imprint of male genitalia.

It wouldn't have been so bad if the pranks had remained physically harmless. They hadn't. When Eve was a freshman in high school, the cinch of her saddle had been cut before a barrel race at a local rodeo, and she'd broken her arm when the saddle broke free. Eve could remember how enraged Leah was in the moments before the ambulance carted her away. The Flynn boys were competing at the same rodeo in calf roping. They should have known to check their cinches, but Eve supposed they hadn't expected Leah to retaliate so quickly. When Aiden roped a calf his cinch broke—along with his leg.

The mischief escalated into attacks involving other people. Taylor's and Victoria's prom dates were kidnapped by a couple of boys wearing hoods, who tied them to a tree so they never showed up. The twins were devastated. The fallout afterward was even worse. The kidnapped boys made it clear that it wasn't worth the trouble to date a Grayhawk when it meant putting up with all the horseshit being shoveled by those crazy Flynn boys.

Since Eve had lived in the same small town her whole life, the "harmless" high school prank involving her name had been a continuing source of irritation. Most of the kids who'd gone to high school with her still lived in Jackson, and there was always some jerk who couldn't resist prodding her, hoping to get under her skin.

Like now.

Eve wasn't looking to hook up or make waves. All she wanted to do was sit at the Million Dollar Cowboy Bar on the square in Jackson, along with the tourists who'd come to enjoy the last of the black-diamond ski season on the Grand Tetons, review the digital photographs she'd taken that day of the herd of wild mustangs she'd rescued, and enjoy her martini.

"Is that an *apple* martini, Eve?" a man called from behind her.

Eve turned to find Buck Madison, the former Jackson Broncs quarterback, grinning like an idiot at one of the pool tables in the center of the bar. Two of his former teammates stood shoulder to shoulder with him, giggling like teenage girls. All three were obviously drunk. She purposefully turned her attention back to the digital shot of the only colt in her herd. With any luck, Buck would give up and shut up.

Eve smiled as she studied the image of Midnight frolicking with his mother, his black mane and tail flying, his back arched, and all four hooves off the ground.

"You look good enough to tempt a man to sin, *Eve*."

Buck's voice was loud in a bar that had suddenly become quiet. Eve shut off her camera and laid it on the bar as she dismounted the Western saddle on a stand—complete with stirrups—that served as a bar stool. She glanced at Buck in the mirror over the bar as she gathered her North Face fleece from where it hung off the saddle horn. She wasn't going to get into a war of words with a drunk. It was a lose-lose proposition. She had one arm through her fleece when Buck stripped it back off, dangling it from his forefinger.

"Uh, uh, uh," he said, wagging the finger holding the fleece. "I'm not done looking yet."

She turned to confront Buck, her chin upthrust, her blue eyes shooting daggers of disdain. "I'm done being ogled. Give me my coat."

She held out her hand and waited.

She felt a wave of resentment toward the Flynns, who'd started that whole Garden of Eden business in the first place. She couldn't help the fact that she'd developed a lush female figure in high school. At twenty-six, she'd made peace with her body. There was no easy way to conceal her curves, so she didn't try. But she did nothing to emphasize them, either.

She was dressed in a plaid western shirt that was belted into a pair of worn western jeans. She had on scuffed cowboy boots, but instead of a Stetson, she usually wore a faded navy-blue-and-orange Denver Broncos ball cap. She'd left the cap in her pickup, but her chin-length, straw-blond hair was tucked behind her ears to keep it out of her way.

"My coat?" she said.

As she reached for it, Buck pulled it away "How about a kiss first?"

Eve had opened her mouth to retort when a brusque male voice said, "Give the lady her coat."

Eve hadn't heard anyone coming up behind her, which surprised her. She photographed wild animals in their natural habitat and prided herself on her awareness of her surroundings. In the wilderness, missing the slightest sound could result in being bitten by a rattler or attacked by a bear or mountain lion. She glanced over her shoulder and felt her heart skip a beat when she recognized her unlikely savior.

Connor Flynn.

Connor was third in line of the Flynn brothers, but he'd been at the top of the teenage troublemaking list. He was thirty now but, if anything, his reputation was worse. He'd done three tours as a Delta sergeant in Afghanistan before leaving the military with several medals to prove his heroism in battle.

He'd paid a high price for his long absences from home serving his country. A year ago his wife, Molly, who'd been

Eve's best friend, had died in a car accident while Connor was overseas. After the funeral, he'd agreed to let Molly's parents take his kids into their home while he served the nine months left on his final tour of duty.

Now they were threatening to keep them.

Connor had ended up in a court battle to get his two-year-old son and four-year-old daughter back. So far he hadn't been able to wrench them away from his late wife's parents. They'd argued to a judge that Connor was a battle-weary soldier, a victim of post-traumatic stress, and therefore a threat to his children. According to all the psychological tests he'd been forced to endure to prove them wrong, he was fine. But seeing him now, Eve wondered for the very first time if Molly's parents might not be completely off the mark.

Connor looked dangerous, his sapphire-blue eyes hooded, his cheeks and chin covered with at least a two-day-old beard, and a hank of his rough-cut, crow-wing-black hair resting on his scarred forehead. His lips had thinned to an ominous line.

If she'd been Buck, she would have handed over the coat in a heartbeat. But Buck wasn't known for his smarts.

"Butt out!" Buck said. "This is between me and Eve."

Without warning, Connor's hand shot out and gripped Buck's throat. Buck dropped the coat to protect his neck, but Connor didn't let go. His inexorable grasp was slowly choking the big man to death. Even using both hands, Buck couldn't get free.

Eve looked around the bar, expecting someone, anyone, to intervene. No one did. She wouldn't have interfered except she knew that Connor might be turning the lock and throwing away the key where custody of his kids was concerned. She didn't step in for Connor's sake. Ordinarily she wouldn't have thrown a glass of water to douse a Flynn on fire. But she cared very much about the future well-being of her dead friend's children, who needed their father alive and well and out of jail.

Despite Connor's long absences, Molly had been convinced that he would take good care of their children if anything ever happened to her. Eve owed it to her best friend to make sure Connor didn't ruin his chance of becoming the wonderful father Molly had always believed he could be.

As carefully as if she were approaching a feral wolf, Eve laid her fingertips on Connor's bare forearm, the one that led to the hand grasping Buck's throat. She turned so she was looking into his narrowed eyes. "Connor," she said in a quiet voice. "This won't help. Let go."

She watched his upper lip curl as though he was snarling while his gaze remained focused on the helpless man in his grasp.

"Think of the kids!" she said more urgently. "For their sake, let go. Please."

He turned to look at her when she said "kids" and then seemed to hear the rest of her sentence. He looked at his hand and seemed surprised to discover that he was still choking Buck. Suddenly, he let go and took a step back.

Buck gasped a breath of air, and with the next breath croaked, "Molly's parents are right. You should be in a cage!" Now that Buck was free, his two football buddies, each brandishing a pool cue, moved up to flank him.

Connor stood as though in a daze, rubbing his forehead where the scar from a war wound loomed white against his tanned skin. Eve realized that if Connor didn't leave in a hurry, there was likely to be a free-for-all. She grabbed her fleece from the floor and her camera from the bar, gripped Connor's hand, and pulled him out the door after her.

She headed away from the bar in case the three drunks decided to follow them outside into the frosty March evening. She hadn't realized where she was going until she reached her Dodge Ram pickup, which was parked under the colorful neon cowboy on a bucking bronc that lit up the bar. She let go of Connor's hand in order to hang her camera by its strap around her neck, then pulled on her fleece. She shook her head in disgust at his behavior in the bar as he frowned back at her.

"What were you thinking?" she said. "Were you trying to get arrested? Don't you want to be a father to Brooke and Sawyer?"

"I was thinking that son of a bitch was being a pain in the ass, all because of something I started in high school."

Eve stared at him in shock. *Connor* was responsible for all those cruel taunts about her name?

He shoved a hand through his hair, but a hank of it fell back onto his forehead. "Thanks for getting me out of there."

"I wish I hadn't bothered, now that I know you started that 'Eve' business. Do you have any idea how much aggravation you caused me in high school?"

He shot her a mutinous, unapologetic look. "No more than you caused me by telling Molly I'd take her to that Sadie Hawkins dance her freshman year. No thanks to you it turned out all right."

Eve felt a stab of shame. Molly had been crazy about Connor Flynn in high school. So had Eve. But she might as well have aspired to date the man in the moon. Not just because Connor was a senior and she was a freshman, but because Connor was a Flynn. A broken arm. A broken leg. Ruined dreams. Too many years of hurt and harm stood between them.

Molly had desperately wanted to ask Connor to the Sadie Hawkins dance, but she'd been too shy to do it. Eve had told her friend that she would ask for her but then chickened out. Besides, she didn't want her best friend dating the boy she had a crush on herself. She'd lied and told Molly that she'd asked Connor and he'd said yes, figuring that Connor would blow Molly off when she came running up to him, excited that he'd accepted her invitation, and Molly would be humiliated and never speak to him again.

Admittedly, it was not her finest moment.

Instead, Connor had met Eve's gaze as she stood by her locker across the hall while Molly smiled up at him, delighted that he'd accepted her invitation to the dance. His eyes had narrowed at Eve, as though he knew she was the one responsible for this further bit of Grayhawk-Flynn monkey business. Then he'd smiled down at Molly as though he was glad to be going to the dance with Eve's best friend.

To Eve's dismay, Molly and Connor were going steady by the time Connor graduated at the end of the year. He'd told Molly not to wait for him when he enlisted in the military, and Eve had felt a flare of hope that they might break up. But Molly called or texted or emailed or wrote Connor every day while he was away learning all the skills he'd need to fight a war.

When Connor was home on leave, he and Molly picked up where they'd left off. He took classes in warfare for two years, and not once was there a break in Molly's devotion, or in Connor's, for that matter. With a sinking heart, Eve had realized that once Molly graduated from high school, they were probably going to get married.

Eve had no one to blame but herself. She should have spoken up. She should have said something to Molly about her feelings for Connor, no matter how unrealistic they were. After that freshman Sadie Hawkins dance, it was too late.

Eve stared at the man for whom she'd felt a hopeless love most of her adult life.

Both Connor's jaw and his fists were clenched. He was trouble looking for a place to happen. But despite all the damage he and his family had caused her and her family in the past, she couldn't leave him here. She didn't want her efforts in the bar undone. She made a face. "Get in. I'll drive you to your truck. Where is it?"

"I left it at the Snow King Resort. Aiden dropped me off in town before he headed back to the ranch. I planned to spend the night with—"

He cut himself off, and Eve realized he'd planned to pick up some girl in one of the many Jackson Hole bars and spend the night with her. He was good-looking enough and rich enough to attract locals, but it was more likely one of the ski bunnies would have carted him back to her hotel room.

"I have to be in town for court early tomorrow morning," he explained, "so I figured there was no sense making the drive back out to the Lucky 7 tonight."

Eve gave him a once-over from head to foot. He stood more than six feet tall and looked rock solid, his broad shoulders braced like a soldier ready for battle. Unfortunately, his impressive fighting skills were hardly likely to impress a judge deciding his children's fate. He needed to look like good *father* material. "Is that what you're planning to wear?"

He glanced down at the white oxford-cloth shirt, sleeves rolled up to expose sinewy forearms, comfortable jeans, western belt, and cowboy boots he had on. "What's wrong with what I'm wearing?"

"It's not a suit, for starters."

"My navy sport coat is on the back of my chair at one of the bar tables. There's a regimental tie in the pocket."

Eve stared at the door to the bar, wondering if there would be a scene if they returned for his sport coat. Of course there would be a scene. He was a Flynn, wasn't he? She sighed. "I'll take you home, and you can get another one."

"Don't bother. I'll call one of my brothers to come get me."

"And wait in a bar, I suppose," she said, pulling her fleece more tightly around her to ward off the chill. *Getting into more trouble.* "Let me take you home. You don't want the police finding you on the street in this condition."

"This condition? Meaning what?"

"You're drunk. And if Buck makes an issue of what just happened, disorderly. You don't want to give Molly's parents any more ammunition than they already have to shoot you down."

"Perfect metaphor," he retorted. "Because that's exactly what it feels like they're doing. Killing me with supposed kindness. I gave them my kids because I thought they'd be the best caretakers while I was gone. Now I have to fight to get my own kids back! And I'm not drunk."

She shot him a skeptical look.

"It was lime and Coke. No rum."

"Then why would you do something so stupid as to assault Buck?"

He palmed his eyes and made a guttural sound of frustration. "It's this custody hearing. I want it over. I want my kids back."

Eve heard the anguish in his voice and felt her heart wrench. But it was the kids she felt bad for, not their father. While he'd grieved the loss of his wife, Connor had shut himself off from Brooke and Sawyer. When he'd returned from overseas after an absence of nine months—an eternity to children only three and one when he'd left—Brooke and Sawyer had barely recognized him.

Eve knew how hard it was for vets to reinsert themselves into their former lives. Over the past couple of months since he'd returned home, Connor had more than once exhibited questionable behavior, like the attack tonight, which might have ended badly if she hadn't been there. She could understand why Molly's parents were concerned.

But she could also see Connor's side of the issue. He

hadn't been able to take his kids with him while he was serving his country. Now that he was home, and had proved to the doctors that he was of sound mind and body, he had the right to raise his children.

During the months-long custody battle, Connor had only been allowed supervised time with his kids, who weren't quite sure where he fit into their lives. Their grandparents were the only stable thing in their world right now.

Except for me.

Eve had spent a lot of time with Molly and the kids while Connor was deployed. Being essentially a single parent of two kids had been a crushing responsibility for her friend, and Eve had more than once taken Brooke and Sawyer for a walk in the forest or on a picnic to give Molly a break. After Molly's death, she'd done the same for the children's grandparents. She understood why Mr. and Mrs. Robertson were so worried about Connor wanting to raise two young children, who were just getting to know him again, all by himself.

It might have been different if there was a woman in the Flynn household, where Connor had been staying since he'd returned to Jackson Hole. But it was all men, from Angus on down. After the stand Molly's parents had taken, if Connor got his kids back, he was unlikely to ask the Robertsons for help.

Molly would have hated the tug-of-war over her children, but she'd left no will stating her wishes, and her parents had argued to the judge that not only was Connor an unfit parent, but that their daughter had wanted them to care for her children if anything ever happened to her. Eve knew better.

Which was why, despite the hard feelings between their two families, Eve planned to testify on Connor's behalf in court tomorrow. When her sisters had demanded to know why she was helping a Flynn after all the nasty things they'd done, she'd made it plain that she was only speaking in court to ensure that her best friend's final wishes were carried out.

Eve sympathized with Connor's suffering over the loss of both his wife and his children, but his conduct tonight had been worrisome. Was she making a mistake helping him to get custody of Brooke and Sawyer, even if it was what Molly had wanted? She knew he must be terrified that the court would take his children away tomorrow. Surely that explained, even if it didn't excuse, his overwrought behavior.

"I'd appreciate a ride up the hill to the Snow King Resort," Connor said. "I'm staying in the suite my dad keeps available for out-of-town business associates."

"Sure," she said. "Let's go."

The cab of the truck was frigid, and Eve let the engine heat up before she put the vehicle in gear. Their breaths fogged the cabin, and Connor shivered with the cold.

"The heater should have you warm in a minute," she said.

He rubbed his hands together. "Feels like Afghanistan in here."

"I thought it was mostly desert there."

"Deserts are plenty cold at night, but I spent most of my time in the mountains."

"Did they remind you of home?"

"Nothing compares to the beauty of the Tetons. Besides, I wasn't there to admire them. They were filled with places for hostiles to hide, which made them an unfriendly place to be."

It was the first conversation of more than a few words she'd had with Connor Flynn since he'd "accidentally" run into her on the fairgrounds at Old West Days at the end of her junior year of high school, knocking her ice cream cone out of her hand. The news had been all over town that he had orders to go to Afghanistan. He was still dating her best friend, who didn't happen to be with him.

Eve had figured the jarring collision was one more example of Flynn harassment, until Connor apologized and insisted on buying her another cone. He met her suspicious gaze with laughter in his eyes and said, "Molly would never forgive me if I didn't."

She felt warm everywhere his eyes touched her. She trembled when he slid an arm around her waist to move her out of the way of a bunch of rowdy cowboys. And a shiver ran down her spine when he gently thumbed a bit of ice cream from the side of her mouth after she'd taken a bite of her new strawberry cone.

His infectious grin. His surprising kindness. His incredible blue eyes. His muscular shoulders and lean hips. The knowledge that he was forbidden to her because he was a Flynn—and her best friend's boyfriend. All of those things had conspired to make her fall even more deeply and completely and irrevocably in love with him.